ARMORED WARRIOR PANZERTER

EVE OF BATTLE

T. E. BUTCHER

TERMS TO KNOW

Panzerter: Bipedal war machines developed for urban combat in the early twenty-first century. Their incredible versatility led to them eventually dethroning Main Battle Tanks as the armored vehicle of choice for many nations. Often paired with Infantry fighting vehicles and/ or dropships, they've become a decisive force in 29th Century combat.

Tubers: Artificial humans named after the birthing chamber they gestate in, The Union of Martian Republics mastered the science of creating them in response to a crisis early in their development. Forcibly sterilized and raised from birth to master a single profession, they make up 45% of the Union's population.

The Union of Martian Republics/ The Union: Founded by five colonies who wanted to share a fair and just future, the Union stretches from the Boreal Ocean to the edge of the Tharcian subcontinent. As time went on, the Union's government grew more corrupt and manipulative, eventually resorting to drastic measures to put down a series of protests. This led to a war with Tharsis where the other nation annexed the Gallacian Martian Republic (Now Galla-cia) and the Erie Martian Republic became the Rosevelt Republic.

The Mobile Assault Guards/ MAG: Founded after the War of 2112, The MAG stand as the most elite arm of the Union army. Using the best equipment and trained as thoroughly as possible, they are one of the most formidable forces on Mars. Tubers who join the MAG are granted reproductive rights and voting rights after serving ten years.

Tharsis: Founded by refugees from Eastern and Central Europe in the aftermath of World War III, the Tharcians have taken eagerly to their new home on the Tharcian subcontinent. After suffering for seven years under the Nazis and then fifty under the Communists, they are a resilient if defensive people. After just over a century on Mars, The Republic of Tharsis has grown into one of the most pros-perous nations in either the Earth or Mars sphere.

Vinland: A Mars country founded by Scandinavian colonists. Their homeland rests across the Mariner sea from Tharsis.

Olympia: An ally of Tharsis, they were mostly defeated in the opening months of the Red World War.

Avalon: an ally of the Union. An archaic society ruled by a king, they're mostly a space-based nation. However, their capitol is on a small island west of Olympia.

1

He staggered through a snowbank. Bitter winds whipped at the young man's face as he soldiered on. A machine gun chattered in the distance. In response, a Panzerter's rifle roared. The trees that still stood lacked leaves. With the young man coming closer, Captain Paul Reiter noticed something on his back. Another soldier.

From the jagged green and gray lines over off-white, Reiter could tell the young man was a Tharcian, likely a pilot due to his lack of heavy clothing. As the snowstorm howled outside, Reiter pressed his own machine forward. His Lowe, perhaps the most advanced panzerter the Tharcians had produced, stomped through the frozen woods like a giant out of fairy tales.

"Fox 7, do you have ID?" he asked. His 1st Sergeant, Master Sergeant Adamski, followed in a Panzerter IV. The venerable machine had seen two refits since the start of the war, and at the moment could go toe-to-toe with any Union Machine.

"That's Merlin Jr, and it looks like he's carrying Zorro," he replied. "Gold 3, get them inside, I'll call up the MEDEVAC."

Reiter looked ahead. Panzerter rifles intermixed with auto-cannon and machine gun fire. *Somewhere White Team is taking a beating.*

"Stovepipe, on me," Reiter said. "We're going to relive White team and the scouts, Fox 5, fall back to Landfall, and prepare to receive more wounded."

"Roger Fox 6," Stovepipe replied. "I'll be on your 5." Despite the temptation to run, Reiter kept the Lowe at a brisk walk so he didn't leave Stovepipe's tracked Iglaiso behind. "Are you going to commit Black Platoon?" Reiter shook his head despite the other man's inability to see him.

"No, if we commit more forces to this skirmish, we risk escalating it, and that could turn into a battle," he replied. "And we know what our orders are."

"Yeah yeah, defend your positions, but don't get decisively engaged," Stovepipe growled. "Biggest crock of shit I ever heard. Some Uni fuckstick is sitting in my easy chair in your home, but don't bother trying to go fight them." Reiter sighed. Their regiment had been part of the Gallacian Provincial Watch before that province had been overrun by Union forces during their initial offensive. Now they'd been integrated into the regular army's chain of command, but the long retreat to their current position still stung.

Switching to thermals didn't do a lot of good in an active snowstorm, so Reiter was surprised when his passive thermals picked up a hit. Another Iglaiso, a recon type, plowed through the snow towards them. The IFV's tracks squeezed over the howl of the wind as it rushed past them.

"Nomad element. Fox 6, report," Reiter snapped. The Iglaiso ignored him and continued running away. Another Iglaiso followed it, this one with a split turret.

"I don't think the nomads are doing to well," Stovepipe replied, but Reiter ignored him. Instead he broke into a run, crashing through trees as he went. Up ahead he could see the battle. A lone

Panzerter IV just barely held off three tinhats. She was belching smoke and already down an arm. Wrecks littered the snow covered forest. Some Panzerter IVs, a pair of Iglasios, and a tinhat. *Steele.*

Reiter charged the nearest tinhat. In one hand he raised his shield, while the other took aim with his new rifle. With a high-pitched ping, a 90-mm heavy metal slug punched right into the Union machine. The ugly thing crashed to the ground.

Its companions opened fire. Reiter grunted as shells hammered his shield. Firing a second time, he smashed a shoulder off one. To his surprise, the first one began struggling to stand back up. *I must have hit nothing vital.*

"White 4, fall back," Reiter barked. "You did your job, the Reece platoon lives."

"Can't do 6," She replied. "Nomad 3's stuck." Reiter put another round into the first tinhat. This time its hips shattered. *Damn it, she's right, we can't leave them.*

"Gold 2 can tow them," he snapped. "You fall back, I'll cover you." The final intact tinhat backpedaled, unleashing a furious barrage as it did. Reiter returned fire. A hammering auto-cannon signaled Stovepipe catching up to him.

While the lighter weapon could do little against a panzerter's thicker armor, it proved more than capable of smashing a tint's sensor ring. Blind and down an arm, the second tinhat lay still. By now the last one had given them the slip. Reiter looked at the tinhats he'd knocked out.

"Union pilots," he called over the external speakers. "Surrender, you'll be treated with all the respect according to the Geneva convention of 1995." Sure enough, the pilots crawled out of their downed machines. "Stovepipe, you got room for two more?"

"We'll have to have some of my guys ride in the scout track, but yeah we should," the infantryman replied. "When do we get a fancy magnetic gun system?" Reiter chuckled. With Steele limping back to base, Stovepipe's riflemen dismounted. After a few minutes of shouting and bribes, they had the scouts and POWs helping them hook tow cables and dig out the recon vehicle.

Reiter focused on the surroundings, ever wary of a follow-up attack. When none came, and the scout vehicle had been freed, he gave the order to mount up and move out. He let Stovepipe's Iglaiso precede him as they made their way back to base.

"Raptor X-Ray, Fox 6, our screen revived contact," he said. "Inform Early company of the changeover." He never wore gloves in the cockpit, as he'd always preferred the greater sensation of his bare hands. With the Lowe's sensitive controls, it made sense, but the weather made his hands numb. *That's what I need to recommend next, heated controls. At least my bum warmer works.*

"Hey 6," Stovepipe called. "You're not obligated too, but do you mind explaining why you came out here instead of sending Black Platoon?" Reiter grinned as he switched his mic back to the company net.

"A few mark IVs could be any Tharcian armored company," he said. "But the Lowe? That's us, and it freaks out their rookies." Even though his machine traded the all black paint job that'd made it infamous among the union for added splotches of green, gray, and white, captured soldiers still identified it as "the Black Knight."

After an hour slogging through snow and mud, they arrived at the town of Landfall. The municipality still had people living there somehow, despite about of the building being damaged or knocked down. Once he'd parked the Lowe in a kneeling pose in an empty lot with the rest of Fox company, he donned his gloves, killed the engine, and climbed out.

As the frigid wind met his face, he shuddered and pulled his jacket on. Gray clouds hung overhead, casting snow on the town. Landfall itself consisted of a couple blocks stretched along the main road, a provincial highway that led to the city of Grunbeck.

While dismounting his panzerter, Reiter noticed some of his soldiers hard at work with snow shovels and sandbags. *This ought to be good.*

"Hey gents, what's going on here?" he asked. At the start of the war, he'd been Black Platoon's leader, but the ferocity of the initial Union Offensive saw him take over the company during the desperate scramble to stem the tide. At Twenty Seven, he was not much older than most of his soldiers.

"A little something I cooked up," Sergeant Mondragon said with a grin. "The laser weapons the Union tends to favor don't mix well with water, you know, dispersing the beam in all." He pointed at his platoon mates, Corporal Merlin the elder, and PFC Smith. The two held sandbags high so Reiter could see they'd been packed with snow.

"Union laser hits our handy snowbag," Corporal Merlin began.

"And the snow turns to steam, scattering the beam," Smith finished while demonstrating the scatter with his hands. Merlin glanced towards the area where white platoon's machines normally parked.

"Hey, sir, is White still out?" he asked. Reiter hadn't given Col. Hawke his After Action Review and Battle Damage Assessment yet, but he could see the other man's concern for his brother.

"No, they're back," he replied. "None of their machines have been recovered, but Invincible is working on that." He held up a hand before Merlin could get a word in. "Ernie is ok, we had to MEDEVAC him and Zorro, but she needed it way more than he did."

"What happened?" Merlin asked. Reiter clapped him on the shoulder.

"You should be proud of him," he said. "Unis shot them both down, Ernest was able to bailout, Zorro couldn't. When we picked him up, he'd carried Zorro ten clicks in the snow." Merlin sighed in relief.

"So he's not too bad?"

"He's being treated for early stages of hypothermia and frost-bite," Reiter replied. "But he'll be biting at your heels before too long." Mo grabbed the taller man's shoulder.

"Hey man, if you need to take a walk, we got this," he said. Merlin shook his head and retrieved his shovel.

"Thanks Mo, but nah," he said as he returned to work. "If Ernie comes back and I'm slacking, that's hardly the example a brother should set." Reiter turned to leave, but stopped himself. *One more thing.*

"Before I leave, you stooges should be getting a new LT before long," he said. The pilots of Black Platoon shrugged. Their last LT had been killed during a patrol along one of the highways north of Landfall. As his soldiers went about their work, Reiter made his way towards a mom and pop diner centered on main street. With the regimental command post in sight, he took a deep breath and entered the building.

———————————

THE CLINK OF WHISKY GLASSES WAS A SOUND DECLAN KENNEDY could get used to. The newly minted Guard-Lieutenant Colonel sipped his fiery drink in the company of his MAG benefactor: Guard-Brigadier Chaney. The two occupied a lunge suite in the underground city of Congregation, the capital of the Congaree Martian Republic. The older man pointed at the new medal adorning Kennedy's dress uniform.

"That Order of the Martian People blends nicely with the rest of your collection," he said. Kennedy shrugged.

"They really are collectibles at this point," he admitted. "I mean, the first one was special, but this is past ridiculous." Chaney nodded as he sipped his own whiskey.

"So humor me this," he asked. "I have a theory, that a medal can only be earned once before it loses all value to a unit, for example, if someone else in the 100th received an OMP, it wouldn't hold as much value because you already earned one, and would be worthless in the 75th Panzerter for the same reason." Kennedy mulled it over for a moment.

"A counter-point," Kennedy said. "If so many high honors are awarded inside a regiment, it raises the standing of the Regiment itself as well as individuals outside of it." He set his whiskey down to talk with his hands. "So like G-SGT Dan earns an OMB, he'd be compared to me and the rest of the 'heroic regiment that earns these awards', so the value would go up." Chaney pointed at him.

"But do you value your medals?" he asked. "Like your old ones?" Kennedy shrugged.

"I guess not as much," he said. "I mean I earned them, but it all built me up to the point where I earned this one, but I'm also not pinning for more because at the end of the day the rewards I want aren't medals." Chaney smiled as he stirred his whiskey.

"Well, my friend, those are the rewards we don't discuss with the public," Chaney said. "Which reminds me, your valor in securing the Tarnotów pocket really got the attention of First Minister Pennington, Ballard is going to be able to see his daughter." Kennedy leaned forward in his seat.

"So the Union officially recognizes her as his daughter?" he asked. Chaney twisted his open hand.

"More or less," he replied. "The Union at large is, but the Cascadian MR isn't." Kennedy clenched his fist.

"Then sick the IRS on them!" Kennedy cried. "They're actively impeding the war effort by harming the mental health of a guard-soldier!" the older man shook his head.

"They both sit on the oversight board for major logging cooperatives," he said. "It's not that simple, and we're lucky Pennington forced them to allow Ballard to see his daughter for a weekend." Kennedy rose from his chair as he knocked back his whiskey.

"It's bullshit, he's doing more for that young girl's future than those two are sitting on a board somewhere safe."

"They're elderly Ken, it's not like we can draft them," Chaney said. "Besides, their counterargument is no matter how well he does, he's doing what he was bred to do, same for you." The cackling fire filled the silence. Though Kennedy and Ballard looked the same as any other Union citizen, they'd been born in batches and grown inside artificial chambers instead of a woman. Like all tubers, they didn't enjoy the same rights as natural born union citizens, but rather had to earn them back through state service.

"Still no sign of Fletcher?" Kennedy asked. Chaney shook his head.

"Our intel suggests she was sent to the rear," he said. "Possibly a prison camp, possibly a direction table. We really have no way of knowing." Kennedy plopped back into his easy chair.

"They should include some escape or evasion training in case our pilots get captured," he said. Chaney sipped more whiskey.

"The party line is, don't get captured," he said. "Granted, it seems like it would have been hard for Fletcher to do unconscious inside a downed Martian." The older man rose from his lounge chair. "Come on, if we're not careful, the whiskey's going to start doing the talking, let me show you around more of Congregation." He rose and motioned for Kennedy to follow him outside.

The hotel they stayed at felt more like a section of a larger building than its own building in a larger city. Along the ceiling, pipes circulated the hot gasses from the fireplaces to heat the floor above them. Even through his boots, the tile he walked on felt warm.

"Everyone knows Congregation is underground," Chaney said. "It's common knowledge, but you need to appreciate it in full you need to see it yourself." They walked down a series of winding hallways, eventually coming to a large atrium. The atrium led to an even larger open area. High above his head, a massive glass like dome held the snow and brutal winter away.

"I can't get over the size of the dome," Kennedy said. More levels extended towards the moist dome, with more people going about their lives. Chaney chuckled.

"Trust me, if you saw the outside of a habitat, you'd be speechless," Chaney said. "Of course that comes with working in space occasionally." Kennedy leaned over the railing, staring down at the abyss. Voices echoed endlessly through the underground city.

"How's your particle weapon project going?" he asked. Chaney grimaced and shook his head.

"It's a great weapon system," he said. "We're just lacking on efficient power sources, or scaling down to panzerter scale, but it works." Kennedy sighed.

"I'm not going to lie, things seem to move so fast at the front," he said. "You blink and a week, a month has gone by, but here everything's so slow." Chaney smiled.

"We're in an island of peace, Kennedy," he said. "The war hasn't reached here, even as the people create goods to aid the people on the front, Roosevelt has been pacified, and the Olympians are collapsing." He pointed to the dome overhead. "We're out of the range of Tharcian bombing, Congregation enjoys a level of peace and security unobtainable elsewhere in our country." Kennedy stood up and stretched.

"So what you're saying is I'm getting a glimpse of the postwar world?" he asked. Chaney nodded and clapped him on the shoulder.

"Put on something comfortable, we're going to take a look at something below," he said. "But first, I need to pick up some guests."

"HOW MANY NEW MACHINES?" REITER ASKED. ACROSS THE TABLE from him, Lieutenant Colonel Hawke held a personnel roster and an update to his TO&E. Tapping the latter document, the older man slid it over to him.

"Not a lot," he said. "A couple tracks for the scouts and infantry, and a refurbished Panzerter IV, but that's the price you pay for more parts for the Lowe." Reiter sighed.

"What about these lieutenants?" he asked. "Know anything about them?" Hawk glanced around the personnel roster for a moment before shaking his head.

"No, they're both fresh out of college, haven't even been to OLC," the regimental commander replied. "On the downside, they couldn't be greener, but on the plus side they'll be easier to develop."

"Assuming they live," Reiter said. "Which the way things have been going is hardly a guarantee." Hawke leaned back in his chair and stretched. At that moment, Reiter noticed the bags under his eyes.

"Their odds are better if they're riding a Lowe," Hawk said. "Most panzerters don't have that level of durability." Reiter shook his head.

"The controls are too sensitive for a rookie pilot," he said. "Especially if they expect it to be slow and cumbersome. No, if we get another one it will go to one of my Sergeants, I've had them sim piloting mine in case I went down."

"Not an unreasonable plan," Hawke noted. "This whole war has been an absolute meat grinder and we're not even two-and-a-half months in." He looked up at the theater map on the wall of his office, really the manager's office in the diner serving as the Regiment's command post. "One and a half million dead, wounded, or missing, and it's only December."

"I wonder how many losses the Union's taken," Reiter replied. "If they weren't hurting too, they'd be doing more than probing us here." Hawke shrugged.

"Not sure, they knocked out Roosevelt and most of Olympia with ridiculous speed," he replied. "But you're right, at what cost?" He handed the documents to Reiter. "Anyway, maintain your company's position, I suspect when Olympia finally crumbles, they'll renew they're efforts against us, and I'm not sure we hold out." He pointed out the door. "We're already rotating Early Company to take over your scouts sector, your remaining forces will serve as Regimental QRF until you get stood up, understood?" Reiter nodded.

"Well, thank you for the reinforcements and equipment," Reiter said with a sharp salute. "Merry Christmas, sir." Hawke smiled as he returned his salute.

"Merry Christmas Captain, you're dismissed," he said. As he left the diner, he checked his watch. With his 1st Sergeant buried in paperwork related to their wounded and dead, he decided to check on the scouts. The mechanized scout platoon had been a recent addition to his company since they'd reorganized themselves. *I don't know a ton about scouts, so I might as well go use them.*

He found them in a smaller parking lot near the lot containing their panzerters. Point Defense turrets scanned the skies for enemy drones and dropships while the scouts mulled about near their tracks. They'd started with four infantry fighting vehicles, but we're down to three now.

"Gentlemen," he called. "How are you holding up?" The scouts stopped talking amongst themselves and starred. *Hardly a warm reception.* "Who's in charge here?" One of the scouts approached him. The man sported greasy black hair and a powerful mustache. Though he hardly came up to Reiter's chest, he still seemed formidable.

"I am," he said. "Master Sergeant Lysak, I'm the platoon sergeant around here." Reiter nodded.

"Captain Reiter, I apologize we weren't able to talk to your group much before you set your screen." The other man shook his head.

"It happens," he said. "Chaos of war and all." Reiter motioned the other man to follow him.

"So how are your boys holding up?" he asked. The older man stared in the distance as he walked alongside him.

"They'll survive," he said. "They have to if we're going to win this war." Reiter frowned.

"That's not what I'm asking, Sergeant," he said. "I need a picture of their headspace."

"With all due respect, sir," the Sergeant said. "The only thing you need to know is if they're ready to fight, and how they're fighting." *This guy's a piece of work, but I have to work with him.*

"Well, your people are scouts," Reiter said. "So I'm going to need all kinds of information from you because my intelligence priorities are different depending on the mission." He stopped and turned on the other man. "And we're refitting right now, so my intelligence priority is who are these scouts I have attached to me and how can I help them accomplish their mission." The Master Sergeant's glare was colder than the surrounding snow.

"We're Tharcian scouts," he said. "Simple as that, you don't need every sob story from these whiney privates that don't know anything to know where to put us, and as to accomplishing our mission? You stay out of the way." *When Adamski gets a chance, we need to look into these guys.* He looked back to the other scouts and sighed.

"Well, if you need anything from us, you know where the TOC is," he said before walking away. As the sun began to sink towards the horizon, he stuck his head in the Company TOC, just to make sure they were ok in there. A heater with an image of a fire place warmed the small storefront they used. 1st LT Comidus, his executive officer, manned the main monitors while Sergeant Steele pecked away on a keyboard. The young woman rubbed something in her left hand while typing with her right.

"Everything ok Steele?" he asked. "Your hand hurt?" She shook her head and showed him a small strand of prayer beads.

"They were Bartonova's," she said. "She gave them to me before we lost her, because she wanted me to be safe." On hearing Bartonova's name, he laid a hand on her shoulder.

"It's ok, you're not doing anything wrong," he said. "Carry on." He retrieved a laptop from a small computer bank. "Deuce, I'll be out in the Lowe if you need me, Steele, I'm going to take care of Merlin's citation, you just worry about Zorro." The pair acknowledged him and Reiter ventured back out into the cold.

It didn't take him long to get back to their motor pool. Passing the snowbag laden panzerters of Black Platoon, he crawled into the cockpit of his own machine. Switching the Lowe into idle, he turned on his bum warmer and opened the computer.

Before he went to work, he glanced to his right. Bartonova smiled back at him, her muscular body soaking the sun. Vargas cheered from the sideline of a children's hockey game, a clipboard in his hand. He sighed. *I still have more pictures to add, and this wall is getting crowded.*

"IT'S BEEN SOMETHING WE'VE BEEN COORDINATING FOR A LONG time," Chaney said. "The mining unions in Cascadia have struggled for decades, ever since we broke into asteroid mining, but since we need so much of those materials for shipbuilding and panzerters in space, we contracted several of the mining unions to provide the raw materials to the foundry here."

The MAG officer led Kennedy and their special guests down a long hallway. Much to the pilot's surprise, their 'guests' had been none other than the First Minister himself, along with the Secretary to the National Committee.

First Minister Pennington's best years were long behind him, the elderly minister sat a few years from a three digit age. While his faculties had been sharp through most of his career, he'd slipped up on occasion recently. Forgetting a name here, fumbling a story there, the stress of the war seemed to have already taken a toll on the man.

Secretary Pearson had come up through the Internal Review Service. Serving as the internal security apparatus of the Union of Martian Republics, the IRS made sure Union citizens upheld their natural responsibilities while also guarding against any future cases of secession. Pearson made a name for herself, winning the loyalty of the Union citizens living in space in Phobos and space habitats.

"The result is just one shining example of the resilience of the United Martian people," Chaney finished. *He's laying it on thick for the politicians,* Kennedy thought, *and they look like they're lapping it up.* They paused to allow security to clear them.

"You'd think they'd recognize us," The National Secretary muttered. "It's not like our faces aren't everywhere." Chaney shook his head as the guards ran a metal detector over him.

"Same rules for everyone, Comrade Secretary," he said. "Anyway, we're seeing a coming economic boom, Boreal Locomotive expanded their facilities here into panzerter production, and the new facilities are having a ripple effect." Once they'd cleared security, Chaney led his group to an observation deck.

Stretched out before them, a procession of Jupiter Heavy Panzerters rolled down an assembly line. The powerful machines seemed naked without their armor plating. As workers below coordinated robotic manipulators to add armor to the legs, Chaney turned to face the group.

"This is just one stage in the assembly process," he said. "If you'll follow me, I'll escort you to one of our finished models." For the first time since they'd collected him, the First Minister spoke.

"I don't recall seeing this model before," he said. "Is the Martian being replaced?" Chaney shook his head as he walked.

"Not at the moment," he replied. "We're currently conducting studies for our next generation general purpose panzerter, by the end of the month we should have a call for our unions to submit proposals."

"Why would you prioritize panzerter development?" Secretary Pearson asked. "We have multiple other needs that need addressing, and our last update led us to believe the Martian and Martian Trooper were more than sufficient for our forces." Chaney held up a single finger.

"You must have read an old report," he said. "But I believe Comrade Kennedy can explain the necessity of newer panzerters and the Jupiter itself better than I can." *Gee thanks comrade.*

"Around the beginning of November we began running into issues," Kennedy said. "Not only could the Tharcians counter our laser weapons, but they also began fielding heavy panzerters of their own." They rounded a corner and Chaney swiped a badge in front of a pair of double doors. "These panzerters had enough firepower to disable or destroy Martians before they could get into effective range, and thick enough armor to shrug off counter attacks."

The double doors opened to reveal Kennedy's personal Jupiter. With the shoulder mounted cannon replaced by a rocket pod, the armor had been strengthened, including the "belt line" where spare magazines for the Jupiter's handheld weapons were stored. As for those handheld weapons, the Jupiter could be equipped with a 100-mm Marksmen rifle, a 75-mm submachine gun, and a 76-mm strobe laser that didn't require ammo.

"These Heavy panzerters, like the Jupiter, are specifically made to destroy fortifications and other panzerters," Kennedy said. "And in my experience, it's an excellent unit."

"Panzerters aren't the only thing the R&D department is working on," Chaney added. "We're also researching improvements to our Infantry Fighting Vehicles and Armored Troop carriers, we've reexamined a lot of our vehicles and weapons with soldier survivability in mind." Secretary Justice snorted.

"There's a reason our doctrine before 2112 emphasized expendable troops," she said. "Our founders would roll in their graves if the military held too much political influence." Sharing a look with Chaney, Kennedy choose his next words carefully.

"With all do respect, comrade Secretary," he said. "If you don't want the military to have political influence, staying out of wars would be the way to do that." He looked back at the Jupiter. "I understand what the founders wanted, but soldiers and sailors are workers too, we've never sat on a TUC on any level, but civil authorities don't trust us to not overthrow them, yet they trust us to protect them from forces that would see them toppled." Kennedy met the Secretaries fierce gaze with a stoic stare.

"Are you insinuating the military could rebel?" Pearson asked. Kennedy shook his head.

"I'm merely pointing out military personnel should have the chance to represent themselves with unions, same as every other citizen," he said. "The thing tubers would also like." Before Secretary Pearson could utter another word, the First Minister held up his hands.

"Listen here," he said. "I'm aware of the deals that have been made, trust me, it is inexcusable that tubers are effectively second-class citizens in our 'classless society,' and the military stuff is true as well." He looked at his watch. "I'll be holding a rally at Foundation in a few days, I'll address our tubers, no, I'll address all of our citizens, tune in, you'll here something good, I guarantee it." The two allowed themselves to be escorted out of the plant, leaving Kennedy and Chaney alone with the Jupiter.

"I don't think you're out of the woods yet," Chaney said. "She still has hooks in the IRS, I'm sure." Kennedy shook his head.

"You saw the way she looked at us and the men working here," he said. "They couldn't wait to get back to their homes in Foundation." Chaney walked over and set a hand on his shoulder.

"I know what you're thinking," he said. Lowering his voice to a whisper, he continued. "They're not the enemy."

"Could have fooled me," Kennedy hissed. "This war is predicated on revenge and envy, we cannot sustain a society with that." Chaney tightened his grip on the younger man's shoulder.

"Than survive," he said. "And when you change things for the better, remember the people the authorities have forgotten." Kennedy nodded.

"I took an oath, the same one you did, and mark my words, I'll keep it until the day I die."

2

Reiter couldn't help but flash a grin. He'd gathered the company in a basketball court and now they stood in front of him, formed up by platoon. Adamski stood beside him and nodded.

"PFC Merlin, post," Reiter called. The young man scampered in front of him, adjusting his glasses before snapping to attention. As Comidus read the order, Adamski and Reiter removed his old rank from his collar and snapped on a new Corporal rank onto his collar. The burnt orange regimental colors contrasted with the green-gray of his CVCs. The two men shook his hand, but Adamski stopped him before he could fall back in.

"We're not done yet," he said. Reiter grasped the medal in his pocket.

"Attention to orders," Comidus bellowed. "For heroic actions during combat on 2 December 2135 in defense of the homeland, PFC Ernest Merlin has been recognized by the Field Marshal Adam Haussner as worthy of The Order of Tepes, 1st Class." Reiter pinned the medal just above the young man's name tape, before spinning him around.

"Give him a hand," Reiter called. When the clapping stopped, he continued. "If I'm being honest, Merlin the younger here has no business on the front lines, and no business defending his homeland." He looked at the shocked gazes of his soldiers. "I say that not to degrade or take away from his performance, but to illustrate a point, he should be studying for finals. All the pilots we got from OMI prep, should." He looked from Merlin to Smith and shook his head. "Merlin, Smith, and Zorro should be worried about prom dates and passing next semester, not whether they'll live to see tomorrow."

He stepped away from Adamski and Merlin so he could see his formation better. "Unger should be looking forward to her last soccer season instead of being buried in a shallow grave West of here," Reiter said. He pushed aside the rage that welled up within him. "The Union has done nothing but leave shattered and broken lives in its wake, their friends in Avalon are hardly better if not much worse." He turned back to Merlin jr. "Congratulations Corporal Merlin, keep up the good work, all officers and senior NCO's meet me in the TOC in fifteen, the rest of you are dismissed."

He left for his office immediately. *I have to look at my notes and review my maps for a minute.* After collecting his things, he hustled to the TOC. Adamski beat him there and already had a pot of coffee brewing for their meeting. Comidus fame in the back and went to work putting up operational maps on their monitors.

"Ski you're not the hero we deserve, but you're the one we need, " the XO said as he sipped his coffee. The other man chuckled as he helped Reiter set up his notes.

"Hey man, Army runs on food and coffee," Adamski said. "As

long as we're fed and awake, we can fight." Even though the man was joking, he reminded Reiter of Lysak Sergeant's words.

"Hey Ski, did you ever get the personnel files for the scout platoon?" he asked. The 1st Sergeant nodded.

"Yeah, I got a lot of stuff from higher on them," he replied. As he talked, the others began arriving. "But we can go over that later with Deuce." The Panzerter platoons, represented by Mo, Steele and their LTs, came in as a crowd followed shortly by Stovepipe and LT. Zukal. Sergeant Lysak rounded out the group as the mortar sergeant walked in after the infantryman.

"Alright," Reiter began. "Before we get started, I'd like to formally welcome Lt. Wesser and LT. Kozma to Fox, as well as MSG Lysak, Black and White Platoon have some good ones with you." Lt. Wesser played with her bun as she smiled nervously. Lt. Kozma simply grinned and raised a hand in greeting. Reiter looked over at Comidus. "Now that that's out of the way, if you would all turn your attention to the main monitor.

A detailed map of the 7th Panzerter Division's area of operations filled the main monitor. rugged forests surrounded two major metropolitan areas: Grünbeck and Swiezin. Reiter pointed towards their own position.

"As you can see, our regiment's in Landfall to prevent Union Forces from crossing the Grenze river to our East, and thus prevent an attack on Grünbeck," he said. "To our North, 4-14th Cav is screening the approach to these two bridges here and here." Icons appeared on the screen as he pointed. "To our South, 7-4th Cav is running recon operations out of Riverside, a little town most of us are more familiar with then we'd like to be."

"Now the axis of our defense is along the Gallacian side of the Grenze river, Division HQ is holed up in Swizen, our sister regiment 1-11th is protecting the main highway leading to Grünbeck from the North as well as backing up the 4-14th Cav." Kozma raised a hand. "Yes, Kozma?"

"Yes sir, excuse me if I'm asking something dumb," he said. "But why are you informing us of all this other stuff going on?" Reiter nodded.

"Not a dumb question at all," he replied. "I'm providing context for our current mission, we're the QRF for the West side of the river, and it's important that we know who we'd be working with and what we could be running into, Deuce, if you would with the OPFOR report?" The XO nodded, gulped down the last of his coffee, and turned to the monitor.

"Alright ladies and gentlemen, they got a mechanized division lined up against us," he said as more symbols populated the map. "That means IFVs, Panzerters, dropships, the whole rainbow of Union military equipment is being arrayed against us." Adamski took the XO's coffee cup and began pouring more. "Except battle-ships and things of that nature." That got a chuckle out of the room.

"So what does that mean?" Comidus asked. Images of Union vehicles in the field appeared on the screen. "That's their standard panzerter, reporting name Tinhat, and their heavy panzerter, reporting name Fatman." He pointed to a wedged shaped tracked vehicle. "This ugly fellow is their IFV, reporting name Ratte, these seem to be spread thin, so also be on the lookout for these 8-wheeled monstrosities reporting name Jalopy as well." After identifying the enemy vehicles, Comidus took a seat with a fresh mug of coffee as Reiter retook the floor.

"Now that you know our mission, here's how your days are going to look," he said. "I need at least three hours of rehearsal out of our platoons per day, barring that they're on REDCON 2 all day and night." Adamski stood up as well.

"To that end, I advise checking your comms every hour. This will keep the radio chaos from rearing its head when you get ready to roll out," he said. After Reiter dismissed their soldiers, he sat in his chair while Comidus returned to watching the monitors and listening to the radio. Adamski also remained to clean the coffee pot.

"Have either of you guys heard anything about the war in space?" Reiter asked. The other two shook their heads.

"Last I heard, Avalon switched from accidentally destroying colonies to outright attacking them," Comidus said. "Could be bullshit, could be a gamble to force Olympia's space holdings to surrender." Reiter shook his head.

"That's a bad gamble," he said. "They're more likely to unite the Olympians against them than anything else." He leaned back in his chair. *If we value life so much, why did we send children to their deaths at the first sign of trouble? How many lives are going to be lost in this conflict? And for what?*

———

KENNEDY LEANED AGAINST A COLD WINDOW AS THE TRAIN rocketed along. *As the old saying goes, if you're tired enough, anything's a pillow.* Though he lay as comfortable as he could, sleep still evaded him as a stag dodges a huntsman. Just before the rolling of the train and the howl of the snow outside could finally lull him to blissful sleep, Chaney tugged on his arm.

"Kennedy," the older man said. "There's a battle report here, says your regiment fought a nasty skirmish recently." Kennedy groaned as he sat up straight.

"We're at war, Comrade Chaney," he said. "Those things tend to happen." The Research Colonel handed him a tablet. Kennedy squinted as his eyes adjusted to the brightness. The lights had been dimmed and blackout panels over windows allowed the train to avoid being detected from the air.

"So they ran into Tharcian pickets and took some losses," he said. "I'll have a word with whoever incompetently…" He stopped as his eyes reached the words *Black Knight.* "So, they managed to refurbish it."

"I assume so," Chaney said. "There wasn't a lot left to repair after your last battle, though of course, we were more concerned with recovering you than trying to salvage either machine." Kennedy shook his head.

"I'm still amazed anyone came to rescue me," he said. "After all, every Union soldier should be prepared to give up his life for his country." Chaney lit a small pipe.

"You know, that would be the case if you were regular army," he said. "But you're a MAG, and we value talented individuals." Kennedy raised an eyebrow.

"Do we?" he asked. "We've spent so many lives just getting to where we are now, and the TUC and the National Committee demand more say in how we do things."

"Tell me something, Ken," Chaney said as he puffed on his pipe. "You have 70 people in your battalion, all 70 of them must die, would you rather they die moving the front line a few meters or die moving the front a few miles?" Kennedy held up his hands.

"I'd rather they not die, period," Kennedy said. "I'd rather they live to fight the next battle." Chaney nodded.

"And that, my friend, is the big mistake," he said. "No, not on your part, but on the TUC and NC, they expected a quick victory." He took a long drag on his pipe. "Because they don't understand logistics, manpower, or attrition."

"We've nearly won," Kennedy said. "Olympia is out of the war, all they have left are holdings in orbit that Avalon continues to seize, Roosevelt lasted a mere two weeks before being overrun, Tharsis is it, why slow down now?" Chaney shook his head.

"Because Ken, they don't like military heroes," he said. "Military figures with any kind of a following are a threat to their own power base, that's one of the many reasons we lost the last damn war, because they did not understand how a military needs to operate and tried to spring one out of thin air."

"So what now?" Kennedy asked. "Are they trying to swoop in at the last second and claim credit for victory?" Chaney shook his head.

"I honestly don't know," he said. "There are still people in the TUC and NC that believe a United Mars must happen for the syndicalist-unionist state to remain uncorrupted, but to unite all of Mars would require military force to an unsustainable degree." He removed his pipe so he could speak more clearly.

"But what of our allies?" Kennedy asked. "Are we eventually going to ask Avalon to join us in worker solidarity?" Chaney snorted.

"If the TUC and NC really cared about the founder's ideals, we would have never allied ourselves to a country ruled by a king," he said. "As to what I was about to say, if this war strains our economy too much, it doesn't matter how well we prepare, we won't be able to take on the First Nation or Vinland." Kennedy stopped to process everything he'd heard.

As far as he'd been aware, the solar system remained divided between the major powers of Mars: The Union, Tharsis, Avalon, Olympia, the First Nation and Vinland; and the major powers of Earth: The US, Brazil, the Central African Union, the North Sea Alliance, the SSR, and Japan. Four of the big players on Mars remained locked in combat, with war with the others a definite possibility.

"I might need another drink," Kennedy moaned. "But let's just focus on the obstacle in front of us." Chaney nodded as he puffed on his pipe. "Or obstacles, the black knight isn't something to take lightly." He returned Chaney's tablet to him. As he leaned back against the cold window, Chaney looked at his tablet.

"Huh, the First Minister is speaking," he said. "I'm going to put his on if you don't mind." Kennedy waved him ahead and the Minister's voice filled the train compartment.

"I know you folks have suffered as this brutal war enters its third month," the old man said. "Now we're promised a quick win, and the MAGs and regular forces have delivered us not one, but two! Olympia and Roosevelt have ceased all military activity, but despite this a vocal minority of Olympians have fled to Tharsis claiming to be the 'Government-in-exile', which of course we know they aren't because Olympia has totally surrendered unconditionally." Kennedy raised an eyebrow.

"I thought their space holdings were still fighting?" he asked. Chaney nodded.

"They are, maybe he's trying to break their spirit?" he replied.

"Tharsis still has us by the throat," the Minister said. "Recently, we've heard they're targeting our tuber service members for medical experiments, I have no words for how disgusted I am by the barbarism the Tharcian people display towards artificial people, in response we're going to increase the pay of our military members by 50% during wartime, and to all tubers by 30%." Kennedy blinked. Chaney grimaced.

"Are you kidding me?" the older man spat. "That's a dangerous precedent, 1 labor equals one hour of work, for *everyone.*" Kennedy shrugged.

"I don't see the issue," he said. "We're making more money." Chaney shook his head.

"Labors are backed by time because it's the one thing you can't alter," he said. "People only live for so many hours, but if you increase the value of one person's labor, you decrease someone else's." Chaney leaned back in his chair. "I've got a bad feeling about this."

"Further more," the First Minister added after ranting about rationing. "The TUC will be establishing a citizens oversight committee to manage the General staff and ensure the war is fought humanly by our forces, there will be no atrocities committed by the Armies of the Working People."

"I've heard enough," Chaney said as he ended the feed. "Personally, I'm convinced the TUC and NC are either uninterested in winning this war or unable to grasp what victory will take." Kennedy shrugged. *The war's ultimately flowed in our favor, who's saying we've won before something bad happens?*

REITER SMILED. FOX COMPANIES PILOTS AND INFANTRYMAN PLAYED an intense game of pickup hockey in a local rink. Stovepipe shouted plays and formations from one side, while Adamski did the same from the opposite. Comidus laughed as he held a steaming mug.

"What's the score?" Reiter asked his XO. Comidus kept his ungloved hands glued to his mug.

"5-4, Infantry," he said. "Ya'll are more skilled, but my boys are more physical." Steele knocked away another shot into the goal. One of the riflemen snagged the puck only for Smith to swipe it and pass it off to Merlin JR.

He bore down on the goal as Mo and his elder brother checked and blocked defenders. He found an angle on the goalie. He raised his stick, ready to shoot. Then passed it off to his brother, who scored immediately.

"5-5," Comidus said. "Everyone gets a little sloppy." The infantry ultimately won in a score of 6-5, but everyone involved seemed to be in high spirits. As the pilots filed past him to change back into winter boots, he high fives and patted them on the back.

"We're going to have to have a rematch," Mo said. "I needed to blow off some steam." Reiter nodded as he walked with him.

"I'm glad, and it's good to see Merlin is fully recovered from his hypothermia and frostbite," he said. "How'd rehearsals go?"

"A little slow at first," Mo said. "She thought it was weird to walk around with a broom, but she got the idea pretty quick, Merlin SR is her wingman so she should be fine." Reiter noticed Wesser standing near the rink a few yards from where they walked. Clapping the younger man on the shoulder, Reiter walked over to the new leader.

"How have your rehearsals gone?" he asked. Wesser shrugged.

"I felt silly holding a broom at first, but staying indoors warmed me to the idea," she said. Reiter smiled. Her green eyes glistened even under gray skies. "Also, are they messing with me? Because my panzerter looks silly with all those sandbags filled with snow." Reiter shook his head.

"No, that's actually a clever idea," he said and explained to her how it countered the Union's laser weapons.

"Oh, I see," she said. "So you were a lieutenant during the retreat towards the Grenze?" he nodded before tapping his rank.

"I got this because our old captain died and our company needed to rebuild," he said. "I was the senior living officer, so I got the job." He gestured to the others changing into their boots. "Mo, Ski, Steele, Comidus, Stovepipe, and some other infantry are all that's left of the old Fox company." Those green eyes flicked to the ground.

"That bad, huh?" she said.

"The Union aren't a bunch of cartoon bad guys," Reiter said. "We're not beating them with songs, nor are they just going to keel over." Remembering his last battle with Kennedy, he shivered.

"They've got some damn good pilots and leaders, and they're persistent as all hell. If that wasn't the case, we wouldn't be having this conversation here."

"Well, I haven't been to OLC," she said. "How can I hope to be a good leader if I haven't even learned the basics?" Reiter held up a hand.

"You don't necessarily need an alphabet course," he said. "First, focus on becoming a good pilot, focus on being able to survive, then we can worry about shaping you into a good leader." Wesser folded her arms.

"Panzerter school said they taught us everything we needed to know," she said. Reiter raised an eyebrow.

"Did they teach you about snowbags?" he asked. "Or to go after an opponent's limbs in hand to hand combat? Or their sensors?" She hesitated slightly. "By the way, under those bags of snow, every member of Black Platoon has five plus kills painted on their hulls." He began walking towards the hotel that served as their barracks, and Wesser followed him.

"They're all aces?" she asked. "Even the kid?" Reiter snorted. *A twenty-year-old calling a seventeen-year-old kid is rich.* He nodded.

"Yeah, all of them," he said. "Hell, Mo was an ace piloting an antique Panzerter III." He looked back at her. "That's why its important you learn from them, they know all kinds of tricks and are good at creating more." Before Reiter could enter the barracks, one of the infantrymen ran him down.

"Sir!" he called. "XO needs you in the TOC!" Reiter sighed as he turned and walked towards the rifleman. As he left Wesser by the hotel entrance, he turned back to her.

"Could be nothing, but we could be fighting," he said. "Prepare your platoon accordingly." He followed the rifleman as the young man ran back into the TOC where his suspicions were confirmed.

"Recon from the boys north of us have enemy movement,"

Comidus said the second Rieter walked in. "Motorized infantry with a few panzerters," he said. Whipping to the rifleman, Rieter took control.

"Radio all of Fox, get them ready to move," he said. Turning back to Comidus, he approached the map. "Has 4-14th asked for us to jump in?" The XO nodded.

"The Unis are using these two main roads," he said. "They're running right for the bridges, the Cav is setting ambushes all along the approach and would like us to counter their armor, and prevent reinforcements from coming." Rieter nodded.

"Let's get mounted up," he said. "Keep me updated from the command track." Rieter turned and bolted out the door. Pilots poured out of the hotel and a few other buildings. They spilled into the motor pool and Rieter clambered into the Lowe. Strapping on his helmet, he ran the Lowe through its start up sequence.

While his Lowe started, he called for all leaders to meet him near the command track. He dismounted among the noise of idling Panzerters. As Comidus's track pulled into the middle of the motor pool, Rieter and other leaders ran to the back of the track while Comidus lowered the ramp.

"Ok, listen up," Rieter said. After he'd briefed them and set a rally point, he sent them back to their machines. "We move out in five," he said as they dispersed. *Here we go again.* Reiter climbed back into the Lowe. As he looked over the pictures of his fallen soldiers, he looked to his left at his new battle map. A single picture of a woman with silvery hair and dark eyes hung over the image of the battle space. *No matter what happens, I'm glad I was able to save someone.*

KENNEDY SALUTED HIS EXECUTIVE OFFICER, A SHORTER MAN NAMED
Halphen. Snow lazily descended from soupy gray skies above him.
Wrapped up in their winter gear, the pair walked through an aisle of
Union panzerters and vehicles. In total, the battalion currently held
two panzerter companies with 9 Martian Troopers each. In addition
to their panzerters, they boasted two companies of infantry mounted
in Capricorn IFVs, as well as a section of air defense and standard
artillery each incorporated into their support company. As he passed
the machines and soldiers stoically lined to greet him, he stopped to
gawk at something he missed on his TO&E.

Three Jupiter's stood at attention across from his own. Where is
own bore snow camouflage with muted gold highlights, these new
machines gleamed scarlet and purple in the lights of the Forward
operating base? Kennedy whipped around to face his XO.

"Who's machines are these?" He barked. "And why aren't they
properly camouflaged?" Halphen hesitated, looking at the machines
himself.

"They're aces, Comrade Colonel," he said. "The Red Guards
they call themselves, their combat record rivals your own."
Kennedy stepped closer to Halphen, his buttons scrapping at the
man's face.

"Who are they and who do they answer to?" he asked. The XO
stepped back.

"You comrade," he said. "They're assigned to the headquarter
company, I was told to think of them as elite forces." Kennedy
folded his arms behind his back.

"We're the Mobile Assault Guards," Kennedy said. "We're all
elite forces." Halphen looked away.

"Well, I was told they could serve as bodyguards, shock troops,
whatever you need," he said. "It's hard to argue with a document
signed by the NC Secretary herself." Kennedy sighed. *So this bitch*

is keeping an eye on me. He turned and walked towards the command center.

"Return the battalion to duty, I want all units inspected for combat in an hour and five," he snapped. "Oh. And send these Red Guards to my office once their checks are done, I need a word with them."

As he entered his office, he was relived to see a simple set up. Particleboard walls ring to a small room with a simple desk and chair. No extra furnishings. No pictures on the wall. Simple and spartan, just how his predecessor had his. *Blake kept his office like this and Myer kept the tradition. So who am I to change anything?* After about an hour of settling his things in, there was a knock at his door.

"Enter, " he said. Three pilots walked into his office, two men and a woman. The man in the middle stood a head taller than the rest. *He must be 7 feet tall.* As they stood in front of his desk, he saw they all wore Guard-Major Rank. "I assume you all know why you're in here?" The tall one, Knight his nametape said. Nodded.

"Yeah," he said. "that squirrelly XO said you didn't take kindly to our fighting colors." Kennedy nodded.

"If you're fighting colors were a natural color, then it wouldn't be an issue. Unfortunately, lobster red is far from a natural color in the Tharcian Hinterlands," he said. "You'll need to alter your machines to a more natural hue."

Knight shook his head. "With all due respect comrade Col, it's our right as aces to paint our machines as we see fit," he said. "If you're worried about being spotted from the air, we can use camouflage nets same as everyone else, but we want the enemy to know who we are."

With a sigh, Kennedy stood and paced the area behind his desk. "I'm sure on the Olympian front you three seemed invincible," he said. "Particularly after you received Jupiters, but rest assured the Jupiters aren't invincible."

"Oh, we've heard of the Black Knight," the woman, Snow, said. Her hair short hair seemed purplish in the light, but not enough to be deemed out of regs. "We've also been dying for a challenge, mopping up Olympians just got so, boring."

"Well, prepare to be bored a little longer," Kennedy said. "The 88th and the Motor regiment are about to seize the bridges north of Landfall, and once that has been accomplished, we will anchor their flank while they bypass Grunbeck and Swiezen."

The Red Guards all moaned. "That's no fun!" Snow protested, but Kennedy held up a hand.

"This is how wars are one, by everyone doing their part in the plan," he said. "You are dismissed until further notice." He returned to his chair once the Red Guards had left and sighed when they closed the door. *I put them in their place, but is that how Blake would have done things?*

He leaned back in his chair and closed his eyes for a moment. *I wish he was around to ask, and of course Riverside is just south of here. Those bastards Mondragon and Rieter are around here somewhere, I just feel it.* He shifted in his chair as he heard footsteps on the floor above him. With a click of a remote, he turned on his heater.

For a moment, he considered ordering the techs to repaint the Red Guards machines to standard winter colors, but changed his mind. *Pearson's toadies can keep their red machines, if it causes their death, then it's their fault.* Soon, he received his combat checks from his companies, including the Red Guards. Aside from minor defects, every machine was capable of fighting.

I would hope so, it's not like they've done any heavy fighting in a while. Grabbing his helmet on his way out of his office, he headed towards the motor pool. *If anyone needs me, I'll be in my cockpit.*

3

S now whipped around the panzerters of Fox company as they marched through thick woods. The howling wind carried away the sound of metal joints, clanking tracks, and growling engines. Switching to thermals did little to help visibility in the powdery haze, much to Captain Reiter's chagrin.

"All units," he said on the company's net. "4-14th is set, we'll wait south of these two main roads." Black Platoon took the lead out of Landfall, with White Platoon taking the rear. Gold Platoon split themselves between the two panzerter platoons, and the scouts went wide with a section on each flank. Rieter's headquarters element: himself in the Lowe, Adamski in a Panzerter IV, Comidus in the command track, and another Iglasio for security; anchored the center of Fox Company.

"Fox 6, Black 4, our point man has a spot with decent observation given the weather," Mo said. Reiter acknowledged, and ordered the company to orient on the road, but stay just far enough to wear they could see it. *They probably saw the weather and figured we couldn't use our drones. Little did they know drone recon tipped us off to their movement.*

"Hey Fox elements, I hope your bum warmers work, because we could be here for a while," Reiter said.

"I thought the Unis were attacking immediately," Wesser said. "Won't they be here any second?"

"Negative Black 1," Mo said. "They're probably taking things slow, besides if its those ugly wheeled APCs, the Cav can handle them, we're just window dressing unless panzerters show up." Reiter checked his battle map. Somewhere ahead of him, the track vehicles in of the 4-14th lay in wait for the approaching Unis.

Over the gentle hum of the Lowe's, engine, he made out the distant whine of engines over the wind. The unsightly armored personnel carriers crawled down the main road with their headlights on. *I can't believe it. Are they really that reckless?* Zooming in confirmed the targets.

The Union APCs lived up to their hideous reputation. An angular bottom shaped for crossing water rode eight large wheels over the icy road. Chains covered their wheels, and a heavy machine gun swung about in a small turret.

"They're really just driving down the middle of the road?" Mo asked. "This is going to be too easy." Reiter shook his head.

"Everyone stay sharp," he said. "Black and white leaders, if I ever order you to advance down the middle of a road, you have my permission to relive me of command immediately." The procession ahead exploded into chaos. The lead APC skewed sideways, flames erupting from its hatches. Then the rear vehicle suffered the same fate.

Tharcian soldiers armed with rockets, machine-guns, and small arms hammered the Union motor column. Tracked vehicles supported them, knocking out APCs left and right. Union soldiers dismounted and struggled to organize a counter-attack, but the surprise of the ambush was too much. While the Cavalry treated the wounded and rounded up prisoners, Reiter's forces cast their eyes west.

"Redeploy the company," Reiter ordered. "And for God's sake stay off the road." Fox company maintained their relative positions, but shifted the line to the Cavalry's west. In the distance they heard the sounds of battle: gunfire, artillery, and machine guns. Sounds like another motor company catching the hammer, you'd think they would've brought armor with them.

Now that he was able to get a look at the carnage, he could see how the motor company I have been destroyed so easily. Because of the swamps on either side of the road, the motor battalion wouldn't have been able to get off and maneuver with the lead and rear vehicles destroyed, Trapping them in a shooters gallery. With a shake of his head, Rieter returned his attention to his own company.

"what do we do if more APCs show up?" Kozma asked.

"Let them through," Reuter replied. "I'll warn the Calvary, but for us to engage in would be overkill, We'll save our rounds for Panzerters." The motor battalion's actions had left him questioning what the union plan actually was. *Motorized units don't usually on spearhead, mainly because there armor isn't worth anything. So why lead an attack at such a low speed? They must have relied on the element of surprise, though I don't see them overpowering the Cavalry without extensive prep time.*

"We got contact," Mo said. "Looks like more APCs with some friends." Indeed, more APCs rolled down the hardball, but tinhats joined them. The rugged machines advancing on them possessed thick legs, curved torso armor, and a wide round head with a sensor ring that resembled a great war helmet, hence the reporting name tinhat. "I have three of them."

"They come twelve to a company," Reiter said. "If there's three here, they may have broken up the others, Black platoon, break off

and reinforce the Cavalry company guarding the north road."
Switching to the 4-14th's net, he warned them of incoming armor
and his own platoon stiffening their line to the north.

Shells whizzed past Steele's machine. "They spotted us!" Steele
said. He'd heard the tension in her voice, not fear, but
determination.

"White 3 and 4 advance," Kozma said. The young lieutenant
laid down covering fire while the other two machines advanced. At
their current range, their 76-mm guns only found glancing blows
against the Union's armor. The tinhats responded by spreading out
and advancing towards white platoon.

"They're trying to break through us," Steele said as she
advanced. Rieter grinned. He'd kept his machine on a knee level
with the trees. Now the tinhats charged well within range of his own
rifle, but hadn't yet entered a range where their weapons could
damage him.

As he rose, the nearest tinhat fired a controlled burst at Kozma.
The LT's trigger arm spun away, severed at the shoulder. The
rounds that missed struck Reiter's shield with a resounding clang.
The attacking tinhat hesitated.

With a crack and a flash, the tinhat collapsed with a neat hole
punched through its hips. The other tinhats were still caught up with
fighting Steele and Merlin jr.

One swung a mace wildly. A haphazard swing caught the side of
Steele's head. Steele surged forward. As they crashed through trees
to the ground, a single bang rang out.

A short distance away, Merlin ran circles around his opponent.
Despite pummeling the machine with a flurry of rounds, he'd yet to
hit anything vital. The tin hat twisted to keep him in its sights.
Smoke poured out of it. It's gun arm locked out by a hit to the
shoulder. Leaning to one side as a hip joint melted in a shower of
sparks, it failed to keep its balance while being shot and collapsed.

"We're not out of the woods yet," Rieter said as there more silhouettes appeared in the snow. "White platoon, fall back, we'll take this." He pushed the Lowe into a run as Adamski followed at his 5' o'clock. "I'll get the two on the left."

"Got it, one to the right," Adamski replied. Rieter opened up with his magnetic rifle. Despite only having 33% of the original railgun's range and penetration, it could still easily crack a tinhat's armor. His initial burst missed wide. After correcting his aim, he neatly punched through the lead panzerter. The machine toppled over, crashing through trees as it sprawled across the ground.

His second opponent discarded his rifle immediately and drew a fat tube weapon. *Shit!* Reiter barley had time to raise his shield when the fat round slammed into it. The attack destroyed the lower half of his shield, but spared the Lowe meaningful damage.

Discarding his shield, Reiter drew his Tesla sword. The brilliant sword cackled to life as if the Lowe's sword were a live bolt of lightening. Resigned to its fate, the tinhat drew its mace and charged.

Reiter cleaved through the tinhat's arm before he whipped about and took out its knees. It's body continued forward, demolishing trees and churning snow in its path. Iglasios from gold platoon pulled up on each of the fallen tinhats, securing the pilots and marking them for salvage crews. More Iglasios, these from the 4-14th, drove past them to secure the new perimeter.

A look at his battle map informed him of successful operations all along the front. Reiter bit his lip. *This is too good to be true, there's no way he throttled them at little cost to ourselves.*

KENNEDY STORMED INTO THE WAR ROOM WITH HIS HELMET STILL IN his hand. "Comrade Meyer," he said. "I wish we reunited under better circumstances, but this is a disaster." Guard-Colonel Erika Meyer, his battalion XO when he was a company commander, had assumed command of the 100th MAG Mechanized division while he recovered from injuries from the battle of FOB Blake. She greeted him with a thin smile.

"Comrade Kennedy, welcome back," she said. "I assume you have a solution?" He nodded and pointed out the door.

"I do, allow me to deploy the 75th, we can save what's left of our motorized regiment if I you give the order now," he said. Meyer shook her head.

"We need your people maintaining the blocking position ahead of us," she said. "The 88th was supposed to move out with them." Kennedy slammed his palm on the map table as Meyer leaned over.

"Colonel Todd is a moron. He saw a drone over his position and jumped the gun," he said. "But then he drove slowly down the two main roads to the bridges. If he's not relived within the hour, I'll get in my Jupiter and kill him myself."

Meyer sighed. "His questionable leadership isn't something you can solve by hopping in a panzerter and shooting things." She rose from her position and approached him. Tiptoeing up to his head, Kennedy felt her breath on his ear. "I understand your frustrated, but you can't barge in here and demand to deploy, I need you calm and steady, am I clear?" Kennedy nodded.

"Clear as crystal comrade," he said. Taking a deep breath, he strode over to the map table next to Meyer. "Does the 88th have Jupiters?" his commander shook her head.

"No, those are exclusive to the 75th," she replied. Kennedy pointed to the rapid destruction of the motor battalion's panzerter company.

"I have reason to believe the black knight's involved," he said. "If you would, I would like to propose a compromise." Meyer looked up from the map table.

"I'm listening, comrade Kennedy," she replied.

"I have these three aces, the Red Guards they call themselves," he said. "Transfers from the Olympian front, I need them to get experience against Tharcians, you need help to stop a massacre." Another officer in the room coughed, though not from sickness. "Excuse you, comrade?"

The officer looked up at him. Thick glasses framed brown eyes, and she held a tablet in her tan hands. "You're placing a lot of emphasis on trying to preserve the Motor battalion's strength," she said. "But in the larger picture, they're doing exactly what we need infantry to do: grind the enemy down."

"Guard-Colonel Kennedy, this is Guard-Major Ivy Irving, she's our operations officer," Meyer said. "A rising star among the intelligence arm." Kennedy nodded.

"Very well, comrade," he said. "However, she's categorically wrong." Major Irving stiffened.

"I beg your pardon?" she said. Kennedy jammed a finger at the images representing the motor battalion's units.

"Those men and women down there," he said. "Some of them have served for years, their experience is invaluable, and many more have been raised from birth to perform those tasks, wasting their lives is not what they're supposed to do, they're supposed to hold ground after we've taken it." She stepped up to Kennedy.

"More and more soldiers are coming in from the Olympian front," she said. "Their experience is far more valuable than a motor sergeant who sat around for ten years, and as for the tubers, we're growing more every day, it's not like we'll run out anytime soon." Fire raged in Kennedy's veins, but before he could do or say something he'd regret, Meyer stepped between them.

"We're all comrades here," she said. "Our enemy is the class traitors in Tharsis, not each other." She turned to Irving. "Tubers are a valuable part of our forces, in fact most of our best soldiers are tubers." Her eyes flashed towards Kennedy as she spoke, and his anger died down. "Comrade Kennedy, bring these Red Guards in, you have my permission to deploy them specifically, the rest of your regiment will wait stand by to defend Headquarters if necessary."

Kennedy nodded. "It will be done, comrade," he said. He paired them on the intercom and waited. *I know Meyer respects me, but she seems to think of tubers in general as equipment. That Operations officer, she needs to learn her place. I bet she's never even set foot on a battlefield herself.*

The Red Guards filed in, followed by his company commanders. "We figured it was better to come in here and maintain situational awareness," said Guard-Captain Ballard, one of his hand picked pilots. "And I'm sorry I didn't have the chance to speak with you yet." Kennedy grinned as he clasped the man's hand.

"It's alright, you were busy," he replied. "Ans after I brief the Guards, I want to hear all about your visit with your daughter." The Guards came to attention in a row in front of the map table. Kennedy walked in front of them.

"Alright, listen up," he told them. "The three of you will sortie immediately following this brief." He stopped in front of Knight. "Your mission is simple, support the 88th Battalion as you are able, destroy any Tharcians that get in your way, and if you see survivors from the Motor Battalion, ensure they're rescued." He looked to Snow and then to Khan. "Am I understood?"

"Yes, Comrade!" They cried before snapping salutes. "We serve the Union of Mars!" Kennedy smiled at the display of patriotism.

"Excellent," he said. "You're dismissed." The three turned and ran out of the room. Ballard's eyes followed them out.

"Something about them reminds me of Wake," he said. Kennedy shrugged.

"I don't know, but I'm certain they're not tubers," he replied.

"How was the visit with your daughter?" Ballard grinned, an unusual sight from the normally dour and cynical man.

"She was so excited to see me," he said. "Remembered who I was and everything. She even still call me daddy." He pulled his phone out from a pocket in his vest. Like all panzerter pilots, they wore light pants and an airy skintight top under a padded vest. Due to the weather, they also wore a layer of thermal underwear.

Kennedy couldn't help but smile when he saw the little girl hugging Ballard's broad shoulders. Despite missing her front teeth, she was all smile. He also noticed the doll she held resembled a Union pilot. *I'll have to thank Ballard and his daughter someday, for reminding me what the world after this will look like.*

"THE CAVALRY HAVE PANZERTERS APPROACHING," COMIDUS SAID. "Lots of them, like two companies and a team?" *Shit, I knew things were going too well.*

"Time until contact?" Reiter asked. "Black Platoon, how are you holding up?" He stretched before grasping the Lowe's controls. As he flicked the bum warmer off, he began receiving answers.

"4-14th's screen is breaking contact," Comidus replied. "They're falling back this way." *So we'll see them any second.*

"Contact Regiment, maybe they send us some help," Rieter said. "And pray the weather clears up so our drones can fight." The Lowe held its rifle in its left hand, and it's sword in its other. *If they have more recoilless rifles, I might be in trouble.* "Black Platoon, status?"

"Sorry!" Wesser replied. "We're coming back your way, Black 3 and 4 sustained some damage and are going to fall back with White Platoon." Rieter sighed.

"Roger, you and 2 fall in on me and Fox 7." *We'll form a blocking position here.* "Fox X-Ray, fall back as well, same with

Gold 1-3, the rest fall in on us." Rieter dared to look over his shoulder. Merlin Sr and Mo's machines sauntered past behind him. Though it was hard to tell, it looked like the snow bags had done their job. *I'll need to push that up, the snowbag idea, I'm sure someone will hate it, but it works.*

"1-11th Panzerter is sending Reinforcements," Comidus said. "They'll take the Cavs positions while they regroup, but their fifteen minutes out."

"Everyone here that?" Reiter asked. "All we need to do is hold out for fifteen minutes." Now they could hear the sounds of battle ahead. Iglasios raced past them and he felt his grip on the controls tighten. Wesser took a knee to Reiter's left with Smith on Adamski's 3 'o'clock. Gold Platoon's three Iglasios filled the gaps between them. Finally silhouettes appeared on Reiter's Cameras.

"Those aren't tinhats," Smith said nervously. Indeed, three dark shapes resolved themselves against the powdery haze behind them. They stood slightly taller than the tinhats they'd seen. Broad with thick armor painted in crimson with black highlights, Reiter grimaced at the sight of the fatmen. A beeping in his headset told him they were hailing him.

"I didn't think red was your color Kennedy, ever here of camouflage," Reiter spat. An unfamiliar voice laughed back at him.

"Oh no, he hates our paint job," the voice replied. "But after today, so will you Mr Black Knight." Reiter sprang up with his rifle ready. He missed wide. The fatman to the right returned fire with some kind of Gatling cannon. The shells perforated Wesser's machine, and she collapsed.

Adamski and Smith sent controlled bursts at their attacker with Reiter adding his mag rifle to the fray. Someone managed to hit the cannon's magazine. The explosion obscured the fatmen from view. *Where are they?*

His answer came through the smoke. One of the red fatmen

swung a spear weapon at him. With a swift parry, he knocked the tip skyward. *That's a harpoon! An anti-ship weapon?* The fatman pressed the attack, forcing Reiter to focus on defense.

Without his shield, he had difficulty guarding his flank. To compensate, he kept himself close to the fatman. *I've got to put them down, my people need me.*

"Fox 6, get back!" Stovepipe cried. Reiter sprang away from the fatman engaging him. Two Iglasios with tow cables tied between them rushed past. The fat man stabbed at them with the harpoon, but missed. The tow cables caught on their raise foot and the fatman collapsed. *Good one down.* Then a scream filled the net.

Adamski's panzerter collapsed in a burning wreck. The fatman he'd been fighting whirled on Reiter, blazing away with strobe lasers. The Lowe soaked up the laser fire, and Reiter responded with his mag rifle.

As the rounds punched through his armor, the other fatman tore the arms off Smith's machine before kicking it over. Reiter roared and put two in its head. The fatman stumbled away, hands outstretched like a blind man. His last opponent approached and drew the Sword-axe he'd seen fatmen use before.

"It's just you and me, pal," he said. "Still like your odds?" No answer. Reiter lunged. The fatman parried his initial blow, but the Lowe forced him to remain on the defensive. Finally, Reiter saw his opening, and knocked his opponent's weapon into the air. He held the tesla blade to the fatman's face as it raised its hands in surrender.

"You're finished," Reiter said. "As prisoners of the Republic of Tharsis, you'll be entitled to-"

"I didn't know you were this chatty," the voice from before said. "Did comrade Kennedy talk to you this much?"

"6, behind you!" Stovepipe cried. Rieter heard a crunch below him and fought for balance. The fatman from before had managed to stab his ankle with their harpoon. Something shot into his machine and his ankle exploded. The fat fan in front of him shoved him. Reiter caught a glimpse of the sky before his head slammed against his seat.

With ringing ears, he fired his rifle into the fatman on the ground. The magnetic rounds punched through steel alloy to smash electronics and structure inside the panzerter. Alarms blared. The standing fatman stomped down on the lowe's knee.

Rounds struck the fatman standing over him. The heavy machine staggered back as other panzerters fired on the machine. Iglasio's blazed away with their auto cannons while dismounts crawled onto the downed one.

Reiter struggled to get his machine up and moving. Without a foot on one leg, and his opposite knee crushed, he had no chance of standing. So he rolled over onto his side and propped himself on his arms.

Unless I hit something vital, they'll keep coming. Bringing his mag rifle to bear, he focused fire on the fatmans center of mass. Its movements stiffened as it struggled to escape. The fatman to his left stood and waved its arms as if the infantry were ants biting at it. Rieter noticed a flash and smoke poured from the fatman as it fled. More rifle fire struck its rear, adding to the smoke.

"Fox 6, are you alright?" Steele cried. Her damaged machine ran to his side. "The 1-11th's reinforcements are here!" Reiter sighed, and he realized his mouth felt like cotton.

"Good," he gasped. "Hopefully they help us with recovery, because we're a mess right now."

"ALL THINGS CONSIDERED, I'M IMPRESSED," MEYER SAID. "THE Red Guards not only destroyed several panzerters, but they defeated the black knight." Kennedy tapped a gloved finger on his chin.

"They may have defeated it," he said. "But let's not forget, the black knight was all but destroyed after the battle for FOB Blake, I'm sure it will be repaired soon." Meyer returned to the battle map.

"But it won't be able to stop us," she said. "I would say we press the attack, but Comrade Todd squandered most of our infantry in that area." Irving approached the map with her tablet.

"So Comrade Colonel," she said. "Can you explain to me the role you envision motorized infantry have if not cannon fodder?" Kenedy grimaced and didn't bother looking at the younger woman while responding.

"Motorized Infantry is more useful in holding town and cities then other units," he said. "Their armor forces partisans to use IEDs, but they're cheaper to maintain and replace than say a panzerter."

"But they're also the least trained arm of the infantry," Irving replied. "This compressed training time, when combined with their cheaper equipment, makes them by far the most expendable forces we have."

"They are still Mobile guards," Meyer snapped. "They still have the best equipment and training in all the Union. These aren't old world conscripts you're talking about." Irving raised an eyebrow, but said nothing. "Give me the Battle Damage Assessment." Irving consulted her tablet.

"Well, the Tharcians held the field, so any that had been disabled or suffered a mobility-kill are lost," she replied while tapping on her tablet. "Each company had 11 APCs with a crew of 10, so we're looking at 17 APCs lost, along with nine panzerters, as for bodies it's looking like 200 dead, missing, or wounded." Kennedy shook his head.

"Unacceptable," he said. "All of this could have been prevented."

"With our current stop-loss capabilities, we'll have all casualties replaced in two weeks, as for the vehicles," Irving said. "You'll have to speak to logistics, but most of the APCs can be replaced in about that time, same with the panzerters." Meyer sighed.

"So that's an entire battalion, out of the fight," she said. "I'll have the 88th take up the motor Battalion's position, though I don't want to delay much further." Kennedy looked up from the map at the division commander.

"What do you mean?" he asked. Meyer pointed at the space between Grunbeck and Swizen.

"If we clear the forests through here, it opens up to the plains of Vaterland," she said. "It'll allow the forces North of the border to crash through and trap a lot of their armies, it will be the furthest a Union army unit got into Tharsis." He caught a gleam of something in her eyes. *Is that glory? Or is she seeing the path to victory?*

"So that's our final objective," he said. "How do we plan to get there?" Meyer pointed to the south, at the little town of Riverside.

"Of the two, Riverside is the tougher nut to crack," she said. "So we'd take these bridges to the north and act like we're going to attack Swiezen, that'll force the Tharcians to abandon Landfall while isolating riverside." She made a hoping motion to the east of Riverside, pointing to the town of Narrowfield. "Then we land raiders in Narrowfield, surrounding Riverside, capturing vital farm-land as well as a hydroelectric plant near Narrowfield." She made a wide arcing motion past Grunbeck then Southeast. "And then we'll make our final move." Kennedy scratched at his chin.

"I like the audacity," he said. "I don't like how many points of failure it has." He pointed to the bridges. "First, Todd bungled seizing these bridges, so if we try it again we'll run into prepared defenses, not to mention the raider attack could go horribly,

Comrade Santana is no Druza, and that's not even starting with us overextending."

"We're relying on the speed of things to overwhelm them," Meyer replied. "And without the black knight, I don't see much stopping our panzerters." Kennedy looked at Irving.

"Do you have a weather report?" he asked. She nodded.

"I do. Fortunately for us, snowstorms will keep Tharcian drones grounded," she said. "For at least another week." Kennedy frowned.

"That hurst our ability to use the raiders," he replied. "But it does keep us safe from drone attack." He looked back at Meyer. "I have a proposal."

"I'm listening," she said.

He pointed to the 88th's position north of them. "Allow me to switch places with the 88th, this disaster is as much to blame on Guard-Colonel Fuller as it is on Todd, my battalion will have no issues moving out when needed, and we have multiple Heavy Panzerters." Meyer nodded, cradling her head in her hand.

"That would add weight to our initial strike," she said. "Yes, I'll accept your proposal. You may move out once the Red Guards have been fully repaired." Irving glanced at her tablet.

"Do I need to request a new pilot, or will you wait for comrade Snow to recover?" she asked.

"What?" Kennedy said. "When did she get injured? Is she in medical?" Irving nodded.

"She is, looks like she was burned pretty bad in the last battle," she replied. Kennedy looked at Meyer.

"Once they're repaired and Snow is fighting fit, that's when we'll move out," he said. Meyer nodded as she issued an order with the battle map.

"Ok, I'm brining the motor battalion remnants here to take over your battalion's duties," she said. As Kennedy made for the door, he stopped and locked eyes with Irving.

"You've never been on a battlefield, have you?" he asked.

She sighed and rolled her eyes. "Just because I haven't doesn't mean I don't make meaningful contributions," she said. Kennedy shook his head.

"That's not what I said," he said. "But if you did, then all those numbers wouldn't just be statistics now would they?" On that note, he left the command center and ran to the sickbay.

To the surprise of absolutely no-one, the other two guards sat near her. Knight looked no worse for wear, but Khan had bandages wrapped around his head. Snow lay in a rickety hospital rack. Her left arm and the left side of her head were wrapped in bandages filled with burn gel. An IV pumped painkillers and saline into her arm.

"How bad is she?" Kennedy asked. Knight stood and saluted before facing Snow's bed.

"Third-degree burns to the side of her head and her arm," he said. "Were it not for the medical staff here, she might have died from her injuries, still she managed to bring her Jupiter back under her own power." Kennedy nodded.

"I'll have to put all three of you in for an award," Kennedy said. "Dispatching the Lowe is quite the feat." Knight nodded.

"If I hadn't been lucky, he would have killed us," the giant admitted. "He bested all of us in hand to hand combat, fortunately we had him outnumbered until the very end." Kennedy looked from snow to Khan and then back to knight.

"Well, you'll have more opportunities for honor and glory," Kennedy said. "I convinced Meyer to switch us with the 88th up north, so we'll be the teeth of the next offensive." Khan muttered something. Kennedy didn't catch wind of it, but Knight pointed to the door.

"Go back to your quarters, Khan," he said. "I'll bring you dinner when the mess opens." As Khan passed them, he said nothing else and left. *That was odd.* Knight was either telepathic or he noticed the shift in Kennedy's demeanor. "Don't mind that, he just really needs his alone time." Kennedy nodded.

"An introvert, huh?" He checked his watch. "I hope you didn't plan on eating with him, because I was going to have you and Ballard join me in the war room." He looked at Snow while gripping the edge of the bed. "I have to admit, I wasn't thrilled to be working with you guys, but you've proven me wrong, and I'm not afraid to admit it." Knight smiled as Kennedy offered him his hand to shake. "I look forward to working with you." The giant took his hand in an iron grip.

"I'm honored," he replied. With that, Kennedy nodded and left the sick bay.

4

"Where are they?" Reiter asked as medics rolled him into sick bay. "Did I lose anyone? I need to know if my soldiers are ok!" He lay on a rolling table in a neck brace with bandages around his head and restraints holding him down.

"Captain Reiter, you need to calm down," one of the medics said. "You need to lie down."

"Calm down or lay down?" Reiter asked. "What do you need me to do so I can check on my soldiers?"

"Yes!" a medic said firmly before bringing him to a stop. Reiter clawed at the straps holding him down.

"Captain Reiter, was it?" a soft voice asked. "I need you to lay down, we're not sure if you suffered a neck injury or not, so please be still." Reiter spotted dirty blonde curls at the edge of his vision, but the neck brace prevented him from looking further.

"Please," he gasped. "I just need to know if my soldiers are ok." *I know we lost some infantry, that fatman definitely plastered some of them.* He heard shoes click on the tile floor of the department store that served as a field hospital.

A young woman entered his field of vision. She wore a white nurse's uniform with her matching Tharcian Red Cross cap barely containing her curly hair. Now that she stood closer, he could see shades of auburn in her hair that complemented her dark green eyes and olive skin. Freckles spattered across her warm smile as she held up a notepad.

"Give me their names and I can check for you," she said. "You're the last one they brought in." Reiter tried to nod, but couldn't in his brace.

"I told them I was fine," he said. "Tessa Wesser, Akchetka Smith-"

"I'm right here, sir," Smith called from the other side of the curtain to his left. "A little banged up, but I'm ok." Reiter sighed in relief.

"Walter Adamski, Lionel Musat, Zukal, Henrietta Schottenheimer and the crews of the following vehicles, Gold 1, Gold 2, and Gold 3," he finished. "I'd give you their names, but those last three were all crew commanders." She scrawled down the note on her pad.

"Ok, I think we took an Adamski back for surgery, but I'll double check," she said. She walked around to Rieter's left and he heard the curtain pull back. "There, now you can see your friend." Rieter turned his head as much as he could to see the young man waving from his own bed.

"Aw they got you in a neck brace, sir?" Smith said. "Those suck." Rieter rolled his eyes as the nurse walked out.

"Tell me about it," he said. "How roughed up are you Smith?"

"Sprained back and a concussion," he said. "Nothing too bad, I was worse after the battle for three rivers, would probably be dead if the Merlin brothers didn't pull me out of my panzerter back then." Rieter sighed and relaxed, but only slightly.

"For what it's worth, Smith, I'm glad you're here," he said. "In the context of being in Fox, I'd rather you weren't in a hospital bed." Smith chuckled.

"It's not all that bad," he replied. "That Nurse Amelia, she's pretty timely with food and apple juice, she's also just plain pretty, or was back in the day." Reiter squinted.

"What are you talking about?" he asked. "She didn't even look like she hit thirty yet."

"I mean she's probably at least ten years older than me," Smith replied. "That seems pretty old." Reiter felt like rolling his eyes until they generated lift.

"Smith, you're like 17," he said. "Why are you talking about anyone in their twenties like their your grandmother?" He tried to shake his head. "Besides, you don't actually know how old she is, you're guessing at best."

"Good point, I'll ask her when she gets back," Smith said.

"What? No!" Reiter replied. "Full stop, you never ask a woman how old she is or how much she weighs."

"Really?" Smith replied, "Huh, who would have thought?"

"Literally anybody who's been around a woman," Reiter replied. "Didn't your mother teach you anything?" Smith chuckled nervously.

"I grew up in a house with 12 brothers," he said. "Mom didn't really have time for me."

"Oh, well, I'm sorry I assumed," Reiter said. "Though I will never pass up an opportunity to learn more about my soldiers." He tried to look back at Smith. "You had twelve brothers?"

"Who has 12 brothers?" Kozma asked as he walked in with Wesser. Reiter smiled, seeing Wesser with a bandage on her arm and one around her head, but her expression was downcast.

"I do, sir," Smith said. "Oh ma'am, Captain Reiter wanted to know if you were ok, hey sir, LT Wesser seems physically ok, but she looks sad."

"I see that Smith," Reiter said. "Wesser, if you need to talk, pull up a chair." He strained to look over at Kozma. "I'll get you in a minute, talk to Smith for now." He tried to sit up more. "And teach him how to address women, politely." *I wish I could take this damn thing off.*

As if summoned by magic, Amelia appeared at his side. She nimbly undid his straps and removed the neck brace. "You're X-rays from the medevac came back negative for a neck or spinal injury. You definitely have a concussion, however." She stood over him. "Two days bedrest and light duty along with some prescribed meds, oh and your Adamski friend was the one in surgery."

Reiter sat up. "What happened? How is he?" Amelia set a soft hand on Reiter's.

"I'm sorry, but he lost both of his legs," she said. "He'll have to go to the rear to be fitted for prosthetics and receive physical therapy." Reiter's stomach sank. He slumped back into bed. "And the others?"

"Well Ms. Wesser is here, and your infantrymen are mostly ok, the ones you named have their own lists of dead," she said. Reiter closed his eyes. She set a soft hand on his forehead.

"Thank you for everything," he said. Amelia gave him a warm smile before vanishing to assist some other wounded soldier. Reiter looked over at Wesser, propped up on his elbows.

"Alright, so what is it?" he asked.

"To our best knowledge," Kennedy began. "There's a Cavalry Regiment screening the bridges, just behind them is a Panzerter Regiment." He marked the relative positions of company sized elements within the zoomed in section of map on the holographic battle map. "I don't doubt for a second that our Battalion is the best in the division, but taking on two regiments of Tharcians head on is more than we can chew."

Ballard and Knight sat across the table from him. His other company commanders were otherwise occupied. G-SRLT Irvin was running her company and the Motor battalion remnants through base defense drills while G-SRLT Spears spent the day reviewing the defensive fortifications with his subordinates.

Each of them ate out of their own paper box filled with a pasta made from local ingredients. He'd never eaten lamb before, more had he drank the sweetened tea Gallacians seemed to love. Nevertheless, he held a tall can of the stuff, same as the two other men who ate as they worked.

"If there's one thing I learned about Tharcian scouts, it's that they always have artillery on the phone," Ballard said. Knight pointed to the two main roads that led to the bridges.

"If that's the case, why didn't they use it earlier today?" Knight asked. Ballard shrugged.

"Maybe they thought it would be overkill to use on a motor batt," he replied. "And our reinforcements surprised them."

"Either way it's safer we assume they do have that capability," Kennedy said. "So we should keep our formations dispersed." He tapped on an access road that ran between the two main ones. "They'll use this to reinforce one side or the other quickly, it's best we do something about this." Ballard scratched at his chin.

"The bridges are mostly for our support vehicles, right?" he asked. "Because our combat vehicles can ford these rivers, we just need to watch the ice." Knight raised an eyebrow.

"I believe that's correct," he said. "Are you implying we forgo using the bridges entirely during the operation?" Ballard shook his head.

"Not exactly, what are the odds they've rigged them to blow if it looked like they'd lose?" he asked.

"I'm not taking that bet," Kennedy said. "They're definitely rigged to explode." Ballard tapped on the more Northern of the two bridges.

"So let's only seize one," he said. "There's no point in wasting effort trying to take both bridges when the one will explode when the other falls."

"And if we seize that bridge, it will keep our supply line away from enemy strongholds like Grunbeck," Knight added. "Though there's still the matter of reinforcements along this road."

"So we feint," Kennedy said. "We'll concentrate the bulk of our forces on the North Bridge, but our initial wave will seize both of these intersections." He traced his finger from the southern intersection to the Northern one. "Once this intersection is clear, our follow-on forces will clear this access road and join the other half of the attack." Kennedy took a swig of his tea. *It's an interesting taste, I've never eaten a mango before, but I guess I could get used to it.*

While the other two men paused to eat, he labeled their objectives. The Northern road became route 34 and the Southern Route 35 with the access road Special Route 105. With the need to take it first, Kennedy named the Southern intersection Objective Alpha, and the other Objective Bravo. Finally he tagged the Northern Bridge as Objective Charlie.

"Now there's the approach," he said. "Now to assign objectives."

Ballard raised a hand. "I'll volunteer my company to take Objective Alpha," he said. "We've got more veteran pilots and can hold off a sudden counterattack." Kennedy nodded.

"I'll have the Recon platoon follow you," he said. "That way it looks like you have infantry support and their sensors can help clear the SR 105." Knight pointed to the Objective Bravo.

"That lives the other panzerter company to take this," he said. "I assume you'll send the infantry company along with them?" Kennedy pointed towards the bridge.

"Yes, and your Red Guards will be right on their heels," he said. "We believe they have a panzerter regiment across the river, your team will blunt any counterattack to retake the bridge while the infantry disable the explosives."

"Are you worried about remote detonation?" Ballard asked. Kennedy shook his head.

"For something like this, the Tharcians are more likely to use a command wire," he said. "And if they didn't, the IFVs have the same short range jamming equipment panzerters have, so I'm not worried about radio controlled bombs." He zoomed out of the map, revealing the entire AO. "Threats of follow on attacks here and here should keep them from committing to retaking the bridge."

"So now the big question is, how do we avoid another ambush?" Knight asked. Kennedy zoomed back in on their specific battle map.

"So Todd took to the main roads and did so slowly," he said. "We will not do that, but rather use the roads and a few other landmarks to guide ourselves." He looked at Ballard.

"Ballard, when your group passes a lumber mill, you'll be halfway to your objective," he said. Pointing at the center of the wooded area, he continued. "The rest of us will proceed to the center until we run into an estate." He pulled up a compass on the battle map.

"From there, Irvin will lead off at 42 degrees North-Northeast with the infantry and red guards behind her." He looked from one man to the other. "Those scouts will be watching the road, destroy them quickly and as quietly as you can, we don't want to sound the alarm too soon."

Taking another swing of tea, he pointed to the estate. "This manor will serve as our headquarters and medevac point as well as a rally point for your companies to retreat to if they get overwhelmed." Kennedy looked at his watch. "I'll take care of some administrative things, but let's round everyone up for the Battalion mission brief at dinner, I want maximum time for your people to conduct drills." The other men nodded.

"Drills with the whole Red Guard will have to wait," Knight said. "But I will coordinate drills with Spears' people so they get used to working with us." Kennedy nodded and they threw out their trash. *No better time to receive information than when you're eating after all.*

"Alright, I'll see you two in a few hours," he said.

RIETER STOOD IN A WAREHOUSE SERVING AS A MECHANIC SHOP, gazing up at the Lowe. The towering black machine lay covered in mechanics like parasites. Just as he'd thought, the entire right knee needed to be replaced along with the left ankle and the parts immediately around it. Fortunately, they'd recovered his damaged foot, so they were able to salvage most of that leg.

Other Panzerters lay in the massive facility, some were being stripped for parts, others were hurriedly being repaired. *At least we have plenty of spare parts.* Whatever parts of the Lowe team in Garden City had been hurriedly donated to the regiment as they moved their data and team east.

"It doesn't look too bad," Wesser said. "It could have been much worse." Reiter hadn't heard her approach over the shriek of torches and welding. He waved her to follow him and they left the facility.

"As far as the tactical situation goes, it's not good," he said. "The Lowe and Drones are the only hard counter we have to the Union's fatman units, hopefully those red ones aren't looking much better." They walked out of the massive bay doors, normally used for loading products.

"I heard the infantry managed to take one down," Wesser replied. Reiter gestured, more or less.

"Iagar threw a thermite into the cockpit," he replied. "The pilot survived long enough to crush him, but they're most certainly dead from these injuries." They walked down a winding sidewalk that took them back towards main street. "About our conversation the other day."

"Yes sir?" She replied. Rieter set a hand on her shoulder.

"You didn't fail," he said. "At least not in the sense that matters, I know people way over our heads will blame us for the deaths of our soldiers, but my attitude is a little different."

Wesser twisted a stray strand of hair hanging out of her bun. "Well sir, in your words, why didn't I fail?"

"We don't shoulder 100% of the blame for enemy action," he said. "The enemy is still out there doing their best to kill us, sometimes they're just competent." He patted her on the shoulder. "Anyway, we did our jobs, and without drones in the air, we didn't have any warning for what happens, but that's nature of this war."

"The nature of this war?" she asked.

Rieter shook his head. "Don't mistake me for saying this, but we have yet to score a single major victory against the Union," he said. "All we managed to do is get a few ugly draws, things don't go our way most of the time and we need to plan to beat adversity when it happens." Looking up, he smiled.

A second Lowe rolled in on a massive flatbed. He recognized its silhouette from its large body and similar shape to his own. "Is that the second Lowe?" Wesser asked. Rieter nodded.

"One weapon rarely decides a war," he said. "But we start churning out more of these, and our odds look a lot better." He stood by and watched as the second Lowe disappeared into the repair bay to be fitted for combat. "Much better."

He turned to walk back to the main road when his foot slid out from under him. His ass struck the sidewalk hard, and he cried out. Behind him, Wesser stifled a giggle. "I'm sorry, you just reminded me of something that happened in my ju-jitsu class back home."

Rieter ground while his hips and back throbbed. "Ju-jitsu?" he asked.

Wesser nodded. "Yes, I learned Olympian ju-jitsu when I was a teenager," she said. "I'm a small girl, I need to defend myself somehow."

Before Rieter could comment, he pictured a ju-jitsu fighter. Catching an attack and redirecting it. Then it struck him. He lept to his feet, brushing the snow from him. "I need to talk to Hawke," he said. Wesser's eyes widened.

"I didn't mean to laugh!" she cried. Rieter shook his head and patted hers.

"You're not in trouble," he said. "Quite the contrary, if I weren't worried about my career, I'd kiss you."

The LT stepped back as Rieter rubbed his lower back. "I don't need to use ju-jitsu on you, do I?" Reiter grinned and shook his head.

"No, but the visual gave me an idea," he said. "One I need to push up." Carefully avoiding the ice he just slipped on, Rieter ran towards the diner. As he ran, ideas began forming in his head. Like the funnel of a tornado, his mind spun, gathering steam, until it whipped about at F5 speeds.

The Union would attack again. It was inevitable. They only seemed to have two settings: attack and preparing to attack. In the war's current state, the Union would advance little by little, preparing to attack as Tharcians scrambled to mount a defense.

But, what if, like a martial artist, they managed to use the

Union's own aggression against them? Rieter's thoughts grew clearer and clearer. They could create an opening, a planned channel for the Union to attack along. Meanwhile, they struck at their command and control, attacked their supply chain. *And while that happens, we trap their spearhead in our channel.*

It could work. It was realistic. He didn't have absurd visions of driving the Union all the way back to their own border, just throwing them out of this province.

As he stumbled into the diner, the welcoming bells chimed. "I need to speak with Col Hawke," he said to an orderly. "I have a plan I want him to hear." The administrator, a sergeant, grunted.

"I'm sure if he wanted to hear a plan from a company commander, he'd ask," the sergeant said. "As it stands he's in a teleconference with the other regimental commanders, so he's busy, return to your duties and maybe he'll ask for you." Reiter's eyes narrowed.

"To be clear, I don't have an issue with being turned away," he said. "What I won't accept is a complete lack of respect or discipline from an NCO." The sergeant rolled his eyes.

"Look, I just wanted free college," he said. "I didn't sign up to get involved in this stupid war." Maybe it was the raised voices, maybe it was some kind of old NCO sixth sense, but a towering Master Sergeant walked out from behind the bar area.

"Hey pal," the Master Sergeant said. "You know that's an officer you're talking to, right?" The Sergeant in front of him stiffened.

"I apologize," he quickly said. "I meant no offense, uh, sir." Reiter smiled.

"Apology accepted," he said before walking over to the bar where the Master Sergeant stood. "If it's possible, I need to speak to Colonel Hawke, I may have come up with a plan to kick the Union out of Germania."

The old MSG cracked open a soda, a Highland Sap, and leaned

over the bar. "He's in a meeting right now, but I'll let him know you're here." He pulled a pen and pad out of his shoulder pocket. "Here, you look like you're 'in the zone', jot down your key points before you forget them."

Reiter thanked the gal MSG, Friermann his nametape read, and scrawled his thoughts across his notepad. When the door to Hawke's cramped office finally opened, Rieter had multiple pages filled with notes and thoughts.

"Captain Rieter, Friermann said you had something for me?" Hawke asked. Rieter grinned and held up his notes.

"Ye sir, I figured it out," he said. "A way to kick the Union's ass and throw off their mojo."

CHANEY CHAFED IN HIS DRESS UNIFORM. THE GREEN COAT WITH ITS elaborate red-gold piping wore too tightly on his broad shoulders, a hair too short on his arms, and much too tightly around his neck. *It's like whoever made this never saw another human being before, or they were lazy.*

Deep under the dome of Congregation, he sat around a large oak table with other general officers and a few surface side admirals. The conference room featured elaborately paneled wooden walls as well as four marble fire places. Soft lamps, including the small chandelier above the table, filled the room with an almost red glow.

Sitting at where the head of the oak table would have been was none other than the Secretary of the National Committee. For the occasion she'd chosen to where a simple sea green gown that went down to over her ankles. A turquoise necklace accented the dress and her bronze skin and hair.

"I apologize for the first minister's absence, but he recently lost a family member in the bombing raid on foundation," she said. "For the time being I will sit in on the general staff meetings, no let's get down to business." Admiral Marlin cleared his throat. With the Fleet admiral preoccupied in space, he stood in as representative for the new year.

"Despite our best efforts, The Tharcians continue to give us the slip in the asteroid belt," he said. "Without a foothold there, we will not be able to attack their assets in the Jupiter sphere." Pearson narrowed her gaze.

"Why bother with their belt forces when they sit on Deimos?" She asked. The Admiral cleared his throat.

"Because the defenses around Deimos are strong," he said. "We wouldn't engage them until their forces outside the Mars Sphere have been neutralized." He brought up a holographic image of the solar system and zoomed in on Jupiter. "And those forces are substantial, without a point to fall back to, any task force we sent to Jupiter would become stranded even if they did prove victorious, it's what we believe happened to the lost fleet in the last war."

Secretary Pearson leaned over the table. "Listen comrades, the First Minister rattled quite a few cages when he announced you people would be represented in TUCs. The National Trades Union Congress has a significant faction that want's signing an armistice with Tharsis," she said. "I assume you all know what that could mean?" Every head in the room nodded in agreement.

"Another war in ten years," a general near Chaney muttered. "We can't have that." The Secretary looked from the Admirals to the Generals, some MAGs, but a few regulars as well.

"We need a significant victory," she said. "One that convinces the pro-armistice faction to go along with the war." General Dunlap scratched at his chin while he spoke.

"Are the Avalonians going to take over the pacification of Southern Olympia?" he asked. "We could use those forces against the Tharcians." The secretary's mouth quivered slightly, to Chaney it looked like she was about to scowl. Instead, she smiled.

"We'll leave that up to our ambassador's union," she said. "We can't ask too much of them, otherwise they may ask for more concessions than we would want to give." *Just like I thought, they're our allies, but not our friends.*

"What do they want?" another General asked. "All I've heard them do is destroy colonies resisting them."

"Habitats," Secretary Pearson corrected. "They're destroying Olympian habitats, we don't use the language of colonizers." *Bad move, man, you got to remember she's a politician.* The General cleared his throat.

"I apologize," he said. "But my point still stands, Avalon and her mad king are making choices we can't condone, millions of people are dying in these 'habitats' and we look complicit if our allies act in this manner."

An admiral across from him shook his head. "That's Tharcian propaganda, they're destroying partially built or derelict habitats as a demonstration of strength, to show the Olympians in space what they could do," he said. *Yeah, I don't buy that.*

"Enough," the Secretary snapped. "I've already heard enough bootlicker lies today, perhaps the ground war is on the precipice of the victory we need." She looked at the Generals to her left.

"Well, the northern front remains static," one of them said. "We've set up air defenses in the hope we'd be able to stop their strategic bombing, In addition, we managed to wrest control of the Wilhelm islands on the East Coast of Tharsis."

The Secretary sighed. "A dozen tiny islands isn't a major victory," she said before smiling. "But it's a start." She looks further down the line. "I take it there's been little movement out of Gallacia?" The two generals to Chaney's left shook their heads.

"We've made some progress," one said. "We believe we can

capture Vaterland by spring if our plans progress as they are." She smiled. "Would that be the victory you were looking for?"

"Definitely," Pearson replied. "Mind you, the armistice faction isn't large enough to stop us from continuing the war, but it is large enough that it could prove problematic when the time comes to recognize the military in the national Trades Union Congress." She looked directly at Chaney. "Although many of them would sign on if perhaps they received a military procurement contract?" Chaney picked his next words carefully.

"The Unions we have are working from proven designs and adding onto it," he said. "It's far more efficient to build 1000 of everything we have right now, then to add in different designs made by Co-Ops with no experience." He raised his hand. "For example, if a Co-op that made bikes in the PMR wanted to build rifles under license from our current manufacture, That would be fine, but what I'm seeing is bicycle Co-ops sending me panzerter designs they want to build just because they have someone mildly artistically gifted and nobody is buying a bike right now."

The Secretary chuckled at his remark. "I understand your frustration," she said. "But if there's an opportunity to expand production, I think we should take it. Our economy needs to be fully tuned for all out war, and I've considered asking the First Minister to invoke the Milita clause." That elicited gasps from around the room.

"We can win the war just fine," one of the generals swore. "We don't need help from poets and artists!" Admiral Marlin leaned over the table.

"Are you sure comrade secretary?" he asked. "The long term damage to our economy might be irreversible." Slamming her hands on the table, Secretary Pearson glowered at them.

"You think I don't know the consequences?" she asked. "Because I do, my nephew is in a news union. He would be called to battle if the situation called for it, but like I said, I'm going to talk to the First Minister about it." She gave one last look around the room before adjourning the meeting. Chaney wandered out in the hall, desperate to avoid the other brass nagging him about prototypes.

Voices came from around a corner a short distance away. "I don't care what the repercussions are, It's Tharcian territory, its fair game," said the Secretary.

"But Melissa, those habitats are among the Orkney and Kami archipelago," Admiral Marlin replied. "It's all too easy for an international incident, besides how are panzerters supposed to enter a habitat if the docking bay is closed."

"Figure it out," the secretary growled, followed by the click of her heels on the marble floor. *Fuck, what is that woman getting us into?*

5

R ieter backed away from the operational map that hung in Hawke's cramped office. He'd rearranged the pins just to show his superior officer the idea he had brewing in hi head. Slowly, Hawke nodded as he took in the information presented before him.

"I like it," he said. "This war has gotten to stagnant for my liking, it doesn't play to our strengths." He leaned back in his chair and folded his hands behind his head.

Rieter circled the map with his hands as if he was washing a window. "Well, there's the matter of finding a place to create this 'channel' and convincing the Union they're not being had, but aside from this, that's all I got," he said. Drawing his phone, he snapped a picture of the map and did the same for Hawke before restoring it to the current situation.

Hawke rose from his creaking chair and edged past Reiter to get to his computer. "This is something I'll have to bring up to General Orban and the other Regiments," He said. Sitting back at his desk, he opened his computer and went to work. "It's ultimately Orban's call, but the other regiments might have other ideas we didn't think of. That being said, it's a damn good idea."

Reiter scratched at the back of his head and grinned. "LT Wesser inspired me, she mentioned Olympian Ju-jitsu and the mental picture led me to counterattack the Union while they're attacking."

"Really? I think you pictured Judo," Hawke said with a chuckle. "I don't think Ju-jitsu has elaborate counters or throws like you imagined."

As he shrugged, Reiter stepped towards the door. "I'm not a martial artist sir, I just pilot a panzerter," he replied. Closing the door behind him, he tipped his hat to Friermann and left. He'd barley made it a block down the road when Mo came bounding across the street.

"No way," the younger man said breathlessly. "Why does it say Lowe-arms type next to my name on the ready room? Did you have something to do with this?"

Reiter nodded and clapped the excited young man on the shoulder. "You're by far the best pilot we have, besides it means your old Mark IV can go toe to toe with any Union tinhat." *Although now I have the logistical problem of having two advanced machines with limited parts.* He gestured for Mo to follow him. "Not to curb your enthusiasm, but what have you thought of your new LT so far?"

Mo shrugged, Still smiling at the thought of the heavy panzerter waiting for him in the motor pool. "I mean, she's been alright so far," he said. "She's been sour since that last battle, but its whatever." Something about his tone caught Reiter's attention.

"Sour, but it's whatever?" he drawled. "How so?" Mo shrugged.

"Like she stays in her room while I run drills, she rarely comes out, and I need to drop off food to make sure she eats," he replied. "I would not say anything, you know I figured I'd just deal with it." Reiter furrowed his brow.

"I'll have a word with Kozma and see if he can talk to her," he finally said. "I don't think it would be appropriate for me to get on her case immediately, we need to work up to that."

Mo walked a little further away. "You know, not to second guess you or anything, but why didn't you assign Wesser to White platoon?" Reiter glanced at the younger man. "You know, get some girl power concentrated over there, Steele would probably be better at getting her used to combat than I am."

Rieter sighed. "You're right to have your questions," he said. "As long as you keep that between us, based on the profiles I had for both of our lieutenant I tried to pair them with a sergeant who's personality complimented there's."

He pointed over to the motor pool, where Kozma laughed with Merlin JR and Steele as they stuffed sandbags with snow. "Kozma profiled as an airhead with a brash streak, not exactly a hothead, but still fairly impulsive." They waved when they noticed him, and Rieter and Mo waved back. "Someone who paired nicely with your girlfriend's even-heeled personality."

Mo's cheeks turned red, though not from the cold. "We're not-uh-she's not-uh-it's more complex than that," Mo replied.

"Oh," Reiter said, letting the thread of that conversation die right there. *Probably something to do with Bartonova's death, I'll be more careful next time.* "Anyway, Wesser profiled as your typical wallflower, so we paired her with the most tenacious and hot-blooded sergeant I had."

Mo snorted. "Considering there's two of us in the armor platoons, that must have been a straightforward choice," he said. He folded his arms and looked back at white platoon. "So, you're going to have Kozma talk to her, huh?"

Reiter nodded. "Yeah, is there an issue with that?" What had started as work had turned into a snowball fight across the street. Steele giggled and yelped as Merlin and Kozma pelted her. Reiter chuckled, but Mo remained silent.

"Yeah, if its alright with you, I want to sit down and talk to her," he finally said. "If I need to give her a dressing down, I can do that and stay professional, but I think Black platoon should solve Black platoon's issues."

Though he couldn't pick up on it, something about Mo's words made Rieter uncomfortable. "I'll sign off on that," he said. "So long as Black Platoon's problems don't become Fox Company's problems." Mo nodded and before Rieter could look back up, a snowball struck him in the face. Gasping from the sudden chill and the thump to his nose, Rieter held his face while Mo bellowed.

"Merlin! Get over here now!" Rieter looked up to see Merlin's horrified face holding a second snowball. Kozma and Steele were also prepared to throw snowballs, but now looked worried.

"Bring that snow ball with you," Rieter said. Mo glanced at him. Their eyes met and the younger man already knew what Rieter was going to do. He held his face where the snowball had hit him, but now it was to hide his smile.

"Sir," Merlin said. His gloved hands trembled as they held the snowball in front of him.

Rieter took a deep breath through his hands. "Don't smile or laugh," he whispered. "I'm not mad, that was a textbook perfect ambush." Mo stood beside him with a stern expression, nodding enthusiastically. By now, Kozma and Steele had dropped their snowballs and began walking over to hear what he was saying. "Kozma is crossing the street to your 5. On my signal, whip around and hit him in the face."

Merlin's horrified face broke into a shit-eating grin. "Yes sir, yes sir, understood sir." His face was delighted, his tone was scared shitless. *Perfect, I wish I could put this kid in for an Actor's List Award.*

"Now." Despite sounding muffled through his hands, Merlin

had heard him loud and clear. As Merlin turned, Mo and Rieter dropped to their knees.

"Son of a bitch!" Kozma cried as Merlin's snowball struck him in the forehead. Steele laughed as the others pelted her and her lt.

"Traitor!" she said between giggles. Rieter caught Mo smiling out of the corner of his eye. After a moment, Kozma and Steele held up their hands.

"Alright, you got us," he said as they walked up. Rieter patted Merlin on the back.

"Frosty here needs an award for his acting skills as much as anything else," he said. Merlin looked confused.

"Frosty?"

"It's your war name," Rieter said with a grin.

Steele laughed. "Like that old cartoon! I love it!" They stood there on the sidewalk, laughing and calling Merlin JR Frosty. *With all the death and violence, I don't mind these comments of levity. Not at all.*

KENNEDY PULLED UP HIS GAITER TO BETTER COVER HIS MOUTH AND nose. *The Storm's getting bad, it would on the night I'm supposed to move out.* Knight, recognizable from his massive silhouette, saluted him as he approached the FOB gates.

"I double checked, the Red Guards and the Headquarters company are ready to move out," he said. Kennedy gestured the man to follow him as he reviewed the convoy. Their four Jupiter Panzerters idled in the center of the formation. Three scout cars formed the lead element. The two-seater four-wheeled vehicles were best suited for the security/ recon role they were being used for.

Beyond them, four bulky supply trucks followed. The box

looking trucks each carried vital supplies: a field kitchen, a mobile HQ, and two ammo haulers. Behind the panzerters, four more supply trucks carried spare parts and recovery equipment. Each supply truck towed a water tank containing filtered water for their soldiers. Three more scout cars brought up the rear with an additional three going to each side.

Kennedy turned to face Knight. "You already briefed them, correct?"

The big nodded. "Halphen did most of it, but I took care of actions on." They walked back to their Panzerters idling in the falling snow.

"It might suck, but I'm ok with moving the entire battalion in this snowstorm," Kennedy said. "If nothing else, the Tharcians won't wanna fuck around in the snow." He had to yell to be heard of the howl of the driving snow.

Knight pointed to the sky in response. "You're not the only one who thought that." Kennedy looked back to see Dropships rising from the short tarmac that served as an airstrip. The drone of their engines blended with the howling snow around them.

Kennedy shook his head. "I need to talk to Meyer, that's asking for disaster." Knight grabbed his shoulder.

"Hey comrade, they can handle the wind, what's your problem?" he asked. Now both men were shouting to be heard over the wind and the noise of engines.

With a finger jabbed at the dropships leaving, Kennedy rounded on Knight. "It isn't they can't fly, its navigation."

"What?"

"It's navigation, without GPS or visual landmarks, how the hell do they now they're in the right place?"

"What?" Knight shook his head and shrugged him. "Can't hear you, but talk to Meyer if it's an emergency." Kennedy turned and ran as fast as his bundled legs could carry him. The temporary and hasty setup of FOB Nike would have made it difficult to navigate. After sticking his head in a secondary mess, the clinic, and a group therapy lounge, he finally found headquarters.

I've been in here a dozen times. If I calmed down a tad, I would have found it. He rushed into the war room with such a flurry, everyone looked at him as he stumbled in.

"Kennedy," Meyer said. "I thought you had moved out already." He yanked down on his gaiter, exposing his mouth and nose to the warm room.

"What are the dropships doing?" he asked. "Because without a reliable way to navigate, sending them up is inviting disaster." Irving reared her condensing head, lurking behind Kennedy as the man approached the map table.

She scoffed, and he turned to see her hold up her tablet. "This operation has a high chance of success," she said. "The raiders got their heading from us using our mapping software. As long as they fly straight and low, they'll reach Narrowfield."

Kennedy shook his head. "Young comrade, do you have any idea how difficult that is?"

"How hard can it really be?" she replied. "All they need to do is go straight, even if they deviate slightly they should end up at their destination." Kennedy looked back at Meyer.

The older woman folded her arms. "Now listen, I had my misgivings, but she took the plan to Santana and he enthusiastically approved," she said. "And he's the expert on what his people are capable of."

Kennedy sighed. "Roger, we'll be on our way then." Irving smiled as he turned around.

"Don't let the door hit you on the way out," she said. Kennedy made his way back to Knight. The man had walked far enough away from the panzerters that he could be heard.

" Don't see any of them turning around," the big man said. "I take it things didn't go well?"

Shaking his head, Kennedy pointed towards the war room. "No, that bitch Irving gave the plan to Santana and of course he went with it." Knight shook his head.

"Guy sounds like an old school soldier, the 'do as I say and if it's impossible figure it out' type, hated those guys," he said before patting Kennedy on the back. "Glad you aren't one comrade."

Kennedy grabbed the biplane that would take him up to the cockpit hatch. "Let's get mounted up and out of here, the faster I can get away from that Operations officer, the faster I can breathe easy." The handle of the biplane clicked, then a winch pulled him upward.

Once he strapped himself in, he relaxed. *It feels so natural, without a doubt, this is where I'm supposed to be.* As the gate opened, the vehicles rolled out, followed by the plodding panzerters immediately afterward.

He felt overstep as if it were his own, his crash chair rocking gently with every step. The control grips conformed to his hands after countless hours in the cockpit. *The last time I sat here, we'd just held of the Tharcians at the Battle for FOB Blake. Those opening days seem like years ago, the rapid movement, the feeling of invincibility, and as soon as we hit Riverside, all those things came crashing to a halt.*

"Red 1, do you know the name of the river?" He asked. "The one that runs north-south, not the branch beyond narrow field."

After a moment, Knight gave him an answer. "I believe it's called the Grenze, comrade, It means either wall or barrier, I'm not sure which, but it used to be the border before the War of 2112."

Huh, barrier or wall, maybe it's fate? Is some force beyond my understanding keeping me from entering traditional Tharcian territory? Kennedy shook his head, despite being certain he was alone in his cockpit. *No, there's no fate, if there was, Union scientists would have quantified it, measured it, and enabled it to be distributed equally.*

Kennedy let the gentle rock of the Jupiter comfort him. Alloyed plating shielded him from the elements and bullets, alloys created by Union engineers. Union Physicists refined the theories that allowed the Jupiter's I3 Nuclear Combustion engine to operate and do so safely. Skilled biologists and doctors built the machines that had formed him and grown him while proud Union workers in the distant past donated aspects of their DNA. Indeed, himself and everything around it had been made and guided by breakthrough Union Science.

But do I really believe that? Kennedy's reverie came to a sudden and sharp halt with a single word screamed over the radio.

"Partisans!"

AS HE STIRRED IN HIS BUNK, RIETER HEARD POINT DEFENSES. THE distinct sound, not unlike a massive roll of paper being torn, echoed through Landfall. *Are they really testing them again?* A loud crashing sound rocked the hotel and Reiter sprang to his feet. He'd gone to bed wearing sweatpants and an old OMI (Ostlan Military Institute) shirt.

Don't have time to change. He threw his flight vest on over his shirt, grabbed a coat, and hopped into an old pair of running shoes. Retrieving his handgun and holster from his doorhandle, he ran outing the hall. Everyone else in the hall also rushed out of their rooms.

Soldiers of all stripes poured out of the doors. Infantry ran towards their base rally points, rifles and kit dangling in their hands. Like him, the pilots ran towards the motor pool.

A PD turret on the roof of the diner opened up on an approaching dropship, showering them with hot brass. With a shout, Reiter directed them to the motor pool as the dropship crashed into the ground. Despite the violence of the crash, Union Raiders rushed out of the wreckage, eyes filled with violence.

Reiter dumped an entire magazine from his sidearm. While he hit nothing, he encouraged the raiders to seek cover. The pilots ran faster now. Reiter dove behind a parking barrier to evade return fire from the raiders.

Reloading, he snapped back more from his handgun. Either he still hit nothing, or their body armor was tough enough to shrug off his handgun, but Raiders began maneuvering after the pilots. While one group moved, another would focus their fire on Rieter.

Despite its concrete construction, the barrier cracked under the intense fire being poured at it. He dumped another magazine before realizing, to his horror, he'd spent his last one. *Shit, I need to get to the Lowe.*

Absent other options, he tried to track how many raiders threatened them. Four currently entered the motor pool while three more help Reiter pinned. A roar to his left caught his attention. An Iglasio rolled down the road as if a madman drove it. Opening up with its coaxial machine gun, the tables suddenly turned on the raiders. Outmatched against the IFV, the raiders could only hunker down and seek cover.

Infantry ran out the back of the metal brick. If a general saw them, they'd lose their minds over the body armor over night clothes that seemed to be the uniform of the hour. They came around through the building behind the raiders on the street. Pinned against their own cover, they didn't stand a chance.

Rieter waved to the commander as he sat in an open hatch near the Iglasio's turret. "Hey, Hey! Friendly!" The commander waved back.

"I fucking know, sir!" Stovepipe replied. "With all due respect, get your ass in the robot!" Reiter grinned and saluted the man. One of the infantry tossed him a rifle from a fallen Raider. "Just I case" he'd said. Reiter ran into the motor pool with his rifle up, and the infantry followed him.

Inside the motor pool, things had devolved into a running battle between the raiders and pilots. The Raiders had better weapons and more ammo, but would be screwed if a pilot managed to mount up. To that end they tossed grenades at joints or units clearly under repair.

Stovepipe's dismounts covered him while he ran towards the Lowe. *She's got twin .50 cals in her head, specifically for this shit, aircraft, missiles, and infantry.* He stumbled and slipped across the snow. Not to be outdone, the raiders returned fire. Reiter glanced back just in time to see a young man eat a bullet.

As fire filled his blood, he scrambled into the cockpit of his Lowe. With a hum, the engine roared to life before settling into its natural hum. Rieter disengaged the safeties and looked for the raiders.

To his horror, they emerged from cover with a struggling Merlin JR looking at him and the infantry. One pointed a rifle at his head and another smiled at Rieter and shook his head. *They're desperate, why? Are reinforcements not coming? Is this not the precursor to an actual attack?*

"Union soldiers, stand down, you'll be treated fairly if you surrender," he said over the loudspeaker. As he shifted the Lowe into a kneeling position, he looked around. The infantry had taken up position across from him, they had cover, clear shots on the raiders, and their weapons couldn't damage the Lowe.

He noticed Wesser waving to him from behind the leg of a panzerter. The small lieutenant stood in her bathrobe, her coppery hair a ragged mess. She held a finger to her lips and made a circle motion.

The Raiders focused all of their attention on either the Lowe or the firing squad across from him. While one stood up on a palette stack, presumably to address Rieter, something moved under a stack of spare parts.

Like a pair of linebackers, Kozma and Merlin sr took one raider to the ground. As their attention snapped away, Mo grabbed Merlin. Steele tackled the one holding his gun on the kid, but as she did, the one on the pallettes drew his gun on her.

So Rieter punched him. With the Lowe's fist. As soon as the others had gotten Merlin away from his captors, Reiter set his other hand between them and the raiders. The Infantry opened up on the doomed men, cutting them down. Reiter relaxed, slightly.

His radar didn't pick up any returns, but in the driving storm, he didn't expect any. "Thorne X-Ray, Fox 6, SITREP?"

"Fox 6, Throne 3," Friermann replied. "Actual's getting patched up, but it doesn't look like we were the intended target."

Reiter furrowed his brow. "What do you mean? Was it a diversion?"

"Looks to be that way," Friermann replied. "We got word the 1-4th is getting a contract from a whole gaggle of dropships with a few ending up over the CAV in front of them." A sharp click filled his ears, a sound Reiter assumed to be another Highland Sap. "The situation's developing, but the word right now is the raiders are landing pretty disorganized. If I had to take a guess, the weather threw a wrench into their whole plan."

The last thing he said stood out to Reiter. "Why would they bother attacking then? Wouldn't it have been smarter to just wait?"

Friermann chuckled. "I don't know, and the person who does is way over our pay grade." Reiter collapsed back into his chair. Outside, he saw his pilots huddling together for warmth.

"Do you think? We'll see a second wave?" he asked.

"If you want your people to change into warmer clothing, go

ahead," Friermann said. "The rest of the regiment is stood up and ready, if we receive a second wave then we'll send Fox to the thick of it, but for now rest, change, and recover, it's going to be a long night."

———————

KENNEDY GRIT HIS TEETH AS HE SCANNED THE SNOWY WOODLINE. Small arms and rockets, no threat to his panzerter, but he wasn't the target. With his laser set to strobe, he swept the woodline back and forth. Trees burst into flame and snow turned to whisky steam.

A rocket screamed out of the forest. It struck one of the ammo carriers, turning the rugged truck into a mushroom cloud that rattled his ears. *Damn it.* He fired a burst of laser fire where he thought the rocket had come from, but failed to see any effect.

"We've already lost five scout cars and an ammo carrier," he said over the net. "We'll have to push through, we don't have time or the equipment to go chasing rats." The two remains lead scout cars raced out of the woods to his right and took to the road. Following close on them were the remaining supply trucks, their light PDCs blazing away at shadows in the forest.

The Red guards stayed back with Kennedy, providing covering fire and big targets for the partisans. Unlike the lighter Martians, their Jupiters were dedicated solely to anti-panzerter combat and thus lacked anti-infantry weapons. *But we can make do.*

Snow and Khan followed the next wave of supply trucks, while Knight and the remaining scout cars covered them. "They're fucking everywhere and nowhere," one of the scout car crews cried. "It's like trying to cath rain in a net!"

"Calm down," Kennedy snapped firmly. "You're MAGs, you're the greatest soldiers in the mars sphere, and farmers will not overcome us with pitchforks." As if to undercut him, a fleeing supply truck skewed sideways after a machine-gun punched into its cab. It hit a tree and remained there.

From the view of his panzerter, the partisans blended with the snow and trees. He shot at anything moving in the woods, but could not stop them from lighting the wrecked supply truck ablaze. *I hope that's not the field kitchen.*

Finally, he and Knight fled with the last two scout cars. The odd chattering of a machine gun followed them, but no more Union soldiers died. Kennedy sighed. "That wasn't as bad as it could have been. We only lost a few vehicles," Knight said.

Now that they had escaped immediate danger, Kennedy checked his Command Matrix. With a groan, he replied to Knight. "We obviously lost an ammo carrier, and several scout cars, and one of the parts vehicles." His matrix chimed with an update. "And our field kitchen wasn't lost per se, but that vehicle is saying they shot their cargo compartment up."

"All those things by themselves are bad," Knight said. "But we didn't suffer the loose of anything we can't easily replace."

"Still, this area's crawling with partisans, and we don't have a mission profile that's equipped to deal with them," Kennedy replied. "It's like we used to have a unit out this way that did."

"Yeah, like the motor batt they threw away," Knight replied. "This changes how we conduct our mission."

Kennedy nodded. "Exactly, if the partisans warn the Tharcians of our movements, we could be in serious trouble, and that's assuming they don't attack our headquarters during the operation."

They traveled for about three more miles before coming to their pre-planned rally point. Once their headquarters element had been encircled in the protective circle of their subordinate units, Kennedy ordered the field kitchen spun up. "I want hot meals for the entire battalion and 50% security."

While their soldiers ate, Kennedy had the red guards and all of his company commanders meet him by the mobile HQ. Unfortunately, some things like the tablet chargers had eaten a few bullets, but their maps remained intact.

"So the partisans change things, but only slightly," Kennedy said. "We'll continue the plan as normal, but I want the recon platoon to leave their dismounts with headquarters."

Ballard nodded. "I don't think that will affect the strength of my group securing Objective Alpha, but should we be concerned?" Kennedy shook his head.

"No, the Capricorns and Martians are great at dealing with infantry," he said. "I don't think they would do much besides try to warn any nearby Tharcians, but that by itself affects our tempo." He pointed at the map and traced their routes. "I'd originally wanted to be deliberate about this, making sure each point was secure before heading to the next, but now we're going to have to blitz them."

Irwin raised a hand. "So you think they'll blow the bridges before we have time to take them?" Kennedy nodded.

"That's correct, I believe the only reason they didn't before was they didn't believe the Motor battalion had a realistic chance of taking the bridges, but if they hear a panzerter batt supported by heavy types is barreling down on them-"

"They won't hesitate to blow both bridges," Ballard finished. "Well, our job just got harder."

Knight raised his hands. "Well, what are we waiting for? They might already know we're here!" Kennedy nodded.

"That's my concern," he said. "Which is why as soon as everyone has been fed and given water, we'll move out." He checked his watch. "Let's call it, thirty minutes, we move out from here, Spears, in need the infantry to do a quick sweep of the estate before your forces move out from there."

They acknowledged their tasks and left to update their respective units. Feeling his own stomach growl, he fished a ration pack out of the mobile HQ. Knight noticed his odd choice in cuisine. "You're not going to get a hot meal?"

Kennedy shook his head. "Not until we've had a successful mission and we stand on the other side of the old border," he replied. "Besides, if they're serving eggs again, I'm better off with this, anyway." He looked more closely at his ration pack. "Even if it uses meat substitutes instead."

Knight laughed. "Alright then comrade, we'll let you enjoy your lab grown food." Kennedy narrowed his eyes.

"Are you implying lab grown things are inferior?" he asked. Knight shot him a confused look.

"No, I would just rather eat something real," he replied. *He's talking about food, there's no reason to believe he's talking about tubers.*

With a shrug, Kennedy smiled. "To each his own, I guess, I don't mind it." As he warmed up his "beef and barley stew" he couldn't help but wonder what the wider Union thought of him. He'd never interacted with a tuber outside of the MAGs. Those tubers he knew, from Ballard to Fletcher, and even Wake were hardly a monolith. But was that also true of tubers outside his sphere? The lumberjacks, the farmers, the fishers, miners and other labor intensive duties they fulfilled for the Union.

There's no way fighting the seas for fish, or cutting down trees is as hard as writing a damn newspaper article or fixing a computer system. Before he could follow the thought thread to its conclusion, Halphen interrupted him.

"Comrade Colonel, battalion has been fed and watered, we'll be ready to move out in five," he said.

Kennedy nodded. "Make it so then." As he downed the rest of his stew, it left a bitter taste in his mouth.

6

As a working party cleared the wreck of a Union dropship, Reiter watched with Col Hawke at his side. The older man's arm hung in a sling while a booster poured nannies into his system to fix his broken arm.

"We only avoided disaster because so many of them got lost in the weather," the Colonel said. "They destroyed some mass green-houses in Narrowfield, even though they attacked with no sense of organization."

Reiter furrowed his brow. "Are we going to face starvation?"

Hawke shook his head. "No, not yet anyway, but many people will go hungry when you combine this with no imports from space."

As they walked down the street, they noticed broken glass littered the area. Reiter kicked a piece of rubble into a large shard. "Think they'll attack again?" he asked. "Was that just a precursor?" Hawke nodded.

"I'm not sure where, but General Orban is considering ordering us to fall back to Grunbeck," he said. "It's not like higher has done much else, there's no grand plan, there's no penultimate strategy, it's just keep holding out until something happens." They continued walking down the road. "Honestly, I think the rot started after the last war."

Reiter looked at the older man. "What do you mean?"

Hawke stared at the shattered rubble. "I think they got complacent, the War of 2112 was won so quickly and easily on the ground that our general staff failed to take the Union seriously for decades, even as the Union overhauled it's military and ground forces."

"I'm not sure how much I buy into that," Reiter said. "Someone had to be aware they could pose a problem again. We had a bit of a naval arms race with them for a while."

Hawke shrugged. "I don't know, and remember it wasn't just us, Olympia and Avalon got in on that too, and the US, Japan, and Brazil." He gestured to the motor pool where Merlin, Jr and Smith helped clean debris. "But look at things like that. They will call up schoolchildren because they didn't have a plan to recall veterans to service." He sighed as the young men waved and they waved back.

"Well, if there's no grand plan," Reiter said, "All the more reason to push up my idea." He began walking towards the pilots cleaning the motor pool.

"Here's the thing about that," Hawke replied. "The other Regiment commanders love it, but General Orban is worried about excessive casualties. She doesn't want to be held responsible for a massacre if things go sideways."

As they reached the motor pool gate, Reiter turned to face Hawke. "She's aware that we'll lose people and ground if we just continue to sit here, right?" Hawke turned his palm like a doorknob.

"I think the battle in the woods reinforced her ideas," he said. "Although personally, I think its flawed to expect your enemy to make constant mistakes, especially when they have a track record for competence."

"Good afternoon, sirs," Smith said as he carried a garbage can full of glass and rocks. "I hope you could sleep well?"

"No," the two men said in unison. Hearing a splash and a hiss, Rieter turned to see Merlin jr. Throwing a second bucket of steaming water onto the ground. "What are you up to, frosty?"

Merlin turned with an empty bucket in each hand. "Oh, I'm trying to get rid of the smell, it reeks over here." Reiter raised an eyebrow when the bitter wind blew the scent of strong disinfectant in his face. Then he realized that the spot Merlin was trying to sanitize was where he'd punched a raider with his panzerter.

Shaking his head, he looked away. "I think it's good, Merlin." The younger man gave him a confused look.

"But It still smells." Rieter shared a knowing look with Hawke.

"Well, why don't you take a break," he said. "I'll give smith a hand, you go lay down or something." Merlin hesitated, but let Rieter take his buckets from him. "Merlin, that's an order, go decompress, and if someone takes issue, send them to me."

As the young man walked to the barracks, Hawke set a hand on Reiter's soldier. "See what I mean?" he asked. "We've all made our peace with what happens here, with training, conviction, or whatever else we have to do, but their young impressionable minds can't fully distance themselves from what they have to do."

Reiter nodded and set the buckets aside. "Alright Smith, what do you need me to do?" Smith raised an eyebrow.

"Shouldn't you be telling me what to do, sir? You're the officer." He leaned on his broom as he spook to Reiter.

"Well, you've been working in here, so you know what needs to be done," he said. "I won't sit here and pretend I know everything."

Before he went to work, Hawke patted him on the back. "I'd have your people ready to leave," he said. "That withdrawal order is coming." Reiter nodded and retrieved a shovel.

After an hour under gray skies, he and Smith had cleared the debris, checked the panzerters, and assisted the mechanics with any repairs that they needed. As they walked back to the hotel, Smith gave him a curious look.

"Why did Smith stop working?" he asked. "Was he needed else-where?" Reiter bit the inside of his lip. *I'm their leader, I can't be spread rumors or alter their perception of another soldier artifi-cially.* "Did I ask something I shouldn't?"

Reiter looked at the younger man and shook his head. "Oh, I'm sorry I was thinking about something else. He didn't look to well and because he recently had hypothermia, I didn't want him out working in too long in this weather."

Smith nodded. "Oh, how very considerate of you." Reiter waved him off.

"If you don't take care of your people, they won't take care of you," he said. "When you're in a leadership position, and I have a feeling you will eventually, remember that." Even as Smith nodded along with the advice, it stirred Reiter's own thoughts. Was he being taken care of? Was Hawke?

We're alive, but the enemy is sitting in our homes. How did the General Staff intend to win? Outlast the Union? Hope that eventu-ally their armies would just collapse? He recalled meeting the late Field Marshall Skara while he was still at the Academy and shud-dered. *No matter what, I'll never be that man.*

"ALRIGHT PEOPLE, SPEED IS THE KEY HERE," KENNEDY SAID AS HE set his stopwatch. "Incubus Company, move out." Ballard's company marched into the woods, the four Capricorn IFVs of the recce platoon following. He sighed and monitored the watch. *And now we wait.*

Even in the dark of night, the full clouds overhead hung low in the sky. Snow fell, the accumulated masses on the ground reflected what little light there was. He'd heard that movies and television lacked color at one point in history, that they'd all been shown in black and white. With the white snow the only thing he could see with his optical cameras, he assumed they looked roughly like that he was seeing.

The seconds and minutes dragged. Kennedy swore this was the longest five minutes of his life. He tapped his foot on the floor-boards of his Jupiter. He sipped water. He looked around. Every-thing just felt so quiet. *Is this a prelude to a more peaceful world?*

Finally, his comms came to life. "We're passing the lumber mill," Ballard said. "No signs of life, but that doesn't mean there aren't any." Kennedy nodded.

"Roger proceed as planned, Harpy, Jericho and the Red Guards, move out." As they left the manor, a once grand structure that had been devastated by neglect, stray shells, and looting, Kennedy noticed something in the trees.

He heard a low barking, followed immediately by an eerie green glow. "We're in contact," Ballard said. Kennedy gripped his controls more tightly. Their lasers were invisible in direct sunlight, but could be seen more easily in reduced visibility. In the dark night against white snow, they were as subtle as a freight train.

"Roger, keep me updated and don't slow down," Kennedy replied. Then an all too familiar whistle filled the air. Artillery hammered the forest ahead of him. He winced. It would take a direct hit for artillery to destroy a panzerter or IFV, probably a few for the Jupiter. But those shells would annihilate any dismounted infantry.

"X-Ray, what are the trajectories for those guns?" he asked. "We need counter-battery fire!" Shells still pummeled the woods ahead, but also in a wide cone around them. *The wind must be scat-*

tering the shells. More shells rushed overhead, some coming towards him, some going out towards their batteries.

His radio buzzed again. "We've reached Objective B," Irwin said. "Red Guards and Jerico are proceeding to Charlie." The light of flares and fires lit up the night.

"We're at Objective A," Ballard said over the radio. "But the Tharcians are responding with an armored counterattack, we're not sure if we can hold them." Kennedy grabbed his control sticks and put pedal to metal.

"Hold on, I'm on my way," he said. "X-Ray, you're in charge of defending HQ, don't muck it up." After pushing the Jupiter into a run, he crashed threw trees and small buildings without a care in the world. *If the Tharcians want to escalate this fight into a bigger one, then who am I to stop them?*

He broke out of the woods and onto the main road. Now he could clearly see the fighting at the intersection. And the Tharcians could see him. As he charged down the road, he raised his laser and fired a burst at the closest Tharcian panzerter he could see. A cloud of steam erupted from them.

Is this some sort of new-anti-laser system? As he closed the distance, he switched to his sub-machine gun. Union panzerters had employed a similar weapon in the war of 2112, but it's small caliber round rendered it ineffective against the Tharcians they faced at the time. This model had been designed with greater penetration and range in mind.

75-mm slugs pounded the Thracian until it fell, unmoving. Kennedy fired another burst. This time he smashed the head of an enemy panzerter. As soon as he'd made it clear, he presented the greatest threat to them; The Tharcians focused fire on him.

Two more fell from Incubus company. Shells struck the Jupiter, but had little effect beyond angering Kennedy. In return he swung his SMG back and forth, hosing down more Tharcians with shells.

As their wingman fell, a Tharcian grew increasingly desperate. Drawing their sword, they lunged at Kennedy. Kennedy evaded their first swing, but their second cut through the body of his SMG. He tossed the weapon away as the heat from the Tharcian's blade cooked off the magazine.

He side stepped another swing. Lunging for his opponent, he missed and received a slash to the side for his trouble. As he grit his teeth, Kennedy struck the errant Tharcian across the face.

The smaller panzerter toppled. He fell onto them, but their blade came up and through his left arm. Twisting their sword arm to the side, he managed to pull the limb completely away from the Tharcian. Then they went for his laser.

The weapon discharged, once, twice, three times, and then a burst. Kennedy gasped as the air in his cockpit grew hot and thick. They'd managed to penetrate his armor twice, but h'd won his weapon back and rewarded his opponent with a burst into the cockpit.

Carefully, he stood himself up off of the wrecked panzerter. "This is Red 1, we've taken the bridge, the infantry are working to disarm the explosives right now." Kennedy heard a loud crump in the distance. *They must have blown the other bridge, so they did have a radio controlled detonator.*

"Roger, With the other bridge down, we'll head that way and center our defense on the bridge," Kennedy said. Switching channels, he got Halphen on the line. "Call Division and tell them we've secured bridge over the Grenze." The Tharcian panzerters retreated back across the river, they'd be licking their wounds for a while.

As Kennedy turned north, Incubus company followed him. "We lost three panzerters, two more damaged, our lasers were rendered ineffective."

Kennedy nodded. "I noticed, it looks like they had some kind of laser defense system," he replied. "We'll have to report that to higher." With the approach into old Tharsis secure, they took over secu-rity of the northern intersection while Harpy doubled back to secure headquarters. *I'll have to set up security patrols for our supply lines.*

His stomach sank as he heard a distant, smaller crashing sound. *NO, No, No, no.* "Red 1, Sitrep?" he asked.

Knight responded immediately. "Looks like they had some secondary explosives placed. The good news is the bridge isn't destroyed."

"And the bad news?" Kennedy asked.

Knight's sigh echoed in the radio's static. "The bridge will need repairs before we can use it, we'll need to call up engineering teams from headquarters." Knight didn't need to continue for Kennedy to understand the implications. Those engineers would need to be escorted, and even then would still be subject to attacks by partisans.

"You know, it'd be great if we had an intact Motor Battalion," he said. "Never the less, we'll do whatever we need to do, Halphen, make the arrangements for an engineering team to investigate the bridge. I will assign all companies to protect the bridge or our temporary headquarters, Reaper 6 out."

REITER TURNED THE LOWE TO BETTER OBSERVE THE BRIDGE FROM Landfall. The column of panzerters and armored vehicles walked shamefully over the Grenze river. When the last vehicle crossed, a nearby engineer team detonated their explosives. Just like that, a seventy-year-old bridge collapsed into a pile in the river.

Reiter sighed. "Alright, Fox, form up around the engineers and hospital staff, we're moving out." The engineers fell in behind a column of civilian and military ambulances as well as a van filled with medical records. Black Platoon took the lead while white platoon took the rear, leaving Gold and headquarters to disperse themselves among the escorts.

"Well, I guess this is better than running for our lives," Mo said. "Still not a fan of retreating."

"Why even are we retreating?" Kozma asked. "That raid really didn't do much actual damage."

Reiter glanced back at White Platoon's panzerters. "It's not just the raid," he said. "The scouts got mauled by panzerters North of us, at an operational level they had us on three sides."

"I don't know if general staff is aware, but our homes are way back in Gallacia," Mo said. "I'd like to go home at *some* point." *I understand the sentiment, but orders are orders. If Orban thinks it's best we pull out of landfall, then she has to have a good reason.*

After fifteen minutes traveling down the main road, they began seeing their first glimpses of Grunbeck. Spires of glass and stone reached towards the sky, dwarfing even their panzerters. He couldn't see them, but Reiter knew the domes of Garden City weren't but a few miles from their current position.

"It's massive, and so beautiful here," Wesser said. Since the Union seemed to lack a strategic bombing campaign, the lights of the city remained on. Their soft glow cast the gray clouds overhead in a pinkish orange. "I'd hate to see all of this leveled."

"I don't think you'll have to see it at all," Rieter said. "If there's anything we learned about Union strategy, it's that they started avoiding large metropolitan areas after the battle of Polaski."

"Why is that?" Kozma asked. "I thought the whole reason panzerters replaced tanks was they were better suited to urban combat."

Reiter nodded. "They are," he said. "But look how tall those buildings are, you could have infantry twelve stories up and never see them."

"So why aren't there any panzerters built for enormous cities like this?" Kozma asked.

"I can answer that," Steele said. "Because I paid attention in 6's class, panzerters average around the height of a four story building because that's the height of most buildings in ninety percent of cities and taller than any buildings in the countries panzerters were originally created to operate in."

He smiled. For just a moment, Reiter's mind was back in the classroom teaching history. Then he snapped back to the present. "The other reasons are tactical considerations, the Union does their best fighting in open or sparse spaces at mid-range, at long range we have the advantage for the most part, while at close range it's a pretty even fight."

"So you think they'll avoid Grunbeck?" Kozma asked.

"And Swiezen," Reiter replied. As they approached the city, Reiter picked up movement on his sensors. Civilians. Life continued as if there was no war here. He saw the occasional closed store front, but other than that, very little indicated an approaching Union threat.

Older buildings mixed with the newer glass and steel construction. Brick and mortar stores and apartment blocks still existed. *Some of these buildings are made from recycled dome materials and probably look newer than they actually are.* Wreaths hung from lampposts and Christmas Lights shone from many a balcony overlooking the street.

"It's all so peaceful," Wesser said. "It's like there's no war."

"And then we come strolling in," Mo said. "Dum-de-dum-dum, sorry to stomp all over your pretty streets, we're a bunch of war-displaced watchmen, have you seen any other sixty ton war machines lately?" Then he paused. "I've got people applauding us, kids are out here saluting."

Wesser laughed. "They probably think you're six, you're rocking a similar panzerter." Reiter chuckled as people began noticing him in the column and hurriedly also saluting.

"What are they even celebrating?" Mo asked. "For God's sake, we're *losing.*"

"People need heroes," Reiter replied. "And even if you don't feel like it, you are one to them, Mr. Top scoring ace." They stuck to their predetermined route, which took them to a large concrete building with a massive bay door tall enough for a panzerter. "They used this place to set up parade floats, hence the bay door."

They ducked into the massive warehouse. Once inside, they lined up against both walls, where scaffolding had been placed to allow mechanics to work on them. Reiter crawled out of his unit and lowered himself to the warehouse floor.

With the panzerters situated, the medical personnel left to take their patients to the hospital. Rieter gathered his soldiers on the warehouse floor. "I understand this is less than ideal, but this is where we are now, I'm proud of your resilience and your dedication to fighting for our homes." He gestured to Comidus. "XO is about to find out the living situation, I'm about to have a meeting with Colonel Hawke and learn the new plan, for now, relax here as best you can."

With that, he turned and left for the management office for the warehouse. There, one engineer told him the headquarters company had relocated to an office building across the street. After making the short walk over, Reiter entered the front door of the marble office building.

The building itself seemed depressing compared to the surrounding buildings. Its windows were recessed away from the exterior with the marble around them jutting out, casting shadows over the glass. The effect created an oppressive mood as Reiter stepped inside. Chos rolled about before him. Civilian office workers did their best to pretend soldiers weren't setting up shop around them while also answering the occasional question from one.

Noticing Friermann directing the setup of tables and files, Reiter approached the massive NCO. "MSG, have you seen Colonel Hawke?"

The towering figure looked at him after a team of soldiers set up a bank of computers. "He's upstairs getting maps set up, I offered him two guys to give him a hand, but he shot that down." The older man cracked open a Highland Sap. *How many of those does he have?*

"Is he hard to find?" Rieter asked.

Friermann shook his head. "Just follow the sound of paper and swearing." Reiter nodded and took the stairs up to the next floor. The floor itself was broken by multiple glass doors and cheap walls. Before long, he found himself stuck behind a door that required a badge to open.

"Excuse me," he said as a woman holding stacks of folders walked past. "I need to get in here, could you open this?"

She blinked at him. "Why?"

Rieter took a breath. "I need to speak to Colonel Hawke, it's urgent, and he's through here." Without saying another word, she held up a badge and opened the door. Reiter stepped through and found Hawke after a moment.

He'd commandeered an entire conference room. On a monitor dominating the main wall, their situation map was on full display. Hawke unfurled multiple Maps to put together the surrounding area and was placing markers when Rieter walked in.

"Need a hand, sir?" he asked.

Hawke looked up with a smile. "Captain Rieter, just the man I was about to send for," he said. "Yes, I'd love a hand." As he set to helping his commander, he noticed the woman from earlier mean-mugging him through the glass before carrying on.

"What's the deal with the people here?" Rieter asked. "The civilians outside loved us coming in here."

Hawke sighed as he placed more map markers. "As you know, we can't demand a private business or residence quarter us, Constitution and all, that being said, this is the office for Vaterland Department of the Interior, so the Province can order them to house us if it chooses, which they did." He ended his last sentence with an edge to his voice. "Were we had multiple businesses willing to house or quarter other parts of our regiment, they ordered the DOI building to serve as our headquarters."

"But they don't like that?" Rieter asked as he opened a box with map markers and computers. "I mean they care about the war right?"

Hawke shrugged. "These kinds of people, low to mid-level bureaucrat, they think they're above having to share space with us, because on some level, they feel like they're above us."

Rieter nodded, remembering a Senate's aide who'd made a deal with them for a POW. "I know the type, sir," he said. "The guy they sent to take Fletcher for her surgery, he just seemed slimy."

Hawke chuckled. "I forgot you had to deal with that self-important clown, he talked to me about pulling strings for a second Lowe." He shook his head. "Anyway, we've got enough here for us to go to work. By now the other company commanders should be on their way."

Reiter took a seat at the conference table. "Why is that, sir?"

The older man grinned. "Because Rieter, we're going to call the other regiments and figure out a counter-attack."

―――――――

―――――――

UNION VEHICLES ROLLED DOWN THE DESERTED STREETS OF Landfall. Kennedy watched them in his Jupiter as he and Incubus company maintained the perimeter. Despite the feelings of triumph radiating from the headquarters battalion, he felt sour. *We didn't take this ground; they gave it to us. And where was our triumphant entry to Vaterland?*

Radio chatter chased the thoughts from his mind. "No signs of prisoners, including-"

"I know," Kennedy replied. "She's going to be further to the rear, if not in the Tharcian Capital."

Ballard sighed. "I just hope she's not on a dissection table, you know they think she's an abomination." Kennedy nodded.

"Listen, fletcher's tough, she proved as much on the Olympian front," he said. "I don't think she would let them take her apart that easily." He cast his gaze to the east. Grunbeck's light glowed in the distance. "The Black Knight's out there, we need to be careful."

"Why aren't we shelling the city?" Ballard asked. "It's practically begging us." Kennedy shook his head.

"Because the city is more valuable to us intact, besides I doubt the Tharcians would station troops inside the city," he said. "Our big lesson in Galicia was they'll go out of their way to keep civilians out of harm's way, I doubt they want a repeat of the battle for Polaski."

Ballard got quiet for a moment. "I know we won that won, but we got our ass kicked doing it."

"We were due for a battle like that," Kennedy replied. "The Tharcians had improvised ways to counter our laser weaponry, Polaski provided them a great opportunity to use it." Rapid beeping from his comms panel told him he was being hailed. "Hold on Ballard, I think division is calling."

He tapped on the panel and found a text message from the command team. They require your presence in the new War Room- Operations. *Huh, does Meyer have big plans already?* Their previous endeavors, while successful, were only mildly so. *Guess I'll go find out.*

"Ballard, you're in charge," he said as he walked his Jupiter towards a parking lot and took a knee. Searchlights blinded him as his eyes adjusted from the dimly lit cockpit. Once he could see, he climbed down to find the new war room. A nearby mechanic indicated command set themselves up in the town hall.

The building presented itself with a rather quaint structure. A Round dome capped a squat marble structure while Hellenic columns lined the steps. As he approached, he noticed most of the windows had been boarded up and the columns seemed to be carved and polished tree trunks rather than marble.

How excessive, using all of this genuine wood for a municipal building. He climbed the steps and was directed to the war room. What was formerly a planning and zoning room had been converted into a twenty-second century war room. Monitors displayed various maps and reports related to the units that made up the 75th panzerter.

Unfortunately, he'd missed Meyer by mere moments, but Irving was more than glad to bring him up to speed. "They have brought the Motor battalion up to adequate strength," she said. "We'll begin using them to disrupt this partisan nuisance shortly."

Kennedy nodded. "Good, they can begin by bringing engineers up to our bridgehead, it is absolutely critical we repair that bridge."

With a glance at her tablet, Irving nodded. "They actually have a mission planned already, one that minimizes risks to our engineers, but it will require you to hold that bridgehead against a possible counterattack."

He furrowed his brow. "Why are we delaying?" he asked. "It is absolutely vital we get that bridge operational."

"You know that, I know that, and comrade Meyer knows that," she replied. "Know who else knows this? The Partisans." She showed him her tablet. "Which is why we leaked to partisan sympathizers we were brining bridge layers from further west to simply bypass the damaged bridges."

Kennedy took the tablet from her soft hands and read. "You're pulling a platoon from the mechanized company?" she nodded.

"They'll be disguised as bridging vehicles until they get ambushed," she said. "Than they drop the disguise and destroy the partisans."

Kennedy studied the plan she's outlined on her tablet. "So we're gambling the partisans go all in on this and we can crush them." He nodded as he handed her tablet back. "That's a risk I would take. If they're not dealt with, they could prove as serious a threat as the black knight."

Irving scoffed. "You pilots seem to overvalue the Black knight as a military asset, if anything it's greatest impact is psychological." Kennedy shrugged.

"If you fought him, or saw him in action, you'd want to avoid him too," he replied. His response elicited a raised eyebrow from Irving.

"What are you avoiding?" she asked. "One high performance machine, or the man at the controls?"

Kennedy looked back at their situation maps. "I'll remind you that Captain Reiter is responsible for the battle we came closest to losing, I have a feeling-"

"General Mate was responsible for the attack on FOB Blake," Irving said. "And we had him assassinated via drone, an operation that cost us countless such craft and also happened to kill Field Marshall Skara himself."

Kennedy sighed. "You wouldn't understand," he said. "But Rieter took people from me, friends, mentors, sisters, and brothers, the closest thing I had to family in my life and he took it from me, all save Ballard and a few others in Incubus company."

Irving didn't snark. She didn't belittle him. Instead, she approached him and looked more closely. "That's not professional, that's personal, but I understand." She hesitated. "In a weird way." She sat down in a chair.

Kennedy pulled one around and sat as well with his forearms resting on the back of the chair. He snapped at two sergeants on computers. "You there, leave us, take a dinner break or something." He turned back to face the Operation officer. "I'm listening."

"During the initial stages of the invasion, we went undercover, posing as research and engineering students," she said. "Our objectives were straightforward enough, steal Tharican military research and designate targets for assassination."

Kennedy winced. "That's rather underhanded. Irving shook her head.

"As they say in intelligence, there are no bad tactics, only bad targets," she replied before looking away. "Well, we picked a terrible target, this guy, husband and wife team, Anna and Woody Pete. They worked on the black knight."

He sat a little straighter in his chair. "So that's how Chaney got data from the Tharcians." He shook his head. "I'm sorry continue."

"Anyway, they had a pretty customary routine," she said. "He'd stay late at the office working on the black knights' weapons. She left in the afternoon to run their errands after working on the black knight's engine." She looked down. "Me and my partner Melissa went through our officers course, MAG training, and intelligence branch training together, we were good, on this mission we got paired with this guy, he had one eye, his codename was Thorn and that was all he told us about himself."

She took a deep breath. "Sorry, this isn't easy for me."

Kennedy held up a hand. "I understand, we can train ourselves into suppressing certain things, but there are times when the cracks show."

Irving nodded. "We fucked up, like actually fucked up, instead of staying late, Woody Pete leaves to visit his in-laws, Thorn had gone to his office to assassinate him while he was there, but his wife showed up waiting to drop something off while we waited for her with an injection."

Kennedy raised an eyebrow. "An injection?" She waved a hand.

"Neurotoxin faster than the nervous system, she would have been dead before she felt the needle, but we never used it, and since she was with Agent Thorn, he tortured her to death in her office and made it look like a robbery, while we found out Woody had gone to tell his in-laws she was pregnant." Something like regret passed over her young face.

"So he broke," Kennedy summarized. "And?"

Irving looked away. "The war started day later, while we tried to pull out, he found us, and the surrounding cells, we couldn't escape him, I only escaped because Melissa covered me in flame retardant blankets while our safe house burned down."

Kennedy looked down. "If you could stop Woody Pete, would you? Or would you rather avoid him?" She shrugged.

"I couldn't tell you," she said. Kennedy stood and put a hand on her shoulder.

"Well, here's to building a bridge," he said. "I didn't like you at first, but I think we've come to an understanding." She smiled.

"I look forward to our renewed professional relationship."

now fell gently on the lawn of the Presidential Manor. Field
Marshal Adam Hausnerr would have thought the scene
outside was serene were it not for the fact he dreaded the meeting
he was about to walk into. With his tablet in his hand, he double
checked to make sure his dress uniform remained in top condition.

He'd always hated the white coat that went with their winter
dress and how easily it could stain or accumulate dirt. His black
pants ran a tad tight, but his coat hid that. With a sigh, he straightened his tie and entered the conference room on the south lawn.

High carved ceilings gave the room a far more spacious feeling.
Within its center, the ceiling rose into a dome that had been painted
with a depiction of their people's exodus from Earth. Below the
ceiling lay a heavy wooden table, around which sat the other
members of the Tharcian General Staff as well as Madame President herself.

President Isabel Reinhardt sat at the head of the table. Her
excellency had chosen a comfortable, but casual business dress for
these meetings. To her left sat the general officers in charge of

personal, intelligence, Operations, and Logistics; while to her right the Generals in charge of Plans, Civil Affairs, communications, education and training, and financing and contracts. Hausner gingerly took his seat at the foot of the table and nodded to the President.

"Alright Ladies and Gentlemen," she said. "We've got a war to win, so let's get down to business." She looked immediately at Hausnerr. "once again, I'd like your strategy outlined and I want to know why we aren't halfway to Foundation by now." The Field Marshall steeled himself as the other Generals leered at him.

"My predecessor's initial strategy revealed itself within the opening days," he said. "He guaranteed a quick victory and couldn't be more wrong." The head of Operations raised his hand.

"I hate to interrupt the Marshal, but that strategy was developed by the entirety of this Staff in conjunction with Marshal Skara," he said. "It was the best plan possible for our forces given the situation." He smiled at the Field Marshal.

"Yes," Hausner said. "The best plan that had never once been war-gamed by any of the leaders involved with it, never took into account our enemy's rearmament and doctrine, and never considered the possibility of its own failure." He opened his tablet and brought up a projection of their current situation on the table.

"With all due respect to Hausner, we had no idea the enemy would be as effective as they were in the early stages of the war," The head of intelligence said. "Nor did we evaluate their equipment as highly as it actually should have been considered."

Hausner held up a hand. "This leads me to our current strategy after the previous one fell apart, play defense and wait for the navy to save us, otherwise known as the Union strategy circa 2112, and that is unacceptable." He locked eyes with the President. "Unless one of our allies in exile whips up something, we're on our own ,and have to plan for it that way."

"So what are you proposing?" the Chief of Operations asked. "Because we have no path to victory unless you have a lot more trained forces waiting around somewhere we don't know about."

A stern glare silenced the man. "The answer is to quite using the forces we have like a blunt object and use them like scalpels. We need to reintroduce maneuver into our battle plans and strategy," Hausner said. "We will hit back at them, we will force them back, and we will win."

President Reinhardt smiled. "Good, I'm tired of the loser mentality from my officers, there's a couple of things I want to run by you though."

The Chief of Contracts and finance leaned forward. "We're all ears, Madam President," the man said.

"I want the bombing campaign to target the Union's orbital elevator," she said. "I hate seeing pictures of it, I hate seeing it reaching up to Phobos, and I especially hate that the Union can cheaply move resources between the surface and space."

Most of the general staff frowned. "I would advise against that Madame President, that repercussions to our international image would be severe," The Chief of Civil Affairs said with her fingers tented. "We might as well order the Effiel tower or the pyramids on Earth destroyed, it's a universal symbol of human achievement."

The President snorted. "They tore down Christ the Deliverer from the slopes of MT. Olympus, Avalon has destroyed multiple O'Neil colonies, each one a continent sized example of that same human achievement."

The Operations Chief shook his head. "If we take to destroying our enemies' symbols, how does that make us any different from the Soviets?"

"I think Madame President has a point," The Logistics Chief said. "The Eiffel Tower doesn't transport millions of tons of metals, gasses, and water for the North Sea Alliance, I think the comparison is apples to oranges."

Hausnerr raised a hand. "I would endorse the option if we maintained the moral high ground. If it were Avalon's Space Elevator, we wouldn't be having this debate." He looked back at President Reinhardt. "There was something else you wanted us to hear?"

She nodded. "Yes, I want Gallacia liberated by the end of spring." Before any of the General staff could object, Hausnerr nodded.

"We'll see to it," he said.

———

"THIS IS A DAMN NIGHTMARE," KENNEDY SAID. HE AND KNIGHT walked around the burnt remains of a supply convoy. A pile of charred bodies lay next to each other a short distance away, while two more had been shot in the head further down the road. MAG MPs took pictures, labeled evidence, and currently worked to identify the bodies. The sergeant in charge of the investigation approached the pair.

"Nightmare's one way to put it, comrade," he said. "Preliminary analysis had some kind of sedative or paralyzing agent as well as alcohol in their system."

Kennedy scowled. "They were drunk on duty? Is that what happened?" The MP shook his head and led them to the back of one of the supply trucks. He opened the double doors to reveal an empty, cavernous space.

"This truck was hauling rifles, machine-guns, rockets, and ammo to boot," the man said. He pointed to a burnt crater a hundred meters down the road. "And that one carried panzerter ammo and artillery shells, but I wouldn't be surprised if they napped a few of those to make IEDs."

Knight held up a hand. "Wait a minute, so how does the alcohol or sedatives play into this?" The MP jabbed a finger at the pile of charred bodies.

"We think someone lured them over with some local spirits and used the alcohol to hide the taste of the sedatives," he said. "Those two though, they were tubers, and that played into their ability to resist whatever he put in there. They make a break for the truck, and he shoots them."

They walked back to the command car Kennedy and Knight had taken to get from the scene. "So this was calculated," Kennedy said. "Whoever did this watched our convoys for a considerable amount of time."

The MP nodded. "We believe the man responsible for this is a guy going by Woody Pete, we've connected his group to multiple incidents of partisan activity." Kennedy shook his head and sat on the hood of the command car.

"Our Operations officer has a plan to put an end to partisans in this area," he said. "Its pretty genus, but I won't say too much out here." He looked back at Knight. "Ready?"

Knight looked back at the torched bodies. "I've seen and smelt enough." They climbed back into their command car and followed their escorts back to battalion headquarters. "You think Irving's plan is going to work?"

With a shrug, Kennedy looked out the small bullet-proof windows next to him. "You can never know anything one hundred percent, but I'm confident in her little scheme." He checked his watch for the date. "And in a few days, even if she doesn't nab this partisan, she'll have crippled their efforts enough that they won't pose much of a threat."

Their command car pulled into a garage beneath the manor they'd been using as headquarters. As they removed themselves from the cramped command car, Kennedy noticed the row of cars in the garage. Luxury sport utility vehicles, sleek supercars, muscle cars, and even a few antique models lined the opposite wall from the command car.

"Who do you think owned this place?" Kennedy asked. "And why do they need so many cars?"

With a shrug, Knight walked over to the cars for a closer look. "Someone who doesn't mind hoarding resources, that's for sure." He stopped at an SUV. As he looked at, its sharp angular body, sleek lines, and White paint job, he whistled. "I have to admit, there's a certain appeal to this one though."

Deciding to get a closer look himself, Kennedy walked behind the big man to the passenger door. Gingerly, he rested his hand on the door handle and traced the lines of the door frame. "The people that made this put their heart and soul in it, they must have." He pointed to the outline of the hydrogen tank. "See how it's all clean lines, the attention to detail is something else."

Slowly, Knight nodded in agreement. "I just hope they weren't exploited, they're damn fine craftspeople, that's for sure." As they reluctantly walked away from the SUV, Kennedy caught a whiff of something.

"Do you smell that?" he asked. Knight took a sharp inhale and nodded. They followed the nauseating odor to one of the many supercars parked in the garage. "Is that what I think it is?"

"Petrol," Knight spat. "Talk about excess." With one last look of disgust, the two men ventured upstairs.

"I have some ideas about our next target," Kennedy said. "I got a taste of the Tharcian homeland, but I'm not satisfied."

"So what are you about to propose?" Kennedy grinned.

"That we target the provincial capital: Neus-Koingsburg."

LEANING OVER THE MONITOR AHEAD OF HIM, REITER SCRATCHED AT his chin. "Kozma's underestimating his opponent, if he keeps trying to tempt Mo into melee combat he'll regret it." He tapped on the minimal in the corner. "He'd be better off keeping them at a distance and ganging up on the Lowe when it's isolated." Comidus, also observing the simulated battle, shrugged.

"Maybe he's seeing something we're not?" Comidus offered as they focused the camera on the duel between Kozma and Mo. "Or maybe he's trying to take our top pilot down a peg by beating him in his element?"

Rieter shrugged. While Kozma engaged Mo in melee combat, the rest of white platoon attempted to circle around a hill and capture their objective: A massive Panzerter sized flag. However, they'd run headlong into the rest of Black Platoon. Smith, Merlin, sr, and Wesser formed a firing line on some high ground beyond the flag.

With most of White team effectively suppressed, Rieter looked back at Mo and Kozma. Mo circled his opponent, striking with the flat of his blade. While his attacks remained persistent, their predictability made it easy for Kozma to block each blow with his shield.

"Why is Mo attacking him like that?" Comidus asked. "I'm no pilot, but I'm pretty sure you're supposed to use the sharp end of the thing."

Rieter snickered, but leaned in more closely. "I honestly couldn't tell you," he said. "What I can say is Wesser played Kozma like a fiddle." An alarm went off. Merlin Jr's panzerter collapsed into a smoking wreck, and with a frustrated growl, he climbed out. "I think his brother got him."

"Sibling rivalry at its finest," Comidus said. White Platoon continued to sustain damage from Wesser's firing line while Kozma tussled with Mo. "This whole skirmish looks like a wash for White." Rieter nodded in agreement.

"We have some good lessons learned, though," he said. "For one, Kozma shouldn't through himself into the biggest threat present and expect his platoon to carry on." Mo's Tesla blade bounced off Kozma's shield with a resounding gong.

"Oh, so he shouldn't do the thing you keep doing?" Comidus replied. "How should he act then?"

With a sidelong look at his XO, Rieter wagged a finger. "I don't do that," he said. "I hold off the biggest threat while you guys retreat, at least that's what I've done up to this point." He pointed to the screen. "Kozma threw his plan out the window, attacked the biggest threat, and left his platoon to figure it out themselves." Steele went down, the alarm punctuated by a sigh from her. White's newest addition, a young woman named Magyar, followed shortly after.

Rieter leaned over the intercom. "White Platoon, head to the ready room and standby for your AAR." Kozma's attacks began coming faster and faster, but Mo blocked them and kept up his own. Finally, he struck Kozma's shield and held his blade in place. Sparks raced across the older panzerter's shield arm and the limb went limp.

Kozma swore and sprang backwards. The tip of Mo's blade carved a trench in Kozma's frontal armor, but he lived. He wasn't lucky enough to dodge Mo's twin .50 cals. The fat rounds punched through his exposed cockpit cover and the battle ended in a Black Platoon victory.

"Black Platoon standby," Comidus said. "You'll be called for you AAR in a minute." Rieter rose and walked into the room behind their sim control center. Their ready room had been some form of classroom before, a dozen desks and a white board up front made it easy to covert to its current purpose.

Once Kozma had taken a seat, Reiter pulled up stills and video from their sim battle. "Alright, White Platoon, what was the plan?"

Steele raised her hand. "I was going to set up in the neutral zone with my sniper rifle and provide over watch. The others would have split up and attacked from three different directions."

Reiter nodded. "I'll get to the issues with your plan in a moment. What happened next?"

With a sigh, Kozma shrugged. "We got played, we expected Wesser to use her forces more conservatively and hold her Lowe in reserve guarding the flag, but instead Mo ambushed us as soon as we entered the neutral zone." The process went on for about forty-five minutes. Rieter dealt out criticism as well as praise where it was deserved.

Magyar performed well for her first sortie with White Platoon. He reminded Merlin jr that Steele and Magyar were grown women in panzerters and didn't need him to save them. Captain Reiter ended the AAR by taking an axe to Kozma's plan as well as addressing his own behavior.

As White platoon filed out and called for Black Platoon, Rieter prepared his notes for the next group. *I wonder if Kozma's actions have anything to do with Mo's attitude? If so I need to praise Wesser for that plan. Not only did she win the battle, but she put a bandage on those jealousy issues, for now at least.*

Reiter shook his head as Black platoon began coming in. *They're both grown men, I should just sit them down and solve the issue right there.* As they took seats, Reiter checked his notes one more time. "Alright, so what was the plan?"

AFTER A LONG DAY OF ARGUING WITH TRADE UNION REPS, Generals and various project heads, Guard-Brigadier Chaney preferred to cap things off with a whiskey by the fire while he read proposals. The alcohol usually lubed him up for a chuckle or two at some small co-ops expense. *What's next? A chemical union proposing to build blue-water ships?*

He shook his head. *They need new drone interceptors so the Tharcian's damn air fleet can stop doing whatever the hell it wants.* He thumbed through proposal after proposal. New rifles, new grenades, new panzerters. After an hour of not a single "boring" proposal, say for a new drone, supply truck, or Armored car, he tossed the first stack into the fire.

Seizing the next stack, he almost chucked the first proposal into the fire until he glanced at some specs. Parts commonality with the Martian. A new engine. Specialized close quarter weapons. *That's interesting.*

He set aside the rest of the stack for a moment while he looked over the new panzerter. A lighter power plant with the same output as the standard Martian engine allowed for greater mobility with the same level of armor. From close to mid-range, a shotgun allowed the panzerter to use multiple ammo types. Once it had depleted its ammo, the panzerter could continue fighting with a sword-axe and spiked knuckles.

Chaney took a swig of whiskey. *Most of the parts could be made out here in congregation as well. The main hurdle would be expanding production to include the new shotgun, engine , and these arm joints.* He set the proposal aside, but noted the proposal had been submitted by the Blackburn Locomotive Group. *Definitely not a bike co-op.*

Believing he'd found a diamond in the rough, he didn't set his hopes too high for the rest of the second stack. Much to his surprise, he found a proposal from a pair of auto unions he liked. Not only did they propose an upgrade to their existing Gemini Scout Car and

Leo Armored Car, but they offered to manufacture and refit them under license. *Maybe I'm getting lucky.*

Before setting it aside, he checked both auto unions. While their cars were well received, the labors to make them failed to match their sales numbers. *Well, they're good workers, it wouldn't hurt to throw them a bone.* He tossed out the next few proposals until he found one he'd never seen before: a variant for the Martian that didn't turn it into an unrecognizable mess.

The proposal called for a variant of Martian more suited to long range combat. A powerful sensor package ingeniously designed to slide around a Martian's sensor ring tripped its sensor range. On its back, the backpack had been redesigned to accommodate a backup power plant to power its main weapon: a Superlaser based on the field refit applied to Kennedy's Jupiter the previous month. To compensate for the increased weight, the Martian's armor had been reduced to the bare minimum to keep out auto cannon fire.

We can probably switch their proposed back up for the other designs lighter engine. He frowned. *Hell, I'd switch the entire Martian line over if it didn't hurt parts commonality with the Jupiter.* He set the proposal aside and returned to the stack.

Inspiration struck him at that moment. *I don't need to swap all of them to the lighter engine, just some of them.* As he grabbed his own tablet to take some notes, his mind began spinning into overdrive. *Why stop there? We can create a new line of Martians with enhanced performance with the lighter engine. Remove or reduce the limiters on the joints.*

While working on his notes, he glanced at the rest of the proposals. A few naval ones, none of them particularly stood out except a refit for the *Cosmonaut*-class Cruisers. *Their value is more in the fact they're still intact rather than their actual combat ability.* He set the proposal aside.

After tossing the last of the rejects into the fire, he took another swig of whiskey. *Four to Five good proposals is a good night, I need to stock up on more of this whiskey.* Gently stirring his drink, he gazed into the flames. Ridiculous and outlandish projects burned alongside nightmarish and horrific ones.

I have my issues with the way things are done, but I won't allow this Union to become the monster the Tharcians believe it is. As the last mad science project turned to ash, he knocked back the rest of his whiskey and closed his eyes.

GRENZE RIVER BAR AND GRILL SEEMED LIKE A REPUTABLE PLACE. Brick and mortar construction and the sound of laughter and music carried into the street outside. Reiter smiled as he and the rest of Fox platoon's pilots walked in.

"Remember everyone, two beers max," he said. "If there's an emergency, we need to stay sober." Magyar slapped Merlin Jr on the back.

"You mean MJ here can't be our designated pilot?" she said, getting a laugh out of the other pilots.

Rieter shook his head. "Not on his birthday." Inside they found wooden floors, a long bar that filled the opposite wall, several tables and booths and an opening to a darker area. "I assume the dance floor's back that way, let's get a booth." Before long, they were seated at a corner booth to fit them all.

"It feels like we were at Mario's forever ago," Mo said. "I can't believe it was only a few months ago." Steele pushed him.

"Oh, you mean when you jerks left us to clean the hanger?" She asked.

Mo shrugged. "We got things done." He looked up from his menu. "I assume you and I are going to pour one for Gos and Varga?"

Reiter looked at the menu and groaned. "I honestly don't think my wallet is deep enough to pour one out for everyone, we'll have our moment later, in honor of our wounded First Sergeant, first rounds on me."

"I'll drink to that," Magyar said. "I mean, we *are* celebrating, right?"

Reiter nodded. "Yeah, we've all had time to mourn by now, tonight is about Snowman." Smith clapped his friend on the shoulder.

"Now you can smoke like everyone else!." Merlin sr frowned.

"Maybe not it's a disgusting habit," he said. "Besides, mom would kill me if you picked up smoking, she was already pissed you got caught up in all of this." While ordering food, the waitress arrived with their drinks.

"Dancing sounds fun," Steele said.

Magyar grinned. "I want to go dancing!" She grabbed Smith by the arm. "And I'll be taking this cutie with me!" As she dragged the hapless pilot towards the dance floor. Steele nudged Wesser.

"Wanna go dance?"

"Uh, it's not really my thing, but sure I guess." Reiter chuckled as the two women joined Magyar and Smith.

Looking back at Mo and Merlin sr, he nodded to Smith. "You guys have been doing that man dirty." Mo sipped his beer before answering.

"First of all, Mr baker's dozen over there needs to be able to read the room," he finally said.

"How can he?" Kozma replied. "He's only been exposed to half of it." He looked at MJ. "Did your school have any kind of co-ed activities?"

"More or less," he replied. Adjusting his glasses, he continued. "Smith never really participated though, he always volunteered to be a greeter or serve the punch, or referee."

With a glance at the dance floor, Reiter raised an eyebrow. "I think Magyar's giving him a crash course."

Kozma shook his head. "Crash course could be her war name, women's a wildcard if I ever met one." Merlin nudged his younger brother.

"Didn't you serve the punch a lot?" he asked, getting a chuckle out of the others. MJ's face turned beat red.

"So? What does that have to do with anything?" he replied. "There weren't exactly a lot of girls at school in general!"

Reiter held up a hand. "Look, talking to people really isn't that hard, and I say that as someone who struggled to talk to people for a long time."

"Wait, weren't you a teacher?" Kozma asked. Reiter held a finger in front of the man's face to silence him.

"The army actually helped me overcome all that." MJ looked skeptical.

"Really?" he asked. "How?"

Reiter gestured at all the men around the table. "Because I can go to each of you, at any given point in the day, and this includes our people dancing, and I can say 'man this is some bullshit' and bam, conversation started."

Kozma laughed. "So you got comfortable talking by listening to other people complain?" Reiter gestured 'more or less.' As they laughed at the table, Merlin leaned towards his younger brother.

"He's got a point, now let's turn you loose on the dance floor," he said. MJ clung to the table while his brother tried to push him out of the booth.

"But I can't dance!"

"Maybe Magyar can teach you," Merlin said as he managed to push his brother onto the floor. "Or Steele, or you can learn how to dance awkwardly from LT." Mo, Reiter and Kozma chuckled as they joined the others on the dance floor.

"I think it's only a matter of time before Amy tires to drag the rest of us out there," Mo said. Kozma nodded before pounding his beer.

"Well, no use delaying the inevitable," he said. "Might as well get out there." Mo finished his beer and stood up.

"Bet I can dance better," he said. Kozma grinned, and the two left for the dance floor, leaving Reiter smiling by himself in the booth. *Adamski would have loved to see all this.*

8

Once again, Kennedy found himself surveying the carnage of a partisan ambush. This time, however, the tables had turned severely. Bodies filled ditches along the road and scattered discarded pieces littered the hardball. Knight followed him, as did Irving.

As he approached one of the IFVs, he kicked the fake bridge parts. PVC piping with fabric coverings had been just enough to fool the partisans. Kennedy nodded before looking back at Knight. "Looks like we had a successful mission," he said. "And we didn't have to fire a shot ourselves." They looked over at Irving as she went from body to body.

'Is she looking for someone?" he asked as the infantry and MPs bagged and tagged bodies. "Because we've got things to do, she can look over the MPs' report later." Kennedy looked over his shoulder.

"I think she's looking for their leader," he said. "Or at least someone connected to him." Knight shook his head.

"Within twenty-four hours, we'll have their names, their fingerprints, all their known associates, and their favorite breakfast foods," he said. "What's the point of looking right now?" Irving shook her head as she looked into bodies that had already been bagged.

"She's looking for a really dangerous man," Kennedy said. "Someone who's as big a threat to our plans as the Tharcians themselves." Finally, she returned to them.

"He's not here," she said. "We need to scour this entire area a mile out." Knight raised a hand.

"We don't have the resources to commit to that," he said. "But we've made things safer for convoys, now we can precede with our plans on the 21st."

Irving sighed. "I hope this doesn't cost us in the long run," she said. "But you're ultimately correct." They piled back into the command car and made for Landfall. After a few miles of snowy hinterland, they began to see the town.

"Is there any significance to the date chosen for Operation Indignation?" Kennedy asked. Irving grinned.

"The Tharcian's celebrate a religious holiday on that day," she said. "Gift giving is one of their traditions, so I decided to partake." They shared a chuckle before the radioman interrupted them.

"Excuse me comrades, it's for comrade Major," he said before handing the radio to Irving. She took the receiver, nodded, thanked her comrade on the other end.

"That was Comrade Meyer," she said. "She's agreed to a truce with the Tharcians." Knight leaned forward.

"When and for how long?" he asked.

"Twenty-Four hours starting at Midnight," Irving replied. "Furthermore, she wants Knight and Ballard to go with her to Grunbeck to observe the truce."

Before she or Knight could say anything in anger, Kennedy

raised a hand, silencing them. "Meyer is easily one of the smartest people I know. The only reason she isn't number one is because I also know Chaney," he said. "That being said, I trust her with my life. If she agreed a twenty-four-hour truce, then she must have had a good reason."

Knight's jaw stiffened, and he said nothing. However, Irving raised a finger. "This gives us an opportunity, we can request the MOs begin depopulation measures here." She smiled. "That would educate and redistribute this area's people and negate the partisans ability to hide in plain sight."

Kennedy leaned his head against the command car's small window. "Hmm, that is a cunning plan," he admitted. He glanced over at Knight. "You know, observing this truce gives you the opportunity to really observe the Tharcians, how they think, how they move, how they react, all of that is valuable information for us." Knight shrugged.

"I'm sure they'll have the same information on us," he said. Without replying, Kennedy shifted his gaze out the window. Even under the gray skies, he could make out the distant shadows of mountains. Snow drifted down onto a white world below. *It's so serene, so peaceful.*

"Comrade Kennedy, have you spoken to Comrade Chaney lately?" Irving asked. He shook his head.

"He's a busy guy, I'd hate to interrupt him," Kennedy replied. "Though maybe I should, just to get a feel of the situation in the capital." With a shrug, he looked back out the window. "I would have liked to attacked by now, but I'm sure the Black Knight will be repaired by the time we attack."

The Command Car pulled around to the command center. The three officers spilled out into the wet street and climbed the cold stone stairs up to the entrance. *Soon, we'll win this war, it'll be here before we know it.* With a gloved hand, Kennedy gripped the door handle and held it open for the other two. *So we win. And then what?*

———

As Reiter walked into Col. Hawke's office, he noticed additional maps plastered about the conference room. Hawke himself hovered over one, his good arm resting on a table. "Reiter, good, The Black Lion himself joins us," he said as he noticed the younger man. "Take a seat, I have a few things to run by you."

While taking a seat from the table, Hawke pointed to an area map. "So we've been thinking, the Unis established themselves a cute little bridgehead here, but what if we hit them in Landfall?" He traced his finger down the main road leading out of landfall. "And attacked all the way towards Pulaski?"

Reiter looked from one map to the next. "There are a lot of things we need to consider," he said. "What forces does the enemy have at their disposal?" Hawke pointed to another map.

"They have a mechanized Battalion near riverside that skirmishes with our scouts, a panzerter battalion near this bridge, and another just south of it, with their motorized forces reallocated to internal security."

Skepticism crowded Reiter's thoughts. "How do we have so much accurate information?" To which Hawke smiled.

"There's a lot of Thracian citizens stuck on the other side, they may not be totting rifles, but they're doing a valuable service to the country."

Pointing to the bridges, Reiter traced a long scything line between Grunbeck and Swiezen. "So there's no doubt this is the path their attack will take, and if they continue, they'll eventually break out of the forests."

Hawke nodded. "We can't allow that, although it gives us a believable path to see them on, I actually want to trick them into going into a city, or rather a town." He pointed to a large town north of Grunbeck, just slightly out of the Union's intended path. "If we get them inside city limits, we can slow them down."

"But how do you trick them?" Hawke flashed a cheeky smile.

"I've been talking to 4-14th, they're moving roadsigns around to decide the Unis," he said.

"It can't be that easy," Reiter replied. "I'm sure they have area maps." He folded his arms. "They'll need more incentive." *Like if General Orban herself was standing there in the middle of the Ironton.* Then it hit him.

"What if we leak that our headquarters company is in Ironton?" Reiter asked. "And by not rushing to bolster its defenses, we're hiding it in plan sight." Hawke snapped his fingers.

"We can have your group and the Lowe's there as a 'last line of defense' while the rest of our regiment attack from the south and the 1-11th comes from the East."

Reiter smiled. "Now we just need a situation to leak the location of HQ."

"We may have it," Hawke replied. "Orban want's to call a truce for 24 hours on the 15th, mainly so we can evacuate all of our seriously wounded, but she also wants to conduct a prisoner exchange."

"What does that mean for us?" Reiter asked.

"It means their equal to Orban will be coming here, to Grunbeck, to negotiate the release of prisoners, they'll also bring observers to verify we aren't doing anything shady." Hawke leaned back in his chair and stretched his neck. "Do you have two people that can sit and talk to someone for a while?" Reiter nodded.

"Yeah, I got two," he said. After looking over and signing some paperwork for Hawke, he left for his own quarters. While he'd been in Hawke's *office*, night had fallen over the bustling city. While his breath hung in the air, he stared at the glowing lights of Grunbeck.

Know what, I could use a walk. A nice quiet walk. Children pressed their faces to the glass undoes of storefronts as their parents pulled them along. A whiff of pretzels hung in the air, and he heard music every time a store opened. *The more I smell those pretzels, the hungrier I get. Aw to hell with it.*

Tracking the scent to its source took little time. Another brick and mortar store, but when the doors opened he also smelled chocolate, peppermint, and cinnamon. Garland wrapped around every long surface, and Christmas carols blared in his ears. He turned to leave, but bumped into someone.

"Excuse me," he said. Then he recognized her. "Oh, you're that nurse from Landfall." She brushed a curl out of her face. She wore a brown long coat with a lavender scarf, a matching knit hat did it's best to contain her thick curls.

"Oh, you're that Captain with the rude pilot, Smith," she said. Reiter shrugged and held the door for her.

"He doesn't know how to be a gentleman, yet," he replied. "I guess it comes with the territory when you're the youngest of thirteen brothers." Amelia gasped.

"Oh Lord, help his poor mother," she said. Reiter shrugged.

"He's a good kid," he said. "Incredibly polite, he just can't read the room sometimes." They got in line, kids ran about, looking at chocolates and various other candies being made, while model train circled Christmas trees. "Sometimes I forget it's even Christmas time."

Amelia nodded. "Same, although I'm normally pretty busy this time of year anyway," she said. "Hospitals are normally busy this time of the year."

As they approached the counter, Reiter squinted at the menu.

"You know, I never got to thank you for taking care of Adamski," he said. "I'll buy." Amelia imitated clutching a necklace.

"Captain Reiter, you don't have to to do that," she said. Reiter raised a hand and shook his head.

"No, no, I insist," he said. "Adamski's been in my platoon for a long time, and I can't express how grateful I am that you saved his life." The nurse leaned in and prodded him.

"Is that why you followed me in here?" she asked. "Because you looked like you were about to leave." Reiter nodded.

"Yeah, it was a little loud for me in here, but I saw you and still owed you thanks." She pushed him. She ordered a cream cheese and cinnamon pretzel while he ordered a standard salt and cheese one. Before he could walk back to his barracks, Amelia called out to him.

"I was going for a walk, would you mind joining me?" Reiter shrugged. *Sure, why not?*

"So you like our design?" the representative asked. Chaney nodded.

"We're willing to invest 2.5 million Labors just for a prototype of your engine, but we expanded that to 7 million for a demonstration worthy prototype," he said. "We believe your design will complement our Martians nicely."

The representative nodded and followed him. Chaney led him to a meeting room with a bottle of champagne in a bucket of ice and two glasses. "I take it, you're prepared to sign this deal?" The representative said.

Chaney sat at the table and smiled. "This is a major contract for the Blackburn Locomotive Group, we're not just talking a contract with a single order, we're talking licences, repair training, spare parts, R&D teams, and endless options for renewal." He removed a tablet from under the table, one with the contract he prepared already loaded for the representative to sign.

Tentatively, the representative, a dour woman in her mid-fifties, thumbed through the contract, pausing occasionally to reread something. "You want to use our facilities on Phobos?" She asked. Chaney nodded.

"I do," he said. "Phobos is the most secure location in the Union and has been a full Martian republic for twenty years." He stood and reached for the champagne.

"Not so fast," the representative said. "This would be the most profitable contract Blackburn Locomotive has ever signed, assuming we hit all of these *incentives.*"

With a smile, the General popped the champagne and poured himself a glass. "Your Union has never worked with MAG research, have they?"

She folded her arms. "We can't agree to an exploitive contract like this, if you want our technology, you'll have to fold your incentives into the main contract."

Chaney poured himself a glass. "In the MAG, we pay for quality, we reward hard work and competence." Setting aside his own glass, he reached for the other. "Taking this contract will increase the Blackburn Group's labor share, tremendously in fact, your workforce, and by extension Phobos itself will prosper."

"Assuming they meet your deadlines and match your quality standards," she replied. "It is unfair to the people working hard in our facilities if they must break themselves to meet the arbitrary standards of the military."

Chaney raised his glass to her, then took a sip. "We are in an arms race comrade, our standard ensures we get an advanced machine to the front lines instead of a metal coffin that's obsolete the second it rolls out."

The representative folded her arms. "Our society places the worker first," she said. "Our institutions risk falling into ruin if we abandon that."

Chaney sighed and rose from his chair. As he paced the table, he held his glass near his face. "You see, that's interesting, because the implication, in your own words, is that the soldiers on the frontline aren't workers in the sense your factory workers are."

He took a sip from his champagne, focusing his eyes on the stern woman before him. "Your workers who operate in total comfort and safety, the second of which is provided by our soldiers and sailors on the front." He spread his hands and smiled. "Now, they can support their comrades by making a safe quality product, *and they will be rewarded when they do.*" He leaned over on the table and moved to hand her her glass. "Do we have a deal?"

Snatching the champagne from his hands, the Representative downed the glass immediately. "For the most part, I want to talk through the timeline, some of these smaller pieces we'd like to negotiate." Chaney smiled.

"We will not alter our combat performance requirements, or our choices in test pilots," he said. "But anything else is up on the table." After looking over the contract with the Representative from Blackburn, Chaney agreed to several minor amendments before they signed the contract.

"I hope you're not taking advantage of our labor pool," the representative scowled. "If even one person is forced out of work, you'll have a lot more than me to deal with."

Chaney wagged a finger. "Your workers will gain the same healthcare and benefits as the military," he said. "It's called protecting our investment." He took another sip of champagne. "Would you like a refill?" He poured another glass for her. "To our successful partnership."

She nodded and took the drink. "We'll lay the groundwork

before I'm even back in Cascadia," she replied before taking a swig. Chaney nodded.

"I already have a test pilot in mind," he said. With a smile, the representative finished her drink and left. Chaney relaxed. As he looked at the remains of his champagne and abruptly tossed it into the fire.

REITER LEANED OVER THE RAILING IN FRONT OF HIM. BELOW, Mechanics crawled all over the Lowe performing routine maintenance. They serviced magnetic joints, tested its subsystems, and cleaned sensors. His black machine stood apart from the panzerters around it. While the other panzerters resembled soldiers from the 21st century, at least superficially, his called back to a long bygone era, a time of chivalry, honor, and pageantry.

At least, that's how people remember it. He sighed. The Lowe's head passed an odd blend of traditional aesthetics and more modern ones. Most of it resembled a knight's helmet with its round flared shape and single spear tip antenna, but beneath its brow sat a sleek visor and an air filter resembling a gas mask.

"May I join you, sir?" Wesser called. Reiter glanced over at the young lieutenant and nodded. As she approached the railing next to him, her gaze turned to the Lowe. "It seems so…out of place."

Reiter grinned. "Funny you say that, I was just thinking the same thing." He looked back to the other panzerters in the warehouse. "I wonder if that's the look of the future panzerter force."

"From what I heard, it's appearance has a psychological impact on the unit," she said. "Whether that's from it's mostly black paint job, it's unique head, I'm not sure."

"You forgot its insane durability," Reiter replied. "Even now, most of the Union's weapons barely scratch it, it took three elite heavy panzerters employing a reckless but well-coordinated strategy just to get a mobility kill."

Wesser looked at him. "How does it feel, sir?"

"How does what feel?" he replied.

"Being invincible," she said.

Reiter sighed. "I'll let you know when I find out." He pointed to the Lowe itself. "In the cockpit, I have pictures of everyone we lost in this damn war." He looked back at her. "I'm only one man Wesser, I can't save everyone, as much as I'd like to."

"You don't have to," she replied. "We're all capable fighters, with good, reliable equipment." She set a hand on his shoulder. "With all due respect, sir, you need to take your own advice."

With a shrug, Reiter stood up. "Kozma is a good dude, but his drive to save the day will get him killed if he's not careful." He looked down at the warehouse floor. "This isn't about how I behave, this is about someone else." He turned and walked towards the stairs.

"Sir, where are you going?" Wesser asked.

"To the cockpit, want to help with maintenance?" he said. As she blinked in confusion, she followed him down the stairs. "The mechanics will need a pilot to check the range of motion in the hands and arms, I want to show you what it's like to be me, even if its only a few minutes."

After a short walk across the warehouse floor, they came to the feet of the Lowe. A maintenance ladder reached up to its upper chest. Reiter waved to the head mechanic before pushing Wesser towards the ladder.

"Get up in their," he said. "I'll sit in the jump seat." She crawled up the ladder, and he followed. *She could very easily lead a company or higher before this is over, she needs to understand the weight of that.* As they climbed into the cockpit, Wesser gasped at the wall of pictures.

"All of these people," she said. "This was the old Fox company?" Reiter nodded as he sat down.

"Yeah, that's our old Captain and XO right there, that's my platoon sergeant and Lugosi," he said with a bitter smile. "The last thing I said to him was chewing him out for smoking while we mustered." He pointed at a tall chestnut haired woman with an arm around Mo and Steele. "That's Bartonova. She was like an older sister to most of the company."

"What happened to her?" Wesser asked. Reiter sank into the jump seat.

"Her, Mo, and Steele engaged this guy Kennedy, he's some kind of super soldier," he replied. "He was seconds from killing Steele, but Bartonova ended up taking the hit instead." Reiter rested his head in his hand. "We barely had enough to bury her."

Wesser recoiled from the photo, and her arm bumped another one on the opposite wall. She looked back to see a raven haired woman in sweats looking shocked with the Merlin brothers on either side. "Who's she and why is she over here?"

Smiling, Reiter leaned forward. "That's Claire Fletcher, Union super soldier and POW, and also the only person I've definitely saved." He tapped her on the shoulder. "French is probably getting pissed, so let's hurry up and take care of this." With that, Wesser took hold of the controls and relaxed. *I hope you're still safe, Fletcher.*

HE'D BEEN EXPECTING THIS ANY DAY NOW. WHILE KENNEDY wasn't necessarily a pessimistic man, he did have a nose for murphy about to strike. *Or as Ballard calls it, I'm Properly Paranoid.* So here he was in a Martian again, of all things, pretending to not be inside.

Riding in a panzerter on its back had been a continuously unpleasant experience up to this point, but he volunteered for the task for two reasons. The first being he could secure the engineer teams transporting the new Martian against partisan attacks. Irving had provided his secondary reasoning. She's reasoned that since the partisans stole things every time they attacked, they'd love nothing more than an intact panzerter.

So he lay on his back, in a crash chair, jostling with every bump in the road. *I hope she's right.* Despite his discomfort, there was something nostalgic to him about sitting in a Martian again. *When I first entered service, this machine was the bleeding edge of panzerter design. Five years later, it still holds up even if it's not top dog anymore.*

Suddenly, the transport ground to a halt. "Comrades, we have a log blocking our path." *Here it comes. Submachine gun and laser are in the truck ahead of me, and I have a mace on me.* A scream filled the net, followed by a crashing sound.

"We're under panzerter attack!" Kennedy threw the tarp off his machine and stood up. They'd stopped on a winding road far from landfall. Snowy pine trees surrounded them. Among the shadows of the trees, Partisans fired automatic weapons and rockets at the convoy while gloomy silhouettes lurked in the snow. Grabbing his SMG, he razed the nearest group of partisans before looking at the panzerter threat.

Four machines. Older models. *Salvaged machines?* He fired a burst at the nearest one and went for his laser. *I don't have time to dick around too much.*

Shells struck his armor. Most bounced. *Nothing vital.* Kennedy retaliated with submachine gun and laser fire. The 75-mm shells wouldn't do much on their own, but their high rate of fire allowed them to exploit holes in the armor of his enemies.

Within seconds of standing, Kennedy had destroyed two of the attacking panzerters and severely damaged a third. *This isn't even a fight, more like an execution.* Then the last one changed tactics. Instead of continuing to fight him, the panzerter opened fire on the engineers and their escorts.

Kennedy whirled on his last opponent, leaving it's crippled friend for the infantry. With a sickening clack, his SMG ran dry. Ditching the weapon, he brought his laser to bear only for a sword to cut through the barrel.

Leaping backwards, he went for his mace when his opponent charged. He managed to catch the tip of the blade in the Martian's hand. With a mighty swing, his mace crashed into the panzerter's elbow. Metal shards and broken magnets scattered across the woods.

With a crunch, he noticed the partisan grab his mace hand and struggle for the weapon. Kennedy used his machine's greater weight to pull and shove theater panzerter in a vain attempt to break loose. *I need to finish this quick.*

He drove his broken stump into his opponent's cockpit. After following up with two more blows, the panzerter fell back dragging him with him. Metal scraped metal. Kennedy's teeth rattled and his restraints cut into him.

As soon as the sparks and crunching stopped, he drew a machine pistol from under his chair. *That pilot can't escape. I need to know where they got those panzerters.* Clutching the carrying handle in his teeth, Kennedy scrambled along the ladder to the Martian's crown hatch only to find the door stuck.

With a few solid kicks, he managed to open the hatch and climb out. Bullets pinged of the Martian's armor and the panzerter below. Kennedy hopped out of his crippled machine down to the one beneath him. *Those last few blows opened the cockpit I'm sure.*

His feet his the armored panzerter below with a jolt. Kennedy grunted and soldiered on. A bullet whipped past his head, and he flattened himself against the cold metal. More rounds cracked by him from multiple directions.

The partisans were routing, but it wasn't stopping them from firing wildly on the advancing Union soldiers. Several rushed towards the very panzerter he crawled across. *They're certainly not making this easy.*

A head poked above a rent in the panzerter's armor. Kennedy sent a burst his way. The pilot opposed up and fired a pistol. After firing another burst, Kennedy crawled across the surface of the panzerter.

He paused and took a breath. As he trained his sights on where the pilot had hidden, he focused on his breathing. Just barely, he could make out blonde hair cresting the torn armor. *Got you.*

"Hey!" Kennedy lurched sideways. A partisan trained a rifle on him. They fired simultaneously.

As a bullet ripped through the back of his leg, Kennedy cried out in pain. His own burst perforated the partisan, an older over-weight man, like a sieve.

"Dad!" the pilot cried. Kennedy grit his teeth and fired another burst at the pilot.

"Micah, stay down!" another man cried. Before Kennedy could react, a partisan vaulted the opposite side of the panzerter and kicked him in the ribs. A steel toe cracked a few of his ribs. "You bastard!" he hissed.

Kennedy raised his machine pistol, but the partisan kicked it away. As he lunged after the strap, a boot came down on his hand. *I need an advantage. Somehow.* With a roar of pain, Kennedy swept his injured leg under his opponent.

After rolling onto of the other man, Kennedy wrestled with him for his rifle. The surrounding air cackled and snapped with the sound of bullets from both sides. "Micah, tell them to go!"

With a final tug, Kennedy wrested the weapon free. In one swift motion, he cracked the partisan across the face with the stock of his own weapon. Union soldiers climbed onto the panzerter to aid him and arrest the partisan. Finally, the pain across his body grew too much for even his enhanced nervous system to bear. As his adrenaline wore off, he blacked out.

9

Another snowy December day. Another long morning in Hawke's office. Reiter left the marble building and made for the warehouse. *We can make all the preparations we want, if we don't actually execute anything, the Union will attack again and we'll be screwed.* He sighed as a child walked by with her mother, proudly holding a shopping bag.

What kind of future will we have if we lose? He remembered his conversations with Fletcher, but her story still seemed unbelievable. He briefly imagined babies gestating in glass chambers, the cold sterile upbringing Fletcher had been through. *They only taught her how to read, write, do math, and pilot a panzerter, filled her with propaganda, called her a number until she was 14, then slapped a rank on her and said 'go kill Tharcians, this is normal.'*

Reiter shook his head and slammed his fist into the concrete wall of the warehouse. *They deprived her of a childhood, of a family, that's so fucked up.* It dawned on him that Kennedy had been created the same way. *No, not created, born.* The more he contemplated Fletcher's situation, the angrier he got. *It's not enough that they're ruthless killers, but they've created an entirely new strain of humanity just to be cruel to.*

As he entered the warehouse, his gaze fell upon an alarming site. Mo and Kozma paced each other with broom sticks held like clubs while the other pilots and a few of the infantry cheered. Wesser blew a whistle, and the pair lunged at each other. *Oh, they're training.*

After a fury of blows, Mo overpowered Kozma and struck him in the side. The other man howled in pain and swore at Mo. To Reiter's dismay, he saw a few Krones being passed around. *Training is one thing, gambling is another.*

"Wesser, Kozma, Mo, what's going on here?" he asked as the group took notice of him. Now that he could see Mo and Kozma more clearly, he noticed multiple welts across both of their arms. "If this is training, I hope you're learning something."

Wesser blushed. "Sorry sir, we have our pilots refreshing on their hand to hand fundamentals, Mo and Kozma just got a bit competitive." Reiter frowned before Steele spoke up.

"In our defense, we learned a lot about our techniques that weren't working," she said. Reiter nodded and softened his stance.

"Very well, we could all learn something from each other," he replied. Then he shed his jacket and CVC shirt, leaving just his undershirt. Reiter took a moment to stretch the lean muscles of his arms and chest. "Mo, may I?"

The young man tosses him his broom stick and Reiter caught it rather easily. Kozma turned and offered his to the crowd. "Who wants to be the commanders first victim?"

"I'll take him," Merlin Jr said. "I've got youthful energy on him."

Reiter shook his head. "For the record, MJ, I'm six years older than you." Melin JR advanced with reckless abandon. Wide swings. Choreographed movements. Sloppy footwork.

Evading and parrying each blow took minimal effort from Reiter. Every time they clashed, he felt MJs broom rattle against his. *He'll tire himself, even in a panzerter, fighting like that would be exhausting.*

Finally, Reiter felt it was time to conclude things. He responded to MJ's attacks with a few of his own, disrupting whatever groove the younger soldier had. With a final clash, Reiter twisted and flicked his wrist. Merlin's broom flew high into the air.

He stopped his blow inches from MJ's face before raising an eyebrow. "Youthful energy, huh?" Gently. He tapped him on the top of his head. "Bonk." Behind him, Steele snorted.

"I think we pretty clearly have our winner," she said. Reiter tossed his broom to one of the infantry.

"Melee combat between panzerters isn't like the movies," he said. "It's all choreographed, it's fluff, I implore you all to study a martial art that includes the use of weapons, it will give you an edge over the guy or gal that swings a sword like a baseball bat."

After watching the group break off into pairs to train, he left with his two lieutenants following him. He'd wanted to go over more team based drills when Kozma brought up another issue. "What's Mo's deal?" he asked Wesser. "Seriously, he's given me the third degree at best since we landed here. Why can't you rein in your soldier?" Reiter sighed.

"Mo's attitude does need to be addressed," he admitted. "I'm tempted to speak to him myself, but I feel like this is an opportunity for you to assert yourself."

As they entered their own planning room, Wesser took a deep breath. "Alright," she said. "What do you recommend?"

KENNEDY GLARED THROUGH THE ONE-WAY MIRROR BEFORE HIM. IN what had formerly been a recording studio, Woody Pete sat in a makeshift cell. He looked like he was in his late thirties to mid-forties, with his dark hair running silver near the temples. The side of his face where Kennedy had struck him remained swollen as he stirred his veggie soup.

For all his trouble, Kennedy would never sit correctly again due to the scar across his left cheek. In addition, medical tape bound his ribs so they could heal as well as his hand. Knight and Irving stood with him, watching the most valuable prisoner ever captured.

"I can't believe it," she said. "All that time, and we finally caught him."

Knight folded his arms. "And a good thing, too. This should put an end to all of their partisan raids." Kennedy shook his head.

"They got panzerters and were able to operate them, I want to know weather they stole them or someone gave them to them," he said. He looked at Irving. "You think he did it himself?"

She shrugged. "There's no way to be one hundred percent sure, but he was a panzerter engineer." Kennedy looked back at their prisoner.

"He was trying to protect one of the pilots, knew him by name," he said. "The pilot knew another partisan as well. Did Woody Pete have any connection to someone named Pa?"

Both of his comrades raised an eyebrow. "Pa's a slang term for father," Irving said. "Did the pilot call this other partisan that?"

Kennedy nodded. "Yeah, yeah he did, and Pete called him by name, Micah." Knight shook his head.

"Did you not have a dad?" he asked.

"No, nor a mother," Kennedy replied. "The Union is the only legal guardian I've ever had." He looked back at them. "Make of that what you will, but we need to know where they got those panzerters."

Irving took another look at Kennedy before approaching a microphone hooked to the sound system in the booth. "Woody Pete, you're guilty of crimes against a United Mars, however your sentencing will be lenient if you provide us with the information we seek."

Woody Pete didn't bother looking up. He merely continued to stir his veggie soup. *Is he messing with us? Or does he just not care about his life?*

The train of thought barreled forward at full steam. *I value my life; I want to live. But my homeland doesn't.* He stared at his injured hand and flexed it as Irving continued her questioning. *Yet, the Union could remake me entirely if they choose to do so, and they likely have before.* He clenched his fist. *No, I'm different, as much from them as they are from each other. My life, my experiences, those are all my own, something I don't share with anyone.*

He looked back into the booth. *It's because of that, that I fight to make things better for everyone like me.* Knight groaned. Despite her best efforts, Irving didn't make any headway with Woody Pete.

"Hey, Irving, let me try something," he said. The other officer shrugged.

"Go ahead," she said. Kennedy took her seat in front of the mic, grunting as he sat.

"We have Micah Woody," he said. "If you don't cooperate, he'll suffer for it." The man in the booth laughed.

Setting down his spoon, he looked over to where Kennedy sat. "You must be that pilot from the battle," he said. "Nice try, but I doubt it."

"We captured him shortly after we detained you," Kennedy replied. "If you don't tell us where you obtained your panzerters, then we'll break off his fingers and send them to you one at a time until you cooperate."

Woody Pete whistled before chuckling. "Jesus, you're a ruthless one." He shifted his jaw from side to side. *Maybe it's hard to talk after I hit him in the face?* "The Provincial Watch abandoned a few at a graveyard, we had just enough gear to get them working again." He leaned back in his chair. "There, tell Micah he can keep his damn fingers, that is, if you really do have him."

Irving looked at him. "That was brilliant, unfortunately, I don't think we learned anything he cared about keeping from us." Knight leaned on the chair behind Kennedy.

"What about Comrade Chaney?" He asked. "Maybe they can talk shop or something, get him a bit more in his comfort zone?" As they talked amongst themselves, Kennedy couldn't help but notice their captives behavior. He kept his head down, but Kennedy noticed the corners of his mouth. The man was smiling.

———

"WE'RE TWO CLICKS OUT," WESSER SAID OVER THE NET. "BREAK off into teams and stick to the plan." Mo looked out over the snow covered scene before him. Pines obstructed his view of the river, but he could make out the top of the bridge in the distance thanks to the work lights on it.

"Anyone else think it's weird they don't have any kind of screen out here?" Mo asked.

Merlin sr replied immediately. "Maybe they're sticking close to the bridge?"

"Hey, we're here for information," Wesser said. "Just another thing to take note of." The Recon platoon deployed ahead of them. Their tracked vehicles and their lower profile made them a much better fit for their current mission. "Recon 1, how do things look?" No answer.

Mo shifted uncomfortably in his seat. *Are they dead? Out of range? Or just being stubborn?* He keyed up his own mic and kept his eyes peeled. "Black 1, do you still have them on your sensors?"

"Roger Four," she replied. "They're just being quiet." Merlin followed him at a shallow angle to his four' o 'clock.

"You feel anything strange three?" he asked.

"Yeah," Merlin replied. "Something just feels wrong." They received an answer to their uneasiness a short moment later. A green eerie light flashed in the trees. A recon track ahead of them vanished in a ball of fire.

"Contact!" Mo cried simultaneously with Merlin. The pair stood just off a state road leading to a North-South highway behind them. The scouts ahead of them lay in a staggered line, while Wesser and Smith stuck to the southern side of the objective, forming a large L with Mo and Smith.

"Recon 1! Break contact!" Wesser cried. "3, and 4 cover them!" They acknowledged and stood forward. As the scouts threw their tracks in reverse, Mo made out further movements beyond them. Tin-hats.

Ghostly lights swept towards them. Snowbags burst into steam with a violent hiss. Mo's Panzerter, a newer iteration of the Mark IV, housed an additional generator to allow it to use Magnetic weapons. In this case, a 50-mm SMG.

A red glow in the tree line caught his eye. The ominous red ring crashed through trees like some kind of a mythic giant. *There.*

Mo's weapon flashed. The blue glow hurt his eyes, but he heard the tin-hat topple. A crash like thunder ruptured his ears, and a second tin-hat went up in a column of fire.

"Didn't think I could touch you at 1600 meters, did ya?" Merlin said.

Mo smirked as he overtook the retreating scouts. "3, I appreciate the shit talk, but don't shoot me in the back." He glanced behind him. Merlin's machine lay prone, the barrel of its 155-mm sniper rifle still smoking. The scouts almost reached him.

"Don't worry four, I'm paying attention," he said. "You got another one approaching." Mo looked back to his front, switching between thermals and optics.

"Where? I don't have anything," he replied.

"That's a big motherfucker," Merlin said. A shell leaped past Mo and deflected off something nearby. "Damn it, shot bounced."

Now Mo could see it. Under the weak starlight, his sensors revealed a large red fat-man. *Shit, it's one of those guys.* The fat-man squared up to him as Mo backpedaled. Instinctively, he fired controlled burst after burst into the fat mans chest.

Then one burst didn't stop until the weapon emptied the magazine. An alarm told him the barrel had melted and warped. As Mo cleared the enemy, Merlin fired again. This time his shell smashed into the fat-man's head.

"Tharcian soldiers," a voice said over the net as they retreated. "I'm going to kill all of you one day." *What the hell?*

After an hour of running at full tilt, they regrouped north of Ironton. "Is everyone here?" Wesser asked. It turned out they'd lost Recon 3. Recon 1 simply refused to talk t them unless he deemed it "absolutely necessary."

"Other than them, we're all here," Recon 1 said. "No, thanks to your people." *What planet does this dude live on?*

"What did you expect us to do?" Mo replied. "We don't deploy recon tracks to stand in front of them."

"The hell do you know about recon?" Recon 1 asked. "Nothing, your Black 1 senselessly got a track full of decent men killed for no good reason." Mo couldn't believe what he was hearing.

"No good reason?" He said. "What are you even going to report?"

Recon 1 replied immediately. "The contents of my report don't concern you, only me and the commander, but Black 1's inadequacies will be included." Mo's head pounded.

"Fuck you," he finally said, and killed his radio.

CHANEY FOLDED HIS ARMS AND SCRATCHED HIS HEAD. "WELL, I don't know what to say, how did you catch this guy?" Kennedy sighed as he sat awkwardly in a folding chair in the former recording studio. "And why are you sitting like that?"

"Well, him, or at least one of his comrades shot me in the ass," Kennedy said. "And after a long struggle, I overpowered him and detained him." With a shake of his head, Chaney looked back at the man on the other side of the one-way mirror.

"I can't believe you nabbed this guy," Chaney said. "His knowledge could accelerate our progress on the particle weapons project." He looked back at Ballard. "Oh and did you tell Ballard to meet us like I asked?"

Kennedy nodded. "I told him, he's not about to get bad news, is he?" Chaney shook his head.

"No, it's actually good news, for him anyway," he replied. As he spoke, the door opened. A taller woman with yellow green hair entered holding a tablet, Ballard followed her.

"Comrade Brigadier, Comrade Colonel, here's comrade Ballard, just as you asked," she said. "Now about this frontline inspection-"

He raised a hand. "It can wait, comrade…"

"Major, or Irving if you desire to be informal Comrade," she replied. *Well, I certainly wouldn't mind being informal…*Chaney shook his head.

"Sorry if I've disrupted things here, but Comrade Ballard, I have an amazing opportunity for you." He handed Ballard a tablet he'd been holding. "I'd like you too look it over." He looked back at Woody Pete. "As for this guy-"

"We need to execute him," Irving said. "He's too dangerous to risk going free."

Chaney raised an eyebrow. "He's also a brilliant engineer. We could use his expertise." He glanced back at the partisan. He sat in his cell, flexing his jaw from side to side. *That's weird, but it looks like someone hit him in the face. Maybe he's relocating his jaw?*

"You want me to be a test pilot?" Ballard finally asked. "You mean I'm leaving the front?" Chaney looked at Kennedy.

"I pulled a few strings so that there's always a spot among Kennedy's people for you," he said. "And I twisted a few arms while vastly overselling how dangerous being a test pilot was to get you the best part." He paused and grinned.

"What did you do?" Ballard asked before Chaney took the tablet and revealed a different document. "Am I getting Penny on week-ends or something?" Then he saw the words and his jaw dropped. "No way, you can't be serious!"

The MAG scientist raised his hands. "Do I look like some cruel dick to you? No, you earned this, to hell with any non-tuber that thinks otherwise?" Irving raised an eyebrow.

"Is there something I should know?" she asked. "Like an illegal child?" Chaney shook his head.

As Ballard collapsed into a chair and sobbed, Chaney explained his situation to Irving. "It's a good thing comrade, the little girl that thought of him as her daddy this whole time has been legally adopted." He gestured to Ballard. "In a huge win for tuber's rights, the Union and Congaree legal recognize Ballard as her father."

Kennedy patted Ballard on the shoulder. "Better back your snivel gear," he said. "It's chilly this time of year." Ballard hugged his commander.

"You better not start half assing things," he said. Kennedy looked incredulous.

"Have you seen my rear end? What choice do I have?" Out of the corner of his eye, Chaney thought he glimpsed Irving smirk.

"I hate to put a downer on things," Irving said. "But we still have a dangerous partisan here, and a frontline inspection to conduct."

With a nod, Chaney dismissed the statement. "Yes, yes, we'll get to that," he said before walking over to her. "Your duty is a vital part of the war effort, but let's be serious this is historical, let's just soak it in for a moment."

Both tablets suddenly buzzed loudly, like a weather service alert. Chaney looked over Irving shoulder as she opened the notification.

"Tharcian surrender is imitate," Irving read. "As of 2300 Peninsular time, Demios's defenses have been invariably compromised by a raid that used torpedos carrying Nerve agents, Union ships bombarded the second moon with said torpedos in a hit-and-run attack, estimates run that 60% of the moon's working population have died."

As Irving read the last part, Chaney whistled. "That's like 70 million people, hell the war could be over right now!" Briefly, he remembered the words of the NC Secretary. *I hope your big victory's worth it.* Despite his own stated confidence, Chaney felt uneasy about the turn of events. *If it wasn't then we just did more harm than good.*

FIELD MARSHALL HAUSNERR LOOKED AROUND THE TABLE. STARING back at him, sat representatives of the Roosevelt government in exile and the Olympians. A monitor displayed a tenuous link to the woman who'd assumed leadership of Olympia's space territories, while diplomats from Vinland also sat at the table. Hausnerr eyed them suspiciously, as the country to the south, across the Mariner Gulf, remained neutral in the current conflict. *Perhaps they look to gain something by brokering a peace deal?*

One of the Olympian reps snorted. "Let's just skip the formalities, we know why we're all here," he said. "We've lost."

Hausnerr shook his head. "We will not surrender, Tharsis will never surrender." Another Olympian rep nearly spat her drink.

"That's hardly reasonable," she said. "If you don't, you'll continue to waste your people's lives."

The Marshall looked at the Roosevelt contingency. "And what is your opinion? Would you waste your forebears's hard fought independence just to put the boot back on your neck?"

"Well, we have talked about offering a separate peace to the Union wherein we maintain a protectorate status," the leader of the Roosevelt group said. "We hardly have a leg to stand on."

Hausnerr narrowed his eyes. "You lot remember the terms of the Alliance, correct?" The rep held up his hands and nodded.

"Yes, yes, yes," he said. "No separate peace arrangements, we understand."

"And what of your mighty fleets?" The Space administrator asked. "How can you protect us from the Union and Avalon when you can hardly protect yourselves?"

He looked away from her, as he still needed time to process the attack on Deimos. "I've been unable to reach Admiral Von Braun, but I'm sure once things at Deimos have been sorted out, he'll be able to answer your questions." *Damn it man, what the hell happened up there?*

"Marshall," the Vinland delegate said. "We understand your president is unavailable while she addresses your Congress, but I'm inclined to remind you that we're available to negotiate a peace agreement between your two sides."

With a sigh, Hausnerr stood and paced the room. "Excuse me if I come off as an old man ranting, he said. "But allow me to briefly address our people's history and why we won't surrender."

Some Olympian reps rolled their eyes, but the other delegations seemed to listen earnestly. Hausnerr took a breath and began. "Our people were utterly devastated by the world wars of Earth, the first two ruined our economies, and killed off much of our future." He looked at the Olympian delegates. "Then our people were dominated by the Soviets, we had autonomy in name only, all of our blood, treasure, and youth fed the Soviet machine."

Shaking his head, he continued. "Then there was the Prague Spring, the Berlin Rose, the Warsaw uprising, we told our oppressors we'd had enough, so the Kremlin made examples out of our capital cities, atomic fires ruined our homelands, and set us on a long exodus that would eventually lead us here."

"Yes, but just because they both call themselves a Union doesn't make them the same!" Another Olympian delegate said.

Hausnerr looked at the Roosevelt delegation. "Did anything I say sound familiar?"

"We're all old enough to remember the Acadian Martian Republic," the delegation leader said. "If we had to choose, we'd stay the free state of Roosevelt."

One of the Vinland diplomats leaned over and whispered something to his boss. Her face suddenly tightened. "Are you sure? Where? When? Why?"

"Is their something we should know?" Hausnerr asked. "If so, please share." The lead diplomat hurriedly stood up and left the room, her phone in her hand. He narrowed his gaze on the whisperer.

With a grimace, the young man explained himself. "We just

received a report from our homeland, we've been ordered to cut ties with Avalon, the Union, and any of their allies." *Whoa, that's interesting.*

"Are you at liberty to share why?" The Space Administer asked before she looked at someone off screen and her eyes widened. "God, Almighty." She looked back at them. "It's the Orkney archipelago, Avalon attacked one of the colonies with those same gas torpedos."

The whisperer turned red. "Supposedly a Tharcian hospital ship caught refuge there, Avalon demanded they hand over the vessel and its crew, they cite their neutrality and the Geneva convention, and then they attacked them and breeched the colony.

Hausnerr shook his head. "Well, on behalf of the Central Alliance, we're willing to extend membership to Vinland." On that bitter note, the Ostlan Conference ended, no closer to peace, and much more embroiled in war.

10

"Why did you stay?" Irving asked. Kennedy watched their prisoner's reaction carefully. Woody Pete simply stared at the floor.

"Because my home is here," he said before doing that odd thing with his jaw. *Maybe it's a personal tick?* As Irving continued with her questions, Kennedy paced about. *Chaney thinks this guy is super valuable, but I have the impression I'm staring at a caged wolf.* He shuddered. The only other people to give him that particular feeling were Wake, and Knight's two subordinates.

"Why did you attack us?" Irving said. "The Union military never harmed you or your family, so why attack us?"

Pete snorted. "We both know that's a crock of shit young lady, I know you were at my house the night my wife died." Irving recoiled from the mic.

"How did he?"

Kennedy sat down and took the mic. "He could have seen your face and recognized your voice," he said with a hand over the mic. "Let me try talking to him." Lifting his hand, he addressed

Kennedy. "What I think she means Pete is why didn't you remain peaceful when our forces entered your territory, I understand there was some unpleasant business with your family, but you could have petitioned the Union government for redress and left our armed forces be."

For a moment, Pete sat silently. Then he chuckled. The man's chuckle grew into a haunting laugh. "Do you really think I'm that naïve?" He paused. "Though I guess I could potion for redress, I studied your people in civics, doesn't seem to bad."

"So you would be interested in working for the Union government?" Kennedy asked. Pete wagged a finger at him.

"I said it didn't sound bad," he said. "I mean granted you people manufactured a slave caste and anyone that steps a little too far out of line gets crushed, but yeah, seems like a great system." He propped his feet up on his table. "Yeah, I guess it wouldn't be too bad, I could live the high life while the tube people do all the actual work."

Kennedy took a few deep breaths and realized he'd been gripping the mic stand hard enough to leave impressions of his hand. "Well, it seems like you'll need to be re-educated so that you can fit our society better, but the Union would be proud to have you."

"Re-educated, huh?" Pete replied. "I think I'll pass, I might lose all of this valuable physics know-how you need, but let's talk more about you Mr pilot, since you know so much about me, I think its time I learned more about you."

Irving covered the mic. "We're playing a dangerous game indulging him," she whispered. "I don't like this, how does he know so much about me?" Kennedy raised a hand.

"I think he recognized you," he replied. "He's trying to intimidate you, but I'm going to shift his focus." Setting a hand on Irving, he looked back at Woody Pete. "To satisfy your curiosity, I'm a simple tuber who happens to be a pilot, that is all."

The Partisan cocked his head. "Really? I don't believe that's it." Leaning back in his chair, he folded his arms. "You see, you fought incredibly hard, not just well, hard, which tells me you're fighting for something more than mere survival."

"It was you or me," Kennedy said. "I choose the most efficient way to end the fight." Pete spread his arms and rocked in his chair.

"Now see, there's training, and then there's conviction," he said. "I fought the Union to avenge my family, including my brother you killed personally, Mr pilot, but you fought even harder. If you wanted to live, there was no reason to leave your panzerter."

Kennedy licked the inside of his teeth. *This guy's digging for something, but what?* "I'm just a good soldier," he said. To his surprise, Pete shrugged.

"If you say so," he said. "A shame too, such a skilled and brilliant warrior. Too bad you can't even get a seat at the table." Shaking his head, he stopped rocking his chair and rested his elbows on his knees. "You see man, they took my family from me, but they have denied you that and so much more."

As he leaned away from the mic, he allowed Irving to resume her line of questioning. *I don't need him to tell me the score, they have given us a raw deal. Though I guess, even if we win all this, can we trust the First Minister? Or the NC Secretary? What about civilians? Surely they won't care for it.*

"I'm going to get us some water," he said. "We might be here awhile." *Of course we can trust them, why would they lie to me?*

———

"That has to be the worst Christmas tree I've ever seen," Mo said. Reiter clapped the younger soldier on the back.

"Don't rain on their parade," he said. "It's great that the Merlin brothers are feeling festive." A short Christmas tree occupied an empty corner of the hanger. The brothers had "salvaged" some cheap ornaments and made some out of junk they'd found around the warehouse. Reiter's favorite was the empty pack of cigarettes stuffed with tinsel.

Steele smiled as she set a star on the top. "My parents used an angel as a tree topper," she said. "But I couldn't find one worth the money." Kozma sat on an ammo can, shuffling a deck of cards.

"My parents used to hide a pickle on the tree," he said. "Whoever found it would earn a candy bar."

With a nod, Reiter sat down on another ammo crate. "Yeah, my old man used to do the same thing for us," he said. "You know it's a good thing we're observing the season and not letting it just slip away, hell two hundred years ago there was a truce on Christmas day."

Wesser smiled. "It's a nice thought, sir, but I don't think the Union shares our traditions." She pointed to the cards as Kozma shuffled. "What games do you know?"

"Eucher, Spades, War, Bridge, Kings, poker, jacks, slap, spoons-"

Mo held up a hand. "Ight, we get it, you know a lot of card games," he said, adding "sir" after a delay. "Does anyone else know spades?"

"I'll sit out," Reiter said. "Even better, I'll referee."

Wesser raised an eyebrow as she sat across from Kozma. "What kind of game is spades that you would need a referee?"

"You've clearly never played a card game in the military," Mo said as he sat next to Kozma. Steele took a seat across from him and they began playing. Reiter pulled out a notepad and pen to keep score.

Wesser-Mo proved to be a much more effective at communicating while Kozma-Steele drew good hands routinely. Reiter smiled while clarifying rules and providing the occasional commentary. Eventually, Kozma-Steele bagged out, allowing Wesser-Mo just enough points to win.

"Well, great game you two," Steele said as she helped clean up the cards. "I think I'm going to lie down for a bit if anyone needs me." While she left, Reiter looked up at the Lowe.

The mighty panzerter loomed ominously in the improvised hanger. *Soon, we'll have to fight again.* He thought about the red panzerters he'd encountered before. *Which reminds me.*

"Mo, Kozma, I will not have any issues with you two observing the truce, am I?" he asked. The two soldiers slouched slightly. "Look, you two are grown men, whatever issues you have need to be pushed aside so you can be professionals, so let's talk about this."

Kozma took a deep breath. "Mo has been hostile or abrasive since I landed here," he said. "I know you've got a big opinion of yourself, because you're the first Tharcian ace in twenty years, but I'm an officer damnit! You should respect me!"

Before Mo could say anything, Reiter raised a hand. "Is that all Kozma? There's no other reasoning for your behavior?" the lieutenant shook his head. "Ok, Mo, now you may speak."

Mo stood up and pointed at Kozma. "Look, I did nothing! This dude shows up out of nowhere with a degree and acts like he's the shit when he barely knows anything, and hasn't really done anything."

Reiter narrowed his eyes. "So this has nothing to do with Steele?" His words caused the younger man to stammer and stutter. "Look, I'm not great with social ques, but if *I* picked up on that without being told, I know for damn sure that everyone else did."

Mo and Kozma looked at the floor, causing Reiter to sigh. "Look, think of this truce thing as a get along shirt, I need you two to cooperate, even if you're in different platoons, am I clear?"

"Yes sir," the pair answered and saluted. *Alright, that's taken care of.*

Reiter stood and stretched. "Alright then, now I'm going to go lie down for a bit," he said. Just before reaching his quarters, Wesser stopped him.

"Hey thanks for ultimately handling that," she said. Reiter shook his head.

"No need to thank me, you did the legwork, got your facts, and came up with the solution, I just did as you asked," he replied. Relaxing slightly, he stepped away from his door. "We're supposed to get a new first sergeant tomorrow, that should be interesting."

Wesser's back stiffened. "Well, I hope I make a good first impression," she replied. He waved her off.

"I wouldn't worry too much," he said. "A first sergeant serves mainly administrative purposes anyway, he shouldn't have a huge impact on your specific duties."

Mo and Kozma sat in a small restaurant booth with some very awkward company. Across the table from them sat two union pilots, one of whom rode the one of the red machines that had given Reiter trouble. They stared at menus and tried to avoid talking to each other.

"I've never had beef before," one of them finally said. "Is it any good?"

Mo shrugged. "It'd put it above chicken, but under lamb if I'm over here ranking meats," he said. "Do they not have a ton of cows in the Union?"

The other pilot, the one who drove the red one, shook his head. "Not particularly, most of our meats come from the ocean or are lab-grown."

"That doesn't sound appeasing," Kozma said. The Union pilots shook their heads.

"It isn't," they said. Mo bit the inside of his lip.

"Do either of you know Lt. Fletcher?" he asked.

The pilot across from him, Ballard he believed his name was, raised an eyebrow. "About yay tall, silvery hair, lot of personality?"

Mo nodded. "Stupid good at puzzles, yeah that's her," he said. "She's alive and well if it matters to you." Ballard smiled at him.

"Well, that's nice to hear and hear our people were saying she would end up on a dissection table." Mo and Kozma looked at each other.

"Why?" Mo asked. "It's not like it's hard to figure out how she's been enhanced over a regular woman and hampered."

Now it was Ballard, and his friend Knight's turn to look confused. "What do you mean by hampered?"

"Well, our medical staff said her lady bits had been severely damaged," Mo said. "So they sent her to the rear for reconstructive surgery." Concern darkened the Union pilot's features.

"That procedure is expensive," Ballard said. "Not to mention if she returns, she'll face consequences for getting an illegal surgery."

Mo blinked back his surprise and didn't respond until after their drinks came. "Illegal, so all that stuff was done to her on purpose?"

"Yes," Knight said. "She's a tuber, her biology is tightly controlled, she needs to finish her first service period before she can have her organs rebuilt, this is to offset the cost of the surgery."

"Well, here something like that is pretty routine," Kozma said. "People need things find after car crashes and stuff all theme."

"It's regrettable," Knight said. "But it's how things are. She needed to go through the proper channels instead of letting your government subvert her." He took a sip of his drink. "Besides, we at least allow people like her and Ballard to exist."

Mo shrugged. "I think you misunderstand why things like artificial humans are outlawed in Tharsis." Ballard folded his arms.

"Well, if I'm illegal, what is there to misunderstand?" he asked.

"You are not illegal," Kozma said. "The process that made you, however, is."

Mo nodded. "So are there any sports in the Union?" In a vain attempt to diffuse the conversation, he learned that the Union had nothing like sports or entertainment as he understood it. As conversation after conversation ground to a halt, the young soldier sighed in frustration. "It's like talking to a wall."

"Or first sergeant," Kozma added. "Man, that guy is annoying."

Shaking his head, Mo continued. "He won't affect your duties, Reiter said, you'll hardly notice him, the man said." The two Union men chuckled.

"This first sergeant you speak of reminds me of this operations officer back in our battalion," Knight said.

Ballard cleared his throat, and when he spoke, he did so a few octaves higher. "You might be experienced, but I've been educated, your memory doesn't trump my science, the numbers don't care about your intuition." He shook his head. "She's wasted so many lives."

Mo snorted. "Our people are hardly better, 'hey, I've got Union raiders camping out on my lawn can we counter attack?' 'no, hold until relived' and they sit around safe while we fight."

"Ironic you say that," Knight replied. "Irving herself hasn't seen combat, maybe there is something there."

"Well, our 1st Sergeant's seen some shit," Kozma said. "Problem is, it was twenty years ago, and he insists everything we do is wrong." He sighed. "At least I got good people under me."

His statement caused Knight to shift in his seat. "My soldiers are good at killing," he said. "And that's about it, they're probably going stir crazy right now." Mo made a mental note to memorize Knight's hull numbers.

"You know what?" Mo said. "Let's get some beers." He ordered them a round. When the drinks came, he proposed a toast. "To those who couldn't be bothered to give a fuck about us."

MAPS AND MONITORS FILLED THE MAKESHIFT WAR ROOM, AND Kennedy felt himself becoming stir crazy. *We are doing way too much sitting and not nearly enough fighting.* He stood with Meyer, pouring over maps after she'd received orders from higher.

Army Command couldn't be clearer: Capture Vaterburg before the new year. The Capital of the Germania province lay in their invasion corridor, but mountains, rivers, forests and cities stood between them and their goal. *So, how do we get there?*

As he worked with Meyer, it became evident that the quickest path to Vaterburg would be to drive between the cities of Swizen and Grunbeck, seize Narrowfield from the rear. And then drive on to Vaterburg. The problem lay in doing all of that in two weeks.

"This is getting outrageous," Meyer said. "Even if we take Vaterburg, the logistical mess behind us will leave us vulnerable to counterattack."

Kennedy nodded as he looked over the maps. "Here," he said. "Thie medium town called Ironton is the key." He pointed to a town closer to Grunbeck than Swizen, but still mostly between them. "There're highways that pass through here to the other two cities, as well as Narrowfield further south."

As she followed the lines on the map, Meyer shook her head. "They could very easily counter attack along the roads, I would rather attack through this airport." She pointed to a small airport

East of Ironton. "Then we can land cargo planes and draw up supplies and reinforcements much quicker."

"But we'll need to be moving fast," Kennedy said. "Ironton possesses enough infrastructure for us to maintain steady command and control of the operation, and it's defensible."

Meyer shook her head. "Do you remember our initial advance?"

"Yeah, I remember being dropped on the airport," he replied. "I know what you're getting at, seizing that airport when we did dropped a deuce in their coffee, and it allowed us to keep pushing fresh forces right up to the line." He pointed to the airport on the map. "We also benefited in that we didn't have to defend it very long, after that one counterattack, they never tried to retake it because we pushed them so far elsewhere."

"Well, it seems like you just made my point for me," Meyer replied. Kennedy shook his head.

"My point is this airport is exposed relative to our advance, and slightly out of the way," he said. "All that in addition to not airdropping onto it, its likely the airport is severely damaged before we can take it."

Meyer cradled her chin in her hand. "They'll certainly have scouts in the area," she said. "What if we compromise?"

"I'm listening," Kennedy replied. Meyer traced a long line from their bridgehead to Ironton. Then she took her other hand and split from her previous line towards the airport. He nodded. "A feint, I see, with what forces?"

"Your battalion will move on Ironton with force," Meyer said. "When the scouts report your movements, they'll orient their defenses on Ironton, allowing us to slip our infantry into the airport."

"Thus giving us both objectives at once," Kennedy said. "That would leave the enemy from Grunbeck south isolated, and threaten the rest with being cut off." Kennedy scratched his chin. "I don't know, I'd like infantry attached to my forces to stay with them, Panzerters are good at destroying buildings and we need this place intact as much as possible."

"Then we'll use the motor battalion to take the airport," Meyer replied. "I know they aren't at full strength yet, but we need them in this fight, and that may be a simpler objective." She pointed to FOB Nike. "We can use the raiders to sell the illusion of a large attack on Ironton, then have the bypass the city and attack the airport."

Grabbing a tablet, Kennedy checked the status of the raider battalion. On paper, they still looked the elite force they'd been when Druza led them into Tharsis, but most of their best leaders, including Guard-Colonel Druza himself, had been killed in battle since.

As he handed the tablet to Meyer, he scratched the back of his head. "I don't know," he said. "Their setback the other day has me wondering if we can rely on them like we did a month ago." He raised his hands defensively. "Not to say they aren't well trained or disciplined, but the current battalion is run by leaders who attained their position through attrition, and most of them hadn't fought together or participated in an attack like the one we planned."

"You're worried about brain drain?" Meyer asked.

"Correct," Kennedy said. "I think our last plan with them was sound, but a lot of navigational errors created a near disaster."

Merry smiled. "Your concern is noted, I'll inform comrade Walker that she needs to double down on map reading and navigational training." Finally, she sat down, a weary look crossing her features. "Thank you for talking this out Kennedy, sound advice isn't abundant in my position."

Kennedy scratched his head. "Honestly, I've just been imagining what Blake would have done, but I seem to deviate from him quite a bit."

"Of course you would," Meyer said. "Your not a computer

running a program, you're a man with your own different experiences, Blake could have figured out how to win the War of 2112 in
as many ways in his time as a MAG, but we're fighting a different
war."

Kennedy nodded and stretched. "Understood, I'll head back to
my headquarters and draw up som plans, do we have maps of Ironton?" After accumulating a tablet and some physical maps, he made
his way to the command car. *My own experience, huh?*

"WE NEED TO REIN IN OUR ALLY OR OTHERWISE CUT TIES WITH
Avalon," Chaney said. He normally didn't speak out of turn or
comment on strategic or political decisions, but he no longer cared
what the others thought of him. "We can't associate ourselves with
these psychopaths, hell the gas attack on Deimos just blurs the line
between us and them."

Secretary Pearson's caramel cheeks bloomed red. "Brigadier
Chaney, you have no right to criticize foreign policy choices or
grand strategy," she hissed. "If you know what's good for you, stick
to research and development."

"What's good for me is another country not joining our
enemies," he said. "Yes Avalon helped us crush Olympia in a month
and some change, but if we're not careful, they'll piss off, oh I don't
know, Brazil, The First Nation, The Americans, Vinland, Japan, the
NSA, India, all the above, who'd be the worst for us to end up
fighting?"

"That's quite enough from both of you," The First Minister said
before coughing. "While not nis area of expertise, comrade Chaney
raised valid points, we need to be more careful about these things,
I'll have a conference with Arthur V and we'll denounce our gas

attack, call it a necessary evil or blame a rouge admiral, whichever is better."

One of the Commodore's attending the meeting shifted a bit uncomfortable. "That could hurt the fleet's morale if you throw a popular commander under the proverbial bus," she said. "But we're not exactly in a great position to flex our naval muscles at the moment."

Secretary Pearson folded her arms and sank in her chair. *Like a pouting child.* "Please Commodore, explain yourself."

The woman in question looked at the first minister as well as the army staff before sighing. "Until Los Estrella's facilities are finished, our shipbuilding has fallen behind the Tharcians," she said. "They have shipyards in the Jupiter Sphere fully capable of resupplying and repairing their vessels as well as making even more of them, on top of this, we're still working overtime to replace the torpedo boats we lost in the attack on Deimos."

"Aren't those escort vessels anyway?" a general asked. "Shouldn't we have had a lot of them in the first place?"

"We did," Commodore Mendez replied. "But we used most of them in the Mars sphere in a massed attack with the goal of ending the war in a single blow." She looked around the table. "They're not much good in direct battle, we found Tharcians outfit all their vessels with extensive point defenses, but their great for destroying cargo vessels and transports, and a large part of our strategy was to strangle their ability to bring their full economy system-wide to bear."

One of the Generals snorted. "They can have all the cargo vessels they want, we posses a direct link from our greatest space asset to the surface, an ever-flowing pipeline of resources and a monument to our great society."

"An incredibly vulnerable pipeline," Chaney added. "Look, I

get it, I'm the ideas guy, but our strategy is going to need some work, or we run the risk of defeating ourselves."

"Nothing comrade Chaney or comrade Mendez have said has been unreasonable," said Guard-Marshall Baldwin. "I'd like to schedule a teleconference between us, Fleet Admiral Rodríguez, and Secretary Pearson, if that's possible, and then meet with Avalon's leadership." He looked at the First Minister. "If that's alright with you, Comrade First Minister."

The First Minister nodded. "Thank you comrade Marshall, Avalon needs to be reprimanded for their abhorrent behavior and brought into line for the strategy to defeat Tharsis."

"Their forces proved capable enough in Olympia," another general said. "Perhaps we could use them to shore up our forces in Gallacia?" *Finally, people are talking sense.*

"Your conference may need to wait," Commodore Mendez said. "He's currently in the belt and hard to reach."

"Why?" Pearson asked. "Why has our illustrious Admiral deigned to go to the belt?"

To her credit, Mendez managed to not look so nervous. "He grew unsatisfied with our inability to locate the Tharcian base in the belt, so he took up the search himself." She sipped some water before continuing. "If that base falls, it cuts off a vital supply line for Tharsis."

"Pardon my ignorance," the First Minister said. "But why hasn't a fleet set out to destroy the Tharcians in the Jupiter Sphere? If they have resources outside our area of influence, then those resources must be seized or destroyed."

"Because the defenses in the Jupiter Sphere are strong," Mendez replied. "Not to mention such a fleet would be harassed by their forces in the belt and suffer supply issues."

"It seems we've underestimated aspects of our opponent's industry," Baldwin said. "We'll have to refine our strategy in a future conference. If all heads have nothing more to report, then this meeting is adjourned."

As Chaney gathered his things to leave, he felt a hand on his arm. He looked up to see the First Minister standing inches from him. "I'm doing you a huge favor, comrade," he hissed. "Your ideas aren't wrong, but your manners are, if Pearson needs to be told she's wrong, talk to the marshal and he'll tell me." Chaney nodded.

"Yes, Comrade First Minister," he said. "I understand."

11

M aster Sergeant Adamski rolled along in his wheelchair, outpacing the nurse behind him. "Mr. Adamski, please slow down!"

Reluctantly, he brought himself to a stop at the elevator. "Sorry miss, I'm just excited to get fitted for prosthetics." His horse caught up with him as he waited on the elevator.

"I understand, but you're going to have to relearn how to walk," she said. "It's a long arduous process."

He raised a hand. "I just need to walk enough to get into a panz-erter, I'll worry about it from there." Impatiently tapping on his wheels, he watched for the light. *I hate this damn place, so damn sterile.* St. Matthew Regional Hospital in Vaterburg boasted itself as the largest and most advanced medical center in Western Tharsis. The medical megaplex resembled a fortress from the outside, boasting ten thousand beds, and many more labs, offices, and storerooms.

Yet despite its massive size and advanced equipment, Saint Matthew still found itself swamped with injured and wounded soldiers. Modern weapons possessed an incredible ability to maim people they didn't kill, and the hospital's burden testified to that.

Refugees, casualties of battle from both sides piled on top of the standard patients the hospital expected to take at this time of year. Complicating the fact was, many soldiers who lost limbs or eyes often needed the hospital's physical therapy centers to aid in their own recovery. He'd spotted Zorro in one such center, working hard to adjust to her mechanical leg.

"When did it start getting bad?" he asked his nurse as she pushed him into the elevator. A wall of buttons greeted them, twenty-five above ground floors with twelve sub levels.

She sighed as she pushed a button for the eighteenth floor. "Right after Polaski fell, we got so many wounded soldiers and refugees we actually had to send a lot of them to our sister care centers." He felt her grip tighten on his chair's handles. "To be honest, if you came in then, we likely would have turned you away. Missing limbs weren't as serious injuries as the majority of what we got then, but I honestly hated it more when we started getting the kids."

Adamski shook his head. "My company got rebuilt with a bunch of those teenagers they shipped out to the line," he said before shaking his head. "It's a damn shame too. Most of them didn't make it out of the delta, hell one of the ones who did is here getting a new leg."

As the doors opened, his nurse, Nora he thought her name was, wheeled him into an office area. Hushed conversations leaked out of the doors they passed, but a patient leaving one of the rooms caught his eye.

"Well, well, well, I didn't know they just let anyone come here," he said. Like him, she was bound to a wheelchair, though slightly more literally then he was. An MP, though unarmed, watched

Fletcher and her nurse leave an office. The prisoner smiled weakly at him.

"Adamski, how are you?" she asked.

"Not great," he said. "But I might be able to improve that today." At that moment, Fletcher noticed the absence of his feet.

"Oh, I'm sorry," she said. "Kennedy didn't-"

"No," he replied. "It was three assholes in red units, they even managed to make things hairy for Reiter." At the mention of his boss's name, Fletcher looked alarmed, so he held up a hand. "He's fine. He got a little banged up, but he came out more pissed than hurt."

Fletcher looked past him uncomfortably. "You said three units in red?" The MP set a firm hand on her shoulder.

"Come on miss, we can't let you learn anything-" she pushed his hand away and looked firmly at Adamski.

"I fought alongside three pilots who painted their panzerters that color once they became aces," she said. Reaching over to him, she grabbed his hand. "They're incredibly dangerous, Knight is their leader, he more or less keeps the other two on a leash and focuses their aggression, Snow is a true believer, like I was but even more hardcore, she'll kill her own people if she believes they're too complacent."

"Jesus," the MP muttered. The nurses looked horrified. Fletcher leaned forward, an effort that seemed to cause her serious discomfort.

"But listen to me, the third one, Khan, is the worst, he's only joined MAG so he could kill people legally and get away with it, he has no ideology, no hobbies, no dreams, all he wants is to kill." She slumped back down, her rant seemingly draining her. "Please, just tell Reiter, to be safe if you can, all the things he did for me, I can't repay him, but this comes close."

As her nurse rolled her away, Adamski rested his hands on the stump of his legs. *Damn it, they're going up against those kinds of people? And I'm stuck back here. Why the hell did I have to get hurt?* His grip on his stumps tightened. *I'm so damn useless like this.*

REITER LOOKED AROUND THE INSIDE OF THE MASSIVE CAMOUFLAGED tent. *I hope we don't get shelled or bombed, we've got so many leaders in one spot.* He shook his head. *Don't jinx it.* Officers and senior NCOs filled folding chairs set in front of a projector. A map of the region filled the wall they faced.

"Sir, keep your head forward," said 1st Sergeant Klammer. "You might actually learn something." Unable to help rolling his eyes, Reiter looked at Hawke.

"Do you think we're about to counterattack?" he asked.

The older man raised his hands. "Hell if I know, we should because it's stupid to bring us all here just to tell us to die in place." The XO whispered something to Hawke after conferring with Friermann. Leaning back towards Reiter, he nodded. "Rumor is we're getting objectives and General Wolfe's plan here."

"Well, you know what they say about rumors, sir," Klammer said. "They're like assholes, everyone has one."

"That's opinions," Reiter said. "Anyway, I haven't seen General Orban since we got here, and they've got everyone from 1st sergeants and company commanders on up here."

Silence suddenly filled the room, and General Wolfe strode onto the stage. "Good Evening leaders of V Corps, we're pressed for time so I'll skip the pleasantries." He pointed to the map of the region with a laser pointer. "As you all are well aware, we've been on the defensive since the 8th of October when this war kicked off. Within the next week, we're going to change that."

With a gesture to an attendant, the projector slide shifted, now the situation map revealed units, movements, and enemy forces. "By the miracle that is Cyberwarfare and resistance groups, we've pieced together the enemy's plans in this region." He pointed towards Grunbeck and Swiezen. "They intend to force a division through this gap, hug the mountains, and breakout towards Vaterburg, now to keep this gap open, they will create diversions towards Kiefernlucke to tie up units north of Swiezen."

He pointed just Northeast of Swiezen. "Already, we're planting misinformation, suggesting we plan to attack out of Kiefernlucke and have massed more divisions there, including the 12th Panzerter we've held in reserve. In addition, we've increased convoy and rail traffic to the city to suggest a buildup." He pointed to the north. "Now when their feint begins, these forces will come out of position while this mechanized division attacks through the G-S gap." Wolfe clapped his hands.

"Now, 7th division will catch the tip of the Union spear while the 12th, 44th, and 2nd Divisions all attack while the Union is out of position, for maximum effect, we've coordinated this effort with the other two corps adjacent to us, VII Corps will attack out of the mountains while III Corps will attack into the Union."

Wolfe stopped, took a swig from a water bottle someone handed him, and looked at the men and women in the room. "Well, you have your objectives, the Union has played rough in your yard long enough, it's high time we take the fight to their homeland, now if there are any questions, relay runners to corps HQ, 7th panzerter, you'll meet your new commander in Swiezen, dismissed."

The room broke out into chaos as people began discussing objectives among themselves. Hawke tapped Reiter as they made towards the door. "Weird, it's like he saw our plans and said that's great, but let's do it on an Army level."

"Don't give yourself too much credit sir," 1st Sergeant said. "I'm sure he's got his own people telling him things."

Hawke ignored him to talk to Reiter. "Pending what our new boss says, I'm thinking the 3-9th is going to hold Grunbeck to Ironton, and I want to put Fox right in the city."

"You want us to hold Ironton?" Reiter asked.

"I'm not sure why you would, sir," Klammer said. "Nobody's qualified to do anything, and we're dragging a bunch of kids around."

"Who is qualified to do anything?" Hawke replied. "We have plenty of time for career courses and qualifications in peacetime, I don't know if you noticed, but we're at war."

As they climbed into the command car for the ride back to Grunbeck, Reiter looked up at the sky. Through breaks in the clouds, he spotted lights streaking across the sky. Occasionally, a mote of light flared brightly before fading. He couldn't tell who was winning the scale of the battle, or even who exactly was fighting, but somewhere above him, his side still gave their all. *We stand a chance.* With that, he ducked into the crowded command car, and rode back to the front.

"Daddy, look! I can see through the roof!" Penny Ballard cried. Ballard smiled as the little girl clung to the railing and gazed up at the dome.

"Be careful Penny, I wouldn't get to close to the railing," he said. As he set his hands on the little girl's shoulders, he looked back at Chaney. "To be honest, Comrade Brigadier, I think she's enjoying our little tour of this city more than I am."

The older man laughed. "Well, she's asked me at least a hundred questions so far, but I'm not opposed to answering them." As

Ballard led Penny down the long hallway towards their quarters, she marveled at the marble floors she walked on.

"Daddy, does Mr. Comrade bridge Chaney know why the floor is so warm?" Ballard looked at the other man sympathetically.

"You can just call me Mr. Chaney, Penny," the general said. "As for the floor, pipes below it are pumping hot gasses through them and that makes the floor warm."

"Why are the pipes there?"

"Because all the room's here have fireplaces to heat them."

"What's a fireplace?"

Chaney grinned. "Young comrade, you'll find out soon." Penny gave another curious glance at Chaney.

"Why do people call you a bridge?" Her question got a chuckle out of the two men.

"You mean brigadier," he replied. "It's like a general, but not quite as important, it's a word for someone in charge of a brigade."

"He's a really important guy in the army," Ballard said. Penny's face scrunched up in thought.

"Mr. Chaney, what do you do in the army?" Much to Ballard's surprise, Chaney was entirely forthcoming.

"I'm in charge of research, like figuring out how the army can have a better truck or panzerter," he replied. "It's part of my job that allowed you and your dad to come live here."

With that, she looked back at her father. "Does that mean you're not a pilot anymore?" Ballard shook his head.

"No sweetie, I'm still a pilot, I'm just going to be a test pilot," he said.

"What's that?"

"It means I'll be piloting new panzerters to test them, and tell Chaney what I liked and didn't like from a pilot's point of view," Ballard said. "Oh look, here we are Penny."

They stopped at a pair of locked double doors leading up into the ceiling. A steel plate stamped with 2673 marked the home before them as theirs. Chaney handed Ballard a keycard that he swiped.

With a smart click, the doors unlocked, leading to a large lounge style living room. To one side, a marble bar marked the boundary of the kitchen. "Bathrooms are down the hall, and your bedrooms are on either side," Chaney said as he pointed to the lone hallway in the room.

"I have my own room?" Penny squealed as she ran laps around a fully furnished child's bedroom. Unable to help himself, Ballard smiled.

"Her mother would've been so happy," he said.

Chaney set a firm hand on his shoulder. "Someone may not agree with me, but part of me thinks she's smiling on you two right now." As Ballard and Penny got acclimated, Chaney pulled a tablet out of a drawer and pulled up some information. "There's the matter of Penny's schooling, you'll start on Monday, yes I'm giving you the weekend, but Penny needs to go to school or be schooled in some manner."

Ballard sighed. "Her grandparents had her in a union school, she hated it."

Chaney nodded. "Fortunately for you, I'm came up with something new," he said. Crossing over to where Ballard sat, he handed him the tablet. "As you can see, her literary scores are well above the standard for a seven-year-old, but her math and science aptitudes are ridiculously good, to the extent that it was asinine for her grandparents to put her in a school focused on fine arts, and media."

Ballard shook his head. "So what are you proposing?"

"Well, since her math and science aptitudes are so high and considering her curious nature, I called a few members of the research division heading towards retirement, they'll teach her math and science and I'll sign off on the schooling credit." He shrugged.

"Think of it as like a bring your daughter to work day, only very day."

Ballard rested his head in his hands. "This is…this is so much," he said. "I never thought any of this could be possible."

With a smile, Chaney headed towards the door. "This is just a taste of the future to come, where everyone in the Union is treated human." On that note, he left the happy little family to explore their new home.

SURROUNDED BY MAPS, KENNEDY BEGAN FEELING MORE AT EASE. Here in his own battalion headquarters, deep inside the former Tharcian estate, he drew up his final plans for the advance.

"So if the 88th is going to advance first, they'll advance to halfway to the objective," he said to himself. "Then they'll create a corridor for my battalion to advance along, we'll anchor the route and create the corridor towards Ironton for the 88th to take the city while our infantry attack the airport." He cradled his hand in his chin.

"So I'll go Panzerters, infantry, support/ headquarters, and then my last panzerter company, and then they'll make the corridor." Someone knocked at his door. "Enter."

When the door swung open, it revealed none other than Knight, along with the rest of his officers. "I hope we're not interrupting," the big man said. "But we're here for the mission brief."

With a nod, Kennedy invited them to take their seats. "Alright, so we're going to hold this bridgehead while the 88th moves out," he said. As he spoke, he motioned to the repaired bridge and their own pontoon bridges. "When the 88th advances to this crossroad here, we will step off and rush down the corridor they've made and beyond, all the way to this cross road here."

"So what are our objectives?" asked Sr LT Bear, the soldier who filled in for Ballard, as the Incubus Company commander.

Kennedy held up a hand. "Well, it's simple really," he said. "We'll advance a single company at a time to secure multiple objectives along the way, timing and communication will be key to this operation." Pointing to his Recon Platoon leader, a severe man named Jackson, he continued. "Your platoon will patrol the route ahead of Jericho Company, once you've cleared out to this intersection, head south and check these aces roads south of our main road, be on the lookout for enemy recon teams, once the intersection and gas station are cleared, that concludes Phase 1."

"I have a question," Jackson said. "A lot of these areas are open, if I were enemy scouts, I'd have artillery prevailed for these areas. How do we counter that in Phase 1?"

"Stay mobile," Spears answered. "Your Canises aren't to different from our Capricorns, a direct hit will destroy the vehicle, but a near miss should only rock it."

With a nod, Kennedy looked back at the map. "Thank you comrade Spears, now then, your objectives for Phase 2, Jackson I need those dirt roads scouted, Jericho, hold the gas station and the intersection, Harpy, drive down the main road and sun out where there scouts are, I suspect there screen is here." Kennedy traced a long curving line from the hills along the highway to a wind farm west of the gas station.

"And us?" Bear asked.

"You'll head directly from the gas station to this wind farm," Kennedy replied. "The whole way, sweep the enemy out." He looked up at his other attachments: an artillery battery and a Surface to Air Missile Platoon. "SAMs will escort Chimera Battery to the gas station along with the headquarters element. At that point the moment they set the battery up, I want excessive use of artillery." Kennedy scanned the faces of the officers in the room. "We need to

preserve our strength in the even the enemy counterattacks our position or we need to attack one of the objectives ourselves."

"Once the artillery is set Phase 3 begins," he continued. "Harby
will shift Southwest and clear the road leading back to where the
second bridge was, the other companies will advance south until we
seize this southern intersection and this rest area south of it, any
questions?"

Jackson raised a hand. "Yes?"

"What if the enemy is more entrenched in these access roads
then our projections suggest?" he asked.

"Then we'll just have to shift forces from somewhere else,"
Knight answered. "worse comes to worst, myself and the rest of the
red guards can bail you out of trouble if you bite off more than you
can chew, this goes for all of you."

"If I dismount a squad, they can follow you into the woods and
reinforce your scouts, Jackson," Spears offered. "We're headed that
way when this road is clear, so we can pick them up when we pass
you."

"Alright, I'm glad you're all capable of aiding each other, but I
have one other thing to add," Kennedy said. "The cold and clouds
are staying, but the high winds and heavy snow aren't, so keep an
eye to the sky for enemy air." They broke off into their related
groups, Spears and name discussed doing some recon training
together while Day, the Artillery leader, began plotting targets. *This
feels correct, I don't think Blake would have done this, but he's dead
and I'm not. Not yet, anyway.*

A GRAY FORM SHAPED LIKE A TORPEDO DESCENDED FROM THE SOUPY
clouds overhead. As the Pegasus dropship touched down, Reiter
turned his face so the heat from the VTOL engines at the rear of the

craft wouldn't burn him. While the four engines, each paired and mounted on fin like structures on the roof of the airframe, wound down, the ramp lowered itself before Reiter.

A line of men and women wearing armor and toting large rucksacks filed out to either side of him. When they noticed his rank on his chest, many of them greeted him, but most kept their heads down. Finally, the lines ended as one last trooper rushed out of the dropship with his head down.

"Are you LT Webb?" Reiter asked as the man approached him. The trooper looked up when he got closer and offered his hand.

"I am! You must be Captain Reiter!" He shouted, still a little deaf from the engines. Nearby, the scene Reiter just witnessed played out with two more dropships full of soldiers. "Sorry we took so long! It was a month and a half to get us all spun up, and then we had to wait a couple more weeks for our escorts."

"Escorts?" Reiter asked.

Webb fumbled for his watch. "They're probably an hour or so behind us, they're moving them by truck because they didn't want the enemy to catch a glimpse of them flying around."

After some of Webbs hearing had returned, Reiter led him to a waiting command car. Because of the nature of his current headquarters, they had forced Reiter to meet his new dropship platoon in the parking lot of a supermarket.

"Let me take a guess, they gave you guys some top of the line shit because you happened to be around where they made it," Reiter said.

Webb flashed a toothy grin. "What? What makes you say that?" Now it was Reiter's turn to grin.

"Alright, I'll show you mine if you show me yours," he said. It didn't take long for the command car to pull up at the warehouse. "As soon as whatever you're waiting on gets here, we should be ready to start planning. The mortars just got here a few hours ago."

Reiter stepped out of the car and smiled. Webb's jaw dropped when he saw the Lowe being prepped for combat. "It's not like I've never seen a panzerter before, but damn is that thing scary." When Webb felt like the shock of seeing the Lowe wore off, he finally denied to show Reiter what they were waiting for.

"Ok, that's worth waiting a couple hours for," he said. The images on Webb's phone displayed a savage, shark-like gunship bristling with armaments and flying on two VTOL engines. "The armaments aren't even the best specs, they carry two drones as well, that's why it's a two-seater."

Shaking his head, Reiter whistled. "Well, I'll never turn down more firepower." As he led him across the hanger floor to show him the officer's quarters they'd made, he stopped to introduce him to Mo and Wesser.

"Well hey there, glad to make your acquaintance ma'am, Sergeant," he said. Then his eyes narrowed. "Ey, I remember you from the news, you're that crazy bastard who took down like three tin-hats at Riverside."

With a smile, Mo raised his hands. "My sisters were on a boat like ten feet away, no way I was losing."

Folding her arms with a fake huff, Wesser looked at him. "You never told me your sisters were there!"

"You didn't ask?" Mo said.

Webb elbowed him in the ribs. "Yea-hah, brother bear over here, I love it."

"You know, you look familiar too," Mo said. Now that they stood inside and Webb had taken his helmet off, Reiter agreed. The black hair slicked to one side and pale, wide face looked like someone from a news article. "You said your name was Webb?"

The drop trooper sighed. "Yeah, I am that Dave Webb, I helped raise those rovers from the floor of the Mariner gulf."

Mo clapped his hands. "That's where I saw you! You did that

and helped with the coral reef expansion project!" The other man shrugged.

"I'm from Mars and I have a degree in Archeology, what else would I do?" He gestured to his body armor and rucksack. "Besides this." Mo offered to take the man's ruck, and they agreed to sit down for dinner with the rest of the leaders and get everyone up to speed. As far as Reiter concerned himself, everything was coming along nicely.

12

W hile Meyer collected her notes for the call, Irving found herself unable to focus. *Woody Pete is planning something. Up to something. What is he doing? Did he let himself get captured? I doubt Kennedy butt stroking him across the face was part of his plan.*

"Irving! Do you have that spreadsheet? The one for ammo count by Battalion," Meyer said. Irving's cheeks flushed red.

"I apologize, Comrade Colonel, It's right here," she replied. Meyer took the spreadsheet without another word. After eyeing it over a couple times, she set it down, took Irving by the hand, and led her to a corner of the room.

"What's going on?" she whispered. As far as Irving knew, Meyer was the only person on the planet to whisper to get her point across. "You haven't been right since we took that partisan prisoner, I know Chaney put a non-executable tag on him, but maybe he can have an accident…"

"I would very much appreciate that," Irving said. "Something isn't right about him, how we got him, or what he's said since coming here."

Meyer gave her a warm smile and patted her on the shoulder. "We'll take care of it, after this conference call, now if you can set up the host we can-" She stopped cold.

That's weird, is someone whistling? Fortunately for Irving, Meyer recognized the sound. The older woman struck her like a speeding car and dove under a table with her. Then someone tossed the world into a blender.

She tried to run. Tried to crawl away. However, the amazon woman with her held her firmly on the floor. Irving screamed, but she couldn't hear her own voice. She lost it in an orchestra of destruction.

When the world began to still, her head rang. Everything rang. The walls of their wing of town hall had been blown away. Thick smoke drifted into gray skies outside the range of her vision.

Blinking, she realized her eyes stung. She felt something in her leg. As she tried to sit up and look, Meyer pushed her back to the floor.

She couldn't hear her commander's words, but she knew she didn't want her to look. Meyer signaled to her to "be still" and she tied a tourniquet made from her sleeve onto Irving's leg. Then she darted off, possibly seeking help, possibly establishing order, likely both.

Irving closed her eyes. She worked her mouth and felt her ears. Her left, the one facing the blast, bled while the other didn't. As her hearing slowly came back to her, she heard cries of pain and shots all around her. Beneath her pain, perhaps as a method of preserving her sanity, her tactical mind kicked into gear.

Why did they hit us with artillery? How did they know we were here? Are we about to receive a follow up attack? She glanced over to a broken monitor. In its cracked reflection, she could see over the fallen wall next to her. She also saw the long piece of rebar pinning her leg to the ground.

Irving screamed, jerking her head away as to not look any more when the colder part of her mind took over. *The damage was limited to a few areas, how could they conduct such a precise bombardment on our control centers.*

Turning her face back towards the sky, she nearly screamed again. Until a large meaty hand clamped over her mouth. "Sh," Woody Pete hissed. "Don't freak out, miss Ivy Irving, I won't do anything to you." He leaned closer. "Not yet, anyway."

He stomped on her injured leg's ankle, crushing it and causing her to cry out. Pete laughed and leaned back over her. "I just want you to know, your life was in my hands right now." And then he stood up and left.

"Hey civilian!" A guard cried. "What are you-ack!" Irving heard a faint yet sickening snap and a thud. She waited for the man to return with a weapon. A knife, a gun, anything that could finish her off. She closed her eyes and accepted her fate.

But he never came back. Meyer returned with a team of engineers who cut the rebar, allowing her to be slipped off and carried onto a stretcher. With as much strength as she could muster, she grabbed Meyer's hand.

"They knew," she gasped. "Comrade Meyer, they knew where the command center was, our ammo depot, our field kitchen, I think Woody Pete let them know somehow." Tears welled up in her eyes. "I wanted him captured, my plan brought him here, this is all my fault." Her voice cracked on the last word.

Meyer held her hand tighter. "You need to heal, and let your head clear," she said. "But mark my words, you will be safe."

———

As he leaned over the railing of the upper section of the warehouse, Reiter kept a close eye on Gold Platoon preparing for the mission. The "hanger" floor was just large enough for them to simulate their mission: Occupy a few homes and set charges in the surrounding sewers. Squad and team leaders walked their soldiers through each phase of their own plan, occasionally pausing to ask an individual soldier what them or a teammate would be doing or where someone would be.

When he walked away, he caught a glimpse of Weber and his men sitting on one of the walls waiting on their turn to use the space. Moving on, he walked past the map room. Inside, the mortar platoon and gunship pilots pre-plotted targets and rehearsed their radio calls. *Everything is coming along nicely, which means something will go powerfully wrong during the mission.*

Finally he came to the "barracks" area. Formerly a large conference room where sponsors rubbed shoulders, the Panzerter teams walked around pieces of paper that marked real buildings in the town.

"Remember," Mo said as he entered. "Buildings can stop shells, but if you need to get somewhere, don't be afraid to walk through a few."

Smith looked uncomfortable. "Uh Sergeant, are we sure we're ok with destroying someone's home?"

With a smile, Reiter entered the room. "If it's someone's life over the building, choose life," he said. "Minimizing the damage to homes is nice, but most of the population is in Grunbeck or further West." He paused, glancing at their "buildings" all over the floor. "Just don't destroy the foundry, we need that once we toss the Unis back across the border."

"Excuse me, sir," Wesser said. "Since you're here, would you like to show the teams where you will be?" Reiter paced around their "map" until he stopped of the autobahn behind a hotel.

"I'll be about here," he said. "That way I can support anyone who needs it quick, but I'm also guarding the approach to our Medevac point." He spun to his right and pointed at Magyar. "PFC Magyar, where is our casualties collection point and what is our Medevac plan?"

The excitable young woman stumbled over her words for a moment. "Well it's, uh…" She looked at Reiter and the surrounding space. "It's where the dropships are, right?"

Reiter nodded. "Correct, Smith, what's the nearest friendly unit to your position?"

"That depends on where I stand and where the drop troopers are, sir," he replied. "If they occupy a building near me, it's their first squad. If they're away from me, the scouts are about 800 meters to my ten."

"Good, it's important for all of you to be aware of friendly forces," Reiter said. "We're going to be working with a lot of forces we normally don't, so it's important to be aware of them and what they are doing." He looked around the room. "Who hear is confident calling in Mortars?" When no-one raised their hands, he sighed.

"Alright, that's an issue," Reiter said. "Fortunately, Brunnen is pretty cool, when you guys are done here, I want you to go practice calling for fire with the mortars and the gunships, that's a skill all of you should know but especially team leaders and team sergeants."

As Reiter spoke First Sergeant walked in. Having caught the last bit of Reiter's speed, he added his own two cents. "To piggy back off what the commander said. If you tape an index card to your monitors or firewall, you can load it with the lines you need for fires and the lines for a Medevac."

As the panzerter teams returned to their rehearsals, Reiter and Klammer stood back to observe. Kozma, Wesser, Mo, and Steele would occasionally interject with some kind of disaster or unforeseen action to gauge their team's reaction. A team getting wiped out by artillery, enemy contact from a weird direction. Between the four of them, the pilots talked out every foreseeable monkey wrench that could be thrown at them.

Which means there's something else out there we won't see coming. He shook his head. *Where does this dread keep coming from?* Leaving the pilots to their work, Reiter headed back to the officer's quarters. Alone in his room, he paced about, mulling over his previous plans.

I'm not a world beating tactician or strategist, I'm clever occasionally, but I know that's not enough to keep everyone alive. He sank onto his bed and lowered his head into his hands. *Lord, if you're hearing this, we're going into battle soon.*

Snow whipped past his face, though not as often as Kennedy had recently seen. He stood in the open cockpit of his Jupiter, watching as his battalion mobilized to attack. Except his order to move didn't come down. Scowling at his watch, he keyed up his helmet radio.

"Something's wrong, we're past the point where Meyer should have given us the order to advance," he said.

"Is there a chance you misremembered the time, comrade? Or maybe she did?" Halphen offered. Kennedy looked down at the mobile command post that the smaller man occupied.

"No, if Meyer updated her timetable, she would have said something," Kennedy replied. "And I'll grow fangs and howl at the moons before Meyer misremembers anything." He looked off over the hills. Was it just him? Or were some of the gray clouds…off?

Spears jumped on the net. "My command matrix isn't updating

outside of our battalion. When I ask for information from division HQ, I get an error message."

With a frown, Kennedy ducked inside his own machine and ran the same request. Sure enough, he got an error message: no data available. "I'm going to try raising someone on division net," he said. As soon as he switched back, he heard the other battalion commanders trying to raise contact with somebody.

Someone needs to take charge of this mess. "This is Reaper 6, who's closest to Landfall?" He asked.

"I've got a patrol nearby," The Motor Commander replied. "I can send them to go check it out."

Why didn't you think of that before? "Roger Snowback, keep us updated," he said. "Until we establish contact, we'll delay twenty-four hours, Reaper out." Switching back to his own network, he updated his leaders. "Until we get some answers, we stay put, but I'm beginning to suspect something bad has happened at HQ."

Knight's Jupiter pondered over the ground trembling with every step he took. Popping his hatch, the giant stepped out of his equally massive machine. "Think they got hit?"

"If the Tharcians launched an attack through Landfall and we don't know about it, the whole division is fucked," Kennedy said. "That being said, if we rush down there and it's something as stupid as their comms acting up at a bad time, we'll be way out of position to attack and will probably lose the bridges."

"So it's a lose-lose situation then, huh?" Knight replied. Below them, soldiers mounted on trucks began breaking out rations. Kennedy stepped back into his cockpit and grabbed a beverage pouch out of the warmer.

"I was saving this for when we got to the intersection," he said. "But I guess I'll have time to make another one." He sipped the hot beverage and shook his head. "I think this is my last good one though, the other two I have are ok."

"What kind are your other two?" Knight asked. "I have an Acadian Cream one, but that's too sweet for me."

Kennedy looked back up. "Yeah, I'll trade, that's what I'm drinking now." He ducked back inside, grabbed a hazelnut pouch and tossed it to Knight. In return, the other man tossed his Acadian Cream. "I don't know what's taking the Motor battalion, they said they had a patrol nearby."

"Think it's partisan related?" Knight asked. "What if they tried to spring that Pete character free?" Kennedy shook his head.

"I doubt it," he replied. "We killed a lot of them in that trap we set, and he seems to be their big leader, I doubt they'd be able to organize without him." Snow whipped past him. "I don't miss the wind on my face, but I'll miss it when we start seeing Tharcian drones."

With a snort, Knight pulled his jacket tighter around him. "Are they really that big a deal? The Olympians really didn't use a ton of drones."

"Absolutely," Kennedy replied. "During the initial advance it seemed like Tharcian drones always showed up to bail them out of trouble, and unlike ours, the Tharcians have one multipurpose drone that can bomb you, but also dogfight."

"Didn't you guys have drone support then as well?" Knight asked.

Kennedy nodded. "Yeah, but there's always seemed to be better integrated," he said. "When the Tharcians bring their A game, they bring the entire house with them, if we prevail we need to be the same way." He looked east, where they'd previously fought. "I'm sure you got a taste of it last time you fought them." With a curt nod, Knight told Kennedy he'd tasted it alright.

THE PEGASAI RUSHED BY OVERHEAD. SEATED FIRMLY INSIDE THE Lowe, Reiter smiled as they raced off to Ironton.

"What's the rush?" Magyar asked.

"They're setting the perimeter," Steele replied. The Scouts rode out the previous day, leaving Black Team to take the lead out of Grunbeck with Gold platoon shortly behind them. Reiter and Klammer followed with Comidus in his command track. The Mortars and White Team brought up the rear.

"Alright, Fox, everyone switch to platoon and team networks, Leaders leave a channel open on Company and give me an up when all units are checked in," Reiter said. *Alright, then keep the team chatter off my radio.* As much as he liked the Merlin brothers, Smith and the rest, he needed the company net for leaders only during combat, if anything else so information flowed better.

After a few moments, all teams came back clearly on the radio and reported no issues. Even the dropships. With their communications clear, he focused on the route. Once they hit Autobahn 12, they turned north until they arrived at Ironton.

Beginning it's life as a mining town, Ironton turned to metalworking when it's mine ran dry. The massive foundry, built over the old mine and extending deep underground, created a very asymmetrical landscape relative to the highway. Between the highway and the foundry on the eastmost part of town, most of the towns' shops, offices, and service centers found their homes.

Just south of the area Reiter called the "market" district, townhomes and apartments extended south while north of the district found itself dotted with more expensive manor style homes. West of the highway, a big box store took most of the space on the north side while more traditional single-family homes extended south before curving west away from the autobahn. Pine trees intermingled with more barren ones in yards and the spaces between buildings.

He turned off the highway, and brought his Lowe into a kneeling position just behind a large church, easily the biggest of Ironton's three. About a mile ahead of him, the scouts maintained their screen line north of the town.

"Fox 6, Mortars are set," Brunnen said. As the man spoke, the Pegasi touched down in a parking lot south of Reiter's position. *Looks like everything is coming together.*

"Fox 6, Fox 7, I'm set," Klammer said. Reiter nodded and glanced to his four 'o'clock. Klammer's machine rested a sniper rifle on the roof of a mechanic's workshop. In the distance to his nine, Gold Platoon's IFVs set a defensive line in the parking lot of the Big and Lo's with their dismounts setting a screen to the southwest.

"Black Team set," Wesser said somewhere north of him.

"Gold's up."

"White's set," Kozma said near the refinery.

"Red Platoon, all squads set," Webber added, his own forces setting charges and dispersed throughout Ironton. "Take care of our ride home alright? We'd rather not walk back."

Despite the tension in his head, Reiter chuckled.

"Roger Red 1, will do," he replied. "Wolfhound, are you set?"

"Roger Fox 6," The gunship leader replied. "We're idle and up for a bit of trickery." Reiter acknowledged and let out a deep breath.

"Leaders, make sure your people eat," he said. "The 4-14 is going to let us know the Unis are coming long before we see them." Taking his own advice, he heated up some ration lasagna and mixed an electrolyte drink.

"Fox 6, White 1," Kozma called.

"Go ahead for 6," Reiter replied as he opened a pack of reese's pieces.

"I think 2 has a case of the nerves," Kozma said. "What should I say?" *Seriously, Magyar? For all her bluster, she gets nerves.* He shook his head. *I didn't really have a chance for nerves, none of us old hats did.* With a glance to his memorial wall, Reiter mulled over his options.

If we were still in Grunbeck, I might've said something more gentle. He sighed as he keyed up his radio. *Too late for gentleness now.*

"Be understanding, but make it clear she needs to step up," Reiter replied. He glanced back at his map. *Our last intel has them attacking in less than twelve hours, I wonder how long we'll be sitting here.* As he unbuckled his restraints, he opened the lasagna. Hot steam hissed out of the pouch and warmed his face.

"All posts, begin rest plan for the next six hours," he said. "Be ready to stand to at 1800 hours." With that, he took a few bites of lasagna and relaxed.

"AM I IMAGINING THINGS, OR IS 4TH ARMY ABOUT TO LAUNCH A counteroffensive?" the Operations Chief said. Field Marshal Adam Hausnerr cradled his forehead in his hand. After the shock of the attack on Deimos, an emergency meeting had been called to reevaluate the war effort. Much to Hausnerr's chagrin, there seemed be no effort to seize the initiative from the enemy. *Because they want to play it safe, it's easier to keep your cushy job when you don't take risks.*

"So what if they are?" Hausnerr replied. "Good on them, its about time somebody did something about the enemy at our door."

"But such an operation would be reckless and wasteful," The Chief of personnel replied. "The losses on our side will shock the people into surrender!" Hausnerr hammered his fist onto the table.

"Then damn it we deserve to fall!" He snapped. "And don't you pretentious fools pretend you're concerned with our soldiers lives, I can see you're all out for your own hides, and frankly it disgusts me." He jabbed an accusing finger at the General staff.

The Chief of Logistics rose from her chair. "This is outrageous! How dare you accuse us of-"

"Of serving your own twisted self interests?" Hausnerr hissed. "Yes, I'm disgusted that I've been shackled with such a spineless staff who would rather see their homeland dismantled brick by brick than put their comfort on the line to see her saved."

"You're replaceable," the Personnel Chief said. "We can find another former warfighter-"

"I. Am. A Warfighter, all of us should be!" Hausnerr said. "But instead you disgusting creations are only interested in furthering your careers while sacrificing the very force that gave you those careers."

"We've already lost a Marshal to enemy action," The Operations Chief said. "We have the ear of the president, she can have you and the entire head of 4th Army relieved."

Hausnerr took a deep breath as the chefs muttered among themselves. "I was in the trenches in the last war, I still remember the name of every man and woman in my platoon we lost, where the hell were the lot of you then?"

"That's a ridiculous question," The Chief of contracting said. "Most of us weren't even old enough to commission yet."

The Field Marshall shook his head and turned away. "All of you allowed this magnificent fighting force to grow complacent," he said. "You thought the Union was beat, that they would never again threaten our people." He turned back to face the General Staff. "We failed this country, we neglected the army, and by extension our national security."

"Whether it was failing to update our doctrine and strategy for the future, pursuing better and better equipment for our soldiers, or even bothering to allocate adequate funding to maintenance, or bothering to fully evaluate the MAG as a threat, the bottom line is every General officer for the past ten years has failed this country." Hausnerr leaned over the table. "I'm not saying this as the Field Marshall, a veteran, or even just a soldier, I'm saying this as Adam the Tharcian man."

He pointed to the door. "You either help me turn this around, or get out, there's the door, if you're not with me, you're fired." Before anyone could react, General Markos, the head of Cyberwarfare, burst through the doors to the staff conference room.

"I apologize for interrupting, but you need to turn on your main monitor," he stammered. When nobody moved, he went to the control panel for the monitor himself.

"Markos, what's the meaning of this?" the Chief of Operations snapped. "You'll be reprimanded for interrupting a high level meeting-"

"Enough," Hausnerr said. "Markos, I'm sure you have a good reason, but do you mind explaining yourself before barging into a general staff meeting?"

"Again, I apologize," he said. "But you'll see in just a few moments, well ok it's Admiral Von Braun, he's alive on Deimos, and he's putting out a broadcast any minute now." Before long, the Cyber Chief had the secure line to Deimos open.

The Admiral's bald head shone under the light of what looked to be a control room. He stood by himself in a work uniform, a black jumpsuit and jacket along with his ship's cap, a baseball style hat with a silhouette of a battleship with the words TNV-*Franz Ferdinand* embroidered on the top.

So he is alive. Somehow, I was certain a gas attack of that nature would spell doom for all on the moon. The old man cleared his throat and began to speak.

13

Reiter couldn't believe his ears. *How did the Fleet Admiral live? More importantly, how is he getting this broadcast across the Mars Sphere?* As soon as Comidus picked up the broadcast, he patched the rest of the company through so they could all hear as well.

"Friends, Allies, Countryman and women, first let me begin by informing the Mars Sphere that Deimos's civilian and military population narrowly avoided disaster. Over four hundred thousand souls have gone before our creator today, and I will soon join them."

"Here, at my life's end, I am not afraid for my own sake, but for the fate of my homeland. It has been over a century since our people fled their homes and eventually fled across the ocean of space to find a new home, free from tyranny, whether that tyranny came from a swastika, or from a sickle and hammer. But, tyranny lives in the hearts of men, and thus we shouldn't have been surprised when tyranny reared it's ugly head, bearing the banner of a gear and atom." The old man sighed, and across the vast distance, Reiter could feel the weight on him.

"Even as I speak, we face an adversary that grinds its own people into the dirt, they disregard their lives to the extent that they manufacture them, stripe away their humanity as best they can, only in naming these poor souls does the Union give them any dignity. Even as their hordes sweep over Roosevelt, Swallow Olympia, and sink their vile claws into my homeland, even as I stand here, moments from meeting the great architect of creation, I urge not just the Tharcian, not just the Olympian, the Rooseveltier, or even the Vinnish, who find themselves attacked, do not let all of our lives go in vain."

Von Braun's voice rose on the last word and began building to a crescendo. "I urge the lot of you, to fight in Tharsis, to bring them to battle in the belt, in every sphere of mankind, and if, and I do not believe it, even if, Tharsis herself fell, every colony and even this moon itself, would not bend until the Union has been broken. Godspeed Tharsis! Godspeed Vinland! Godspeed to every man, woman, and child that cries out for a freer world!" The broadcast suddenly cut off.

"He looked rough at the end there," Comidus said. "And I thought I saw gas leaking into the room." Reiter shook his head.

"Well damn, I want to go after the Unis right now," Webb said. "Can they hurry up and come to us?"

"Ride that high, everyone," Reiter said. "The unis will be here before we know it." *The casualties were supposed to be way higher up on Deimos. Maybe he had something to do with the lower numbers?* The Regimental network chimed.

"Heads up, people," Hawke said. "Intelligence has multiple offensives along the front, they're taking the bait." *Which means we'll be under fire soon.*

"Alright everyone, I hope you made your peace with the Lord,"

Reiter said. "Because here they come." *Are we really prepared for this? What if those 'Red Guards' show up?* He took a few steadying breaths. *If they do show up, they'll learn a thing or two about gunships and mortars.*

"Forward elements of 4-14 got activity near the bridges," Hawke said. "Operation Coal Stock has begun." Reiter's grip on his sticks tightened.

"Did you take care of those nerves white 1?" he asked.

"Roger Fox 6," Kozma replied. "I feel like these boys and girls wanna take on the whole Union army by themselves."

He grinned. "Let's settle for the division ahead of us," he replied. Reiter glanced at his picture of Fletcher and then back at his map. *Now there's nothing to do but wait.*

SOMETHING HAUSNERR LONG THOUGHT DEAD STIRRED INSIDE HIM. Watching Von Braun's final words left the man with a cool relief, all the tension left him and a cool smile played across his face. "Muster the air fleet," he said. "Commence Operation Babel, Markos, as soon as the fleet is launched, prepare to launch Operation Mayhem as soon as they break off their attack." He turned back towards the General Staff. "After hearing that man's last words, if you still want to cower in your office while our nation fights for its life, there's the door."

The Signals chief immediately rose from the table. "You've lost your mind," he said. "I'm taking a principled stand against you."

"So be it," Hausnerr said. "You'll do so from the unemployment line." He looked around. "Anyone else?"

The Operations and personnel chiefs also stood to leave. "Just you wait Hausnerr, dignity will be restored to the office of Marshall," The Operations chief said.

"Good luck replacing us," Personnel spat. "I hope you're happy wasting lives." Markos moved to follow them out, but Hausnerr stopped him.

"Markos," he said, loud enough for the disgraced staff to hear. "Go ahead and take the signals seat, you're due for promotion, anyway." As the portly general sat, he called in an attendant from outside. "Promote the deputy Chiefs of Operations and deputy Chief of Personnel, we have new seats available." He looked down at the staff table. "Any others."

The Training chief shook her head. "Von Braun's words moved me. You were correct Marshall." The Remaining General Staff nodded in agreement.

"Well then, now we have a lot of work to do," he said. "I want 4th Army's plan on my desk in an hour, nice me the other Army commanders, we need to turn this into a much larger counteroffensive." The General Staff dissolved as they returned to their various offices to whip the Army back in shape, and Markos to wreck the Union's network infrastructure."

"Excuse me, Marshall Hausnerr," a young Major said. "President Reinhardt is on the line, she wants to speak with you." Hausnerr nodded and took the phone line from the man. Motioning for the aide to follow him, he walked into the hallway towards his office.

"Hausnerr speaking," he said.

"I can't believe that man Von Braun," the President said. "Congress is debating an armistice resolution right now, it looks like it's going to be defeated on the floor, but I'd like you to speak on the floor, really drive home the spirt of Von Braun's message."

"How long will they be debating the resolution?" he said. "Because I have to review battle plans and completely redo our war plans, on top of that we have major bombing attacks and a cyber attack underway."

"If the peace faction isn't crushed, then they will continue to be a thorn in our side through this war," The President said.

Hausnerr sighed. "We'll crush them madame President, but it will be with a victory that makes their words hollow and a spirit that makes their faction bankrupt."

"Marshall!" Another aide cried as he ran down the hall. "Marshall!"

"Excuse me, madame President," he said. "What is it, young man?"

"Major fleet engagements, in the belt and at Lagrange 7," he gasped. "It looks like they're trying to avenge Von Braun."

The field Marshall folded his arms. "Well, let's hope they're following an established plan and not simply acting out of emotion," he said. Thanking the man, he returned to his phone call with the President. "Madame President, if they're still debating in two hours, I'll be there to say a few words." He handed the phone back to the aide who handed him a tablet as they walked into the sunny atrium of the Citadel. "What's this?"

"I apologize sir, it's the battle plans you requested," the young Major said. "They were able to set all this up thanks to intelligence gained by guerrillas in the hinterlands." Hausnerr did his best to hide his surprise, but before him lay the entire Union battle plan, as well as the Tharcian one to exploit it.

"This is amazing," he said. "This is the most complete intelligence report I have ever seen, thank you Major…"

"Starnes," the Major replied. "I was your predecessor's aide until I found myself stuck with the front line, took them a while to realize I was there too, bastards."

With a chuckle, the Marshall clapped him on the back. "Well, I think we've found you some new employment, Major Starnes."

As Guard-Brigadier Erika Meyer entered the communications tent, Irving's parting words echoed in her mind. "Landfall is in danger, they isolated us and we're vulnerable," the younger woman gasped as medics loaded her into a truck and sent her to the rear. With her mind snapping back to the present, she dragged her boots through the freezing mud to the soldiers struggling to restore a radio set.

"Status?" She asked. The younger of the two, a treacly man, shook his head.

"Negative comrade," he said. "We've got power, but all of our encryption equipment is useless."

His companion nodded her head. "When the shells hit, they lost synchronization with the wider network, even though our radios work again, we can't send out any messages until we load an encryption, which's it stands now is impossible."

Cradling her head in her hands, Meyer rubbed her temples with her bony fingers. "So what you're saying is none of our long range communications can get a message off because we can't encrypt them?"

"More or less," the male comms sergeant said. "If we had even one radio with an active encryption card, we could load the current encryption key before it changes in seven hours." Meyer cast her gaze to the encroaching dusk outside as a chill wind swept through the tent.

Then she had an idea. "You said you needed an active encryption key," she said. "Would there one in my panzerter count?" The younger man raised an eyebrow.

"I though you'd only use it in case of emergency," he said. "You kept the radio keys up to date?"

She nodded. "It was one of your late predecessor's duties," she said. "If I needed to sortie, I would need working and encrypted radios." The female comms sergeant picked up one of the bulky encryption banks from their table.

"If her encryption is still good, we can load the long range radios and talk to the other battalions," she said. "Though I couldn't your panzerter do that if it's loaded?"

"My panzerter has a maximum range of 12 kilometers," Meyer replied. "The long range here more than doubles that, and I want to be sure all the battalions can hear us at once, but as a last resort yes, we can use the panzerters radio."

The comms sergeants followed her to her personal machine. Her Martian Commander knelt in a narrow side street. Even with the shortened distance to the cockpit, the comms sergeants struggled to climb up into it. Meyer rolled her eyes when they finally climbed beside her, gasping for air.

"I don't know how you pilots do it," the male on said.

"They make it look so easy," his companion gasped.

"Can we focus?" Meyer asked as she started her panzerter and opened a panel, revealing the communications hook-ups. While the comms sergeants tested her encryption, Meyer decided to run a test of her own.

She brought the Martian to a standing position, a move that frustrated the comms sergeants. From their, he put on her helmet and keyed up the mike. "Any Leviathan element, this is Leviathan 6, do you read me?" No answer. Curling her lip, she tried again. "Any Leviathan element, this is Leviathan 6, can you hear me?"

"Leviathan 6, Grendel 3, we got you Lima Charlie, Reaper actual sent us to find you guys." Meyer snapped forward. *Kennedy delayed the attack, which is good, we can still attack all at once.*

"Grendel 3, pass on this message to Reaper, attack as planned, all units go." She smiled, satisfied in her work. "Hurry up with the keys," she said. "If they need division level support, we need to be able to provide it, besides we have reports we need to send."

"We're hurrying," they said. "We're just about done."

Meyer smiled. "Excellent, when you finish, crawl onto the hand and I'll lower you to the ground."

"You're not getting out, comrade Brigadier?" the female asked. Meyer shook her head.

"I suspect an attack is coming, and I'll be the last line of defense for this headquarters element," she said. "I want everyone prepared to go mobile, this town could be attacked any moment." *But why hasn't it?* Landfall itself remained incredibly vulnerable since they'd been shelled just before noon. It wasn't like the Tharcians were far, their forces occupied Grunbeck a mere ten kilometers away.

Why shell an urban area if you're not going to take it? You're only destroying the infrastructure you'd need after retaking it. Then understanding dawned on her. *They knew our command post was here.*

———————

"I'M GLAD WE SET ALL THIS UP IN CONGREGATION," CHANEY SAID as he entered a meeting room with Ballard and some other members of the Phoboian team. " A Massive Air Fleet is headed towards Foundation, in fact, that might be the only thing left when they're done."

The Lead Engineer frowned. "Comrade Chaney, please don't joke about the destruction of our great capital, it's tragic that war has ravaged the other founding cities."

Chaney shook his head. "IRS took your sense of humor, huh? Any way how's the simulation going?"

"No sortie's yet," Ballard replied. "They're still adding combat data from the Black Knight and Tharcian units."

"Well, you can relax at some of those numbers," Chaney said. "The Black Knight will beat just about any panzerter we throw at it one on one, which is why we'll focus on beating it twelve to one."

"That seems to callously waste pilots lives," one engineer said.

Chaney shrugged. "As far as we can tell they've only built one that's combat capable, any way please continue." Once they'd loaded all the data they felt they could, Ballard crawled into the sim pod and took the controls."

Someone knocked on the door, rapid fire. "I wanna see, I wanna see, I wanna see!" Penny exclaimed as she bolted into the observation room. Chaney sighed and shook his head.

"Shouldn't you be learning physics?" he asked. Penny pouted.

"Ms. Lopez said daddy was going to be fighting a computer," she said. Chaney glanced up at her tutor and sighed.

"Well, I guess today we can have a more *applied* lesson," he said. "But please don't interrupt your dad when he's working ok?" Penny sat on an empty table as they watched the monitors, her legs swinging over the edge.

The Phobian appeared inside a Central Tharcian cityscape. With its narrow streets and clustered buildings, it more heavily resembled their original homelands in Central and Eastern Europe than a typical Tharcian town or city. The perfect place to test the Phobian's abilities.

To the untrained eye, it superficially resembled a Martian. It possessed the same 360 sensor ring and rugged aesthetic. But a seeker form, a lower smaller head with a rotating AA machine gun, smoke dischargers along the chest and shoulders, a 105-mm shotgun, and laser lenses on the chest marked it as a new breed of Union Panzerter.

Before he could witness the Phobian engage any enemies, an attendant grabbed his shoulder. "Your Special Guest is here, he wants to speak with you." Chaney scowled.

"Fine, I'll go talk to him, save me a replay of this run though," he said. Leaving the sterile simulation room, he walked to his office in the Research Complex. His office, a spartan and bare one compared to the one in his home, sat in an isolated corner of the complex. All the better, so no one would see his guest.

"What do you have this time Agent Thorn?" he asked. The man who sat on his desk, a grizzled man with an eyepatch, leered at him. "We're performing some rather important tests."

The spy stood up and approached him. "I thought you would want to see this," he said. "Could be the key to solving a lot of our problems." As he spoke, he unzipped a pocket on his jacket and handed Chaney a frozen vial. On closer inspection, the vial contained a stalk of grain in cryostasis.

"What is this? And where did you find this?" He asked. Thorn paced over to his desk and turned on the news, cranking the volume as he did.

"Vinland, I was there to scope out some medical technology when I stumbled on that," he said. "To my understanding, it's a strain of super grain that can stay alive even in low-light and extreme cold."

"Like Congregation," Chaney said before frowning. "GMOs are illegal, I doubt we can get this through the National TUC." Thorn just shook his head.

"Which is ridiculous, we can create super soldiers, but not super foodstuffs?" A predatory smile played at his thin lips. "Well, I think the TUC and the NC are going to change their tune soon."

Chaney heard the news cast behind him, but it took a moment for the information to sink in. He turned to see a nightmare playing out on the monitor. Sections of the orbital elevator burned. People below screamed as debris fell from miles above them. Tharcian airships and drones pummeled the massive structure.

Did Thorn know about this? He turned to question the man, but he was gone. *Already off to his next assignment, I guess, best I get back to work too.*

IN THE DISTANCE, A BATTLE RAGED IN THE SNOWY NIGHT. YET Kennedy felt eerily calm in the cockpit of his Jupiter. Under the watchful eye of himself and the Red Guard, their own artillery and AA assets moved down the state road towards Autobahn 12.

A few kilometers away, South of the intersection ahead of them, Several IFVs winked out on Kennedy's Command Matrix. "We're under panzerter attack!" Spears cried over the radio. "

"Incubus 6, take your company and swing south by Southeast," Kennedy replied. "Flank the enemy attacking Jericho." *Spears is a smart guy, he knows to get out of the kill zone.* "Harpy, begin your advance along your lane, Centaur Battery, prepare to fire immediate suppression if Jericho makes contact again."

Thy stopped on the road so the battery's Sagitaruis Mobile Artillery Systems could prepare to fire. Sure enough, the sounds of combat echoed throughout the dark forest, enough to the point Kennedy relived most of the battalion had been engaged.

"Reaper 6, Auger 1, BDA follows," Jackson said. Kennedy gave him the go-ahead, curious about what the scouts had encountered. "Our dismounts used out and destroyed a missile carrier and a recon track with rockets, their actions stirred up another section of two vehicles, of which we destroyed the recon vehicle, but the second missile carrier evaded us, 2 enemy tracks destroyed, five dismounts killed."

Kennedy shook his head. *Good infantry are hard to replace.* The artillery shook his machine as the big guns sent a salvo of smoke shells to cover Spear's advance down Autobahn 12. "Now, let's go," Kennedy said as he brought his Jupiter to a run. He swung his strobe laser south, just to be sure some bold Tharcian didn't slip buy.

"Reaper 6, Incubus 6, We've killed four panzerters, disabled a fish, a destroyed two tracked vehicles after losing three Martians," Bear said.

Before Kennedy could respond, shells struck the gas station and ignited the massive fuel cell below. A clam of fire and noise tossed him onto his back as he screamed. His ears rang as the ground around him pulsed and vibrated. As dirt and debris pummeled his cameras, Kennedy struggled to clear his head and stand.

When the salvo finally seized, He was disappointed to see both Hydra SAM carriers were a total loss. While his Jupiter had taken a beating, it's rugged armor and tough systems held up. As he got his machine on it's feet, he called out to Centaur Battery. "Give me counter-fires now!" He glanced at his command matrix for a better idea of the situation and was disappointed to see the screen spider-webbed.

"Reaper 5, my matrix is out, keep me updated," Kennedy said. "Headquarters, spread out, now." A rapid beep drew his attention to his sensors. His Air Radar tracked four rapidly approaching aircraft from the Southeast. *Drones? Impossible, the weather hasn't been clear long enough for them to launch.*

Despite his objections, four Tharcian drones streaked towards them just over treetop height. Bombs left out from under their wings, savaging the headquarters element even further. The Jupiter's retaliated as the drones circled back for another pass.

One went up in a ball of fire as his strobe laser found it's fuel cell. More vehicles beneath him ignited as the drones cannons punched through their thin roof armor. Another flew to low and Snow managed to maple it on her harpoon.

Kennedy took a quick survey of the damage. His artillery burned alongside Halphen's mobile HQ. The Hydra that survived the fueling station explosion had been lost in the follow son barrage. *We've lost our support units, but now me and the Red Guards are free to maneuver since we don't have to protect them.*

"Red 1, get your people moving," he said. "We're going to shore up Jericho." As the Guard acknowledged him and ran past, he took a quick survey of their armament. Knight carried a strobe laser like he did, while Snow wielded a machine-gun when she stowed her harpoon. Last, but not least Khan carried a submachine gun and a recoilless rifle.

Kennedy followed them, careful to keep an eye out for friendly forces. "Reaper 6, Jericho 6, it looks like the enemy is beginning to with-" Spears was cut off by a hiss of static. A nearby explosion didn't encourage Kennedy to the man's survival.

When they caught up to the infantry, they found them held up on the hills halfway to their objective. Flashes and explosions off in the forest to his left told him Incubus company had found the enemy as well. Smoking wrecks of tracked vehicles of both sides lined the road.

A Tharcian IFV poked out around a hill, only to burst into flames as green light struck it. As they crested the hills, the Tharcains broke into a full retreat. Kennedy noticed the light of engines heading south, but before he could engage them, something flew past his head and slammed into Snow.

Her Jupiter doubled over, smoke pouting out of the hole torn by the shell. More shells left out of the woodline towards them. "Fan out, shield Snow's machine from further damage," Kennedy said.

He could see them now. Four panzerters in the woodline. Three of them welded normal rifles while the fourth lay prone with a sniper rifle. They formed a firing line in the trees just to the southeast of their position. Fortunately, the hills protected Snow from follow on fire.

Kennedy broke left while the two remaining Red Guards went

right. Their strobe lasers filled the dark night with eerie green light as they incinerated trees and vaporized snow. One such pulse found a magazine, and a Thracian panzerter lit up the sky.

Khan poured smaller shells into the sniper as he closed. Despite not penetrating, they dented and dinged its armor enough to convince it to move. After a short, but furious exchange, all four Thracian panzerters lay in burning molten heaps.

After catching his breath, Kennedy realized that the remaining Tharcians had given him the slip. With a frustrated growl, he slammed his fist into his busted matrix and opened the net. "All Reaper elements, give me a SITREP, now, as soon as I have your status, send MEDEVAC and prepare to hold the door for the 88th."

While people he hadn't met personally rattled off the status of their company, Kennedy glimpsed his helmeted face in the reflection of his broken matrix. *I look like hell, but I feel so alive.* He shook his head as the reports finished. *We're a shell of our former strength, I doubt we'd repulse any serious counterattack, but we do what we have to do. We have to win.*

14

As the battered cavalry troop rolled past, Reiter looked on in shock. Most of their frontline units had either been destroyed or broken down as they retreated past Ironton. One of the IFCs, he recognized it as an Iglasio Command Track, pulled off of the Autobahn into his position. The man in the hatch waved his hands and Reiter shifted the Lowe to kneel closer to him.

With a snap and a hiss, the cockpit opened and Reiter stepped out, a few feet above the Troop Commander. "Hey what happened back there?" He asked.

The other Captain pointed north, where Reiter saw the dim glow of fire on the horizon. "They hit us pretty hard, the regiment that attacked us had those heavy panzerters, so good news is you shouldn't see them when they come here, but it looks like another armor regiment is going to roll through."

Reiter nodded as he took in the information. "Roger thanks for the heads up, we're going to try to make them attack into the town itself," he replied. "Do you need help to evacuate your wounded?"

The Cavalry commander shook his head. "Negative, we got

most of them into dropships and got them out of there, hey we're going to screen your rear, what's your radio freq?"

He gave the other man his radio information, then held up a hand for him to wait. "Make sure your guys stay on the autobahn when they pass through. The forest ahead of us is mined, as are most of the streets branching off of the autobahn."

The other man flashed him a thumbs up before rolling off to his south. "Fox 6, Wolfhound 1, our recon flights have another armor regiment heading towards Autobahn 12. Want me to say hello?"

I don't want to overplay my hand, but thinning out the herd does seem tempting. Or, I have a better target in mind. "Wolfhound, do your drones have enough range to get to the bridges over the Grenze?" he asked.

"Roger 6, it would be close because their entire AA support will be gunning for us," the gunship pilot replied. "But it sounds like you want them blown."

"Exactly," Reiter replied. "If you can make it happen, do it." *That should slow down any reinforcements for a while.* Artillery rumpled in the distance, and Reiter checked his map.

The Cavalry troops adjacent to the one that just rolled past launched a local counterattack against the Union salient. Further to the south, a Union Mechanized regiment tangled with the Cavalry at Riverside. Their own Mechanized regiment, garrisoned at Narrowfield, launched a two pronged attack, one aimed at knocking out the command elements, the other seeking to hit the Union infantry in the flank.

A different roar filled the air near them. Reiter looked at his air radar. Multiple bogeys approaching at high angles and high speed. *Drones? No, they're too small. Missiles.*

"Incoming!" Someone screamed into the radio. Reiter made the Lowe as small a target as he could while the ground shook. As the roar of the fire and chaos rumbled around him, Reiter noticed the missiles stayed outside of Ironton.

That wasn't meant for us, that was for Early and Giant. "Fox Company, SITREP?" Hawke asked. After conferring with hie platoon leaders, Reiter's suspicions were confirmed. Fox company, and Ironton were intact.

"Fox 6, we're green to green," Reiter replied. "That didn't look like it was for us."

"No, Early and Giant got pretty bloodied up though," Hawke said. "Good news is it looks like the Union are using those discount tinhats rather than the ones from the initial invasion." *Good, we stand a chance.*

"Listen up, Fox," he said. "The enemy is going to try to encircle us, we need to do everything possible to force them to fight us inside the town."

"We've got 3 watching a firebreak with his sniper rifle," Wesser said. "If they want to flank us, they'll have to cross that kill zone."

"We have a similar setup with the westbound road," Kozma said.

"We may not have panzerter sized armaments," Stovepipe said. "But we do have giant-killer missiles, that'll teach them to fuck around."

"Hey, we have a few of those too," Wolfhound 1 said.

"Good, all the better to keep them from by passing us too easily," Reiter said. "Lysak, if you get a target light it up for the mortars and gunships." He heard a screaming overhead. Looking up, he saw drones fitted with drop tanks flying towards the Union's rear. *Good, it's about time we evened the odds.*

WHILE THE EARLIER MISSILE BOMBARDMENT HAD BEEN IMPRESSIVE, Kennedy frowned when he saw the Taurus APCs roll past him. "Victor 6, Reaper 6, I didn't know you were dragging Taurus's into battle," he said.

"They're great," Guard-Colonel Fuller replied. "They're easier to get then Capricorns and they hold more people." Kennedy looked over from the Taurus's to the Martian Commander across from him.

"You had a choice between the two, and you picked the APCs?" he asked. "Their armor doesn't hold up against most Tharcian weapons. If you use them aggressively, you'll take heavy losses and your infantry will have to walk back from the airport if things go sideways."

"No, they will not," he said. "Worse comes to worst, our drop-ships can evacuate them, but we plan on encircling the city before the Tharcians can regroup, even if they can't take the airport, they have a haven in Ironton a short distance away."

Kennedy furrowed his brow. "So they're going to walk, all the way from here in their kit, attack the airport, and then if they fail, walk to Ironton?"

"Well, that's assuming they fail to take their objectives," Fuller replied. "My soldiers will triumph over the enemy."

Kennedy surveyed his own battalion as the other man spoke. Most of his leadership lay dead. Ivin still lived, but she was down to three Martian troopers while incubus Company was currently being led by a Sergeant with four panzerters under his command. All but one of his SP howitzers burned near the crater that marked the location of the fuel depot, while nothing could be found of his mobile SAMs. *At least my Recon Platoon and a few of the infantry tracks lived.*

He shook his head. A dozen riflemen with half as many tracks along with a single SP Gun and a handful of panzerters hardly made a battalion. "Well, don't be overconfident, the Tharcians did a number on my battalion and we didn't have nearly as many objectives as you."

Glancing back at his forces, he scowled. *If there's any serious counterattack, we won't be able to hold them off, Fuller needs to take his objectives in a few hours or he'll be surrounded when a Tharcian counterattack pushes us across the river.*

"All reaper elements, keep an eye to the sky," he said. "The weather is clearing up, and we're going to see a lot more drones." As the last vehicle from the 88th crossed the southern intersection, Kennedy tightened his grip on the controls.

That Missile barrage was impressive to look at, but did he actually do any damage to the enemy? If Kennedy had access to the Orion MLRS that the 88th had, he would have used their ability to scatter mines or bomblets across the battlefield rather than just pound hypothetical enemy positions with airbursts or high explosives.

He unzipped the shoulder pocket of his CVC shirt and removed a pack of cigarettes and a lighter. *I haven't smoked since the Battle for FOB Blake, guess I haven't been that stressed in a while.* After lighting the thick cigarette, he took a long drag and exhaled. *Not too much, good.*

"Reaper 6, we got movement form the Northwest," Jackson said. "Looks like advanced forces for a larger element." Kennedy took another long drag on his cigarette before putting it out.

"Alright then," he said. "Let's let them have it." The probing force had been sensibly put together: Three IFVS and two panzerters. While his Recon platoon evaded detection, Kennedy held off on using his artillery, preferring to keep his last gun hidden rather than use it right out the gate.

Instead, he and Knight took up a blocking position on the north side of the Autobahn. While the fresh Tharcian panzerters could match the Martian troopers most of their forces used, the Jupiter outclassed them in armament and armor. Sure enough, their shells bounced off his armor at long range while his strobe laser took them apart rather handily.

As their panzerter support died, the Tharcians IFVs pulled back. Relaxing only slightly, Kennedy gazed off into the cold night. *They're coming, they're somewhere out there, but they're coming.* With snow coming to a gentle rest on his machine, he tried to focus.

On the hum of his engine. On the whispers of wind outside his metal shell. On the distant rumble of weapons fire. Anything to make the dullness looming over him. As his eyelids grew heavy, he fought a battle he didn't think possible. A war on exhaustion.

***

UNLIKE ARTILLERY, MORTARS DIDN'T MAKE MUCH NOISE IN THE AIR. The small fact gave Sergeant Mondragon some sympathy for the Union scouts currently under attack by the mortar platoon. *It's also unnerving. If I can't hear them in flight, how will I know when they undershoot?* He shook his head, causing his helmet to shift uncomfortably on his head. *At that point, it really isn't my problem anymore.*

"We got panzerters coming around the hill," Merlin sr said. "Looks like they're looking for an opening." His wingman's panzerter lay prone inside the frame of someone's garage with the rear wall knocked out. Mo's unit itself took a knee behind a large manor style home a short distance away.

"Hold your fire, Black 3," Wesser said over the radio. Their team leader and Smith held a position at the Western end of the neighborhood while a squad of drop troopers crawled about…somewhere. "We don't want to give away your position unless absolutely necessary."

"Is tinhats at 1500 meters necessary?" Their team sniper asked.

"Negative," Wesser replied. "Keep your cool 3."

"Easy for you to say," Merlin muttered. The three tinhats finally came into view of Mo as well. They traveled in the dip between two hills, giving them partial cover.

"They're looking for the scouts," Mo said. "Do we tell grey-hound to move?"

Suddenly a jet of fire whooshed out of the woodline, striking the lead tinhat. The Panzerter staggered and swept the forest with its laser rifle.

Merlin reacted first. A shell smashed into the knee of the lead panzerter, sending it sprawling to the forest floor.

With the leader down, the remaining tinhats split off and ran to either side of their formation. Mo's rifle came up. Two shots. Both glanced. As he blew his cover, Smith and Wesser traded shots with the other panzerter.

While their rifles didn't always penetrate the tinhats armor at range, Mo's innovative snowbags had countered the laser weapons these three welded. When the tinhat's took a shot, their green beams only found a sandbag filled with snow. The Snowball would melt into steam or burst, absorbing and scattering the energy of the laser.

Though he had no issue penetrating their armor, Mo knew Merlin struggled to hit targets actively trying to evade him. The older man's sniper rifle wove back and forth, struggling in vain to line up a shot.

Finally, one of Mo's shells demolished their opponent's rifle in a flash of light and metal. After a brief pause, a 155-mm shell struck the panzerter center of mass. With a roar and a blast of flame, the tinhat collapsed into the woods.

A short distance away, the last tinhat charged Smith and Wesser. Shells pummeled its armored form, occasionally pene-trating to the sensitive components beneath. Even in the dark night, Mo knew the union machine was belching smoke as sensitive parts burned. Their teammate's shells began penetrating more and more frequently.

Without warning, the entire top of the panzerter's head lost itself in a flash of heat and light. Like a puppet with its strings cut, the tinhat went limp before collapsing.

Mo relaxed his rip on the control sticks, not realizing how tight he'd gripped them. As he looked over the smoldering wrecks, he shook his head in disgust. *How many of you are like Fletcher or Ballard, I wonder? They really grew you, raised you, and all for this?* Gingerly, he rubbed his tense hands. *I can't believe it, something like that on that scale, it's just too cruel.*

In a morbid sense, it reminded him of a fish farm. *They've got plenty of those up there, maybe that's where they got the crossover?* He took off his helmet and rubbed the sweat out of his hair with a gloved hand. *Except people aren't fish, you can't do that to them.*

"Heads up, black team," Merlin said. "I've got more contacts, wide formation, and they outnumber us seven to one!" in seconds, Mo clipped his helmet back on and looked at his own sensors.

"Remember the plan, guys," Wesser said. "Bend don't break, Three, how many of those contacts look like panzerters?"

"If I'm spit balling, many twelve to fourteen?" Merlin replied. "Lot's of ground vehicles."

"I'm not worried about ground vehicles," Mo said. "Unless they've got Anti-air, then that's an issue for our gunships and dropships."

Mo heard a click and realized Wesser switched her mic over to the company net. "Wolfhound 1, can you get drones in the air?"

INFORMATION IS AMMUNITION. THE SAYING, ENGRAVED IN THE BACK of Reiter's skull since his days at the OMI, meant exactly that. The more you knew about you, your situation, your enemy, the more the odds ticked in your favor.

However, staring at his map left the man desiring more of both. The approaching panzerter battalion clearly intended to encircle the township, possibly to bypass them and drive on the airport to their southeast. The Mortars already reported using a quarter of their shells to destroy the enemy recognizance platoon and focused on delivering more to the main Union body.

The gunships released their drones in an attempt to gauge the anti-aircraft capabilities of this particular group. As the four triangles sped across his map, Reiter blinked and three of them vanished with the fourth suddenly making a series of dramatic and furious turns.

"Wolfhound 1, what happened?" he asked.

"We're in trouble 6," Wolfhound replied. "2 got a good look at the launchers before his drone went down, it's a mobile SAM reporting name "King Cobra", and the bad news is we can't medevac or fly as long as they're around."

"What?" Reiter replied. "But it's at least five kilometers away!"

"They're bad news, boss," Wolfhound replied. "Us, our drones, and our dropships are out if we can't take care of them." *It's ok, you don't have to, we have other people for that.*

"Black 1, Greyhound 1, did either of you get a bead on where those launchers came from?" he asked.

"They're both pretty well inside the formation," Wesser replied. "We can't really target them without exposing black team to fire from the entire battalion." *Damn.*

"Let me get my Charlie squad on the phone," Webb said. "They've got enough rockets to hunt those damn things down and light them up." Reiter bit his lip and checked his map. If that squad moved out of position, they'd basically ceded the neighboured to the Union as soon as the panzerters moved.

"Greyhound?" Reiter said. "Can you do anything?"

"Nope," Lysak said. "We can't risk our tracks to attack them." Reiter wanted nothing more than to punch the stubborn old fool through the radio. Compared to their dropships, their ticket to the hospital, if things went south, the tracks were hardly a loss.

But I can't demand people sacrifice themselves. How would I be any different from the Union? He looked at the recon platoon on his map. Further forward, than any other element, they sat in a wide line just off the autobahn.

Then two of them started moving. At first Reiter thought they'd just shifted position and his map hadn't updated yet. But they sped on. Directly towards the Union position.

"Greyhound, what's going on?" he asked.

"Mutiny!" The older man spat. "Treason! Insubordination!"

"What are they doing?"

"Giving away my position!" Lysak howled. "They're out to betray us!"

A glance at the map cast doubt on the man's accusations. If they looked to betray them, they'd missed a golden opportunity to slit the throats of the other scouts and leave them blind to the enemy. Now, in search of his own answers, he hailed them.

"This is Fox 6," he said, and as calmly as he could add, "What are you doing?"

"Fox 6, this is Greyhound 3," one of the crews replied. "We've been tracking what's going on with these King Cobras, and we're not about to let them torch our air cover." Reiter sighed.

"You recognize how dangerous that is?" he replied and noticed Wolfhound launch the last of their drones.

"We'll lose the city without gunships," Greyhound 3 replied. "Now, oh shi-" One of the tracks disappeared from his map as the other wove around and eventually broke contact with the union heading west.

As his stomach sank beneath his chair, Reiter looked at his memorial wall, more specifically at his photo of Bruno "Gos" Lugosi. *Here I am again Gos, not making decisions, not being decisive, not being go-*

"Scratch one!" Wolfhound 1 said. "And the other King Cobra looks pretty banged up. We may be out of drones, but we can fly without having to worry about anti-air, at least for now." Reiter sat up in his chair. *They didn't go down for nothing.*

"All units," he said. "Brace for enemy action, Wolfhound, what are they up to?"

"Looks like a big pincer," the gunship pilot replied. "The right flank is about to crash into the seam between Black and White team."

***

MO SHIFTED AND CROUCHED BEHIND A MANOR HOUSE. AS HE AND Merlin played down covering fire, Wesser and Smith moved to get a better angle on their attackers. In the face of about a half-dozen tinhats, their fire wasn't enough to disable or destroy the unit, but enough to keep them ducking.

One hapless Union pilot failed to duck quick enough. For his trouble, a fat shell smashed the machine's hips to scrap. *They. Just. Keep. Coming.*

More shells joined theirs, telling Mo that Smith and Wesser sat in position. "Their main assaults about to begin," The LT said. "Let's hope they go where we want them to."

"And if they don't?" Mo asked as steam clouded his vision. The Union panzerters advanced slowly and steadily, grinding away at the buildings they used for cover. As they implacably marched and fired down a side street leading into the neighborhood, the road beneath them suddenly gave way.

Panzerters staggered and fell, some more than others. One unfortunate tinhat lay on its back after shells had smashed its knees, flailing about like a tortoise. More shells pummeled the Union armored column, but this time from White Team. Kozma charged forward alongside Merlin JR. Their combined fire knocking out tinhat after tinhat in close quarters.

"They're too close!" Merlin sr cried. "We can't provide supporting fire with them at that range." Mo grit his teeth and glanced at Wesser's machine. *This is all going according to plan. Too well, in fact.*

Then a green glow fell across Kozma's machine. Its head vanished in a shower of molten metal and it collapsed backward. A tinhat hoisted itself up with its laser drawn, shifting to Merlin Jr as he ran to recover his team leader's machine.

The world seemed to slow down. Merlin sr, in a desperate bid to protect his brother, fired his sniper rifle. While he'd eliminated the threat to his brother, a closer tinhat realized he had a sniper rifle. This immobilized tinhat retaliated with its machine gun.

An explosion tossed debris skyward as Merlin's magazine detonated. His panzerter crashed to the snow next to him, missing a hand, portions of its head, and all of its snowbags.

Tossing radio etiquette to the wind, Mo cried out to him. "Wes! Wes! Are you ok?" His radio came back with static before they could hear a ragged cough over the net.

"I'm good, nothing a tourniquet and a dentist couldn't fix," he replied. As he updated his team, the serving panzerters broke off their attack. Two machines in the forest laid down covering fire while another tinhat dragged their immobile but operational comrade back into the woodline, leaving three panzerters burning in a collapsed street.

"Black Team, Wildcard 2, we're going to search the wrecks for anything useful and see if we can get White 1 medevaced." Mo nodded as Wesser acknowledged the drop troopers. *It's good to have these guys around.* As he peered over the crumbling manor, he spotted something moving in the woodline.

"Wildcard 2, Black 4," he said. "Do you have people in the woods?"

"Negative 4, we're all in the neighborhood," the squad leader replied. "Got something?" Switching to his thermal sights allowed him to see the figures much better. Against the cold trees, the union infantry stood out like a shark among tuna.

"Yeah," he said. "Looks like we've got some company in the tree line."

"Well hell, there's a big ass pool room in this house," Wildcard replied. "Invite them out of the cold!"

"Yeah," Merlin sr said. "Let's warm them up."

"I'll start at ten, you start at one, meet you halfway," Mo replied as he engaged his chest mounted machine-gun. Red tracers lit up the night like searchlights as they swept through the trees. Thanks to his thermal sights, Mo could see the union infantry diving and dropping into the snow. Whether it was from being hit by their machine guns or an attempt to avoid them remained unclear.

As they let their gun barrels cool, Mo surveyed the terrain ahead of him. Despite not seeing any new movement or heat sources, he still felt uneasy. "Alright Wildcard, go survey the wrecks, see if the Union left anything salvageable." He looked over at Wes Merlin's panzerter. "Black 3, you should fall back since you lost your weapon."

"I was actually going to snatch one of those Union machine guns," he replied. "The panzerter sized ones, not people sized."

"That's actually not a bad idea," Wesser said as she and Smith moved back to their original position. "A panzerter scale MG nest would be something else." Mo looked out ahead of them. *Yeah, I suppose it would.*

15

The left flank of the Union's pincer attack fared hardly better than the right. Their panzerters emerged from the forests surrounding Ironton into the massive parking lot of the Mega Mart. Straight into a pre-planned shooting gallery for Captain Reiter and his First Sergeant.

To their credit, they pressed on when Reiter downed their lead machine with a shot through center of mass. It wasn't until 1st Sergeant sniped a second that they began to waver. *They must realize they're out of range, surely they won't keep pushing.*

"Fox 6, permission to engage," Stovepipe asked.

"Hold," Reiter replied. *I don't want to give away their position yet.* Another superheavy round tore through a tinhat. Then they stopped. "Now!"

Two giant killer missiles streaked from their launchers and dug into the rear most tinhats. One collapsed in a heap while the other, who'd taken the missile in the shoulder, twisted to face his attacker as its arm went limp.

Green light highlighted one of the Cstalios, annihilating the machine. Before further damage could be done, the tracks popped smokescreens and fell back to their next fighting position. Reiter covered them with more fire from his magnetic rifle.

Unable to find the Missile Carriers and under fire from the command team's superior weaponry, the Union panzerters retreated. A few more parting shots destroyed limbs and brought down another tinhat. *Do they have more forces in reserve? It seems like they vastly under-prepared for this.*

"Fox 6, Black 1, BDA follows," Wesser said. Reiter grimaced when she told him they'd lost their sniper rifle, but was glad to hear Merlin Sr could still fight. When Steele called for a medevac, he feared the worst. It turned out Kozma was hurt bad enough he had to be pulled out of his panzerter, and a group of droptroopers were making their way to the vac site with the man on a stretcher.

That can't be it, there's got to be more to their first wave then just that. They'd given a battalion sized element a bloody nose, an impressive feat for a company. Reiter was about to call higher when the scouts got his attention.

"They got armored vehicles infiltrating Ironton," Lysak said. "Wheeled, four axles with angled armor."

"Let them through," Reiter replied. "Wildcard can deal with them."

"We can take care of them too," Wesser said.

"Black team, keep an eye out for dropships or panzerters," Reiter replied. "Wildcard is more than capable of taking on a motorized column." *I have to conserve our strength, we don't know when the 12th regiment is going to begin its counter attack.*

For a moment, Reiter basked in the quiet of the night. Then in the distance, he heard the racket of automatic weapons fire followed by a muffled *crump*. More automatic weapons joined the orchestra of violence, which ended in a crescendo of mortars.

"Fox 6, Wildcard 2-alpha, scratch five APCs," the assistant

squad leader reported. Reiter sighed and, as he expected, received the medevac request comments later. The squad leader and several others were being escorted to the medevac point by their squad.

We've held off this initial attack, but how long do e have before a followup? Reiter checked his map and referenced the BDAs of his leaders. *According to the latest information, we've savaged them pretty bad, they would have forced our frontline to fallback if their advance had been more coordinated.*

He looked at their current strength and positions. *No way the Union is out of the fight that easily, we'll see another more determined attack, maybe from dropships?*

"Wolfhound 1, Fox 6," he said. "Do you have enough drones to get us an air patrol?"

"If we get an air patrol up, they'll be vulnerable to long range AA," Wolfhound replied. "In addition to that, they might not have enough fuel on hand for close air support if they're also flying patrols."

Reiter sighed. "Do you have enough fuel on hand for your gunships?"

"As of right now, yes," Wolfhound 1 replied. "But the drones refuel by siphoning of our main cell. We have drop tanks, but we've already burned through most of those between getting here and doing what we've done already."

With a nervous eye to the sky, Reiter nodded. "Roger that," he said. "Keep everything grounded until we need it, until then we'll just keep an eye on the sky." Switching his mic over to the regimental net, he sent up his BDAs and sitreps.

"Hold your position, Fox," Friermann replied. "Early and Gamble are pretty messed up on your flanks, so we're rushing forces from the 4-14th to buffer them." Reiter acknowledged. Then he waited.

AS ANOTHER THARCIAN PANZERTER COLLAPSED IN A SMOKING HEAP, Kennedy gasped for breath and wiped the sweat from his brow. Though the Jupiter boasted thick armor, shells hitting all night still wore it down. *Eventually a shell will hit just the right spot and the armor won't hold.*

"Red 1 and 3, how are you doing?" he asked.

"Honestly, I'm impressed our panzerters haven't given out yet," Knight replied. "They've taken plenty of abuse."

"I'm worried I'll burnout the lenses on this strobe laser," Kennedy replied. Sweat dripped into his mouth and he gagged at how salty it tasted. "I didn't know the Tharcians had enough forces to maintain this."

"That bastard Fuller should have taken the city by now," Knight said. "We should be getting word to move any minute now." As a familiar whine filled their ears, Kennedy's eyes glanced at the sky. Screaming down from a move came a pair of Tharcian drones.

With a burst of cannon fire and a pair of bombs, they destroyed two more Martians and scattered infantry everywhere. Kennedy and Knight fired on them with strobe lasers as they raced away.

On his second pulse, his weapon suddenly sparked, and the barrel glowed. *Damn it, now is not the time for my weapons to fail!* Another diving pair of drones caught him in their sights. More cannon fire, another bomb.

Kennedy's machine staggered as he fought for balance. Alarms rang in his ears as he upped pedals and twisted stick in a vain attempt to keep the sixty ton panzerter upright. Despite his best efforts, the Jupiter went down. Armor plating crumpled on impact. His helmeted head struck his damaged matrix again, resulting in distorted lights playing across the crumbling screen.

"Comrade, are you ok?" Knight asked as he sent the drones

tumbling to the ground. Kennedy shook away his pounding headache and shock.

"I'm fine, I just need to stand back up," he replied. The Jupiter shuddered as it pushed off of the snowy ground below it. Once Kennedy got his feet under him, the process became much easier. Alarms continued to flash across multiple displays across his cockpit.

He was struggling to tune out the ringing when another group hailed him. "Reaper 6, Peryton 5, are we clear to pass through?" That the advance forces of the 616th were already here surprised him.

"Go for 6, where is your 6 element?" Kennedy asked. "Are you about to move on the airport?"

"Negative Reaper, he's in a dropship en route to Objective Alpha, we'll move on bravo after Alpha's been secured."

"What? Alpha isn't secure?" Kennedy said. "If it's not secure by now, then we need to bypass!"

"Negative, Victor reported being fully committed, but just unable to secure the city," Peryton 5 replied. "We're going to help them finish up, then move on Bravo with their support." Another pair of drones swooped down above the tree line, unleashing missile on the panzerter battalion.

Missiles rose to challenge the drones in the air. Despite their agility, the drones proved unable to shake the missiles from their Hydra mobile SAMs. Kennedy sighed as he looked at the humble four-wheeled vehicle.

"I'd ask you to leave one of those with us," he said. "But I know you need them." As the advance forces passed by, Kennedy realized just how paltry they were. A handful of Capricorn IFVs and Martian Troopers escorted a pair of Hydras and a missile artillery platform. *They really think that will tip the balance? Granted, the rest of their battalion is dropship based, so I'm not going to see them yet.*

"Is their air presence really that bad?" Peyton asked.

"Yeah, now that the weather is clearing up they're using more and more drones, it's only a matter of time before our own drones will need to come forward again," Kennedy replied. "I hate to say it, but I don't think we've been given adequate air defenses."

As the advance forces shuffled away, Kennedy scanned the skies again for any errant heat signatures. On finding none, he switched his mic back to the battalion net. "I don't like this," he said.

"Well, me neither," Knight replied. "Most of our battalion is dead or wounded and we're strung out without much support, I wouldn't like it either." Kennedy shook his head.

"I'm not trying to sound superstitious," he said. "But it's like there's something in the air, this land, these trees, this sky, none of it feel right." *Why?*

As Mo fell back to the Market district, he passed the burning wreck of a Union APC on the road. Hunkering down behind a church, he looked back across the area he just vacated.

"Black 1, we're set," he said as Merlin sr set his machine down in a narrow street. It gave his wingman excellent cover from the sides, but would be difficult to extract himself if they absolutely had too. Scanning with his stolen machine gun, it looked like he had plenty of room to fire the weapon.

"I'm blind from the air down here," Merlin said. "Don't let their raiders get the drop on me."

"Well, my air radar isn't great," Mo replied. "I'll know when their dropships get into the city, but they're pretty fast." The chatter of small arms ahead silenced both of them. Somewhere among the large homes, gas stations and corner stores, The drop troopers were giving the Union hell.

When a gaggle of bodies raced out of a gas station that exploded behind them, Mo trained his chest machine-gun on them.

"Thunder, thunder, fucking thunder!" Wildcard 2-A said. On hearing their running password, Mo relaxed and told Merlin to let them through.

"Enemy back there?" he asked.

"Was a couple of APCs and about a couple dozen guys," the drop trooper replied. "Now it's one APC and about a dozen guys." As if referring to it summoned the damned thing, the APC in question burst through the wall of lames at the gas station, its turret swiveling to find the drop troopers.

While they boasted impressive armaments for their type, the Union machine proved no match for a panzerter with a standard rifle. In a split second, it burned like its comrade. The drop troopers scrambled into the church in front of him.

Lurking off in the dark night, Mo could see shadows moving beyond the bounds of Ironton. *They're about to come for us again, probably more concentrated.* He glanced further to his left to spot Wesser and Smith just inside the perimeter created by market street and the autobahn.

"You sure you should be there, Black 1," he asked. "Wouldn't want to be in 6's line of fire."

"We're fine here," Wesser replied. "6 And 7 are providing over watch to gold platoon, we're safe." *Well, out here safety is relative.*

Shells and eerie green light emerged from the night. While the shells smashed structures, the laser beams melted others and started fires. Mo Leaned over the church and replied with a fire of his own. Merlin fired stream after stream of shells as panzerters revealed themselves.

As suppressing fire intensified, the pair were forced to keep their machines behind cover. "Black 1, we're pinned down!" Mo cried.

"Black 4, we're moving to-" A screech and a hiss of static ended Wesser's voice.

"One, respond, One! Tessa!" MO cried.

"Four, she's ok," Smith replied. "She's bailed out, collecting her now." Relaxing just slightly, Mo flipped to company net.

"White Team, we're pinned," he said. "Need some help."

Rather than a response from Steele, Wolfhound came into the net. "Hang tight, Black Four, help is on the way." Within moments, Gunships roared past overhead. They unleashed rockets, missiles, and cannon fire on the Union forces below.

With the reduced enemy fire aimed at them, Mo and Merlin added their own weapons to the deluge against their union opponents. *I can't believe it, we're about to beat them back again.* As if the thought itself cursed him, missiles streaked towards the gunships.

Luckily, the gunship pilots launched their drones as a barrier. Discouraged, they broke off their attack and launched flares.

"Black 2, do you have 1?" Mo asked.

"Roger, I got her right behind me," Smith replied. After a moment of shuffling, Wesser came over the net.

"A little rattled, but I'm ok," she said. "We need to focus, we haven't held this position long enough to fallback yet." Gritting his teeth, Mo turned back to the chaos ahead of him.

"Alright Merlin, let's even the odds here," he said. While Merlin related controlled bursts onto the advancing panzerters and Armored vehicles, Mo and Smith used precise shots to disable weapons, sensors, limbs, and tracked vehicles.

In return, the Union forces began using cover more than before. While one group attempted to suppress Black team, others advanced on their position.

Suddenly, more intense fire raked the advancing union forces. White team came out of position on their right flank and began advancing on the enemy using the same bounding movements the Union used on them. Before Mo could think of how good things were going, he heard a sound that gave him chills since the first hours of the war. MAG dropships.

CROUCHING IN THE DARKNESS OF A SHATTERED STOREFRONT, DAVE Webb prayed a stray shell from the panzerters didn't annihilate them. With the other 9 members of his first squad, they waited for the Union to reach their position.

"Any Black or White element, Wildcard 1," he said. "Status?"

Sergeant Mondragon replied to him immediately. "Both teams have begun bounding back, you should get company soon." Webb nodded. He'd chosen a planned blind spot in the prepared positions for the panzerter teams. If Union infantry tried to slip by the big hitters, the drop troopers intended to make them pay.

"Wildcard 1, Wildcard 4," his platoon sergeant, an intense man named Ausgebucht, called. "We got White 1 to the vac point, but the birds won't fly with that anti-air around." *Damn, we could hunt them down, but then we'd be abandoning this ambush point. Fuck it, if we don't kill those SAMs, killing a few APCs won't be worth it.*

"Roger 4, we're gong hunting," Webb replied. As soon as he got off the radio, he crawled over to his squad leader. "Listen up Szabo, Union has some nasty anti-air in the AO, it's up to us to sun them out."

Szabo shrugged. "Are you sure, LT? We only have so many rockets." LT tapped the older man on an armored shoulder.

"We got mortars on speed dial, as long as they're not licking their tubes, we can destroy them and not even be seen," he replied.

With a few terse hand signals, they rose to their feet and scurried out of the store.

Each trooper wore an armored exoskeleton that completely covered their legs, though at the torso the exoskeleton served more to brace their back with a lightweight armored vest protecting their vitals. A helmet fully enclosed their head and provided comms, optic overlays, and other support systems to the drop troopers. Each man carried an MK-35, with the exception of one squad member toting an MG-2. A third of them also carried antiarmor rockets slung over their shoulders.

While rushing across the shattered market district, the ground trembled beneath their feet and Webb heard the sound of metallic foot falls.

"Get down!" His squad leader snapped. They threw themselves into bushes, behind cars and through store fronts. As the footfalls approached, they increased in pace. A massive rifle thundered nearby.

A tinhat rounded the corner at a run. The hair on his neck stood on end as the panzerter's rifle hummed. Ghostly green light lit up the street, bringing it an intense heat with it. Most of it. Something orange flashed behind them.

One of their panzerters staggered sideways. A red-orange trench glowed in its shoulder. Even with his helmet on, the return fire threatened to rupture his ear drums. The tinhat rang like a gong as the shells pounded its armor. While the panzerter's duked it out, Webb prayed for it to end, ideally with his machine on top.

Finally, the street buckled. Section broke and collapsed into the sewer below. Both panzerters crashed to the ground like they plummeted from a beanstalk. The horribly disfigured tinhat lie in a crack in the street, jus a block from the Panzerter IV.

"Move, secure the pilots!" Webb cried. *We can kill two birds with one stone, take a prisoner and recover a friend.* Halfway between the two machines, he bolted towards the tinhat.

As he and several others approached the union machine, he caught site of a wheel of the hatch turning. "We got a live on!" One of the drop troopers cried. The unionist emerged with a machine pistol blazing away. He sprayed wildly at them, but died quickly in a hail of bullets. *That's weird. Reports said they were likely to surrender once their machine had been disabled.*

While his troopers searched the pilot's body and machine, Webb pivoted around to find their friendly pilot. Much to his surprise, two soldiers in CVC uniforms were escorted to the medic. Webb followed them into the broken storefront when he recognized one of them quickly.

"You're that cute, lieutenant," he said. Wesser glared at him through her cracked visor.

"While I appreciate compliments, we're in the middle of a battle," she hissed.

Webb held up a hand. "My bad missy, how do they look doc?"

"Some mild bruising from their restraints, but otherwise they're fine," he said.

Webb glanced at Wesser and her friend. "Do you two have weapons?"

They each showed him a sidearm. "We got these and a few magazines," the other pilot, a boy named Smith, said.

"Good enough," Webb replied. "Come with us, we're going to kill Unionists, specifically a SAM unit."

"Ok," Wesser said. "Do you have a plan?"

REITER HELD HIS BREATH AS UNION DROPSHIPS WEATHERED A WALL of auto cannon fire from gold platoon's Iglasios. One plummeted to the ground, but about a half dozen others remained in the air. While dismounts fired AA missiles, Reiter added his head mounted .50 cals to the frenzy. *I might be able to tag a few with the magnet rifle, but I need to save the ammo for the panzerters.*

Blasts of chain guns and rockets nicked that thinking as soon as he thought it. While his machine-guns perforated the Union drop-ships, his rifle shattered two of them. For now, that was enough to convince the dropships to break off their attack, but not before they disgorged their troops.

Cursing, Reiter turned his machine-guns on the bailing raiders, but was unable to see if he hit anything. As small arms chatter rose from Mega Mart, he figured some raiders had made it through, but until he heard a report from Gold, he wouldn't know to what extent.

Shells slammed into buildings across the street. *That came from North.* Reiter pivoted the Lowe and brough hid rifle to bear. Union panzerters surged down the autobahn. When they saw him take notice of them, they peeled off the main road, smashing through buildings in a vain attempt to find the river.

The Lowe's rifle punched holes in their armor. Tinhats crashed through storefronts as smoke and fluid leaked out of the Union machines. *One down, and that's two.* Three more scrambled about, blazing at him with lasers and high caliber shells.

Thanks to MAVAG's engineers, his thermal coating held of the lasers while his armor rested shells. *At this range, their weapons can't do shit.* With a resounding ping, his rifle knocked another Martian out of commission. *Of course, that doesn't matter if they kill everyone else.*

"Fox 6, Black 1," Wesser called.

"Go ahead for 6," Reiter replied. *It's been awhile since I've heard from her.* As 1st Sergeant added his sniper rifle to Reiter's gun battle, Wesser updated him to the status of her unit.

"We lost contact with the rest of Black team, Our panzerter is a loss, and we're running with Wildcard 1," she said. "We're currently hunting the SAM launchers." Despite wanting to tell Wesser and Smith to come back towards him and evacuate on the birds, he reconsidered. Even heading towards danger, they would be safer with wildcard than stumbling about on their own. It also mitigated the odds that they'd be captured or killed by raiders.

"That's fine, Wildcard, take good care of them," he said.

"Roger 6," Webb replied.

He looked back over at his map. "Black 4, Status?" The final panzerter in his immediate vicinity fell, but he could hear more fighting in the market district. "Black 4?"

"Hold on," Mo replied. After a moment, the young man came back. "Me and three are still fighting, havn't seen 1 or White element in a while." Small arms fire leaked in over Mo's transmissions. "We're helping out some wildcards right now, haven't seen panzerters in a minute."

What's their plan? To grind us down? Their losses are far disproportionate to our own, at least as far as I can tell. In all they'd lost three panzerters, a Cstalio, a recon Iglasio along with a standard one, and multiple drones. *If they attack in a third wave, we might not be able to hold them off.*

With a look at his map, he shook his head. *Wildcard needs to kill those SAMs or we're going to lose Ironton and the airport.* Returning to his immediate situation, he checked the skies for anymore dropships. While Gold platoon remained fully capable of beating air attacks, he didn't want them to absorb an entire attack.

As things seemed to be calm for a moment, he reevaluated his position. *If we can draw them directly down the Autobahn, we can set a trap of them.* "Black 4, Fox 6, shore up White team's position, Focus on protecting the flank." "Gold Team, I'm sending 1st Sergeant to aide you, Shore up your flank."

Switching to the regimental net, he called out to the other

commanders. "Early and Harbinger, how are you holding up?" he asked.

"We've seen better days," Early Company's commander said. "But we're still in the fight."

"I'm going to try to draw the Union into a trap," Reiter replied. "Do you think you got enough steam for a counter-attack? Specifically, around the highway?" After a few moments, he got his answer.

16

"We need just a few more forces," Guard-Colonel Fuller said. "There's a gap opening around the highway, we could drive right down and seize the entire municipality!"

Kennedy sighed. *If that wasn't a red flag, I don't know what would be.* "I hate to rain or your parade comrade, but it sounds like you're being drawn into a trap, my recommendation is to begin drawing back, we've bloodied most of our division already, we need to fall back so we can rebuild."

Unfortunately, Fuller wasn't hearing any of it. "Now listen here, comrade," he said. "I know you've been engineered to be the perfect pilot, but I was the top tactician in my Officer training, I'm certain I would be aware of a trap if I saw one."

With a shake of his head, Kennedy looked south. Green flashes amidst an orange glow indicated heavy fighting in what reports described as an old mining town from the days immediately following the domes coming down. *Fo what we've spent trying to get it, I'm rethinking its strategic importance.*

"You're full of adrenaline," Kennedy replied. "You're emotional. You've lost friends and colleges, you're not in the best shape to make a nuanced call, I'm not saying you're bad at your job, I'm merely pointing out you're in the perfect storm to make a mistake."

I hope he listens to reason, this battle is already becoming too costly. "Reaper 6, if we can't take Ironton, then we'll lose any momentum we have on this front, and our soldiers will have died in vain," Fuller replied. "It's imperative that we take this mining town."

Before Kennedy could reply, Surface-to-air missiles left from their launch tubes and soared into the sky. The light of the explosions revealed something Kennedy hadn't seen or heard because of their altitude: a massive swarm of Tharcian drones.

Naturally, a great horde of them broke off the main body and dove on their position. "Victor 6, we're under heavy air attack!" Kennedy cried. Without his stove laser, he stood helplessly to watch as drones screamed by, peppering his battered battalion with cannon fire and rockets.

While he keyed his mic to order a general withdrawal, something floated into his view. A 2000-lb bomb. The explosion rattled his teeth and knocked out his sensors. As he struggled for balance, he felt the Jupiter take hit after hit from cannons and bombs.

The heavy panzerter buckled, arms blared. He lost a knee, a hand, an ankle. Pain exploded behind Kennedy's eyes as the Jupiter fell on it's back. More systems failed as damaged sections crumpled under the sudden impact. Sparks filled Kennedy's vision and he tasted blood in his mouth.

As soon as he could see again, he undid his restraints and seized his machine pistol. Without power, he had to override the door controls and push the heavy door to the cockpit open. Drones still buzzed and swarmed the remnants of the 75th Panzerter Battalion. *I need to get to a command truck or track; I need to get a hold of Meyer, this whole operation is about lost.*

Abandoning his crippled panzerter, he ran as fast as he could across the snowy ground. His ass burned where he'd been injured previously. Unable to run particularly fast, he hobbled in the general direction of his forces. A Capricorn fired helplessly at the swarm above them. *Without radar guidance, that's futile.*

Kennedy loped towards the friendly vehicle, waving his arms. "Hey, hey, it's Kennedy! I need your radio!" At first it seemed like they didn't notice him. Then the hatch at the back popped open and two soldiers ran out.

"Comrade Colonel!" one cried. "Get in the track! We need to get you to safety!" Kennedy waved them off as he limped around to the back of the Capricorn.

"Who's the commander?" he asked.

"I am comrade," a meek-looking man replied. "Guard-Staff Sergeant Maynard at your service."

Kennedy nodded as he got his breath back. "I need your radio," he finally gasped. "I need to contact division, if that's not possible, we need to contact Knight, let him know to rely to Meyer that this operation is a loss and we need to fall back."

As Maynard handed him a transmitter, the world changed in a flash. Suddenly, gravity left the track and everything floated for a brief moment. Then it came crashing back. The turret broke away. Kennedy was thrown headfirst into a bulkhead. And then he knew darkness.

"IT'S AN ABSOLUTE TRAVESTY," COMMODORE MENDEZ SAID. "IT'S outrageous, it's unacceptable, Vinland has made themselves handmaidens to the oppressor class." Chaney nodded as he walked with the woman. He'd invited her to watch a demonstration of a newer development of his particle weapon project, but she'd meet him with bad news.

"A certain associate of ours showed me a sample of a supercrop he got from a Vinnish colony," Chaney replied. "Do you believe his actions could have provoked them?"

The Commodore shook her head. "I doubt it, the sample he acquired would warrant halting all trade with us as well as encouraging neutral countries to join them in an embargo."

They walked down one of Congregation's many wooden hallways. They both wore civilian clothes as to not give away the military nature of where they were going. *Not that we have any reason to believe Tharcian agents are here.* But a directive from the IRS on information control wasn't something they could just ignore, besides, they were more comfortable.

"Perhaps our allies could stay their hand," Chaney said. "Not being so reckless with the lives of anyone not Avalonian would do us all a lot of good in the long run." Mendez scoffed.

"You now how the diplomats are about Avalon, they'd rather not go there, and would rather not speak to them," she said. "Our forces in Olympia have had more contact with Avalon then our own diplomats."

"Unfortunately, that may harm their careers more than anything else," Chaney said. "What good is having an ally if working with them gets you thrown in jail or unpersoned?" They came to a stop before an unassuming little shop. Chaney knocked and an engineer, also dressed in civilian clothes, let them in.

"So this new development?" The commodore asked. "I take it you have a solution for the rapid degradation?" Chaney sighed. Ever since the PFS *Metro* had been crippled following the use of its particle cannons in the belt, he'd increased the amount of time and labors devoted to the project in an attempt to salvage something.

"In a sense," he replied. "We used the exiting science and architecture to transition to a more reliable weapon system." He held up his hands. "Rather than trying to accelerate individual particles, we've made strides in directing high energy ionized gases, or plasmas." He smiled. "As long as we have nitrogen gas, these new impulse weapons will have ammunition and plenty of it."

As they followed the engineer, he led them to an observation deck. Multiple engineers worked at the impromptu control center. Beyond the thick window stood a pair of panzerters. One, a Terran III, stood with a large tube like weapon. Multiple wires and hoses connected the Terran, and its weapon to generators and reservoirs.

Across from the Terran hung a mostly intact Panzerter IV. The battered Tharcian machine was held by multiple cables in a hunched over but still standing position.

"None of the machines we had on hand could handle the power output required," one of the engineers explained. "Unfortunately, all the Jupiters and Martians are for the soldiers on the front."

Chaney waved a hand. "That's fine, we've more than made do with what we have." Aided by the additional power supplied to it, the Terran raised its weapon and fired. A thick red bolt caved in the Panzerter's torso, sending molten metal and sparks everywhere.

The engineers applauded, but Commodore Mendez remained unimpressed. "So your new toy can destroy a damaged panzerter," she said. "I haven't seen anything worth informing the ARF of." The Terran fired again. This time the legs fell away as its arms and head spun from their cables. "Ok, so it doesn't burn out after one use."

With a chuckle, Chaney waved to the Terran. "With this, we can save our metals for warships, vehicles, colonies, and buildings, while all the ammo these impulse weapons will need is a steady supply of nitrogen gas."

"What's the drawback?" Mendez asked. "There's no way you've discovered the perfect weapon."

Chaney held up his hands as if to surrender. "As of right now, these would be expensive to manufacture, and it would take additional refining to create weapons for multiple mission sets, also as of right now, power consumption is to great to produce small arms versions." He looked back at the Terran. "Also they have some mild thermal blooming in atmosphere, nowhere near the extent lasers do though."

"And I assume you have some plan for mounting upscale versions on warships?" She asked. "Because Metro is still in dry dock on Los Estrellas."

With a smile, Chaney waved her off. "I assure you, comrade, the Metro will never need a refit again once we install naval grade impulse cannons."

WEBB DOVE INTO A SNOWBANK TO AVOID DETECTION. A TINHAT stalked past him and the others, it's creepy red ring glowing in the night. *We're almost there, it'd suck to get caught now.* Their target lay just beyond a low rise ahead of them. A four wheeled armored truck with a rotating missile launcher bristling with anti-aircraft missiles.

They'd destroyed the unit's sister about a kilometer away, shrinking the air defenses umbrella the Union possessed. *Good thing we had those pilots with us, I'd never turn down extra hands to carry our wounded.* He still had six men with him and four rockets capable of destroying the track. As he slowly crawled through the snow and dirt, he swore.

His issue began and ended with the shivering Union infantry surrounding the missile carrier. *If we shoot a bunch of rockets at that SAM, it'll give away our position. If we lead with the machine-gun and rifles, the SAM carrier will just run away. If I put rocket teams on its escape route, I negate the problem of it escaping, I'll just keep the MG here and a couple guys with rockets along the escape. I have three rockets I might as well use them.*

His entire stream of thought happened in a few seconds. He motioned to his team leaders, acquired a rocket so one of his riflemen could cover his buddy. After glancing at the SAM, he determined its best escape route out of the clearing would be South of his current position and slightly west.

His rocket teams crawled towards the route. Webb set a timer on his watch and nodded to his gunner. The other man nodded and crawled back towards a tree further from him. *Now we'll look like a much bigger element attacking them.*

As the seconds clicked down, he grabbed the sling of the rocket and braced himself. *Been awhile since I used one of these.* The timer hit zero.

Webb sprang into a kneeling position. The rocket came to his shoulder and ignited. An orange glow trailing smoke streaked towards the SAM. Too high.

The shaped charge blasted a mighty oak tree. It's super half plummeted to the snowy ground below. His machine gunner opened fire.

With sparks pinging off of it, the SAM rushed out of the clearing. As Webb pinged away at the infantry, he witnessed the carrier slow down to avoid the fallen tree. And a second rocket missed.

By now the infantry picked up on their ruse. Already they used bounding movements in an tempt to flank out his gunner.

He desperately attempted to suppress the infantry. While he kept them ducking, they still advanced. *One shot left.*

Then the final rocket streaked past the SAM carrier. Webb felt his stomach sink while his blood boiled. *Fucking seriously? Lord, give me a break!*

Cycling his weapon into full auto, he let loose on the Union infantry. His scattered drop troopers took potshots at the Union squad as the SAM began to clear the log. *I'd call mortars, but we're too close.*

God must have been listening, because with a deafening roar, the SAM carrier vanished in a ball of fire and debris. An Iglasio appeared out of nowhere, blasting the infantry with machine gun fire while a Cstalio trailed them. *What the hell? Did gold platoon get lost?*

Then he realized the Iglasio lacked a turret, the machine-gun held by a soldier hanging out the top. The other markings indicated a recon variant. *Scouts?*

After mopping up the Union forces, Webb approached the two tracks. "Hey, you got room in there?" He asked. In the darkness, he saw a grinning face covered in soot.

"We don't have a ton," the scout replied. "We got a little lost killing a different SAM, some tinhats didn't take too kindly."

Webb shook his head. "Unbelievable, we're about to get shwacked, you came at the right time." He waved over his men. "So you'll give us a ride?"

"Yeah," the scout replied. "Just tell me which direction is Ironton." As they climbed onto the tracked vehicles, they grabbed handholds and sat on flat surfaces. One of the troopers rode in the Cstalio to aide that crew with reloading. Webb and his gunner climbed into the shell where the turret would be with the scout, while the other drop troopers held on. One injured man applied a tourniquet to his arm and sat in the troop compartment.

The tracked vehicles turned about, smashing through fallen trees and churning snow. As they headed south, Webb kept his eyes peeled. *The enemy's out there.*

"Prioritize the seriously wounded!" Wesser cried over the screaming wind. "Casualties that need surgery first!" As soon as she received word the Union's Air defenses had been destroyed, she told the dropships to spin up.

Several drop troopers groaned as Smith and several others moved them onto the waiting pair of dropships near them. While the Tharcian army possessed airborne ambulance versions of the Pegasus dropship that could stow many patients on litters vertically, they could only go two wide on the models they possessed and three deep.

While her impromptu aide teams began loading more patients, Kozma asked to talk to her first. "Hey," he said. "Give them hell Tess Wess, you brainy beauty." Wesser smiled nervously. *Surely that's the pain meds talking.* He winked at her, or blinked? She couldn't tell with the bandages covering half of his face. Gingerly, she took his good hand and squeezed it.

"You just get better, ok?" she said before watching the drop troopers load her friend into the back of a pegasus. Rapid honking drew her attention as two tracks rolled down the road. She realized on closer inspection that the lead vehicle actually sustained serious damage. Webb leaped out of a gaping hole in the roof and stuck the landing in front of her.

"We've got one more wounded," he cried over the whine of the dropships engines. The back of the track opened and another drop trooper clutching his arm trotted out the back. While he ran into the back of another dropship, Wesser looked at Webb.

"What happened to that track?" she asked.

Webb jerked a thumb at the damaged Iglasio behind him. "Oh, you mean the scouts? Apparently a tinhat kicked off their turret, luckily for them it was unmanned." The two dropships they loaded up lifted their ramps and began rising into the air. "We should probably tell Captain Reiter-"

Chainguns ripped through the lead dropship. The stricken craft spun and struck a low building as it spun around and burst into flames as its fuel cell ruptured. The other dropship landed in the middle of the street, but the Union dropship had already seen it. A second burst of chain gun fire permanently grounded the second machine.

Wesser ran for cover, tears streaking down her face as the two ships full of wounded burned. While the union dropship passed over, the Cstalio sprang into action. Antiair missiles streaked towards the ugly aircraft.

Too slow and low to evade them, it took the brunt of the attack and crashed a few blocks away. Wesser's ears still rang when Webb and more drop troopers ran past her, followed by the scout track. *They didn't pose any threat. They were carrying our injured. Kozma.*

"Ma'am!" Smith cried. "Let's get out of the open!" He grabbed her hand and ran with her to the nearest open building. Small arms fire echoed in the streets.

"Our last dropship," Wesser said as they ducked behind a counter. "We need to protect it, otherwise our wounded don't have a ride and neither do we." Smith nodded and hefted a rifle he'd taken from a wounded droptrooper.

"Let's let the drop troopers take care of the raiders for now," he said. "And inform them when they get back." Nearby, the Mortars thundered as they fired on a target somewhere in the distance. Wesser picked up her own rifle and used the counter to stand up faster.

"We need to get back outside, we can't see the dropship or protect it from in here," she said. "We don't have a good angle in here."

Smith nodded, and they ran back outside. The small arms fire sounded closer, but much less intense. As it did down, The drop troopers ran back alongside the recon track.

"So this is our last one?" Webb asked, waving at the drop ship. It sat on the side of the road, tucked out of sight thanks to the surrounding buildings. *Lazy Sue* was stenciled across the front with interesting nose art of a woman being fed grapes.

"Yeah," Wesser said. "That's our ride home." *I feel naked, I hate this, I'm used to a heavily armored shell.* She grabbed at her shoulder and shivered. *I know all to easily how soft and vulnerable my body is, even these drop troopers are vulnerable.*

More rumbling in the distance. Could be artillery, panzerters, mortars, or a dozen other things. *Why is it that we create so many innovative ways to kill each other?*

TWO DROPSHIPS SWOOPED LOW OVER THE ROOFTOPS. MO OPENED fire with his rifle. He missed twice, but the Merlin brothers brought down one of them. The other managed to dump chain gun fire and rockets into the younger brother's machine.

As their airborne attacker flew out of range, Mo looked over to see Steele and Merlin looking at the younger brother's machine. "I'm ok," Ernest Merlin said. "My cockpit hatch it stuck though, I can't bail out." *Damn, we need to get him away from the front.*

"White 4, get Two out of here, we'll cover you," He said. "Wes with me. White three, cover their flank." Mo shifted to put the older Merlin's machine in the center of their defensive perimeter with Magyar taking up the right flank.

It all seemed to be going to slowly. Steele grabbed the immobile panzerter and began the aggravating process of dragging him back towards the aid point. Mo looked to his right towards the Northern end of Ironton. In the distance, he could see movement, but not enough to confirm anything.

"All Fox elements, Wolfhound 1, Air Superiority is back on the menu boys and girls!" A pair of Bellaphron gunships zipped by overhead. They blasted something on the ground ahead of Mo and continued their sweep. *Where the hell were you a minute ago?*

"Wolfhound 1, Black 4, We got a disabled panzerter with a trapped pilot being dragged back to the aid station. Can you keep an eye on them?"

"Roger Black 4, we got eyes on, if you need us, just holler," Wolfhound 1 replied. Mo sighed. *Good, now Ernie and Amy are safe, at least relatively.*

"Alright gang, let's hold this flank," Mo said. "I doubt the Unis got enough juice left for another serious attack, if anything they'll come in drips and drabs hoping we crumble." *Hopefully, I'm right.*

"Well, we got this flank," Magyar said. "But who has our backs?"

"Fox 6 is holding the middle," Mo replied. "Which works in our favor, between him and the Lowe, I'm not worried about the enemy behind us." He looked back North and reevaluated their formation. "White 3, come around behind me and put yourself at an angle behind me."

"Suddenly not confident about 6?" she asked.

"No, I want us be easier to move if we have to support him or assault something," Mo said. "Besides, we have an adjacent unit in front of you, and I don't want another friendly fire incident in the dark." Magyar's machine ran around behind him and took a knee behind a two story strip mall.

"Better?" she asked.

"Better," Mo replied. More movement caught his eye. In the streets to his ten' o'clock, APCs crawled forward hoping they wouldn't be noticed.

They advanced slowly, with infantry stalking down the surrounding streets. Mo flipped his rifle to burst and unleashed 88-mm shells on the column of armored personnel carriers. The three axle vehicles burst into flames as the explosions tossed the infantry like kindling.

Magyar and Merlin joined in the carnage, smashing buildings and vehicles around them. Abandoned cars burned alongside union armored vehicles. In a second, they had reduced the five vehicle column to a burning heap.

So, senseless. He shook his head. *What are they even doing at this point, there's no way they have enough to take Ironton now.* Something popped to his left and Magyar cried out.

"My sensors! I'm blind!"

"Don't panic, did you see what happened?" Mo asked. A twinkle drew his attention to the steeple of a church across the way. Someone was in there. With a blast from his machine gun, he forced the sniper to miss. The 8-mm rounds pitted and scared the old stonework. "White 2, are you ok?"

"I'm fine, but my machine is blind," Magyar replied. Mo sighed.

"Bailout, we can recover the panzerter later," he said. "Here, I'm coming to you." He carefully guided his panzerter over to Magyar's, keeping his eyes on all of his sensors and scanners. Gingerly, he held out his hand for Magyar to step in, while shielding it with another. Bringing her in close, he popped open his cockpit hatch, and she stepped inside.

"Ugh, it smells like rotting meat in here," she said as she slipped into the jump seat behind him. Mo shook his head as he sealed his hatch.

"I haven't exactly had time to put an air freshener or two in here," he said. "The heat doesn't help."

"Why do you have it cranked all the way?" she asked.

"Because it's like ten degrees outside," he replied before looking North one more time. *They're coming, I can feel it.*

17

W hile Knight watched a dropship carry away his wounded commander, he turned to evaluate his battered battalion. Six Panzerters, and about as many IFVs with most of their dismounts, and their single mobile howitzer. And Fuller, still begging for his help.

Kennedy refused him. But I don't have as much leverage with rank. Kennedy believed aiding this man would be foolish, he didn't want to risk their lives and the division by taking down the corridor for everyone else.

"Comrade, do you hear me?" Fuller cried. "We're nearing the deceive moment! We just need a little extra push and Ironton *and* the airport will be ours!"

Knight sighed. "Comrade Kennedy wanted us to respect the greater situation, we can't allow this corridor to close."

"Don't you remember you're training?" Fuller said. "Were you trained to seize the moment, or remain stagnate in the face of enemy action?" *Damn, he has a point. If he is turning the tide of the battle, then I'm failing to support the cause, but he's never called for fire support once since we've had it, despite the battery just sitting there.*

Knight looked back at Khan and growled. *Good soldiers follow orders.* "Red 3, hold the bridge, if it looks like you're going to be overwhelmed, retreat, that's an order, everyone else, fall in on me, we're going to aide the 88th."

He brought his Martian Troopers into a wide arrow formation centered on him with his other vehicles filling the gap. *A single heavy panzerter should be enough to deter the Tharcians for now. At least until the skies clear up more.*

After a short march, he came to a low set of forested hills. Just beyond, he could see fires burning in Ironton. Along with his forces, about ten other panzerters spread out along the clearing. Most of their air defenses lay in tatters, but several APCs and IFVs joined him. In all they had about a battalion's worth of fire power amassed here. *Weren't we about to win this battle?*

"Good, you're here," Fuller said. "We're going to concentrate our entire attack along the highway, the advance forces will lead, your group will take the center, and my battered forces will seal the deal, now we'll move in echelon columns and crush the last of the Tharcian forces in Ironton before pivoting to the airport."

Doesn't seem like a bad plan. Maybe all he really did need was numbers. Knight settled his unit into the center of the formation. The remaining panzerters formed a split column behind him, and the vehicles filled the gap. The exception was his mobile howitzer, which he staged with a couple others and a MLRS towards the rear.

"Alright Comrades, on my signal, advance," Fuller said. Knight watched as the column to his left plodded forward, counting down the seconds to signal his own company to advance over the hills. Shells streaked towards the left column. APCs skidded sideways and crashed. Martians sustained multiple hits before falling.

"Artillery!" Fuller cried. "Counter-battery fire! Now!" The

howitzers and single MLRS unleashed concentrated hellfire on suspected enemy gun positions. *Without spotters, we'll have a hell of a time confirming any hits.*

Dropships harassed targets in the distance, just beyond the mining town. As the last vehicle from the column to his left passed him by, he signaled his own group to advance. Heavy mortars harassed them, damaging panzerters and knocking out his limited IFVs.

Once the Union entered the city, they discarded any pretext of rapid advancement. Much to his frustration, Knight's column about stopped to allow the left column to enter the highway first. Panzerters led the way down the wide roads with armored vehicles filling the gaps between panzerters. Infantry ran from building to building, rooting out any resistance.

Knight himself had just entered the city limits when the head of the column in front took contact from panzerters. Two of them. Staggered line. One even used a Union machine gun.

Martians began falling left and right, knocking over buildings and blocking off escape routes. Knight swore to himself. *I don't have time for this.*

Kicking his Jupiter into high gear, he crashed through a strip mall and several homes like they were nothing, and blasted away with his strobe laser. The one with the machine gun collapsed in a shower of molten metal. Its partner spun on him and began running and dodging.

I'll lead him away from the main body, that'll let them take their objective. Knight found himself in a running battle with the the Tharcian. Though speed wasn't the Jupiter's strong suit, it didn't lose any speed crashing through buildings. *I just need to keep him busy.*

"ALL UNITS, NOW!" HAWKE ORDERED. REITER EMERGED FROM behind the church he'd used as cover. *If I live through this, I'm defiantly making an offering to this church.* Raising his shield and his rifle, he squared up on the advancing tinhats. *This is reckless, but worth it.*

"Let's go, Fox!" He cried as he unleashed the magnetic rifle on the approaching Unis. Sparks flew everywhere. At less than 1600 meters, the 88 mm high-density slugs tore through armor like it was wet paper.

Tinhats crumpled and fell. In all the chaos, he got carried away and his rifle seized up. A blinking readout with an alarm drew his attention. *Coil failure, just my luck.*

His hesitation allowed the Union forces to rally. Advancing two wide, the Lowe buckled and jerked as shells pummeled the big black target. Lasers created welts in his armor, weak points that shells could exploit.

As the shaking and rocking caught his attention, Reiter covered himself with his shield as the tinhats in front of him suddenly parted. Sparks and dust filled his vision as an enormous impact rocked the Lowe.

To his shock, the upper part of his shield had been sheared away. A tinhat between the other two quickly discarded a fat tube and drew a laser on him.

Roaring out of the dark night, his gunships poured fire power onto the flanks of the Union forces strung out on the highway. Rockets and Chainguns shredded the panzerters supporting elements and knocked out several.

"We got ya back boss," Wolfhound 1 said as they peeled away, shells and missiles chasing them. *Wolfhound gave me a breather, I need to make the most of it.*

Smashing the pedal to the floor, the Lowe's nuclear turbine screamed with the rush of power. Reiter drew the panzerter's Tesla sword. The cackling blue blade lit up the night, casting his machine and surroundings in an eerie light.

The highway was just wide enough for panzerters to stand two abreast, great for concentrating fire, bad for trying to dodge an enemy with a sword. Reiter cleaved through limbs, torsos, weapons, and heads. With every swing and the occasional thrust, he connected his attacks, each one flowing into the next. In the relatively confined space, the tinhats behind his immediate opponents had a hard time bringing their weapons to bear. No machine guns or recoilless rifles would threaten him.

His ferocity caught the Union off guard, and before long, they began falling back. Fortunately, for Reiter, they weren't getting far. Forces from Harbinger Company had swung wide and caught the Union from behind, trapping them in Ironton.

Desperation filled the air. The Lowe took concentrated fire from armored vehicles as well as panzerters, all clawing to escape the noose Hawke had made for them. He switched to his twin .50 cals to bust up a trio of APCs when his air radar flashed.

A Union Dropship, trailing smoke and fire behind it, swung into view. Wobbling as it flew, it hammered away with rockets and chain guns. Despite the armor plating between him and the aircraft, Reiter felt every impact through the cockpit frame as the rounds pummeled his hatch.

With his head throbbing, he turned his twin fifties on the incoming craft. More fire blossomed from the craft, Reiter was positive he'd hit the cockpit. But the pilot, even if he was mortally wounded, had a steady hand.

The dropship crashed into the Lowe at full speed. Reiter's head slammed against the sides of his cockpit. He flailed blindly with his sword. His face plate cracked against a bulkhead, his picture of Bartonova sticking to it before cracking further against his picture of Fletcher.

Something was burning. He could smell it. His head throbbed, and he tasted blood. Outside something collapsed, and he felt the mighty Lowe, the titan of Tharcian engineering, fall. As the pictures obscured his vision, he felt oddly at peace as the world seemed to slow down around him.

Bartonova, I'm sorry about what happened to you. If I end up seeing you soon, I'll let you know just how much. Fletcher, if there's any good that comes out of this war, I'm glad we were able to save you.

Father in heaven, it's chaotic down here, and this world is rough. Please protect them.

His head smacked the cack of his chair as if a giant had kicked him. Pain exploded behind his eyes as his vision went red. And then darkness fell.

MUCH TO ADAMSKI'S SURPRISE, FLETCHER SUDDENLY DROPPED HER fork. She'd been patiently listening to him and Zorro explain hockey when her eyes widened. Her hand spasmed, and she let go of her fork.

"Are you ok?" Zorro asked. Fletcher nodded as she gingerly rubbed the back of her head.

"Yes, I'm fine, I just… don't feel as good all of a sudden," she said. "Nothing to be alarmed about." Adamski straightened himself in his wheelchair. None of them had been cleared to walk yet, although Fletcher was making excellent progress. *Yeah, you would too if you came out of the gate a superman.*

He shook his head. "You're not getting homesick, are you?"

Fletcher shook her head. "No, there's a lot I like about home, everything is really clean, all of my needs are within walking distance, but my life focused around my duties so much I never really got the chance to become attached to where I was stationed."

Adamski swatted the table, startling their guest. "Well, let me tell you," he said. "Southern Gallacia and Germania, Ostlan? Gorgeous in the winter, during peacetime, skiing is so good there." He frowned when he remembered his current condition. "I mean, I won't be doing of that anytime soon, if ever again."

Zorro changed the subject. "So what are schools like in the Union?" she asked. Fletcher shrugged.

"I'm not sure, the only schooling I ever had was my basic education and duty training as well as MAG training," she said. "but from what I understand schools are cultural centers, future writers, journalists, scientists, engineers, and managers are given a comprehensive education that allows them to be the best in their careers."

"Huh, I can kinda relate," Zorro said. "I got sent to a military prep school when I was 14, so I got treated to the whole drill and ceremony number pretty early on, then they call my name, give me a list of jobs, tossed me into a pilot program and then I ended up at Fox troop."

"You were a student?" Fletcher asked. "Like in the middle of learning and they demanded you fight in their war?"

Zorro gestured "more or less." After sipping her drink, she resumed. "I mean, you could go AWOL, I wasn't going to because I ain a little bitch, but I was honestly surprised by who did and who didn't."

Adamski furrowed his brow. "How do you mean?"

With a shrug, Sorrow looked at him. "We expected Merlin to leave, his brother was a big deal back in school and I think trying to live up to that got to him, but Schwartz was a surprise because he was a harass from day 1."

"Really?" Adamski said. "He didn't even show up."

"Guess he got cold feet," Zorro replied. "We all knew Stasiak would bail though, he was way too into some chick that was way not into the military."

Fletcher shook her head. "I can't believe you made kids fight your war."

"I didn't ask for kids," Ski replied. "And I can tell you Reiter didn't either." At the mention of the Captain's name, Fletcher twitched and reached towards the back of her head.

"The Union doesn't have to press kids into service, they just build them," Zorro said before frowning. "I'm sorry."

Fletcher scowled and took her tray. "I apologize, I guess I'm not that hungry." A shout echoed across the cafeteria. They stopped to listen to what they were shouting about when they heard the news.

"Huge battles all across the front," an orderly cried. "You can check the casualty registry to see if you have friends or loved one's dead or wounded."

In a smooth motion, Zorro flicked out her phone and Fletcher rolled back. "What's Fox's CasReg?"

"411789," Adamski rattled off. "I've had that shit burned into my brain."

"Thanks top," Zorro said as she pulled up a list. A lot of names they didn't recognize jumped out at them. "Is this the right list?"

"Has to be," Adamski said. "That number is exclusive to Fox." He suddenly pointed when a name he recognized caught his eye. "See, that's Kozma, our White team leader." Tracing the line, he found MIA.

"Is Captain Reiter on there?" Fletcher asked. Adamski looked up. *That's genuine concern in her voice, she wouldn't want to see him hurt, not after all he's done.*

He shook his head. "No, he's not, but it sounds like this battle is still ongoing."

As Fletcher's face creased with worry, Zorro set a hand on hers. "You could always pray for him if you're worried."

Confused, the other woman looked back at Zorro. "What does praying for someone do?" She asked. "And if it helps, how do you do it?"

As soon as the shaking stopped, Weber looked back at his motley crew. "Alright, let's go," he said. A squad's worth of people followed him. Five other drop troopers, one of the mortar men, and their two downed pilots. Toting a mix of Tharcian and Union weapons, they darted along down the sewers. The sewers themselves were round thick tunnels reinforced by super concrete in some areas. On each side of the sewage, a putrid river that ran along the center of the tunnels, two concrete walkways wide enough for two people, allowed them to move quickly between objectives.

Webb's goal was simple: find the roads the Union tried to use, plant charges on the super concrete supports, and collapse the road above. Smith, one of the pilots, seemed oddly comfortable taking point.

Suddenly, the ruddy young man stopped and raised a fist. "Do you hear that?" He asked. It took Webb a moment, but he heard a low rumble above their heads. *Armored vehicles, the kids a natural.* Webb stepped up and tapped him on the shoulder.

"Good ear kid," he whispered. "Let's get down to business." He looked back at the mortar man. The burly, squat man took off his pack and removed the mortar round inside. One of his drop troopers held up the net cord and Webb nodded.

Motioning half of his group to pull security, he helped unpack all of their deadly tools. Det cord, a spare 120mm mortar round, plastic explosives, and a magnetic detonator. Carefully, they packed their plastic explosives around the net cord in sections, almost like a sock.

The mortar man managed to pry the cap off of his round and managed to ball up some plastic explosive around the fuse. Webb waved over Wesser. The young woman held her nose with one hand and held a captured machine pistol with another.

"What's up," she whispered. Webb pointed at the three super concrete supports around him.

"Which of these looks strongest?" he asked. She nodded to the middle one, and he thanked her. Carefully, they used plastic explosives to stick the loose mortar to the support. Gingerly, they wadded up more plastic explosive to the other supports and connected them to the mortar's fuse with set cord.

Loose dirt from the ceiling startled them as the low rumble stopped. *Did we miss our shot?* Webb ducked down a side passage and climbed a small ladder so he could see the street from the sewer drain.

As he poked his head past the concrete threshold, he saw tires and booted feet running around. Something rumbled in the distance, and the men and women above him grew excited. Scrambling back the direction he came from, he waved them around a side passage further down.

"They're there, but i don't know how long," he said. The mortar man spooled the cord around the alley and attached the detonator.

Very carefully, he handed the detonator to Webb. He nodded and looked to the others with him. Everyone had their weapon up and ready to go. They just waited on him. Motioning for them to protect their ears, he held up his fingers. Four. Three. Two. One.

Dust, dirt, chunks of road, and sewage surged past them as Webb clicked the detonator. The sewers echoed as the explosions echoed off of each other and the walls away from them. Sound like screeching metal and crashing vehicles added to the chaotic symphony of violence.

The drop troopers rushed past him first, guns up and all business. He followed, with the mortar man and the pilot's right behind him.

The sewer drained as its flow had been cut by debris from the street above, as well as multiple APCs plugging the line. Union soldiers cried out for help. Some screamed as rubble pinned them to vehicles or walls, while metallic banging told him others had been trapped in their vehicles.

"Let's round up any wounded we can," he said. "We've got a lot of prisoners on our hands." Movement at the rim of the opening he'd created caught his attention. A rifle cracked. One of his droop troopers, he couldn't see who, spun around with a shattered faceplate and fell into the sewer line.

They returned fire. Despite having the high ground, the aggression of his own forces quickly overwhelmed the sporadic fire of the Union infantry. That is until one of the APCs turrets began moving and haphazardly spraying machine gun fire.

Something stung his arm as he ducked into a side tunnel. He grabbed his arm and felt blood. Grazed, no round in the wound. Clean through.

As he applied a dressing., the pilots ducked into the tunnel after him. "We're pinned," Wesser said. Webb pressed his dressing deep into his arm, allowing the quick clot to do its thing. He looked behind him to see the side tunnel was a dead end, probably for storage or maintenance. *Damn, we might be in trouble.*

Got you. Knight fired his strobe laser. Just as he pulled the trigger, his opponent swatted a massive pile of snow off a rooftop. His beam reflected off the steam it created. *Damn it, he's good.*

Lowering his shoulder, his Jupiter charged into the cloud, laser forward. Something orange flashed in front of him. The Tharcian lunged. The front half of his strobe laser flew high into the air.

Instead of stepping back, Knight threw his machine forward. The Tharcian retreated out of reach. As he caught his breath, Knight drew his sword-axe.

His opponent stayed hunched and circled him slowly. Even still, it took the MAG all he could to turn and keep his opponent in front of him. The Tharcian lunged again, but stepped back out of Knight's reach before he swung.

He's testing my reaction time and headspace. He wants to see how much I'll commit to counter-attacking. Knight spotted an abandoned car on the side of the street. *I need to quit playing his game.*

He kicked the car like a soccer player shooting a goal. The Tharcian destroyed the car with its machine gun, but the cloud of debris and smoke hid Knight from him.

Knight's weapon tore a long gash through the side of his torso. The Tharcian backed off, sparks and static lighting up the damage.

"Usually when the fight get's this intense, they start talking," a familiar voice said. *It's that kid from the truce.*

Knight sighed. "I'm not very chatty," he replied. "But since it's you, I'll give you the courtesy of knowing your killer." He chopped right at the kid's head. Mo, that was his name, parried the blow as he danced away.

"Yeah, big talk," Mo replied. As Knight reoriented himself, he became astutely aware of the weight of his panzerter through the controls. *This machine was meant to fight at mid to long range, its joints probably can't handle sustained hard maneuvers, I need to end this quick.*

Mo approached with his sword raised. What followed was a monotonous slog between the two machines. Knight would attack with a blow or two that Mo would easily parry before backing off again and then approaching to repeat the process.

"What's the matter? Age catching up?" The Tharcian gasped. Between his words, Knight could hear the ragged gasps for breath. *The Kids exhausted, good I can finish this.* The kid was exhausted. His own thoughts sank in. This kid had been fighting desperately for his life all night.

Briefly picturing Mo's face, he was nearly caught off guard when he approached to attack once more. This time he followed up his block with a thrust. His wide blade took out a chunk of Mo's leg. Knight stepped into the attack, slamming his weight into the lighter panzerter, and driving it into the pavement.

Mo's ball mounted machine gun sputtered to life. Knight sighed as the round plugged and plinked off of his armor. *I understand, you're desperate not to die.* He grit his teeth and tightened the controls.

Before he could land the final blow, a round struck his sensors. A black blob appeared on the left side of his screen. *Damn it.* He lashed out. His blade connected with the panzerter's hip, crushing the joint.

Shielding his sensors with his opposite arm, he prepared to finish the panzerter when he hesitated. *He's barley a man, he can unlearn the behaviors the Tharcians taught him.* Rounds continued to chip at his arm. *Am I getting soft? I've never debated killing an enemy before.*

He smashed the machine gun and turned away. Knight sighed as he pushed his Jupiter back towards the main body. *I'm not getting soft, I'm just tired. All these battles just seem to blur together.*

The rest of the Union forces came under fire from panzerters outside of Ironton. With a groan, he pushed his Jupiter to a run. *I need to open the pocket, this battle is lost.* He fired away with his laser, striking several and melting armor plating.

The Union forces had been reduced to a handful of panzerters and vehicles. Their artillery support came in sporadic and unfocused. *They're not ranging in. They're probably getting a lot of calls or running low on ammo.*

"Victor 6, Red 1, begin withdrawal," he said. "I'll open the pocket."

Stubbornly, Fuller refused at first. "We almost have them! Just a little more!"

Knight shook his head. "We need to save every veteran pilot, squad, and crew for future attacks, begin withdrawing now."

18

"Ladies and Gentlemen of the legislature," Field Marshall Adam Hausnerr said. "As we speak, our forces are taking the fight to the Union. Despite the setbacks and disasters that plagued the opening month of our struggle, those episodes did not foreshadow our defeat." He stood at a podium on the floor of the central chamber in the Hall of Law, a massive building cast from glass and marble.

All three houses of the legislature presented themselves. The lowest house, the weakest and composed of lobbyists, sat in the nosebleed seats. The central house, the decisive house, held legislators representing the provinces and colonies, each representative representing roughly ten thousand constituents from their home province or colonies. The upper house, or senate, contained the least people, but each had considerably more sway over legislation than the other houses. Two Senators from each province, and one from each colony.

"No, this offensive, even as they push the Union of Mars across the Grenze, is a new beginning," he said. "The Unis had us out numbered with their ally Avalon two to one for the better part of a year, yet despite their numerical superiority we have held them off even with our back to the Mariner gulf."

Hausnerr looked up at the weathered face of Senator Huber, leader of the Armistice faction. "Some of you served in this congress when we defeated the Union previously, you got complacent, now we need more money to make our military stronger because we have run out of time to do so, while many of you lived in a fantasy, that war would never stain our ground, the Union prepared itself, they cast their envious eyes on our wealth and prosperity, while we expanded our dominion and built one of the greatest economies in the solar system, they poured money and effort into expanding and strengthening their military."

Hausnerr spread his hands. "This will not be a quick war, this is the beginning of a long struggle, some of you don't have the stomach for that, well to that I say quit now!" The room gasped at his statement. "Tens of thousands have died already in the face of an implacable enemy, hundred of thousands of Tharcian citizens, *your countrymen,* struggle under the boot of Union thugs, vile men and women more interested in punishing the people of Gallacia for leaving then liberating anyone despite what they're propaganda says."

He jabbed a finger at Senator Huber. It was a generalized gesture, but say politicians knew he was accusing the man directly. "If you would be so cowardly to betray them with an armistice, to allow the Union and all its vile instruments free rein over the continent, then I beseech you to leave now, for all the rest of you, you have my solemn promise, that the army of our great republic will defend to the death our second home."

He gripped his podium. "Even as our allies and our brothers and sisters toil and cry out for freedom, we will oppose the Union and their wicked Mobile Assault Guards, we will fight them in

Olympia, we will fight them in Gallacia, whatever the cost, we will fight even with the ocean wind at our backs, our navy, with growing strength will challenge them among the stars, and even if, this building is over run Union thugs, and our second home is consumed by fire, then our colonies with all of their heavenly power, will rain justice onto this world until once again we have been liberated!"

Cheers rose from the halls of the legislature. Hausnerr noted that delegations from colony clusters seemed particularly animated as well as younger or were legislators. But the old guard, they remained stoic and unblinking. *What the hell, is patriotism not politicly favorable? We're in a war.*

"Admiral Hausnerr," purred an older woman, one of the armistice faction, from the president's notes. "How do you account for the failure of the army to stop the Union from overrunning Gallacia?"

"Simple," Hausnerr replied. "Skara played ball with your budget cuts, force restrictions, and funding limits, he was just as complacent with you even as our mortal enemy made leaps and bounds in doctrine and technology, I'm not, I'll tell you what we need and expect it done."

"Marshall, what makes you think this war is winnable in the first place?" Senator Huber asked.

Hausnerr locked eyes with the older man. "Senator, we'll win this war because we have to, the Union won't stand for anything other than complete capitulation, if we approach this another way, there won't be a Tharsis."

Another senator asked him a question. "What do you have to say about the Union raids against the colonies?"

Hausnerr nodded. "We've been working with the navy and some allied forces to produce a panzerter for use by the colonial defense forces. These panzerters will be built in the cluster and allow the colonies to fight the invaders on equal terms." An attendant approached the podium.

"The President would like to speak with you on some recent developments," he whispered. Hausnerr thanked the attendant, dismissed any further questions, and followed the young man off the chamber floor.

He led him through a tunnel to the Citadel. The massive structure housed the upper echelons of the Tharcian Army, as well as a good chance of the Navy's presence on the surface outside spaceports. Finally, he found himself in a meeting room with President Reinhardt as well as a delegation from Vinland.

"Our government has come to a decision," The head of the delegation, a blonde woman with a bob cut, said as she approached him. "We're willing to join the Central Alliance and the War against the Union."

Hausnerr smiled, and they began shaking hands and sitting down to hash out the fine details. A Vinnish expeditionary force would mobilize and land in Tharsis before the country openly declared hostilities with the Union. In the mean time, Vinnish diplomats would stall and harass the Union and Avalon with sanctions and embargos while her shipyards began building and refitting warships in a wider push to support their new allies across the system.

All told, a single Vinnish Army of around 300,000 would reinforce Army Group West while 45 Ships reinforced the Tharcian fleet. Vinnish and Tharcian engineers would also collaborate on new methods and equipment to defend their orbiting colonies. Feeling pleased with the entire ordeal, Hausnerr excused himself to head upstairs to the Citadel's nerve center.

I need to find out how the battles across the front are going. Wordlessly entering the vast room filled with monitors, live maps, and readouts, he found himself a chair. And waited.

MORE THARCIAN PANZERTERS ENTERED IRONTON FROM THE NORTH end. *I need to break the ring, we'll all die if we're trapped in this pocket.* Using a captured Tharcian rifle, Knight opened fire. Thanks to the advanced fire control systems of the Jupiter, he easily punched through magazines and engines, rapidly bringing down his attackers.

I need to get to the north end of the highway, like the mouth of a river we can use it to funnel our people out. The Jupiter staggered forward. His earlier battle with Mondragon, with all his hard maneuvering and sudden changes in direction, had been hard on the heavy machine's joints. *I can't afford to get embroiled in hand to hand combat, not with the wear on the joint's so far.*

Like most modern panzerters, the Jupiter possessed electro-magnetic joints. While this negated the strain much of the weight normally on leg joints, the Jupiter's engine didn't quite have the power output to keep the joints as clear of each other as they could be. Even with regulators to prevent the joints from falling under a certain threshold, the joints still "clicked" during hard maneuvers, creating shavings and interfering with the normal elec-tromagnets.

This was normally countered by regular maintenance. Engineers would clear the small amount of shavings built up and replace worn joints. However, Knight's previous engagement had caused the joints to click excessively, building up shavings and degrading the ability of his joints to repel each other.

He felt it with each rocking step of his battered machine. *Come on, just a little further.* As he toggled off damaged secondary systems, his sleeve pulled back, revealing the tattoo of Phobos he possessed on his arm. Even if it was only a glimpse, the reminder of his wife in the chaotic situation brought him some comfort. For a brief moment, he pictured the two of them on an artificial beach within the Martian moon.

I'll be home soon, Sammy, don't you worry. More Tharcian panzerters. More shells streaked his way. The Jupiter rattled with each impact, the heavy machine growing as weary as its pilot. *Come on, just a little more.*

Two went down in a flash of fire and smoke. Knight had forgotten about the Mobile Artillery in all the chaos, but now the last panzerter laid into them with its rifle. Even as fires blossomed in the night, the panzerter collapsed after accurate fire from Knight's rifle.

This is all so wasteful. He shook his head in disgust as the panzerters burned. *How many of those pilots are like that Mo kid? How many are younger? I can't believe these bastards press-ganged children into an adult's war.*

His grip on the controls tightened as he headed towards the highway. *As much as I hate it, I can't separate those children from the vile instruments of their government.* His thoughts turned to his wife. *Sammy loves kids, always wanted them. Would she understand? No, how could she? I've always believed the right things, doesn't that mark me a good person? I just want a fairer world. Then why do I have to do these things that are blatantly unfair.*

Movement on his sensors interrupted his inner turmoil. Friendly signatures under attack. Beleaguered Martians fought off a fresh wave of Tharcian panzerters. Knight turned to bring himself along the Tharcians flank, dumping round after round into the enemy machines.

Surprised by the massive panzerter on their flank, he forced them to split their fire. A fatal mistake. As the last one collapsed, he hailed Fuller.

"Call a full retreat, we need to preserve what strength we have," he said.

A heavily damaged Martian ran past him up the highway. "No need to say it twice, we're all going to die!" The man said. Knight grit his teeth. *Coward!*

Switching his mike to the general net, he called out to the surviving Union forces. "All MAG forces in the vicinity of Ironton, if you want to live, fall back North along the highway, I'll cover your retreat." He blasted at a pair of gunships as IFVs and APCs raced down the highway, desperate to escape the slaughter.

This can't be anything other than a disaster. A dropship crashed into a building to hear him, a law office it looked like. He sent his last shells in the general direction of the missile that had killed it when his weapon clicked empty.

Guess it's just the sword now. With a sigh, he tossed away the useless rifle and drew his sword. *No one gets past me.*

CHANEY SHIFTED UNCOMFORTABLY IN HIS CHAIR. THE RUSHED AND abrupt nature of this meeting wasn't at all lost on him. Many of the generals and officers present had hardly changed out of their night clothes. Pearson herself wore a thick bathrobe over a nightgown.

"What's happening in Tharsis?" She demanded. *Straight to business, then.* Most of the General officers stared blankly, either still asleep or otherwise not up to date on the current situation. Chaney himself had a decent understanding as he'd been awake observing tests on the newest weapon prototypes, but since he wasn't in charge of strategy, he hadn't paid too much attention.

"An intelligence failure," the head of intelligence said. "Or rather a counter-intelligence failure, we underestimated the amount of information and the amount of detail Tharcian terror cells were able to feed to their government." He cleared his throat. "I recommend we reevaluate our center-intelligence and counter-terror strategy."

"It's not just and intelligence failure," The Operations chief said. "The Tharcians were able to plan this entire operation without our plants in their high command having a clue, and their plan was better than the ones we've typically seen thus far."

"What does that mean for us?" Pearson asked.

"It means we can't rely on our knowledge of their high command for insight into current operations," the operations chief replied. "And we can't assume the Tharcians will screw up constantly." Chaney found himself nodding along with the others. Whatever their illusions of swift victory, he couldn't see them winning within a year.

"There's also the issue of embargo," the chief of logistics said. "We rely far too much on imports for food, if something isn't done about these embargoes, then we face starvation."

"Avalon needs to be reigned in," Added Commodore Mendez, herself still wearing a night gown. "Their reckless conduct will bring disaster to our cause."

"I wasn't done with supply issues," the Chief of logistics said. "On top of the damage to the orbital elevator, the surface will suffer for raw materials and fuel, while Phobos, Los Estrellas, and the other settlements will bear the brunt of the food shortages."

"Enough," Pearson finally said. "I'll have to convene with the First Minister and the ARF as well as the Guards-Marshall when ever he returns from his frontline inspection."

"Comrade Secretary, we need decisive action now," the chief of operations said. "This is not a matter we can simply discuss in a future meeting, we must figure out how to subdue Tharsis before Avalon's reckless behavior draws more enemies into the war."

Pearson looked at Commodore Mendez. "Would piracy help our holdings in space?"

The younger women shot the political a disgusted look. "Comrade, our fleet will not lower themselves to the level of pirates," she snapped. "Nor will it have any meaningful impact on our logistics."

"Forget I said anything," Pearson muttered before returning her gaze to the others. "How long will it take to repair the elevator?"

"At least six months before we're sure it'll be safe to move anything," Chaney said. "That's including clearing out damaged sections and making sure we don't accidentally collapse the whole thing. Until then, we may want to build back our spaceports so we can at least get something into orbit and back."

Relief crept over Pearson's stony face. "There's the first solution I've heard tonight, how what do we do with the civilians we've detained?"

"We can't afford for them to become terrorists," the chief of intelligence said. "If we leave them in their own homes, and to their own devices, they'll plot against us."

"Well, we can't just kill them," the chief of operations said. "We're not monsters here." Chaney's thoughts turned toward Woody Pete, a man who'd managed to maim one of their best pilots and was potentially behind the intelligence disaster in Western Tharsis. Before the war, he'd been an ordinary man with a family, but now he was a terrorist mastermind. *No, we're not, but they could be.*

"We put them to work," Chaney said. "Who better than to clear the debris from the elevator? To build our spaceports? To dig ditches and supplant our tuber population? Break them up, move them all over the Union, toss their children in our education centers and completely relocate them."

Pearson raised an eyebrow. "So we'd leave large sections of Olympia and Tharsis barren?" Chaney shook his head.

"No, we put loyal Union citizens in the occupied zones and begin transitioning them into Martian Republics," he said. "I know it isn't my place to make that call, but it's the only way we prevent problems like this in the future."

"His plan has merit," the chief of intelligence said. "If we break up the nuclear families and separate citizens from those in their hometown, then they'll likely become much more docile, and by extension useful."

"If our labor pool suddenly swells," the Chief of Operations said. "WE could have issues paying everyone, and what's stopping us from using their farmers and miners to shore up our own resource issues?"

"Because those farmers and miners could be bad actors," Pearson said. "As for paying people, don't worry about the economic or political ramifications, those are for individuals such as myself and the First Minister to handle, stick to winning the war."

Despite her appreciation of his idea, Chaney found himself resenting her tone. *It's like she believes herself our betters. has she ever worked a hard day in her life? Must be nice to sit your way to the top.*

"Comrade Chaney," Commodore Mendez asked. "Can you please explain your new project to the general staff?" Realizing he drifted off in thought, he nodded.

"Yes, I can, sorry I was just thinking about it," he said. "We're developing new munitions with the intent to fully replace both lasers and ballistics, and the process of feeding said weapons greatly unburdening our supply lines."

"How so?" Asked the chief of Logistics, her eyes filled with curiosity.

Chaney grinned. "Well we all we need for the weapon to operate is Nitrogen in its gaseous state, a substance which I'll remind you is a byproduct of our helium-3 refining."

"So let me get this straight," the chief of operations said. "You made a serviceable weapon out of an element we're breathing right now?"

Shaking his head, Chaney grinned. "Funny you say that, because most of the things you're breathing can already be deadly in the right amount."

"I've seen the tests," Commodore Mendez said. "It looks impressive, but Commodore Masterson is developing a similar weapon based on the particle weapon research, although his uses Red Mercury." Chaney frowned at this information.

"We need to save our Red Mercury reserves in the event that our supply of Helium-3 is cut off," he said. "it has far more value as a fuel reserve then a weapon." While the meeting ground to a close, and the other officers were dismissed and began heading to bed, Chaney mused his own words.

Is that even possible? The war dragging on to the point that we need Red Mercury for our panzerters and warships? He shook his head. *I hate to admit it, but that's how we need to think. At least if we want any chance of winning this war.*

———

"THERE THEY ARE," WEBB SAID. HIS MOTLEY CREW, MADE UP OF downed pilots, dismounted mortar men and the remains of his Alpha and Charlie squads. In front of them lay a crippled and damaged panzerter IV. *Damn, this thing took a beating.*

Molten chunks of armor plating littered the street along with shavings and other chances of scrap metal. Deep gouges in the panzerter's frame testified to the punishment it had taken. Webb shook his head. *My human body defiantly can't stand up to whatever did that.*

"Call the scouts, they might be wounded in there," Wesser said. Gasping for breath, Webb found himself surprised that while he tired, the panzerter team leader seemed unbothered by all the running they'd done.

He turned his attention back to the panzerter. "You there, Smith, is there a way to open this from our end?"

The younger man was already clambering onto the fallen machine. He pulled at something near the hatch and shook his head. "The emergency release is stuck."

From inside the machine, they could hear banging and muffled shouts. A sulfurous odor filled the air. "What's that smell?" a drop-trooper asked as Wesser's eyes grew wide.

"There's a fuel leak somewhere!" She cried. "If we don't get them out quick, they'll suffocate!" Smith squat down and attempted to kick the hatch open.

"Well, don't just stand there!" he gasped as two drop troopers leaped to his side. With assistance from their partial-exosuits, they were able to kick the hatch wide open. They helped Mo and Magyar out of the damaged unit, the two of them gasping for breath.

"Thank God," Mo gasped. "She was breathing all my air."

"Your air?" Magyar asked. Mo nodded.

"My panzerter, my air," he said before looking back at his panzerter. "Damn, that's not going to buff out."

Webb set a firm hand on the younger man's shoulder. "Come on, let's go, we've still got to retrieve your buddy." After shaking his head to clear out the lingering fatigue, he pointed south.

"Last I saw Wes Merlin, he was shot down back that way," he said. *Good, can't be too hard, somewhere in that general direction is a disabled fifty-ton panzerter.* He waved for the group to set off and they followed him. Even in his partial-exosuit, fatigue began to set in. His limbs felt heavy and his eyes throbbed. *It doesn't matter, I can go further.*

True to his word, Mo had been correct about where the older Merlin went down. The massive machine lay doubled over a building, like a drunk vomiting behind a counter. One of its arms reached for the ground while the other had been severed at the elbow. Sparks danced from exposed wiring and magnets while the visor that made up the unit's eyes flickered behind it's cracked appearance.

"I have to admit, that's solid Vaterland architecture right there," one of his soldiers said. "Even when partially destroyed, can still bear the weight of a panzerter." Webb had to agree with the guy. It was impressive, but it also presented a different set of problems for them.

"Think this building is in danger of collapsing?" he asked Wesser. "Because if not, we need to get in there and get up to the third floor."

She shook her head. "No way to know," she said. "Honestly, collapsing the building might be the safest thing to do."

"What if there's another fuel leak?" he asked. "Then we wouldn't;t have time to dig through rubble." Wesser swore and looked at him.

"Then your team needs to work fast," she said. "Because that building can fall any second." Without another word, two drop troopers along with Smith rushed into the building. They could hear the structure groan as they saw their team running through the windows.

Slowly, they began backing away from the damaged building. Broken signage told them this had been the town's bank. More groans rang out as they continued backing away.

Suddenly, something cracked. Loudly. The panzerter shifted with the scrape of metal on concrete. Blurred shapes moved past the windows on the second floor as the groans became more pronounced.

With a final heave, the panzerter fell on its face. Its helmeted head crumpled against the road as its body collapsed with the surrounding structure. Rushing out of the dust came Smith, one of the drop troopers carrying a downed pilot, and...

"Hans didn't make it," the drop trooper said. "He got pinned when the panzerter shifted." Webb sighed and turned away. *This long night just keeps getting a little longer.*

19

As the last Martian past Knight, it handed him it's rifle. Nodding in thanks, he unleashed it on a gunship sweeping in low to attack a fleeing armored column. *Not today, asshole.* The thick rounds rushed past the aggressive looking craft as it juked and dodged, returning fire with rockets and cannons.

While the Jupiter shrugged off the worst of it, several armored vehicles burst into flames, including the command truck containing the XO. Gritting his teeth, Knight zeroed in on the attacking aircraft.

Eventually, the gunship zigged when it should have zagged and a 105-mm round punched clean through the airframe of the Tharcian gunship. *So wasteful.* He looked back as more wheeled and tracked vehicles fled. No more dropships. No more panzerters.

Almost there. Then a shape came into view on his sensors. A panzerter. A Familiar one, not one of his though. Knight sighed and gripped his controls tighter. *The Black Knight. This man that allowed children to die in battle.*

The Black knight had seen better days. It's armor had been

dinged and worn, and his shield was mostly gone. It's glowing blue sword seemed to be working just fine, though. *I'm probably not looking much better.*

Rifle in one hand and sword in another, he braced himself for the coming battle. "Captain Reiter, the black knight himself, how brave of you to face me without your child-soldiers in front of you."

The Black Knight paused in the middle of the highway and assumed some kind of ready stance. "Big talk coming from you, where are your two cronies?" Knight focused on the heavy machine in front of him. *I definitely can't take him on in a protracted battle, especially since it looks like he's ready for close quarter combat.*

"They're indisposed," he said. "They have they're missions, I got mine." He grit his teeth as he stared at the man. *What kind of monster is he? What kind of absolute psychopath orders children to die for him?* "How do you do it?"

"Come again?" Reiter replied. Knight slammed his fist into a console next to him.

"How can you stand by while you send kids into battle?" Knight said. "All of those innocent lives? How many saplings have you burned today?"

The Black Knight stood silently in the night. Its sword hummed as snow drifted by. In the distance, artillery rumbled. "Honestly, no matter what I tell you, there's nothing I can say that would satisfy you," Reiter replied. "But I can tell you, that they *choose* to do this. The act congress passed allowed students in prep schools to volunteer."

"You mean to tell me they choose this?" Knight replied. "All of this madness and death? The suffering? What lies did you feed them?"

"I didn't feed them any lies!" Reiter replied. "Do you have any idea where you are? You're standing in the ruins of somebody's home! Their families are in danger, their friends are in danger, and you think we'd need to lie to them to get them to fight?" The Thar-cian's words hung in the air between them. A dropship somewhere behind the black knight rose into the air, but Knight ignored it. The battle for Ironton was ending with both sides beginning to with-draw. But for him, his battle was right here.

"That you people would get so desperate to even ask disgusts me," Knight said. "None of you actually believe a damn thing you say about the sanctity of life."

"Oh, and the Union is any better?" Reiter asked. "What about the tubers? You're going to raise people from birth to fight and die for your country without any regard to whether they'd want to?"

Knight grimaced at the other man's words. "They wouldn't exist if it weren't for us! They owe us that much!" It dawned on him, as he spoke, that he knew very little of how the tubers had been raised. Despite working with Kennedy and Ballard for the better part of a month, he'd never bothered to ask them about their childhood.

Their childhoods were great, I'm sure, they prepared them for the things they were best suited to do. They weren't stolen. They weren't stolen.

To deal with his own headache, he opened fire on the black knight. Rounds bounced off the other panzerter's thick armor, but Knight knew Reiter was getting tossed around in there. *That'll stun him, but I need to finish this quick.*

As he poured on the rifle fire, he charged with his sword held high in an all-or-nothing attempt to win.

SPARKS FILLED REITER'S VISION AS SHELLS STRUCK HIS ARMOR. *Damn it, I can't see!* As soon as the shelling ceased, the fatman filled his vision, sword raised. *I guess he's done talking.*

He met the sword with his own blade, static flying between

them. While parrying the fatman's blows, he allowed himself to drive back down the autobahn. *Space for time, even though it's damaged, a fatman is still a huge threat to forces without heavy panzerters of their own.*

Despite his opponent's incredible skill and experience, his movements were predictable and followed a pattern. *He's using the minimal movement possible and keeping me to his right.* He attributed the movements to fatigue and noticed the damage to the unit's sensors. It all became clear for Reiter.

More artillery rumbled farther north of him. He knew what it was before Hawke even said anything over the radio. The 12th Regiment was on the attack. The battle of Ironton had been won. They'd have some room to breathe now.

Something slammed into his panzerter and alarms blared. Reiter fought for balance, the distraction resulting in the loss of his shield. Upper Left leg compromised.

While Reiter struggled to stay upright and keep weight off his damaged leg, Knight pressed his attack. Under pressure and fighting for his life, Reiter flipped the script.

He leaned into each of his attacks. Cutting through his enemy's rifle, the sudden shift in momentum caught the MAG off guard. Stumbling backward, he feebly blocked the incoming blows.

Finally, an overhand strike pushed the fatman backwards. As its feet dug trenches into the autobahn, something finally gave. With a rending shriek, the fatman's foot caught itself in the ground, but the leg above it continued. More metal peeled away from the severed limb.

But the fatman did not fall. Instead it lunged forward in a final desperate attempt to seize victory. As Reiter knocked the blade aside, he thrust with his sword. The fatman's arm went limp at the tip, pierced its chest just below the head.

Reiter caught his breath. The fatman seized, moving entirely. No one called out to him to challenge his morals. No one cursed him while vowing revenge. There was just his own breath, and the hum of his engine.

"So stupid," he muttered. All around him, homes and businesses, the things people spent their lives building, lay in ruins. Decades, possibly centuries' worth of blood, sweat, and tears had all been undone in a matter of hours. Panzerters lay where they'd fallen, the smoldering, partially molten wrecks of combat vehicles surrounded him.

As he stood alone, snow gathered over the wrecks, in the ruins, and over the bodies. *From up here, you can't tell the Tharcians from the Unionists, or the tubers from the normals.* Leaning over, he picked his picture of Fletcher off the cockpit floor. *No one is made for this. Because people were never made for this.*

Artillery and missiles roared in the distance. Drones passed overhead in formation. *12th must be moving. It sounds like we're done here.*

"The Union line is breaking," Hawke said. "Twelfth panzerter is breaking through, we're winning, I can't believe we're winning!" Reiter turned the Lowe around as friendly panzerters closed the ring around Ironton.

Iglasio's rolled past him. Reiter recognized them as 4-14th's units. One of the commanders waved to him as he stood in his open hatch. Reiter waved back when he realized the man was trying to get his attention.

"Fox 6, what do you need?" he asked as he switched to their net.

"Hey, thanks for noticing us," came the reply. "Our panzerter platoon took a beating. Do you mind giving us a hand with mop up?" Reiter checked his ammo and status. The Lowe had taken a severe beating, but was still combat operational. Several subsystems had been knocked offline, but he still had most of his machine-gun ammo.

"Yeah, I don't mind," he finally replied. He let the IFVs take the lead, following behind them and watching upper floor windows. When their dismounts stormed into a building, Reiter looked away. Surveying the devastation reminded him just how badly this quaint mining town had been brutalized. In one store, he recognized the burning remains of a Christmas tree.

He shook his head. *It's all so sad, it's easy to see how people get warped by this.* His eyes wandered over to a picture of Szilard stubbornly tacked to his combat wall. *I'm sorry kid, I'm sure you would have loved another Christmas with your parents.*

"You're going to be ok," Wesser gasped ahead of him. Webb held onto the back left end of the stretcher bearing the older Merlin brother. As snow fell gently from the dark clouds overhead, *Lazy Sue*'s engines idled before them.

Merlin coughed. The noise sounded ragged, but it was a good sign. The pressure seal on his right side was working, and his lungs were stabilizing. Pressure dressings clotted the bleeding in savage gouges in both legs.

"Hey hold up!" One of the medics aboard the Sue cried. "We got to make room for more!"

Doc swore and shook his fist at the other medics. "What the hell do you mean? You knew you had more wounded coming!"

"Because we're supposed to have two other Pegasi!" The other medic angrily responded.

On the litter behind them, Magyar groaned. "Aww fuck me," she groaned.

"Can't I'm a little busy right now," Smith grunted him. In spite of the situation, Webb chuckled. He wasn't sure if the young man was joking or being serious, but his comment eased some of the tension and exhaustion they felt. *Exo-frames only go so far.*

He glanced over his shoulder and saw Magyar pat the young pilot's arm with her own. "Smith, get your goofy face down here where I can talk to you."

Smith bent over and Magyar landed a peck on his cheek. "You better be here when I recovery, or I'll be a bit upset." Webb smirked. Then a commotion to his left drew his attention.

"Where is he?" the younger Merlin asked. "Wes? Wes? Talk to me!" Doc grabbed the young man's shoulder.

"Easy lad, he's table right now, but don't go aggrevatin ya brother," the old medic replied. "He'll be fine, just calm down." The younger Merlin nodded and looked down at his wounded brother.

"Wes?"

Wesley Merlin coughed, then nodded. "I'm good," he said. "Just do me a solid and don't tell mom." He shook his head. "Audrey's already going to be pissed enough as it is." His words wheezed out of his throat. He grimaced before sheepishly smiling and giving his brother a thumbs up.

"All clear!" The flight medic called. "Bring them in!" Webb bounded forward, along with the other litter-bearers. Once the wounded pilots and two injured drop troopers had been secured on the bird, they cleared out.

The Lazy Sue lived up to her name, slowly climbing into the air before accelerating away. It was gone in moments, only a noise in the distance. *They're probably taking them to Vaterland Regional Medical, that's the biggest and best equipped hospital near here.*

"Well alright, squad and team leaders, do your BBG checks and let me know when you're done," Webb said. "When everyone's squared away, find a place to shelter down and take a nap."

"BBG?" Wesser asked once the others had gotten to work.

"Beans, bullets, and gas," Webb replied. "In our case, meaning water, do your people need anything?"

Wesser looked at Merlin and Smith and shook her head. "I don't think so," she said. "Although it would be good to get ahold of Captain Reiter or-" The Sound of Massive footfalls drew their attention. "Is that an enemy panzerter?"

Webb grit his teeth as he ducked into a store front. The pilots and doc followed him. "That depends, do you think one got by Reiter?"

As the machine rounded the corner onto their street, Webb's tired eyes struggled to ID the machine. *Damn it, I'm too tired to ID this thing, be looking at its legs, I need a look at its head.* Slowly, he crept forward in a crouch with his rifle ready.

Fortunately, instead of a wide saucer shaped head with a red-ring, he saw a more human like head resembling one of his own drop troopers wearing a helmet. With a sigh, Webb relaxed and waved the others out.

"It's alright," he said. "Friendly, Friendly." As the others cautiously emerged from cover, the Panzerter IV knelt and opened its cockpit hatch. A short but stout woman crawled out and climbed to the ground.

"Hey LT," she called to Wesser as she removed her helmet, revealing strawberry blonde hair. "I could really use some food and a nap." Wesser caught her when she stumbled.

"Come on Steele, let's get you to cover and lay down," she replied. In the distance, Webb heard the distant sound of a pair of .50 cals hammering away at something. He sighed and shook his head. *Does this shit ever end?*

"I HAVE NO REGRETS," MEYER SAID AS SHE RODE IN THE COMMAND truck with Kennedy. He nodded and leaned back, bandages swaddling his head. "Our position is untenable, we have to pull back and regroup."

"You don't need to justify anything to me," he said. "I understand perfectly clear." Dawn broke on the horizon, casting the sky and snow below in shades of orange. Finally, one of the longest nights in their lives was over. "I'm eager to hear Knight's report, I'm fairly certain he'll confirm what I already thought happened at the front."

"And what's that?" she asked. *You've rarely steered me wrong, and have consistently brought clarity to a situation I didn't see, I need to hear this.* Kennedy relaxed slightly.

"We need to do something about Fuller," he said. "I firmly believe his incompetence led directly to our defeat, his actions overcommitted us in Ironton and I believe directly led to our defeat."

Meyer nodded slowly. "There will be a full investigation into what happened, I'm sure the proper culprits will be punished." She sighed. "Although as much as we cast blame, we have to admit one of the culprits was the Tharcians themselves, they had better intelligence and a better plan then they had up tp this point."

"What are you saying?" Kennedy asked. "That our actions didn't have consequences?"

"No," Meyer replied. "Rather, we assumed our enemy would either remain the same or get worse, but instead, they improved." She looked out the window to the breaking light of dawn. "And in assuming our enemies would remain stagnate, we became stagnate ourselves. We need to get back to our roots as an offensive force."

Kennedy grunted. As he fell asleep, Meyer pulled out a tablet. The entire Army was taking losses across the entire front. MAG forces withdrew through the pine gap towards the northern edge of the theater. Divisions had been caught overextended. Out of position, or flat footed by a sudden determined Tharcian coun-terattack.

Of course it wouldn't be easy, these people are fighting to defend their homes. She sighed as she adjusted the tablet to hurt her neck less. *This is an ideological war no doubt, everything's got a little of ideology in it, but the Tharcians aren't shouting slogans or talking points as they march into battle. They're fighting for their homes.*

A notification popped up across the top of her screen. A message from Chaney. Reading it told her he wanted he a complete report from her on whether or not, their doctrine had caused the defeat behind them. *Sure, I'll get right on that as soon as I have free time while I'm rebuilding nearly an entire division. Sure.*

She bitterly tossed her tablet into the seat next to her. There would be time for analytics, testimony, and evaluations later. But right now, she just wanted to escape the gloom of loss around her. It made the air oppressive, heavy, like she was walking underwater. *Maybe things will get better when we return to the rear.*

The whole operation had turned shameful. The kicker was her mechanized rifle battalion had made good progress towards a narrow field, but had been forced to pull out when the other half of the operation collapsed. She shook her head in disgust. *I'll have to make sure they get medals for bravery or something, I don't want them to feel like their efforts had been futile.* But the truth was, they had been. There was nothing to be gained from their rapid advance. When the 25th Mechanized took over their positions, they'd be forced to start from behind where her battalion had started.

I know Kennedy can't help but think otherwise, but this feels like it's my fault somehow. I came up with the plan. I allowed that terrorist to be housed in our basement. Without a doubt, the intel leaks came from him.

Fuller might be overconfident, even incompetent, but I've made the most damning mistakes at the operational level. She shook her head. *I need a smoke or something, I need to get out of this funk.* Finally they arrived at Pulaski, the fallen provincial capital of the Gallacian province. As she stepped out of the command truck, she told a guard that Kennedy was sleeping inside as she dug through her pocket.

Finding her pack of cigarettes, she was glad to find a few left in there. After fumbling for her lighter, she found a corner out of the wind. Eagerly, she lit up and took a long drag.

———————

"Do you have an update from the front?" Ballard asked. Chaney shook his head. In the whee hours of the morning, Ballard showed up for work roaring to go, but Chaney was running on fumes.

"No comrade, I don't," he replied. "I've been in meetings since 0300, but I still don't have any word on the status of your old battalion." He took a deep breath. "I apologize for snapping, it's ben a long night, let's talk about the Phobian."

Deftly he brought up an image of the machine Ballard had been piloting in various simulations. The panzerters squat and aggressive appearance with the more standard looking Martian and Terran. Ballard looked at the projection.

"So I'm not going into sims today?" he asked. Chaney shook his head.

"No, I just need feedback, then we'll make adjustments to the sim model and resume testing," he replied. "Now, what's the biggest problem for you so far?"

"The cockpit," Ballard replied. "I know your modified sim pod isn't exactly the real thing, but it's cramped as hell and several critical gauges are either in odd places to look at and critical functions are difficult to reach." Chaney raised an eyebrow.

"In that case, where should the gauges ideally be in your opinion?" he asked.

Ballard tapped the sides of his head. "At the edge of peri-rebel vision," he said. "Preferably under my line of vision, but some are over my head, and others require me to turn my head to look at, if I'm referencing gauges, the only thing I should move is my eyes."

Chaney nodded, jotting down notes on a notepad as he spun the figure. "That will take some time. What do you think of the weapons?"

"I understand that this is supposed to be a close quarters unit, but some kind of long-range weapon and more anti-infantry weapons," Ballard replied. "I'd rather not burn out a laser lens because I had to engage a panzerter and immediately after defend against infantry."

Chaney sighed. "That may unduly increase the weight of this thing," he said. "And I was already beginning to lose confidence in the new power plant's ability to save weight and even maintain the performance of the other engine."

Ballard stretched his neck. "Well damn, that puts this whole project in trouble," he replied. "And it really answers a need of ours, is the other new panzerter looking any more promising?"

Chaney signaled, more or less. "It's a new Martian variant, so it's easier to test and get us in the development stage. Problem is we were relying on this new engine to help with some of the power plant issues caused by the Superlaser." He switched the image before them to the other new panzerter about to enter frontline service.

Ballard frowned. "This one's less my style," he said. "But I recognize the need for it, especially if we can beat them at their own game." Chaney shook his head.

"This is less about beating them at their own game, and more about leveling the playing field at long range," he said. "Although I admit, it's still not quite in our favor, the Black Knight for example can annotate them before they have a chance of coming into a range that can damage it."

"Belive you me, I get that it's scary looking, but what's your fixation with it?" Ballard asked. "Kennedy I get, for him it's personal, but as far as I'm aware it hasn't killed anyone you know."

Chaney uncorked his water bottle and took a long swig. "Before you ask, yes its water, I'm too dehydrated for that shit, and secondly, it aggravates me because they made a well balanced machine that we can't match without breaking the bank." He immediately pulled up an image of the Black knight. The circle that displayed speed. Protection and firepower flared to life, all three points reaching almost to the edges of the circle. "It's protection isn't particularly complex, it's good on the surface, but our preferred weapons, lasers are practically useless against it and our panzerter firearms are barely better, it's more agile than the Martian with enough firepower to take out a Jupiter clean."

"If the Tharcians just built an amazing machine, why haven't they built more of them?" Ballard asked. Chaney raised a finger.

"Because, it's only weakness is its expensive and too heavy for most bridges," he replied. "That being said, we can't just build a better machine or we'll wreck our own economy, but what if they refine the black knight, reduce the weight?" Chaney wagged his finger to punctuate his point. "Then my friend, they've won the war."

20

After stirring from his sleep, Kennedy found himself in a hospital bed. *This is becoming way too familiar.* As he rose to take in his surroundings, he noticed he was in an actual hospital. His bed possessed guardrails so he wouldn't roll off, and an IV dripped fluid into his arm. A soldier watched tv in the corner.

"About time you woke up, comrade," he said. It took Kennedy a moment to realize it, but he was looking at Khan.

"Comrade Khan, where are we?" he asked. The Red Guard shrugged.

"Some hospital in the old capital, they have Snow down the hall," Khan replied.

"And Knight?"

Khan shook his head. "KIA, keeping the pocket open so we could pullout of Ironton. Word is, he's posthumously being awarded an Order of the Martian People, so there's that." He looked out the window to the snow filled city. "If his wife hadn't been killed in an airline crash, he'd probably have some next of kin to receive it."

With a sigh, Kennedy shook his head. "He was a good soldier, so it's just you and Snow now?" Khan shrugged.

"The whole 'Red Guards' thing was a big propaganda push, if anything he'll have a state funeral," he said. "But I'm not really interested in that."

"What are you interested in?" Kennedy asked.

Khan's features darkened. "Punishing the Tharcians, they've killed our people and provoked us long enough." He looked directly at Kennedy. "I don't care about your struggle, comrade colonel, I don't care about your birth, all I want is to kill as many Tharcians as possible, and if I can't kill them, I want to hurt them."

That's absolutely psychotic, I guess it can't be helped though. Better he kills a worthless Tharcian then stays in Union society and becomes a serial killer or something. Besides, that kind of anger is pliable. Kennedy set himself on his elbows. "Khan, do you have your service pistol?"

"I do," he replied. "Do you want to end someone's life?" Kennedy shook his head.

"Not at the moment," he replied. "But when I'm discharged from here, Meyer's going to want a full AAR with all of her leaders, we've run ourselves with a lot of civility, but we've been leaving a good portion of our disciplinary options off the table, certain individuals need to be made examples and I'll need to borrow your pistol for that."

Khan smiled. "I've always read that line, but it thought it was all talk."

"You've never experienced an officer fail spectacularly enough to warrant it," Kennedy said before looking up at him. "I need you and Snow to augment my battalion, to crush any opponent in our path, I know it's not good for your career, but I need to spend more time in the planning seat and less in the pilot's seat, do you understand."

The other soldier held up a hand. "Just point me at Tharcians, I'll take care of the rest along with Snow."

"I'm counting on you two," he said. "And I expect results. By the end of all of this you both should have killed a whole division's worth of Tharcians." As Kennedy expected, the younger man practically salivated.

"You're speaking my language, comrade," he said. Kennedy nodded.

"Of course, this will probably involve actions against partisans, terrorists," he said. "Do you have any qualms about attacking them?" Khan shook his head. "Excellent, I'll have to talk to Chaney about refitting your machines with anti-infantry weapons."

The other pilot raised an eyebrow. "You can just 'talk' to the head of R&D?"

Kennedy nodded. "I do, in fact it's how I got my Jupiter to begin with," he said. "Even now I know he's hard at work making new weapons. Maybe we'll get something else new when we refit."

With a smile, Khan stood up. "Well, new ways to kill Tharcians will always excite me." Easing himself back into bed, Kennedy smiled.

"Before you leave, I need to ask you something, other than to change the channel," he said. After the younger pilot switched on a music channel showcasing an orchestra, he looked down at Kennedy.

"What's your question, Comrade?" he asked. *Well, here goes nothing.*

"What motivates you to kill people?" Kennedy asked. "I was born for this, but I'm curious what a normal like yourself thinks."

Khan shrugged. "I don't really kill people, just Tharcians. And Olympians. And Rooseveltians."

"And why aren't they people?" Kennedy asked.

"If you're wondering if I'd turn on you and kill you, the

answer's no," Khan said. "Tubers are always people, because they don't have institutional power as a class, Tharcians and Olympians on the other hand brutally press their own people by denying them critical services and enabling others to oppress people."

Good, perfect actually. If things don't go completely our way, I can count on Khan to champion my cause. Kennedy nodded. "Thank you comrade Khan, you know I'm glad your lot got assigned to us, in a sense we're not that different at all." He smiled. "Because I know you were born for this too."

Khan smiled, then saluted. "Thank you comrade colonel, you'll have my positive thoughts for a swift recovery and my service pistol is here when you need it," he said before leaving.

With an exasperated sigh, Kennedy sank into his pillow as the orchestra played. *What a weird saying, you have my positive thoughts, I'd be surprised if he had many positive thoughts to begin with.* As the music flowed over him, he listened. *I've known about this music, like I recognize the instruments that go in an orchestra, but I never realized it sounded so sweet.* Violins danced in his ears while cello and bass belted their own tunes. A piano augmented the other sounds.

Such a sweet song, I wonder what the tune is? He angled his head. A subtitle read Song #251-Winter Collection. *If only the title was as sweet as the music.* A nurse entered his room.

"Need anything, sir? Food? Drink?" she asked. *Sir?* Then he noticed the collar strapped to her neck. *Ah, she's Tharcian. That would explain the compliance collar. Can't have her poisoning my food, can we?*

He nodded. "Yeah, I'll take it." As she set a warm box in his lap and set a box of juice on his nightstand, she began humming along with the song. "Have you heard this song?" he asked.

She nodded. "We used to sing it in church this time of year," she said. "It's called 'I heard the Bells on Christmas day,' though I don't think your people call it that." Kennedy shook his head. *No, we don't, but I have to admit: the name is prettier.*

UNDER A LAZY AFTERNOON SUN, MO SAT ON A CRATE WHILE salvage crews picked apart Knight's fatman. Any parts that could be repurposed for their own machines would be pulled off and all the data from its computers would be sent to R&D along with what they couldn't salvage. A massive rent under the head marked the point where Reiter's weapon had pierced the cockpit. Mo hadn't tried to look inside. He didn't have the heart.

As he sat in silence, Steel and Wesser joined him. "Are you alright Mo?" Steele asked. He shrugged.

"I don't know, to be honest," he replied. The two women took a seat next to him.

Wesser set a hand on his shoulder. "Have you been resting like you're supposed to?" she asked. "Because I'll need you at 100% when we leave to rebuild." For now, their regiment sat in reserve for the rest of the division, but soon another would take up their position so the division could rebuild.

"I have been, light activity, nothing strenuous, just like Doc ordered," he replied. "It's just, I knew him."

"You knew him?" Wesser asked.

Then Steele's eyes widened. "He came to observe the truce didn't he?"

Mo nodded. "I've seen his face, and I have to admit, it made it a lot harder for me to kill him."

"Mo, he nearly killed you," Wesser said furrowing her brow. Mo shook his head.

"But he didn't, he very easily could have crushed the cockpit, denied Tharsis not one, but two experienced pilots," he replied.

"But he didn't, he just tore out my machine-gun and left, the fuel leak that could have killed me and Magyar wasn't something he intended to do."

Wesser stood and stiffened her back. "Do you think he extended the same courtesy to the other pilots out here? Do you think he would have hesitated to kill Wes? Remember the level of oxygen deprivation he suffered could lead to permanent brain damage, he'll never be right for his kids ever again."

"Damn it Wesser, I know," he replied with a grimace. "It's just different."

Wesser put a hand on her hips. "Would it have been different if you'd seen Blake's face first? Or Kennedy's?" Mo shook his head.

"No, They both introduced themselves while threatening or trying to kill someone I cared about," he said. "It's just between him, Ballard, and Fletcher, I can't hate them."

Steele gently took one of his hands. "Javi, no one's asking you to hate them," she said. Mo reflected back to his duel with Blake, how the old man had threatened his sisters if he didn't surrender to Kennedy stabbing Bartonova as she ran to save Steele.

"Don't get me wrong, ma'am," he said. "There are some real monsters out there on the other side, but Ballard and Fletcher, they didn't ask for any of this, hell Knight didn't sound like he wanted to fight much when I got to him."

After sharing a look with Steele, Wesser took her hand off of her hip and set a hand on his shoulder. "We're fighting people Mo, not monsters, we can't forget that," she said. "The second we do, we're no better than they are."

She paused for a moment before looking away and adjusting her glasses. "And I'm sorry I snapped at you."

Mo waved his hand. As he watched the machine before him being broken apart to be rebuilt, his thoughts turned to his own future after the war. "Hey Amy, me and LT got some platoon business to go over, do you mind giving us five?"

Steele let go of his hand and stood up slowly. "Sure, whatever you need." As she trotted off, Wesser shook her head.

"She's too kind," she said before looking at Mo. "Our platoon, is us and Smith, don't insult her intelligence, now what did you want to talk about without Steele around?"

Mo barely took his eyes off the panzerter in front of him. "I want to marry her."

Blinking back her surprise, Wesser stepped away. "Wha? What?" She gestured to the fallen panzerter in front of them. "Did you forget we're in the middle of a war?" Mo just kept staring.

"I want us to have something to look forward to, after all of this." He finally looked up at Wesser. "If I'm going to fight for something, it's going to be a better tomorrow."

As Wesser relaxed slightly, she smiled. "Well, I admit I'm excited at the thought, but maybe you should hold off until we have a home to go back to." Mo raised an eyebrow.

"You're from Gallacia too?" he asked. She nodded.

"Why else would I be in the Gallacian Provincial Watch?" she asked. "But yeah, I just didn't get the chance to actually defend my home."

Mo stood up and stretched his back. "Well, you can help liberate it," he said. "And you're right, I shouldn't ask Amy right now. Besides, I don't even have a ring."

"All of that will get figured out," Wesser replied. They watched salvage crews begin pulling apart the armor plating around the cockpit.

As they worked, Mo stood up. "Alright, sitting here mopping isn't doing us any good," he said One of the mechanics poured kerosene into the open cockpit.. "I suppose this'll be the closest the man gets to an actual funeral." He saluted before leaving with Wesser.

"I wish we had more of a service for Kozma and the others," she said as they passed a row of helmets propped up on entreating tools. Mo nodded as they walked.

"I forgot to ask, have you seen Captain Reiter anywhere?" he asked. Wesser shrugged.

"Last I heard, he was still in a meeting with Hawke," she replied. An armored Mercedes truck sat with its hatch open in the light snow. Smith and Merlin got out and approached them.

"No word on when we're going back," Smith said. "But the Merc here is our ride." Steele emerged from the back with her arms folded.

"Did you take care of your platoon business?" She asked. Mo winced as he approached her.

"Yeah, mainly admin stuff, promotions, awards, etc," he said before leaning in closer. "Sorry, I can't talk to you about it, but you'll love it when it happens."

Steele blinked as she stepped back. "What's that supposed to mean?"

"Don't worry about it," Mo replied as he laid down in the open hatch. "But if we got a ride, it probably means we're getting ready to roll soon." Half laying, half sitting, he closed his eyes as Steele curled up next to him. And before they knew it, both of them were snoring in the back of the truck.

———

"WE'LL BE HERE FOR THE FORESEEABLE FUTURE," MEYER SAID AS she sat next to Kennedy's hospital bed. "It'll take some time to mobilize the personnel and material to be fighting fit again."

Kennedy nodded slowly. *I was kinda hoping to be out of the hospital for this talk, but I guess now's as good a time as any.*

"So first thing's first, we need to do something about partisans," he said. "It's going to get more difficult to continue operations if we have random civilians blowing up train tracks and ambushing convoys."

Meyer nodded. "Well they said IRS agents are being trained to police battalions and theatre's for partisans," she said. "So we won't need to burn as many resources hunting down partisans or rounding up civilians." Kennedy shook his head.

"They should have already accounted for that," he said. "The Tharcians were arming subversive elements on Phobos before the war. They fight dirty and dishonestly." He relaxed and set his head on his pillow. "We'll need to be more ruthless."

"We need to be careful," Meyer said. "There're lines we'd be better off not crossing."

"Are we better off though?" Kennedy asked. "Aren't you tired of supplies going missing or being destroyed? Of the enemy knowing what we're about to do?" The look on her face betrayed her surprise. "Yeah, Khan told me about the leaks, and guys like him and Wake have a point, we have to crush them."

After regaining her composure, Meyer looked out the window. "If we let our most destructive desires drive us, we'll lose our ability to build things."

"I mean, that's great for your kind maybe," Kennedy said. "But I never had the ability to build, so let me give you a warrior's perspective, the Tharcians will never accept that we beat them, that damn Marshall said it in his speech, if we allow ourselves to be ruthless, it will save lives in the long run."

"There's more at stake then just our nation and Tharsis," Meyer replied. "If the enemy blows our actions out of proportion, what will the

international community do? Vinland's already pressuring our economy, The First Nation isn't far behind, and who'd help us if any of the
settlements in the belt join them, or stars forbid the nations of Earth."

Kennedy snorted. "They haven't fought a war in years, for all
intents and purposes their military is largely ceremonial," he said.
"besides the settlements don't pose a military threat, I'm sure we
can make them comply."

With a sigh, Meyer shook her head and sat down. "If you're
thinking about the founder's dream, it'll never happen by violent
means," she said.

"We'll it sure won't happen another way," Kennedy replied.
"Do you think any of the countries you listed would willingly join
the Union?"

"It won't happen in our lifetime," Meyer said. "To accomplish
something of that scale takes decades, lifetimes, I'll give you we
can't just ignore partisans, but we will only be as rough as we
need to."

"Whatever happened to whatever it takes to win?" Kennedy
asked.

Meyer rose out of her chair and jabbed a finger at Kennedy.
"Damn it Comrade Colonel, I am your commander, and my division
will be strong, what we will not be is cruel." She huffed as she
finished speaking. *I'm getting no where like this, she's exhausted,
tired. If I keep riling her up, it will just hurt both of us.*

Slowly, he nodded. "I apologize, just the loss of so many so
quickly clouded my judgement," he said. "You have my word we
will not be cruel."

"Thank you," Meyer replied. As she rose to leave, she paused.
"You know, when the panzerters were first created, the main selling
point was how much they scared their enemies, not their firepower
or mobility, but they terrified the religious extremists that cropped
up in the early 2000s."

"So you're saying what we need is a new weapon?" Kennedy asked, leaning forward slightly. Meyer shook her head.

"Not necessarily, but I wanted to say a lot of historians believed that panzerters prevented the insurrections in the middle east from becoming longer wars," she said. "So not everyone who thought along those lines was a monster, but like I said, it's a tightrope to walk across." And with that, she left him alone with his thoughts.

We can't win with half measures, half measures are why we're here and not on the shores of the Mariner's Gulf. He relaxed into the cheap pillow under his throbbing head. *Meyer's smart, she'll come around.* As he lay in silence in his bed, he fumbled for the remote. *In fact, she may come around sooner rather than later. All I need to do is reveal the extent of Fuller's incompetence.*

While flipping through the channels he had, he stopped on a documentary about Unions. *Good, useless information about how our government operates, stuff every good Union citizen already knows, the perfect thing to put me to sleep.*

As his mind began settling, he began combing for ways to expose his colleague as incapable of holding his job. Were the recordings of his orders available? Most likely in his panzerter's black box. Or he could just ask him to explain what happened in front of Meyer.

Then the lightbulb went off. *Of course I can do that, it'll expose him for a fraud and leaving his soldiers to die. They can't say anything against him, but I can. And I will. He needs to be dealt with for shrinking his responsibilities as outlined in the Constitution. That goes beyond MAG justice codes, that's the standard for everyone in the Union.*

He smiled as he sank deeper into sleep. *Yeah, I got him there, and the second he admits, Meyer will have no option but to order him terminated.* Mow that he believed he had the perfect plan, he closed his eyes and allowed sleep to take him.

Unbeknownst to him, a lone figure entered his room. When they saw the decorated MAG war hero laid up in a bed with bandages on their head, they smiled. A whole universe of possibilities opened up, all the wicked ways they could dispatch this man, but that wasn't what they were here for. Rather, they walked next to his bed and laid a lock of blonde hair on his pillow.

SNOW COVERED THE SURROUNDING GROUND, BUT THE MERCEDES stuck to the wet roads. As Reiter sat in the passenger seat, he kept a wary eye on Smith. "I know how to drive, sir," the young man replied.

"I know," Reiter replied. "But the roads are wet, and Black ice is a thing, besides I need to make sure you stay awake." He reached down between his legs to lift up a green box of sodas.

"Are those Highland Saps?" Smith asked.

Reiter nodded. "Yeah, Courtesy of Friermann, he's driving a different one of these with Hawke and them." He handed the younger man a can, but Smith stopped him before he could crack it for him.

"Sorry sir, I'm superstitious about people opening my drink," he said. Reiter shrugged and handed him the unopened can before opening his own. Ice cold, just how he liked it. And how it would be when the carton had been sitting on the icy ground for two hours.

As they talked, they kept their voices down. The wide Mercedes truck featured three rows of seats. In the middle row, 1st Sergeant slept with his ski cap over his eyes and his head against the window, with Merlin stuffed into the narrow middle seat, his head cocked straight back in a vain attempt to not touch the other passengers. Wesser didn't care, and rested her head on the younger man's chest, not out of anything more than him being softer than the door.

In the back row, Mo and Steel cuddled for warmth under Steele's blanket. Under normal circumstances, Reiter would have had concerns about their ability to keep their hands to themselves, but Webb sat next to them with his head in a pillow. Besides, they were both out like logs. *It's like a weird family road trip.*

"I barely recognize LT without her glasses," Smith said.

Reiter looked at him. "Focus on the road and not your sleeping LT," he replied. But he had to agree. When Wesser wore her glasses, they drew attention to her eyes and the shape of her face. Without them and with her eyes closed, he realized her face was paler than he thought it was and heavily freckled around the horizontal center of her face.

How can I know my soldiers if I barely recognize them without their glasses? At first Reiter considered giving up even trying, but then he decided against it. *If I quit trying, they become names on a spreadsheet, then numbers, then they stop mattering at all to me.*

They'd pounded into his head in OMI of the potential horrors of war, of its dehumanizing effects. On some level, they knew these days would come again. *I have to hold on to those ideals, otherwise, I could become an unfeeling husk. I wonder if that's how Knight felt at the end.*

His memory of the duel was still fresh. Knight's voice wasn't angry, furious, or even self-righteous like the other Union pilots he'd talked to mid-combat. He'd just sounded broken, like a man in a pit of despair. *I can't become like that.*

"Sir?" Smith asked. Reiter blinked, realizing he'd zoned out.

"Oh, sorry Smith," he said. "I was just thinking about something, did you say something?"

Smith patted the leather steering wheel. "This is a nice car, I wouldn't mind owning one," he said.

"They're expensive," Reiter replied. "And if you have a dozen kids like your parents, you'll need a bigger car, anyway." Smith chuckled.

"I don't think I'll have nearly as many kids, I'm not even married," he replied. He took a swig of his Highland Sap and winced. "It's more limey than I expected."

Reiter chuckled. "It's green as green can get, what did you expect?" Smith jiggled the can in his hand.

"It says Lemon lime right under the logo," he replied. "If you put Lemon before lime, you expect it to be the dominate flavor."

"Which is easier to say?" Reiter said. "Lemon lime or lime lemon?"

Smith bobbed his head. "Lemon lime for sure, but its deceptive."

Reiter held up the can and pointed to it. "The can is green, they're not deceiving anyone."

"Then why call it highland sap?" he asked. "Because I doubt there's any tree sap out there that tastes like lemons or limes."

"Oh so you went around licking every tree in these woods checking their flavor?" Reiter asked.

As he kept a hand on the wheel, Smith raised another in mock surrender. "Hey sir, I'm just making an observation. The name and branding don't make any sense."

With a wave of his hand, Reiter gestured to the surrounding terrain. Snowy covered pines and barren trees blanketed rugged and treacherous hills. In the distance to the south and behind them, Mountains reached towards the sky. "Look all around you, there's your highland."

Apparently, their conversation grew a tad too animated. "Are you guys really arguing about a soda?" Wesser asked. "I was just starting to get some good sleep."

"Want one, ma'am?" Smith asked as Reiter pulled one of the

long cans out of the pack. After a groggy look at both of them through squinted eyes, she wearily took the can.

"Where did you guys even get these?" she asked.

"Friermann," Reiter replied. "He was handing them out to everyone taking a little road trip, I grabbed one, Comidus and Stovepipe grabbed one, I honestly have no idea how many of these he had stashed."

"When you're in headquarters, you can make things happen," 1st Sergeant said, surprising the three of them. "How many more of those do you have?"

"Enough," Reiter said as he reached back to hand the other man a soda. Merlin stirred.

"Go to sleep, son," The first sergeant said. Though he was mostly incoherent, Merlin's babble sounded suspiciously close to "yes First Sergeant" before his snoring resumed.

Sipping her soda, Wesser slowly nodded. "I may not have slept as much as I wanted, but at least we're not moving in panzerters of God forbid IFVs," She said.

"Nothing wrong with sleeping in an IFV," Webb said. "There's just plenty of better places to sleep." The drop trooper cracked his neck as he woke up.

Seeing the rest of the pilots stirring, Reiter made a design. "Hey Smith, pull over here, let's let everyone walk around for a bit and piss," he said.

21

"A lright Comrades," Chaney said as he brought his department heads together. "Army Command wants more innovation, so let's give it to them, I want to hear your passion projects, your side gigs, anything you've been working on or want to work on, let's have it."

This will probably be barely better than the proposals I just went through the other night, but I well might as well let them think we hear their voices. His panzerter development chief adjusted her glasses. "We're still running into issues with the Type-VII engine," she said. "So far we haven't been able to safely reduce its weight and increase its output."

Chaney raised an eyebrow. "Safely?" She stirred uncomfortably.

"There have been some accidents, Comrade Brigadier," she replied. "But I would like more funding for that."

After a moment's hesitation, he nodded. "I'll make it a priority," he said. "As far as panzerters go, I have guidance from Army command." He pulled up a model of the Black Knight. "They want a medium panzerter that can perform either as well as the Black

Knight or close enough to its specs, a mass production model that will form the base of the next generation family of Union panzerters."

"That's asking a bit much," the materials chief replied. "Matching the durability of a heavy panzerter on a medium chassis is no small feat."

With a shrug, Chaney dismissed the model. "Well, since the Tharcian's heavy panzerter more than matches our medium panzerter's agility, they don't see the reverse as an arduous task." He around the room. "However, we do have several strategic issues Army Command would like us to tackle, while I don't believe science alone can solve all of our problems, it can give us a much easier time."

"Well, what are these issues?" The logistics chief asked.

Chaney pulled up an infographic of their strategic issues. "As you can all see, there's a laundry list of concerns, environmentally friendly methods of extracting resources on the surface, efficient ways of meeting the nutritional needs of our forces, restoring the orbital elevator, personnel shortage issues, extremist education and rehabilitation, like I said a laundry list," he said as he gestured to the rest of the concerns.

"I firmly believe our Impulse weapons project can aid with our resource issues," the head of weapons development said. "I've been trying to find low ammo or ammoless solutions for all of our needs for a while now."

With a smile, Chaney nodded. "Yeah, and your efforts have been noticed," he said. "Although there are two hard numbers that will doom us if they get too low." He held up two fingers. "One: our personnel, and two: our rations." He looked around the room. "If either of those numbers falls below a certain threshold, nothing else matters."

"I may have some solutions," The head of biology said. "As

long as we have the resolve to see them through." *Newton's laws, what am I about to hear?*

"Go ahead," Chaney said as he gestured to the man. "The floor is open, comrade doctor." Dr. Withers adjusted his glasses.

"Well, as you know, we've begun testing our handicappable cockpit refits," he said. Chaney nodded as he remembered approving the proposal before the war when he foresaw multitudes of pilots' missing limbs.

"I'm familiar with the project," he said. "And that will indeed help our personnel issues." As he spoke, the thought of veteran pilots who'd been maimed returning to service fully capable of performing relaxed his mind.

"Well, given the nature of the technology," Dr. Sinister said. "it would theoretically be possible to fit a still living brain in a specially designed cockpit." An uncomfortable tension rose in the room.

"You said still living brain," Chaney said. "Are you implying that the body is-"

"Dead?" the doctor asked. "Yes, we can use brains of our fallen soldiers to pilot machines." *So would they just live as a machine? It seems like an existential nightmare.*

"It's going to be an uphill battle getting consent from individuals before they die or their families," Chaney said. "That will make testing difficult."

"Well, I was just going to use dead tubers," Dr. Withers said. "Their organs get donated anyway, we only need the one least likely to be used anyway, besides they're state property and we wouldn't need their consent, anyway."

After taking a deep breath, Chaney rested his elbows on the table and tented his fingers. "Let's stick with a feasibility study for now," he replied. Dr. Withers seemed satisfied with that answer and nodded slowly.

"We'll see too it," he replied. "I also want o look into advanced growth techniques on our tubers, compress their development time further." He waved his hand. "Growth hormones, enhanced education techniques, advanced physical training all combined could potentially shave four years off of their growth, making them combat capable at 14."

"Feasibility study," Chaney replied. "Those hormones could make their bodies more greedy for nutrition, remember food is still an issue, which reminds me." He lowered his arms and looked directly at the doctor. "How's the research into those seed samples we acquired progressing?"

Dr. Sinister shook his head. "Our counterparts in space haven't exactly been forthcoming with their own developments, in fact some in my department claim that they have the man who developed the seeds themselves working on one of the belt settlements."

With a sigh, Chaney scribbled a note. "I'll have to talk to my sources about that, but if true, that's an incredible breach of trust on the part of our Naval counterparts." He looked at his head of panzerter engineering. "Halt all data sharing relating to the new engine, change the passwords on the cloud drives, and leave the Naval department in the dark. If they want us to starve, then they don't get a lightweight engine."

She nodded and made a few notes to herself. "They've been pinning for any breakthroughs we get, but never offering us anything," she replied. "All take, no give."

After hearing out a few more less interesting and workable proposals, Chaney adjourned the meeting. As he gathered his things to leave. The good doctor stopped him. "There is one more thing I wanted to look into," he said. "But one I didn't want the others to overhear."

Chaney nodded. On the inside he rolled his eyes, but he was nothing but agreeable externally. "Well shoot, let's hear it."

"I believe we can cultivate psionic abilities in the tubers," Dr. Sinister said. "Nothing dramatic or crazy, but things like negative reaction time, enhanced perceptiveness." Chaney sighed, but held his skepticism in check. *I don't believe in psychics per se, but what he's describing is more akin to pushing human ability to its limit.*

"A feasibility study," he said. "I need feasibility studies for anything that isn't an active project."

AS THE BITTER WINTER WIND SWEPT OVER THEM, FIELD MARSHALL Hausnerr clutched at his hat. The test range displayed multiple pop ups targets approximating troops, armored vehicles, and panzerters. The delegation behind him included senior members of the Vinnish government and military as well as his own general staff.

He led them to a door set into a hill. The room inside had been built from a pair of aluminum cargo containers. Screens and monitors dominated the ceilings and walls while a large table centered the room. Heaters in the back corners proved more than adequate to keep the cold outside at bay.

"Ah, it's about time we got out of the cold," the ambassador from Vinland said. After a look from Hausnerr, she straightened her back. "Just 'cause it's like this at home doesn't mean we love it." He nodded and received a salute from a Colonel heading up the project.

"Is everything ready?" Hausnerr asked. The other man nodded.

"Roger sir, our pilot is roaring and ready to go," he replied before pointing to the main monitor. The whole of the test range was visible to them, with secondary monitors displaying target status as well as that of the new panzerter. Hausnerr waved the ambassador forward.

"You admitted your military hadn't developed a heavy panzerter," he said. "This is one of our newer designs, we're currently fielding two, the Panzerter VII or Lowe, and this model the Panzerter VI or as the test pilots call her, the Tiger."

The ground rumbled beneath them as the massive panzerter strode into view. It resembled the IV, at least superficially. Massive slabs of armor covered its limbs and body. It had the same helmeted head and sensor package as its smaller cousin, but shared the pointed antenna of its heavy panzerter cousin.

"It looks cumbersome," the ambassador said.

Hausnerr chuckled. "They designed the Tiger with armor protection and firepower at it's core," he said. "The Lowe is more of an all-rounder on a heavy frame." He pointed to its squared off frame. "For example, the Tiger's wrapped in super chobam armor, an extremely heavy and heat resistant composite, unfortunate it can only be applied in large flat slabs, it's cousin uses a lighter composite with a thick coating of thermal dampener paint."

"So far you're not selling me on your big cat here," she replied. "Besides, why would we invest in a heavy panzerter to begin with, we need a colony defense model at the moment."

Hausnerr pointed at the Tiger. "This will kill any panzerter that opposes it, at long range, the Union heavily uses panzerters, including their own heavy panzerters. If not this, you'll love something like this."

"Well, let's see it perform first," she replied. The Tiger hefted a massive rifle, a 105-mm magnetic marksman rifle. From his notes, it was heavily based on some notes shared between the Lowe and Tiger teams pertains to the railgun originally fitted to the Lowe.

The colonel activated the gunnery table. As targets popped up up and down the range, the tiger engaged each of them. While the panzerters got the rifle, it peppered the infantry and smaller vehicles with a 30-mm Close-In Weapon System mounted on its head. *Another cue from the Lowe team.*

Looking back at the ambassador, he pointed to the Tiger. "It also makes an excellent commander's unit," he said. "And with the strives we've made in pilot safety, your commanders will be very well protected."

She looked back at her entourage. After sharing a few muttered conversations, she smiled back at him. "When you've cleared it for production, we'd like to order a limited run. From there we would appreciate help to develop our own heavy weapons."

Hausnerr nodded. He'd mostly expected this. Vinland's army and navy were highly professional forces, though that was out of necessity as both forces were much smaller than their contemporaries. Hell, their biggest capital ships were heavy cruisers and they lacked fleet carriers. There force would have to grow, and to do that, they needed material.

"I don't see a reason why our people shouldn't collaborate," he said. "After all, we're all fighting for our peace and freedom here." She nodded and spoke a few more words to her cohorts in Vinnish. They nodded and looked back at him.

"We'd like to meet the pilot if possible," one of them said. "And get their own feedback on the machine, so we can give our pilots a better idea of what to expect." Hausnerr nodded.

"We can do that, if you don't mind going out into the cold again," he said. As the Tiger took a knee and dropped it's ladder, maintenance crews ran out to take a look at it and ensure their fancy toy hadn't been broken. While Hausnerr and the Vinnish delegation braved the snow and the wind once more, they caught sight of the maintenance teams rushing out of a separate bunker.

"I don't envy them," the Vinnish Ambassador said. "Having to come out in this and put their hands all over cold metal." Hausnner looked at the freezing tech team. They didn't look too miserable, and one looked like he had one eye. *Huh, that's good of Ostman Heavy Metals to be giving jobs to our war wounded.*

The one-eyed tech noticed Hausnerr looking at him and smiled. *I'll have to shake his hand or thank him for serving later.* As they approached the pilot, the young woman took her helmet off and smiled. Noticing Hausnerr approaching. She snapped to attention and saluted.

"Relax, Lieutenant," he said. "Our Vinnish guests would like to speak to you." She smiled again before shivering.

"Can we talk inside?" she asked. "Maybe after I get some soup?" They chuckled and Hausnerr began ushering them back to the range control building. Before leaving the mechanics, he looked around real quick for the one-eyed mechanic, but he was nowhere to be fine. *Damn, oh well, I'll find him later.*

With that, he turned around and led his group back in from the cold, the one eyed man fading from his mind as he did. Fortunately for their young test pilot, one of the range control officers had prepared her a soup pouch in control bunker. As she ate, she took questions. The last one apparently hit a bit of a nerve.

"LT. Bartonova, if you're such a skilled pilot, why are you testing machines rather than on the front?" a Vinnish General asked. The young woman stiffened her shoulders and grew stern.

"Here in Tharsis we have a policy," she said. "If you're the last of your siblings, we exempt you from combat," she said. "It's a provision to prevent entire family lines from being wiped out." Hausnerr nodded, more to himself than anyone else. *She has every right to feel any certain way. Her sister and brother died heroes, and her home is under enemy occupation.* He remembered the one-eyed man and shook his head. *This war just keeps on taking and taking.*

Kennedy stiffened as he entered the temporary command center. At one point, it had been a broadcast center for the ice hockey arena they currently occupied. Now, however, maps lined the walls, readouts filled with monitors, and a media Union ran news coverage in the background.

His injuries weren't too severe in and of themselves, but it had aggravated his injured leg when his panzerter fell. *I've already talked to Chaney about my next panzerter, I shouldn't be using a cumbersome Jupiter again.*

Irving had also rejoined their group, as well as Fuller, Guard-Colonel Gomez, who commanded the 509th, and the new motor battalion commander. Along with Meyer, they gathered around a central table to discuss the state of their division.

"Based on the losses we took in the last battle," Meyer said. "Only 40% of the division is combat ready, we all but lost our drop-ship battalion, lost most of our motor and panzerter battalions, and our mechanized battalion also took a beating."

Fuller shook his head. "If nothing else, we'll be able to replace our vehicles and weapons with better models before we return to the front." Kennedy grimaced. *Your decision to use inferior equipment directly led to our loss, among other designs. Hypocrite.* "Are you alright, Comrade Kennedy?"

He nodded. "Yeah, this old partisan injury's been aggravating me lately," Kennedy replied. "And you're right, unfortunately, they have plenty of examples of our gear to pick apart." *And whose fault is that?*

"We may be getting new equipment," Meyer said. "But there's no guarantee we get experienced personnel to replace our losses." She leveled a cold look at Fuller. "Every battle we fight like the last one will only increase the skill gap between our forces and theirs, to the point it won't matter who's at the controls, we've lost."

Irving nodded. "This isn't just an us problem," she said. "It's a doctrine issue. Deep battle theory is brutally efficient with our industrial base and population pool, but it also taxes our resources at a high level." She also glanced at Fuller. "We can't be frivolous with lives." *So I'm not the only one that sees him for what he is.*

"I don't know why you're looking at me, comrade," he said. "I brought us as close to victory as we could have gotten, if it weren't for my actions. The Tharcians would have rolled out of Ironton and up the entire line!"

Undeterred, Irving rounded on him. "Your actions also doomed the entire operation," she said. "That's undeniable, I honestly don't know why you're here and not in a labor center." *Oh, wow, ouch.*

His ratty face turned red as it convulsed. "Listen here Comrade Major, I am your senior, and I will not tolerate this level of blatant disrespect!"

Kennedy raised a hand and leaned forward. "Hold on, comrade, let's give our Operations officer time to explain herself," he said. Narrowing a glance at Irving, he added, "Respectfully."

Gomez nodded in agreement. "I'd also like to hear what she has to say," he said. "It is her duty to review combat data and create our lessons learned, let's hear her out."

After an approving look from Meyer, Irving gathered herself and took a deep breath. She then pulled up the maps relating to the Battle of Ironton. "So at first the plan goes pretty smoothly, comrade Colonel Kennedy's forces slog through a hell of a fight, but manage to force open a lane for the 88th Division." She glared up at Fuller. "It's at this point, the burden of winning falls on the 88th, and not long after, the battle is lost for us."

Before Fuller could protest, Meyer silenced him. "Continue Comrade Major," she said. Irving nodded and pulled up more detailed maps.

"So when we look at the Tharcian disposition, it becomes clear that they wanted us to attack into the township," she said. "Their flanking forces were further forward and offset from the town. This company here merely set a screen inside city limits while the rest waited deeper inside."

"They looked vulnerable," Fuller said. "All I needed to do was kick in the door and the whole rotten thing would collapse."

"What you did was kick every single brick of the house in the hope it would collapse," Irving replied. "And when they chewed through fifty percent of your forces, did you withdraw? Consider a long flanking attack to get around them? Doing something, anything to lure them out of the damn urban area?"

"No," Meyer said. "He called for reinforcements, first from the 616th, a force we were reserving for the airport, then from the 75th, who was guarding their backs and only consented because the acting commander couldn't overrule him in the field." He fell under her stern gaze again. "You not only cost us one of the Red Guards, but most of our experienced pilots from before the war."

At this point, the man was sweating. His eyes darted around the room as if an excuse or escape from the situation would suddenly materialize. "I honestly didn't think we could lose," he replied. "All those big wigs, they all talk about whatever it takes to win, well that means we're going to take some losses, you two of all people should know, right?"

Before Meyer could speak, Kennedy raised a hand. "Look comrade, maybe you're just not cut out to be a combat commander, look, I know some people," he said. "Maybe we can work something out."

He relaxed. "Oh, thank you comrade Kennedy, how merciful," Fuller replied. "You're such a good Unionist looking out for your fellow worker, I thought I was looking at the end of my life."

Kennedy shrugged. "Well it's definitely the end of your career, you're not going to see another promotion with this on your file."

He reached into his coat pocket. "Here, join me outside for a cigarette, I need some fresh air, anyway."

As Fuller followed him downstairs around to the back of the building, his hand bumped into Khan's service pistol while searching for his lighter. When they reached the alley behind the arena, Kennedy stopped and lit up in the snow-filled, damp alley.

Dangling his cigarette in his left as he smoked, Kennedy glanced at the other man. "You know, for what it's worth, I think you're right about the whatever it takes to win line," he said.

"You really think so?" Fuller asked. Kennedy nodded.

"I mean, if we say we're going to win by any means necessary, wouldn't we be hypocrites if we did anything less?" he asked. The other Colonel nodded as he lit up. Kennedy made small talk with him, bu evaded questions on what he thought the other man could do. When the Fuller finished his cigarette, Kennedy looked back at him. "Do you have any regrets about your service?"

Fuller shook his head. "No, none." Kennedy nodded.

"I didn't particularly want to do this," he said and drew the pistol. When Fuller found himself staring down the barrel of the pistol, he didn't attack Kennedy. He didn't fight for his life. Scream. Beg. Cry. He just surrendered. Kennedy grit his teeth.

You're just going to quit? How do you expect to fight for your people when you can't even fight for you? This man is so damn pathetic. I really don't want to do this, but he's making it hard for me not to. A single gunshot rang out in the alley. Kennedy snuffed out the butt of his own cigarette and stowed the pistol.

As Reiter looked over the East bound Autobahn, cars sat bumper to bumper blaring their horns. Many of them had their belongings strapped to the roof or filling the rear of vans and SUVs.

By comparison, only a few cars trickled into Vaterburg. *Probably people with important jobs or things of that nature.*

Standing on the shoulder of The Lowe, he sighed and sat down. *Why does it feel like even when we win, we're still losing?* He fought to tell himself that this was different. He wasn't retreating, rather his unit had been pulled off the line to rebuild. *Hell, I came here in a Mercedes, that's new.*

"Hey sir, I figured you'd be out here," called Wesser. Reiter nodded and climbed down to her level.

"I'm not going to lie, I'm bummed about a few of these," Reiter said as they walked into their temporary offices. "Not because I hate seeing our guys succeed, but because we're losing good people." He sat down at his desk, a stack of papers at least an inch thick drawing his attention.

Fortunately, Comidus had already highlighted the sections he needed to sign. Unfortunately for him, one of these documents was Comidus's transfer to Harbinger Company. *Well, they lost their commander in that last battle, at least they're getting a good one.*

"Looks like we're getting more drop troopers and dropship crews first," he said. "I'm glad we're getting them, but it's a factor I've never had to manage before." Wesser nodded as she was busy working on her own paperwork.

"So, I was wondering, who's going to be your new XO?" she asked. Reiter stopped and thought for a moment. Though he knew Wesser slightly longer than Webb, the drop trooper was her senior and should get the position based on that. Then again, he'd be getting a new slew of officers as well.

"I think whoever I pick now will only be the acting XO," he finally replied. "I need to see who we're getting from division before I make a final decision, but I think you'll be staying with Black Team, besides you and Mo are a great leadership team."

"So you're going with Webb?" Wesser asked.

"For now," Reiter said. "Don't get it twisted, your time will come, and I'll hate every second of it because I hate losing good people." Discreetly, he'd put her in for a high award along with Mo. He had no idea if it got docked at all, but he thought her efforts on the ground after she'd been shot down saved numerous life.

"Speaking of losing good people," Wesser said, and Reiter paused.

"Kozma's family's been informed of his passing," he said. "I hate it a little more every time I have to sign one." After finishing his paperwork, he scanned everything to his computer and emailed it to the personnel shop at Regiment. Stretching, he looked over at Wesser. "The ceremony is at noon, right?"

She nodded. "We might have enough time to get coffee beforehand."

Reiter checked his watch. "Yeah we do, let's go." After donning their winter coats, the pair left their offices at Fort Holzhausen and took a government car off base towards a local coffee shop. "It's so surreal," Reiter said as they headed into town. "Like Grunbeck, life just happens like there isn't a war thirty miles from here." He shook his head. "Just weird."

"They're in their own little world," Wesser said as they pulled into the coffee bar. Grunbeck was probably much less business as usual now. The amount of refugees they'd seen fleeing through Vaterland reminded them of the fact, but still some people were staying put.

After a quick jaunt inside, they returned to the car. A caramel latte for Wesser, a peppermint mocha for Reiter. "I didn't take you for a peppermint guy," Wesser said.

Reiter shrugged as he started the car. "It's seasonal, and Christmas has the best seasonal drinks," he said. While they debated the merits of various seasonal beverages, they pulled up to the gate, flashed their IDs, and drove onto post.

With time to spare, they parked the car and walked on to the drill pad. The rest of Fox company milled about. Their pilots formed a single platoon that the infantrymen, mortars, drop troopers, and even scouts dwarfed. Shortly after they arrived, Col Hawke and Sr Master Sergeant Friermann also arrived shaking a few hands and smiling until 1st Sergeant called the company to attention.

After receiving the company from the 1st Sergeant, Reiter waited while platoon leaders and platoon sergeants switched spots. Col Hawke approached with Friermann. Reiter saluted them and the pair stood next to him in a line. 1st Sergeant read off the orders.

"The following soldiers post: Corporal Merlin, Corporal Smith, Corporal Dudas, Corporal Dohnal, and Corporal Panchenko." As the named soldiers left formation and formed a line in front of Reiter and the others, they walked around in front of them.

He stripped off the two silver stars representing Corporal and replaced them with the three that represented sergeant. "Attention to orders," 1st Sergeant said. "The following soldiers have displayed incredible skill, competence and bravery on the battlefield. In this the Field Marshall has placed special trust in the faith and talent of the following soldiers, and thus they are promoted to the rank of Sergeant."

Reiter smiled, albeit slightly sadly. Merlin was going to Early company, and some infantrymen were going to Harbinger. "The following soldiers post: Sergeant Lionel Musat, Sergeant Javi Mondragon. Sergeant Amy Steele." The three of them came to the front, same as the others. This time, however, Reiter replaced the sergeant rank with the three silver stars in a silver border of Panzerter-Sergeant for Mo and Steele, and a black border representing Rifles-Sergeant for Stovepipe.

Hawke and Friermann shook their hands after Reiter passed them. Then they called up Comidus. Instead of Reiter, Hawke stepped forward and took off the old rank. Three bronze stars arranged in a triangle replied the two that formed a diagonal line. *It's official, he's Captain Comidus now. He earned it.* Reiter shook his hand and smiled.

He smiled even more when Webb, Wesser, Smith, and the rest of their ragtag group from Ironton were called up. When Hawke presented them each with the Homeland cross, one of the highest awards for valor, he was practically beaming at their shocked reactions. *I can't articulate it, but I feel like things are looking up.*

22

"Interesting," Chaney purred. "Interesting, interesting, interesting," A warm mug of coffee with a dash of whiskey in it kept his nerves perked, but also relaxed as he dissected the report on the super crop strains. When confronted on the issue, Masterson, his naval counterpart, at first feigned ignorance, but broke down under pressure. By his logic, as long as the surface had access to the seas, they had no business starving as in his words, "they had more than enough food for them, where the settlements in orbit and the inner belt didn't have that luxury."

What he neglected to talk about was the massive crop output of our dedicated agriculture and aquaculture settlements, not enough to feed us in abidance, but no-one would starve if we had an unbroken chain. On top of that, Commodore Mendez admitted they'd taken food centers from their enemies in space. *So why aren't they using them?*

When he finally twisted something out of Masterson, the data Dr. Withers had combed through yielded some, well, interesting results. They were no stranger to genetically modified food. Hell, they were a prerequisite to terraforming the planet as most of the plants had either developed more efficient photosynthesis or had been changed in that manner to compensate the reduced amount of sunlight compared to Earth.

The super crops had the same developments, but to an extreme degree. This allowed them to reach maturity in an eighth of the time under near-earth conditions. Overall, the plants had been highly refined, using their resources more effectively than standard crops and holding a 70% increase in nutritional value.

This is amazing, with this we can look more closely into the enhanced growth techniques for the tubers. Chaney looked at his watch and elected to give the doctor a call. As his office assistant, a slim tower with a speaker and microphone, called the head of biology, he checked the data again. *I hope we're not reading a bunch of snake oil.*

"Good evening, Comrade Brigadier," Withers said. "How may I be of service?"

Chaney returned to the top of the report. "This report on the super crops, what do you make of it?" he asked.

The other man mused on the other end of the line before answering. "If our counterparts are being honest, they've been holding out on us," he replied. "That being said, I think we'll see our own production of them soon." Chaney nodded.

"I hope so," he replied. "My associate was able to acquire most of the team behind the project, so if they made them before, I can't see why we wouldn't be able to manufacture our own soon." He paused before continuing. "Has your associate gathered anything else interesting lately?"

Shaking his head, Chaney closed the report on super crops. "No, he's indisposed right now, and I don't want to bother him right now, Tharcian cybersecurity is incredibly potent and I don't want to risk compromising him." *Potent enough that he would rather physically go to places to gather intel.* "How are the feasibility studies coming?"

"Well for starters, the same techniques used to create the super crops can be used to enhance our tuber growth patterns," Withers replied. "We could even cut out food requirements almost entirely and make them photosynthetic."

"Not unless we're desperate," Chaney said. "They're supposed to be the pinnacle of human ability in any given field, and I can't approve of things that would make them less human, that would leave them open to discrimination." *That's one of the reasons we stopped making them sterile around the time the MAGs was founded, because if they feel more like us, they'll fight for us.*

"Fine then," Withers replied. "That being said, our other studies look promising, for example, the project I've tentatively called Project IMMORTAL only needs to discover the parameters we need to keep a dead brain active or restart a dead brain, once we've crossed that hurdle, we'll have answer to its feasibility."

"Just because you can keep it on doesn't mean it can perform complex tasks," Chaney replied. "Let alone pilot a panzerter."

Withers chuckled. "That's true comrade, however, even if we can't use them for this, I'm sure we'll find another use for them," he said. "But imagine the possibilities, a brain in a jar doesn't need to be comfortable, or the same amount of life support. You could have a much smaller cockpit module, among other benefits."

He had a point. Most of the kills to the base Martian were direct hits to the cockpit, head, or engine. Even the Martian Trooper, the cheaper "mobilization' variant, suffered from cockpit hits, although ammo explosions were less lethal with a smaller cockpit.

"From the engineering perspective, it is appealing," Chaney finally replied. "But what about your last feasibility study?"

"Ah yes," Withers said. "The psionics, we've done some tests with tuber rats, and I believe we've had some promising results, enhanced spacial awareness, increased reaction times, and so on." The doctor paused. "With your permission, I'd like to start with the next batch of tubers."

"I'll have to see the results myself," Chaney said. "Enhanced performance to a rat is one thing, enhancing the performance of a finely tuned human is something else entirely."

Withers sighed. "As you wish, comrade, we can run more trials here within the next week, what day works for you?" Chaney checked his schedule. He had multiple meetings that week, with the other project heads, with Ballard, and with Penny's tutors. *That little girl takes to math and science like a fish to water.*

"Thursday works," he said. "I have a meeting with Commodore Mendez about the behavior of the Navy's research and development corps, but that's in the evening and my morning is free."

"So be it then," Withers replied. "I'll have the trials ready to go that morning." After ending the call, Chaney returned to his work. *We need fewer projects right now and more results.* He sighed and closed his computer. *The Martian is beginning to show its age. It was five years old at the start of the war, but still state-of-the-art in terms of mass-production panzerters.* Chaney leaned back in his chair. *I hope Thorn comes back with some good intel, because I can already feel our technological edge slipping.*

KENNEDY LEANED BACK IN THE CHAIR IRVING PULLED UP FOR HIM. With his leg in a more comfortable position, he looked at the data she pulled up on the projection table before him. "So this is what I've gathered from the command matrices relating to the Black Knight," she said. "And I've started to see the concern, enough fire-power to destroy any of our panzerter's at range, agile enough to avoid return fire and eel in close quarter battle, and finally enough survivability to withstand whatever we throw at it."

"So what are your observations?" Kennedy asked. "Because so far you've told me things I already learned." His head throbbed. "The hard way."

Irving pulled up an image of Kennedy's Jupiter. "I think you should go back to a base Martian, especially since Fuller was dealt with. We have freed one that should be easier to refit since it needs to be repaired, anyway."

Kennedy furrowed his brow. "That would give me a significant loss in armor and firepower," he replied. Irving held up a finger.

"But it would increase your survivability," she said. "If Tharcian weapons head in the black knight's direction, then it will be much more important for you to avoid being hit period." She straightened herself. "And after reviewing most of the combat data, you're probably one of our best field commanders. We lost a lot of good ones in the initial push, and the last couple months weeded out most of the complacent ones."

"So I should go back to a Martian, huh?" he said. "Fair enough, but how do we overcome the Tharcians?" Irving sighed.

"I'm not entirely sure," she said. "We need to be adaptable, we've seen all sorts of looks and behaviors from them as time's gone on, but we need to focus on us while we rebuild."

As she spoke, Kennedy found himself nodding along. "We'll be getting new faces," he said. "They could be vets or green as grass, but either way they haven't fought together, and we haven't fought with them, so we need to train."

"We don't cross talk as much as we could," Irving said. "The Tharcians clearly excelled here." She pulled up replays from the battle of Ironton. "Look here, these scouts are using mortars to soften the 88th's forces as they advance, when they get inside the city, infantry ambushes and panzerter fighting positions became the rock they broke themselves against."

"At the beginning of all of this we caught them flat-footed all the time," Kennedy said. "We excelled at staying mobile against an enemy that was slow to react and relied on stagnate defensive lines."

Irving bit her lip. "They changed," she said. "Trying to advance against them now is like trying to climb a rope made of razer wire." She pointed at the defensive positions. "They aren't stagnate, they're flexible and just as mobile, more like an elastic band then a brick wall."

"But enough stress and the band should break," Kennedy said. "That's how we fight." Irving shook her head.

"Part of our problem as a division was we attacked along too narrow a front, tried to accomplish too much with a plan that was more complex than it had to be," she said. "We should have attacked along a broader front and gone after their headquarters and reserve, we focused too much on bypassing the enemy force instead of destroying them, of course this is my fault, I came up with the objectives, I could have told Meyer we should refocus."

Reaching out, Kennedy took the young woman's hand. "We live and learn, these mistakes won't be made again," he said. Irving smiled.

"We need to return to the mobile battle we excelled at," she finally said. "From there, we figure out how to avoid incidents like the battle of Ironton." She shook her head. "Losses like that are unacceptable."

Kennedy didn't know whether she meant the battle itself or those who died. Either way, he welcomed her attitude. "Then we'll comb all of the combat data," he said. "We'll look at combat data from other divisions, because we weren't the only ones who took a hard loss, but I'm sure somewhere we'll find the keys to win again."

They poured over the maps and data. The fact the Tharcians knew so much about their plans had played a key role in their defeat, a fact Irving agonized over. "Woody Pete's still out there," she said. "He'll be a problem as long as he is." Kennedy held up a hand.

"Don't focus on that," he said. "We've got new counter terror measures coming online, Woody Pete's little stunt won't be forgotten, or repeated." As they spoke, Meyer entered the room.

"Good, you two are here," she said. "We'll be getting fresh bodies soon, I want them training as soon as we hit the ground." Irving nodded.

"We'll need to refocus on air defense training," she said. "The Tharcians got their drone fleet back into the air alarmingly quick and on top of that they've begun using dropships and gunships on this front." Meyer looked at Kennedy.

"How's the leg?" she asked.

"Better," he replied. "Although I doubt I'm the first half-assed tuber." His commander smirked.

"Funny," she said. "They must have included some comedian in your recipe." Kennedy grinned.

"Only a bit," he replied. Grimacing as he rose to his feet, he looked at the map one more time. "I'm going to double down on maintenance, our vehicles and weapons need to be in excellent working order when we do hit the field again." Meyer nodded.

"It's a good initiative," she said. "Especially if worst-case scenario, we end up having to defend this city." Kennedy looked back at Meyer.

"Have you thought about who will replace Fuller?" he asked.

Meyer shook her head. "His XO died in battle, as did most of his company commanders, I may have to move some personnel around to compensate," she said. "Maybe move Khan over or Snow?"

Kennedy shook his head. "They're Majors more so because of their combat abilities, and not so much their leadership qualities," he said. "Knight would've been excellent, but- "he shook his head. "It's a damn shame, really."

As he left the room, Irving followed him outside. "Shouldn't you be sitting?" she asked. "Or at least not walking around so much?"

"Whatever it takes to win, Comrade," he said. "I need to go get a handle on my battalion." Irving stepped close to him and saluted.

"Well, be careful, the cold can be hard on your joints, especially if they're healing," she said.

"It'll warm up eventually," he said. "And one day, we'll celebrate the warm weather with champagne on the golf shores." As he walked away, he noticed her smile despite trying to look concerned. *One day.*

"SIR?" MAJOR STARNES ASKED. "LIEUTENANT BARTONOVA WOULD like to see you." Hausnerr waved a hand.

"Tell her I'll meet with her before the weekend," he said. "I'll be sure to make time for her." Starnes frowned.

"Sir, she's here right now," he said. Hausnerr blinked and checked his schedule. He had a meeting with Markos at 1700, which gave him two hours to sign the stack of papers in front of him and deal with Bartonova.

"You know what?" He said. "Fine, let her in." Starnes ducked back out of the room and after a brief moment. Lt. Bartonova stepped inside. Smartly, she'd chosen to wear her duty uniform rather than a dress or field uniform. A Green-gray jacket over the same color trousers tucked into black boots. Neatly polished, he noticed.

She gave him a crisp salute, which he stood and returned before they got to business. "Sir, I want a frontline assignment," she said.

Hausnerr blinked and rubbed the back of his head. "I'd love to, but you see policy makes you a lower priority to go to the front," he said. "Unless you know, the Union is overrunning this part of Tharsis."

Bartonova huffed and bit her lip. "My sister joined the Provincial Watch to pay for college. She always thought of herself as a crime scene investigator before a pilot," she said. "My brother, I understand, but my sister had no business dying the way she did."

The Marshall sighed. "Your sister died protecting one of her teammates," he said. "Regardless of how you feel, she died on her own terms." He stood and set his paperwork aside. "Besides, if you go and get injured or worse, there will be investigations, inquiries, nasty things that affect far more people than you, think of your parents even."

The pilot before him steeled up. She looked like she wanted to cry, but was forcing herself not to. After a moment, the strain on her face eased. "Well, don't the Tiger need field testing?"

Hausnerr shifted uncomfortably. "Well, it does, but we'd need to train another pilot and-"

"No, you don't," she said. "I'm right here, I'm already trained, you don't need to waste time training someone else."

After taking a deep breath, Hausnerr looked her in the eye. "I will not allow you to take the Tiger on some half-cocked revenge tour," he said. "You'll do more damage to the Union, training more pilots to fight them, multiply your skills with young incoming cadets." He held his hands in front of him as he spoke. "You can change the course of the war, simply by doing that."

With a frown, Bartonova went to a more relaxed position. "I'd rather change the course of the war by shooting down unis," she said. Hausnerr nodded.

"Most people would, but that's not all that goes into winning," he said. "Training, intelligence, planning, logistics, all of these things have a much greater impact on the course of the war then you're giving them credit for."

Still not entirely convinced, she saluted and left. After she'd left, Major Starnes returned. "You know sir, you could have just said 'I'm the marshall, and I said no.' You really didn't need to draw that out." Hausnerr sighed.

"I could have," he said. "And I would have alienated an amazing pilot, for what its worth I think she deserves to have a shot at ace hood, along with our other top pilots, but policy is policy, I can't in good concise order her to the front or allow it to happen." Starnes nodded.

"That's…reasonable," he said. "I'm not used to that out of a Field Marshall."

He flashed his aide a weary smile. "Get used to reasonable," he replied. "The old guard tended to make things complicated for no other reason then to say they did something." Looking back at his papers, he changed the subject. "Any updates from fleet?"

Starnes shook his head. "None so far, I do have some good news though." He pulled out his tablet. "A refit package for the Iglasio incorporating thermal dampener paint and magnetic weapons, the downside is with our current power supply, there isn't enough to operate all the weapons."

Hausnerr rested his head in his hands. "If only they could use a Nuclear Combustion engine like a panzerter," he said. "Then we wouldn't have this problem."

"Well then, they'd probably weigh 75 tons and be too big to move anywhere," Starnes replied. "On the plus side, things seem to be coming along nicely for us, a few of the field refits for our panzerters are becoming standardized, and our spaceports are moving so much raw material I don't think we'll ever be able to use it all with our current industrial base, even as massive as it is."

"Well, you're right, that is some good news," Hausnerr said. He wiped his brow. "I actually find it hard to believe my predecessor wanted this."

Starnes frowned. "He definitely wanted the attention, but none of the responsibility. When things went well it was all him, when things went wrong it was because someone failed him." He lowered his tablet. "That's how it was, when he wasn't busy sucking up to the president, he was busy getting pandered to by the Defense industries."

"So I've heard," Hausnerr mused. As Starnes left, he returned to signing off on his new sets of orders and authorizing war plans and contracts. Halfway through the stack, he decided to check his email. While clicking through the various mundane messages, he found an odd one from Markos. It read:

Field Marshall,

The Sun walk. 1735. Urgent. Come alone. DNR.

Markos

Well damn, that's odd, I wonder what all the urgency and secrecy is about. He checked his watch and saw he had about ten minutes to get to the Sun walk and talk to Markos. *Well, if it's this urgent, paperwork can wait.*

The aptly named Sun Walk was a large glass hallway on the top central floor of the Citadel. Hidden from the outside by by the high marble walls, it was the ideal place for a tired officer to get some sunlight after spending long hours in front of a screen. Officers like General Markos. Sure enough, the man was sitting on a bench near the center of the walkway.

"Well, Markos," Hausnerr said. "Your message seemed urgent, so here I am." Markos looked around and muttered something into his watch. Then he looked up at Hausnerr.

"Alright Marshall, I've killed the cameras and any electronics in this hallway for two minutes, that's just long enough to update you," he said. "I believe there's a spy in the citadel if not on the general staff."

"WHAT THE HELL'S THIS?" WEBB EXCLAIMED. ROLLING IN ON A prime mover was a stocky panzerter. It looked like a Panzerter IV, but a weapon barrel jutted over one shoulder. It also looked stockier than the standard model.

"That," Reiter said. "Is a Panzerter Kannone, it's a refit of older Mark IVs." He pointed to the cannon. "As you can see, it's equipped for long range combat." Webb looked at the thing and blinked.

"It looks shady," he said. "Like they just threw a cannon on the thing as an afterthought." He shook his head. "And here I was thinking a panzerter IV is a panzerter IV." Reiter shook his head.

"For the most part, the differences are internal," he said. "Better engines, joints, things of that nature." He sighed. "Hell, at this point hardly any of our panzerters are factory issue, you can thank nonstandard spare parts for that." After talking to the prime mover's crew, he signed the paperwork and took the vehicle into Fox company.

"Alright," Reiter said. "It's ours now, help me ground guide this thing inside." Under the milky sunlight, Reiter climbed into the cockpit of the new machine. The controls looked familiar enough. *Hell, this could have been my old one if it wasn't torn to pieces during the battle of three rivers.*

As he started the engine and unlocked the controls, it took him sometime to get the Panzerter Kannone upright. *The Lowe really spoils me, so responsive to its controls.* As Reiter walked the machine into a bay, Webb waved his arms to help him avoid hitting a wall or bumping into something. As he walked it into a berth, he glanced over at the Lowe.

Sheets covered the machine as it underwent repairs. The upside to its modular armor system was it was easy to repair and replace. The downside was new armor modules took some time to come in, but had gotten better since they got the Lowe. As he climbed down a ladder, Webb met him on the bay floor.

"Damn, maintenance on these things must be a bitch," he said. Reiter nodded.

"Trust me, you don't know the half of it," he said. "And this machine doesn't even have a pilot yet, so it'll end up getting some neglect with no one to seriously look it over." As they walked out of the bay, Webb turned back to look at the machine.

"You're not going to have Smith pilot it?" he asked.

Reiter shook his head. "I don't even know which platoon is getting it," he replied. "And it'd be the PL's decision, but no, I would say Smith's skill set is better suited to being the point man."

Webb shrugged. "I don't know man, if that's all he ever does, that seems like it'll hinder his development," he said. "But what do I know? I'm just a drop jock."

"Well, it's with considering when you put it like that," Reiter replied. They found a crate in the motor aces area. The concrete pad they stood on held bays on two sides and a hanger on the third, with the force being barbed wire topped fence with a gate for vehicles. One of the bays contained berths for panzerters while another was a three story parking garage for ground vehicles. The hanger contained the dropships and gunships.

"What else are we waiting for?" Webb asked. Reiter checked a list in his pocket.

"We have two Iglasio Recons-types, An Iggy Mortar, a Cstalio, a dropship, parts for the gunship and the panzerters, and maybe another Panzerter IV," he said. "We're going to be here awhile, and me and 1st Sergeant have a meeting with Hawke tomorrow, so you and a sergeant are going to have to run reception."

Webb nodded. "I hear you, I hear you," he said. "Well, we're a panzerter company, so it makes sense to have one of the panzerter sergeants." After another second of thought Webb said, "Steele."

"Steele, huh?" Reiter said before nodding. "Ok."

"Her new lieutenant could be in the group tomorrow," Webb replied. "Besides, she seems diplomatic." The drop trooper paused. "Do you hear that?"

Reiter perked up. As a kid, his hearing had been pretty good, but his hair metal phase as a teenager and his time in the army had done a number on his hearing. Finally, he heard the faint, but unmistakable cry of a running cadence. "Oh, it sounds like Wesser's torturing them."

Sure enough, Wesser led the way in her pt uniform, screaming the response to a cadence Stovepipe led them in from just behind her. "Do you wanna be a panzer jager?"

"I wanna be a panzer wager," the formation half muttered while Wesser screamed.

"Do you wanna live a life of danger?"

"I wanna live a life of danger," the formation repeated. One of the drop troopers pulled off to the side to vomit. Reiter and Webb grimaced.

"Glad I'm not in that formation," Webb muttered.

"Agreed," Reiter said. "Oh, looks like we got some stragglers." Sure enough, a few ran behind the formation. They didn't experience anything approaching relief, however, as 1st Sergeant and Doc badgered them relentlessly. Reiter shook his head. "Vehicle inventory?"

"Vehicle inventory," Webb agreed, both for once gold that something they were solely responsible for had gotten them out of a brutal PT session. Sure enough, shortly after, a prime mover arrived with the recon Iglasios. This time, Reiter ground guided Webb as he drove both of the vehicles into the vehicle bay, essentially a glorified parking garage with high ceilings.

They parked the recon vehicles on the top floor with the mortar carriers. The middle floor was reserved for gold platoon's IFVs, and the ground floor for the HQ trucks. As they took the stairs downstairs, Reiter shook his head.

"It's crazy to think six months ago we would have begged and pleaded for enough parts to repair some of our panzerters," he said. "And now we get them all the time."

"Yeah," Webb said. "Before this kicked off, we didn't even have working dropships or any gunships, our gun pilots had simulators and that was it, it took us forever to get kitted out and distributed to the line." Reiter shook his head. *Funny how all of that happens.*

23

"So there's no Christmas in the Union?" Zorro asked. "You can't be real." Fletcher nodded slowly.

"As real as I am, sister," the young tuber said. "There's Winter Solstice, but compared to this, it just seems like another day. People just say its special without saying why." She pointed to the Christmas tree in the hospital cafeteria. "That tree look really pretty, but I still don't get why you'd bring them indoors."

Adamski shrugged. "It's just what our parents did, and their parents, and so on," he said, "It's a tradition."

Fletcher raised an eyebrow. "There's still a lot about your superstitious celebration that confuses me, but I have to admit it's charming." She plucked at her beef a little more. "They still give me too much food, if this keeps up I might get fat, that'll make physical therapy harder."

"Somehow I doubt that," Zorro said. "You've been here longer than me, but your waist is the same size as the day I got in here."

"You've been watching my waistline?" Fletcher asked.

Zorro paused with a mouthful of mashed potatoes. "I'm compet-itive," she said.

Adamski raised a hand. "Alright, let's get off that," he said. "Fletcher, you said you didn't have a name until you were 14, you were joking, right?"

Fletcher shook her head. "I was being serious," she said. "L-478, when I graduated my core education they named me and sent me to pilot school." Adamski shook his head.

"Well to us, you're a name, not a number," he said. "I wonder how the rest of Fox is doing, I heard they made a name for them-selves in the last battle."

"Well," Zorro said. "They carted Wes Merlin in here, he didn't look too good."

"Is that the one who rescued you?" Fletcher asked.

"No," Zorro replied. "That was Ernie, the younger brother, Wes is the older one." A murmur spread through the hospital cafeteria. Adamski looked to see what people were talking about and couldn't believe his eyes.

"Well, speak of the devil," he said. Ernest Merlin stood into the room in a freshly pressed dress uniform. His powder blue jacket and matching pant looked fresh and his new shoes were freshly shined. As he approached their table, he smiled sheepishly with a few small boxes.

"Hey guys," he said. "Merry Christmas." He handed each of them a box. Adamski noticed each of them had individual wrapping paper. Black and white for Zorro, red and green for him, and red, white ,and black for Fletcher.

"It looks like your country's flag," she said. "Are you trying to rub it in?" Merlin held up his hands.

"No, No miss Fletcher, it's not like that I swear!" Fletcher smiled.

"I'm messing with you," she said. When Merlin looked stunned, she pointed at Zorro. "She said you were easy to mess with." Zorro blushed as Adamski shook his box.

"I hope you didn't get me socks, kid," he said. Merlin shook his head.

"No, Captain Reiter reminded me before I went Christmas shopping," he said. "My parents and sister-in-law are all here to see Wes, actually." Adamski nodded, and then he noticed the younger man's rank.

"Hey, wait, you weren't just gonna walk up in here and not tell us you got promoted," he said. "When did that happen?"

"After Ironton," he said. "A lot of promotions and a lot of medals after the last battle, hell Smith got promoted too, he's visiting Magyar right now."

"Who?" Zorro asked. Before Merlin could say 'your replacement' Adamski suggested they open their gifts. Thankfully, he didn't get socks, but instead a warm hoodie. Zorro got a book she apparently loved, and Fletcher received a Gallacia Gladiators hoodie.

"I've seen this before," she said. "In Pulaski, what are they? I assumed they were some kind of elite military unit."

"Close," Adamski said. "They're a hockey team." When Fletcher raised an eyebrow, Adamski raised a hand. "Let's get you to Christmas alright?"

She nodded and thanked Merlin. "So I assume this is a big part of the tradition?"

"Yeah," Zorro replied. "Usually everyone puts their gifts to their family under the trees you mentioned earlier, then on Christmas morning everyone opens their gifts, the emphasis is more on the giving part."

Adamski smiled in spite of himself. *She's a grown woman, but it's like explaining it to a child. Why would the Union deprive its people of a simple joy like Christmas?* He shrugged. *Maybe it's a cultural thing, Fletcher's general attitude seems to poo poo religious faith, but she seems wholly unfamiliar with what religious people actually believe.*

"Sergant Merlin," Fletcher said. "Do you know what Reiter would want for Christmas?" Merlin blinked.

"That still sounds weird to me," he said. "And I'm sorry, but I don't." Adamski leaned over the table towards her.

"Books, especially action, adventure, and horror," he said. "Monsters on the loose, that kind of thing. In lieu of that, something practical like socks or a bandanna would be good."

"Why would a bandanna be helpful?" she asked.

"To keep sweat out of his eyes," Merlin said. "My brother actually wore one all the time." Adamski leaned back and rolled his wheelchair away from the table. The younger man shuddered when he saw the blanket over where the stubs of Adamski's legs were.

"If I give you cash, do you think you could pick up a gift for Fletcher here to wrap?" he asked. Merlin shrugged.

"Yeah, I guess, I'll have to talk to you guys to make sure its personnel," he said. "I'll swing by your room and get that, right now I've gotta go see my family." Thanking the young man as he left, Zorro looked back at Fletcher and smiled.

"So the Captain huh?" she said.

Fletcher scowled. "It's not like that, I just haven't been able to express my gratitude for what he did." She blushed. "Though he was much kinder, then he had to be."

Adamski shook his head. "He's a good dude, awkward as fuck, but he's good."

"Oh, it's so hot when someone kicks my ass," Zorro giggled. "Irresistible."

"Except he didn't," Fletcher said. "I'm pretty sure it was Mo or Steele, whichever one fights like a wild animal."

"Mo," Adamski said. "It's not elegant, but it works, he had his back against the wall trying to survive and protect a boatload of civilians, including his sisters, I guess it just stuck with him." *I just hope it's the only thing from this war that sticks with him.*

KENNEDY STIRRED. IN THE DARK OF THE HOTEL THAT SERVED AS A barracks, he thought he caught something at the edge of his vision. A shape. A figure. A human figure. Cold sweat covered his body.

Did Fuller have an ally in the IRS? A Friend? A Lover? He snatched his service pistol and sat up in his bed. *You won't take me!*

"Whoa there," said the figure, raising his hands in mock surrender. "I ain't your enemy ace." Kennedy took deep breaths to slow his breathing and slowly reached over to turn on the lights. He didn't move his pistol off the figure.

"Who are you?" Kennedy asked. "How did you get in here?" Now with the light, he could see the man was about his height at around 6'5" and an eyepatch covered his left eye.

"Intelligence service," he said. "You already know my associate Fuller, you may refer to me as Thorn." Kennedy relaxed. Slightly. He didn't lower his pistol.

"You're the one who turned that Woody Pete character into a monster," he said. "He, and by extension you, just handed us the greatest defeat of this war. Give me one good reason why I don't just terminate you?"

Thorn grinned. "Because I've also given the Union more information about the Tharcians and some other bit players, then you could imagine," he said. "Besides, run a lot of errands for our friend Chaney, so there's that."

Mentioning the General's name caused Kennedy to hesitate before finally lowering the pistol. "There're easier ways to approach me," he said. "More proper ways."

"I'm not one for formalities," Thorn replied and walked over to the armchair in the corner of the room. "Besides, I like to keep my involvement low-key."

Kennedy scowled. "Seriously, what do you want?" Thorn walked over and handed him a data-key. The small thumb sized device could hold several terabytes of information. Kennedy looked it over while Thorn sat back down.

"That key contains everything you need to deal with Gallacian partisans," he said. "Who the Tharcian loyalists are, who fled, who stayed, and who's most likely to collaborate, and of course who will need to be retrained."

"I cam trust this information?" Kennedy asked. "How did you even get this?"

Thorn flashed a predatory smile. "Combing through public records from before and after the last war, scouring social networks, using IRS templates to determine who's most susceptible to dangerous thinking," he said. "All things we'd have to do anyway to prevent another war after this one."

Setting the key on his nightstand, Kennedy looked back at Thorn. "There are less dramatic ways to give me a data-key," he said. Thorn just kept smiling.

"I'm also here to talk to you about your enemies," he said. "You've been directly opposed by two, well I guess three men." Kennedy noticed a manilla folder on the dresser next to Thorn. The intelligence agent stood and picked up the folder, flipping through it as he paced the room.

"The 3-9th Armored Regiment, your most consistent opponent in this theatre, is commanded by a Lieutenant Colonel Walter Hawke, a graduate of Germania War College and a full-time officer in the Provisional Watch, he's bested you and Meyer at the operational level."

"The Provisional Watch," Kennedy said. "Those are those weird not-soldiers, right?" Thorn nodded.

"The Tharcians return to them as part-timers," the intel agent said. "They hold civilian careers with dedicated days ever month to conduct military training, an efficient way to do more with less, but hardly the backbone of an army." He cocked his head. "Yet curiously the best of these units outshines the best of their regular forces while the worst of them aren't even worth mentioning, unfortunately for you, the 7th Panzerter division trends towards the former."

Kennedy shook his head. "You were saying?"

"Yes, anyway, your other rival, this one more personnel, you're already mostly familiar with," Thorn said.

"Captain Reiter," Kennedy replied. Thorn nodded.

"He's bested you as a tactician as well as in personnel combat," the agent said. "He's a history teacher at a Gallacian University, making him not only a dangerous enemy in battle, but a corrupting force on susceptible young minds." He approached Kennedy and handed him a physical photo.

To Kennedy's shock and horror, Fletcher sat among a group of Tharcians, smiling and holding a sweater. As he sat there glowering, he looked up at Thorn. "How did they turn her over to their side?" he asked. "Fletcher was a dedicated Unionist."

"An oversight on the part of our doctrine," Thorn said. "We didn't incorporate counter-POW strategies for pilots in case they were captured, intelligence agents and staff officers? Yeah, line pilots? Not so much." He took the photo back from Kennedy and set it inside the folder. "Rest assured, pilots still in training are receiving said training now."

"Do you have anything I can apply?" Kennedy asked. "Something helpful on the battlefield?" Thorn handed him the file folder.

"As they say, information is ammunition," he said. "Of course, the full capabilities of their armaments are detailed here as well, but you should really look into the notes on their histories, their personalities, their behavior." He smiled ruefully. "That will inform your idea of how they do things and make them more predictable."

"Noted," Kennedy said. "I assume you're not doing this out of the goodness of your heart?" Thorn laughed.

"Oh no, my heart is as black as they come," he said. "As for my compensation, I only ask for a favor in the future, no matter how dirty or bleak." Kennedy rubbed his chin. "Look comrade, I know how internal affairs go with other countries, let's just say that if it looked like tubers place in it, all would suddenly change, I'm the kind of guy you want on your side."

"How do I know I'm not being played," Kennedy asked. Thorn chuckled.

"You don't," he replied. "But your social skills are advanced for a tuber." He flashed another predatory grin. "Fine, I'll clue you in to what I believe is happening." He leaned in closer to Kennedy. "I think the upper echelons of the government are preparing to ditch the surface and move into space."

"Really?" Kennedy said. Thorn saluted as he headed for the door.

"Take that information as you will," he said. "But now I need to go." And just like that, he was gone.

———

HAUSNERR LEANED FORWARD AS HE FOCUSED ON THE DISPLAYS IN the control room. "This was recovered from the Svalbard Cluster?" he asked. Joining him in the depths of the Citadel sat the Vinnish contingent led by the ambassador, along with his general staff. The ambassador nodded.

"Yes," she said. "We got this in a large data stream before losing contact." On the screen, an internal monitor from a colony docking bay replaced footage of the air lock. The massive airlock, the entry point to the colony for various vessels to dock, suddenly depressurized and opened.

A Union ship, long and angular, loomed into the bay, followed by another and then another. Hausnerr scowled. "That's a violation of the Geneva convention," he said. "How were they forcibly able to enter the airlock?"

The ambassador held up a hand. The Union ship lowered a ramp, and it wasn't until panzerters floated out of the hold carrying pods that he realized why that seemed odd. Modern space vessels had their decks arranged perpendicular to the engines to better simulate gravity under thrust, and except for carriers were fully designed around this. Carrier's hanger doors opened along the front to allow panzerters to use the catapults and save fuel. These doors opened as if the panzerter's had been staged on the ship ready to move into the colony.

"It's a landing ship," he said. "Some kind of assault craft." The panzerters, a different design from either the land based models or their space bourne counterparts, opened the pods and they saw marines stream out of the pods. A few cuts later and the panzerters exited the airlock. The colony defense force, typically kitted out to resit pirates at most, never stood a chance.

Their weapons, the heaviest of which were some unarmored missile carriers, stood no chance against the panzerters. Lasers lit the vehicles in great balls of fire while the infantry easily routed the colony defense force. Once they'd secured the area, they began rounding up civilians before the feed cut out.

"Our naval forces were left unable to respond," the ambassador said. "Not with a colony in the cluster being held ransom, and as far as we can tell, our targeted embargos are having little effect." She bit her lip. "In fact, they may end up being irrelevant in the long run."

Hausnerr raised an eyebrow. "What do you mean?" He asked. She nervously glanced over at the marshall as she fidgeted with her hands.

"Our scientists were working on an extensive adaptation program for several of our domestic crops," she said. "Enhanced nutritionally yield, greater survivability, less reliance on sunlight, mainly for our colonies."

"Let me guess," Hausnerr said. "The Union got their hands on it?" She held up her hands in mock surrender.

"It looked like it was just a string of accidents," she said. "But our project head was taken by pirates, or so rethought, and now I believe they're on the verge of circumventing the point of our embargo."

The Marshall shook his head. "I figured they may have food issues," he said. "When you banned halted all exports of grain seeds and livestock to the Union *before* you banned raw materials." He looked back at the screen. "I'll have to confer with our Naval counterparts, they're still in the process of appointing a replacement for the Late Admiral Von Braun, but we will have some kind of countermeasures soon or else we risk losing the colonies."

"What about a blockade?" One of the Vinnish asked. "Wouldn't you be able to force them out of the colony?" Hausnerr shook his head.

"We're the wrong people to ask about that," he said before glancing at his Naval liaison. "But Admiral Bernhard here would be able to give you an opinion."

The admiral also shook his head. "I'm not entirely up to date with the situation in our own system, let alone the belt and the

Jovian system," he said. "That being said, I still don't think I would do that. The amount of support vessels, let alone capital ships, we'd need to devote to a bloackade would cede strategic initiative to the Union and Avalon."

"So there you have it," Hausnerr said. "Don't get me wrong, we're all in on liberating the colonies the Union and Avalon have seized, does this hurt your presence on the surface at all?"

The ambassador shrugged. "More or less," she said. "We have a lot of agriculture in space, but we haven't lost enough ground to endanger our people with starvation, yet."

"Our shipyards are already in full tilt," Admiral Bernhard said. "It's above my pay grade, but maybe we can send some destroyers and cruisers their way. We have some under construction on the surface."

"Let's not get ahead of ourselves," Hausnerr said. "That's a decision that needs the consent of the state department and your colleagues in orbit, but I do think it should be on the table considering our new allies." He looked back at the ambassador. "How long until the official declaration of war?"

"We want to land our expeditionary forces before officially joining the war," she said. "Of course we'll increase our denunciations of Union and Avalonian aggression, put on the whole show and fireworks before we formally announce we have no choice but war." She gave the military men a wry smile. "Hopefully we alienate as many countries as possible from the Union and Avalon."

"That would be idle," Hausnerr said. "Ideally, the First Nation either stays out of the conflict or sides with us, and the Earth nations don't get involved at all." It had been rumbling among the state department, and upper levels of the military, but Hausnerr had learned from the Secretary of state first hand. The Earth's major powers were horrified that within twenty years a major war had broken out on Mars yet again.

As much as they cloth their pearls, they're nothing but a bunch of hypocrites. What are they going to do? Sanction us? Threaten us? Hell, they haven't fought a real war in almost a hundred years. He shook his head, banishing the empty words from a world away. *The less they interfere, the better. The last thing we need is an uniformed third party trying to dictate a bad peace to us.*

24

Ballard set the old book on Penny's nightstand. "There's your bedtime story," he said. "Now go to bed, sweetie." As he rose to leave, the little girl stirred.

"Daddy," she said. "Have you ever hurt real people?" Ballard hesitated as he got to the door. After a moment of thought, he shook his head.

"Only bad guys," he said. "Nobody that didn't deserve it."

Penny only stirred more in her bed. "How do you know if someone deserves it or not?" Ballard felt his tongue swell in his mouth a bit as he struggled for words.

"Well, when you're in the army and your at war," he said. "Everyone on the other side is trying to hurt you, that makes them bad guys."

"But are you trying to hurt them?" she asked.

"Yes, because they're bad guys," he replied.

Penny sat up in her small bed. "But if you're on the other side, you'd be a bad guy because they're there to hurt you too," she said. She folded her arms as her faces screwed up in thought. "But you're not a bad person, so does that mean that other people on the other side aren't bad people?"

Ballard nearly told her that of course they were bad people, but he hesitated. *Too many of their soldiers are children. Hell that Mo character was basically a kid, same with Kozma. Can I really tell her they're all evil even if I know damn well that's a lie?*

"If you don't go, are they still bad guys?" Penny asked. "What if nobody showed up? Would there be any bad guys?"

Ballard shook his head. "No, I guess not," he said.

"Then why do you show up?" she asked. "If you don't show up, it means less people will get hurt." Ballard smiled sadly.

"I have to go," he said. "I was made to do this by the government, even if I didn't want to, I'd have to, or they'd hurt me."

Penny pouted. "Well then, they sound like bad guys," she said. "Why would they make you if you don't want to?" the old pilot took a deep breath.

I can't explain to her they grew me in a tube specifically to do this. He slowly flexed his hands. *They made me for this, yet I hate it, all the struggling for meaning the breeders do, and here I am hating the purpose and meaning they gave me. Am I just defective? Or is there something beyond our genetics and upbringing that makes us, us?*

He shook his head. "Sorry sweetie, I was just thinking about something," he said. "I'll explain it better when you're older."

"But I'm smart," she said. "All my tutors say so."

Ballard sighed. "It's not an intelligence thing it's a maturity thing," he said. "I'll explain it when you're older now go to bed."

"Good night daddy," she said sleepily as she laid down her head.

"Good night, Penny," he replied and shut the door behind him. He walked into their living area and collapsed on his couch. *How long have they been using kids as soldiers?* He looked at his hands.

How many have I killed? How many fathers are mourning the loss of their own Penny?

He sighed and sank into the cushions. *I can't blame Penny for thinking out loud, that's what kids do, but I need to get her to keep quiet on the whole government are bad guy's idea. That might get us both in trouble.*

"I wish I could say I was trying to guarantee a better future for you, kiddo," he mused to himself. "But somehow I don't see it, even if we do win." *What the hell am I saying? I should want nothing else but to win, damn it!* He stood up into a sitting position. *Increased reaction time. Enhanced musculature and bone structure. Numerous other alterations. They made me for this war. They made me to win it.*

He clenched his hands and looked at his fists. *Then why is it that I don't want to do anything other than live a peaceful life with my daughter.* He buried his head in his hands once more, but answers never came.

———

"I'M ALMOST AT A POINT WHERE I WON'T NEED THE CHAIR anymore," Fletcher said. "Although I'd love to not have to do another PT session." Zorro nodded in agreement.

"I swear, I thought a prosthetic leg wouldn't hurt at all," she replied. "but the meaty part above it is another story."

Adamski sighed. "Try learning to walk on the damn things," he said. "Trust me, value the legs you have." He smiled as Fletcher produced a small box carefully, yet simply wrapped.

"I couldn't decide between a book and a bandanna," she said. "So I got a 'monster-on-the-loose' book from the 99 cent pile and a Tharcian flag bandana." She held up her hands. "Remarkably, I didn't burst into flames when I picked it up."

Adamski took a closer look at her wrapping job. She'd chosen a simple brown paper and twine to wrap Reiter's gifts. Every fold had been tucked with a clean precision, all right angles and straight lines. "You know, I'm a little skeptical you haven't been doing this your whole life," he said. His phone buzzed, and he looked down at the text. "Reiter will be here soon, he just got off."

Fletcher's smile brightened when a nurse called her name. "Fletcher, Clarissa? Is she in here?" she called. The tuber twisted in her wheelchair to face the other woman.

"I'm here," she called out. "Is something wrong?" The nurse, a shorter woman with a large head of curly hair, shook her head.

"Oh no," she said. "Not really, they didn't give you enough hormones for your tissue regeneration today, gotta get those buns nice and fertile, you know?" At first the nurse's demeanor seemed to make her uncomfortable, but as the nurse produced a packet and added the vegetable green contents of a glass of water, Adamski started to feel it too.

"Uh, excuse me nurse," he said. "May I see the packet you're holding?" The nurse frowned at his request.

"It's just a hormonal treatment," she repeated. "It's necessary to speed up the healing process." Two things already didn't mesh with Adamski. Number one was the nurse's defensive posture, which he could attribute to patient-caregiver integrity. But all the nurses he knew would drop some kind of acronym or the chemical name of a drug they were giving someone. They usually got away with this because most people weren't doctors or chemists, and thus those things meant nothing to them.

"She's already ahead of schedule," Zorro said, seemingly picking up on Adamski's discomfort. "Why would you try to rush it faster?"

"That," the nurse, her name tag said Amelia, said. "Is Nurse-patient privilege, and I'm not obligated to speak with you about it."

Her face suddenly clicked with why he recognized her. She'd been in the field hospital outside of Landfall and was present for the severing of his ruined legs. *What's an army field nurse doing in a civilian hospital?*

"Hey nurse," he said. "Did you-" He spotted Reiter across the mess hall. His goofball Captain had apparently taken a page from Merlin and elected to wear his powder blues. He had a small gift wrapped under his arm. "Hold off on that drink, Fletch, Reiter's here."

"The Black Knight?" Amelia said, and everything suddenly clicked with Adamski. *If it weren't for that visit from Mo and Steele, I wouldn't have known the critical piece, but Reiter's ace title is the Black Lion of Gallacia, I'd assume black knight was someone misremembering the title or adding their own. Were it not for Mo telling me that the Union specifically refer to the Lowe and Reiter as the Black Knight.*

"Uh, nurse," he said. "How long have you been working here?"

"Amelia," Reiter said. "What are you doing here?"

"Oh, I got transferred," she said. "They evacuated the hospital at Grunbeck, so now I'm here." Reiter frowned.

"I was just in a meeting with my counterparts," he said. "The hospital's still-"

"I'm sorry," she interrupted. "Ms. Fletcher needs to take her supplement." At this point, people around them began paying attention, including the MP assigned to Fletcher. As he began approaching the group, he noticed a pair of hospital security officers approaching from a different direction.

"I'm not taking that," Fletcher said. "There's clearly something wrong here."

"Paranoia is a side effect of hormone imbalance," Amelia replied. "You need this."

"Why would you lie to me about the hospital?" Reiter

demanded. *That's probably the firmest I've ever heard him.* Adamski quickly wheeled himself around to where the nurse and Reiter stood behind Fletcher. "Hey wait, what's that smell? What did you put in there?"

Amelia lunged forward, pushing Fletchers head back and thrusting the glass towards the tuber pilot. Several things happened at once. Reiter punched the glass, knocking it across the table and away from everyone. Fletcher thrust the woman away from her as Adamski lunged out of his chair and tackled her.

She scratched and clawed at his head, but his lower than normal center of gravity made him much harder to grapple with. Before long, he had her hands behind her back. She writhed and struggled and screamed like a madwoman as the security personnel ran over.

"What happened? The MP asked. He looked at Fletcher. "was it you?" Reiter swiped some spilled water and sniffed it.

"I recognize this," he said. "It's a herb based painkiller, suitable only for someone in hospice." He shot an icy glare at Amelia. "With her metabolism, it would have killed her. Why?"

As the security guards hoisted her to her feet, she lunged at Fletcher and screamed. "Traitor!" *Well, that confirms it, she's a Union spy.* While she was led away, Fletcher set her head in her hands.

"I can't go home," she said. "Ever, it's all gone." Reiter set a hand on her shoulder awkwardly.

"Hey, assuming we manage to win this," he said. "Then I'm not opposed to you staying at my dad's beach house. It may not be the homiest place, but it's something." He suddenly remembered the gift in his hand. "Oh, and Merry Christmas."

Hᴀᴜsɴᴇʀʀ sᴍɪʟᴇᴅ ᴀs ʜᴇ sᴀᴡ ᴛʜᴇᴍ ᴄʀᴏssɪɴɢ ᴛʜᴇ ɢᴜʟғ. Tᴏ ᴛʜᴇ untrained eye, they looked like any old blue-water cruise ship or cargo vessel sailing into port. But the Field Marshall knew better. Each passenger vessel carried roughly 800 Vinnish soldiers. Each cargo ship carried dozens of panzerters and armored vehicles, all ready to do battle with a detestable enemy.

From his perch in the harbor station, he could see the disguised transport fleet approaching Tharsis in earnest. He left the harbor station with his entourage and headed for one of the largest docks. The cruise liner *S.S. Vinland* pulled into her berth as gangways dropped not o the receptacles below them. He smiled as the first Vinnish troops disembarked.

The chorus of an old Vinnish tune preceded the march of the marble and fog colored Vinnish soldiers. It always impressed Hausnerr to hear Vinnish. Since the language itself was a close cousin of English, it was easier to preserve their language. The thing they couldn't stop was the eventual blending of Danish, Swedish, Finnish, Samii, Norwegian, and Icelandic leading to Modern Vinnish.

As each soldier sang, a green duffel over their shoulder, Hausnerr's smile wavered. *How long will their spirits be this high? How long before the fighting begins wearing them down.* He shook his head and his smile returned. *No matter if their morale is high, then I won't bring it down.*

He smiled and shook the hand of every Vinnish soldier that passed him on the off ramp as they headed to a nearby warehouse. The first few dozen soldiers didn't immediately realize who he was, but as the line progressed, his guests realized who he was and rendered him a proper salute before shaking his hand.

As the last few soldiers entered the warehouse for in processing, Hausnerr led his entourage in after them. It didn't take him long to find the woman in charge. She stood in front of a large formation of soldiers seated in the bleachers put out for them, surrounded by her own entourage.

When he approached her group, she saluted, snapping sharply to attention. "You must be the man in charge," she said in a thick Vinnish accent. "I'm General Volden, Commander of the Vinnish Expeditionary Force."

Hausnerr returned her salute. "I'm glad to meet you, Field Marshall Hausnerr, High Commander of the Army." He offered his hand. "I can't articulate how grateful I am that you're here." With a firmer grip than most men he knew, she shook his hand. "General Volden, Welcome to Tharsis."

AFTERWORD

Dear Reader,

Amazon lists millions of books, and I'm glad you discovered this one. But if you'd like to know when I release a new book, instead of leaving it to chance, sign up for my newsletter. You'll get a free short story as well as updates on my work.
Yes please-Sign me up!
No Thanks-I'll take my chances.
Either way, if you continue to the next page, you'll get a free preview of the next book in the series: Enemy Front.

PREVIEW OF ENEMY FRONT!

Captain Paul Reiter wiped the sweat from his brow as he sat in the cockpit of his Panzerter. Long gone were his worn-out Combat Vehicle Crew shirt and pants. Instead, he wore a simple vest over a drab t-shirt and splintertarn pants. *At least I have a fresh pair of boots.* While the CVC uniform would've been comfortable, it was just too low a priority on the supply list, so instead, he improvised.

And improvise they did, as he waited in his powered-down Panzerter. He sat and listened for the snap-pop of a flare in the air. Somewhere across from the copse of trees he lay in, LT Webb and his droptroopers slowly advanced on a suspected Union artillery nest in a cluster of hills. Three of his other platoons pulled security while the droptroopers prepared to assault the position, leaving his headquarters platoon in a supporting position.

Come on, any day now. Dangling from a chain above his head hung his memorial journal, a book containing pictures and names of every member of Fox Company that had died since the start of the war. Even after their victory in Ironton, the book still added names and faces. Reiter stared at it as he took a swig from his canteen. *Let's hope I don't have to add any more today.*

Cautiously, he set down his canteen and stood up in the open cockpit hatch above him. His new position allowed him to actually see the hill in dawn's early light. A low fog clung to the hills as cloud shrouded the peaks not too far in the distance. Rather cleverly, he'd hidden the Lowe's head among the branches of the surrounding trees but left the cockpit where he could get an unrestricted view from the open hatch.

In the weak light of morning, it seemed easy enough to forget his machine was one of the most advanced in the Tharcian army. Issues with spare parts had resulted in the shoulder mounts for railgun being used for a pair of 35-mm rotary cannons. The new weapons increased his short-range and close-quarter capabilities, and unlike his last refit, he hadn't lost any weapons. Suddenly, his radio crackled.

"Fox 6, Blue 1," LT Webb said. "We got eyes and hands on the objective. Site's abandoned. It looks like counter-battery fire threatened to blow an ammo dump and they bailed."

Reiter sighed as he held his earpiece tighter to his head, as if he would hear better. "Roger, Red 1. Anything look salvageable?"

"Maybe some of these gun barrels," Webb replied. "I have no idea what caliber artillery they use. I'll have a more detailed report later. I'm calling in the birds."

"Roger 1, see you back home," Reiter replied. "Black and White 1, do you copy that traffic?" When he received an affirmative, he explained they'd leave after dropships picked up their drop platoon.

"I don't get it," LT Major replied. "We've barely had contact with the Union up in these mountains. Are we sure they didn't just starve?"

"That's a negative," Wesser replied. "We have good intel that they still have open supply lines through Olympia. I think they're just biding their time."

Reiter nodded in agreement as he powered up the Lowe.

"Black 1's right," he replied. "Our enemies aren't morons; they won't attack if it will be too costly for them." He heard a low droning echoing off the hills. His air radar sounded an alarm. "Fox Company, enemy aircraft approaching."

As soon as the words left his mouth, the radar resolved a target. Three enemy dropships. He knew from experience that Union dropships carried stupid amounts of firepower, as well as elite raider forces.

They swooped low over the treeline, blasting rockets into White Platoon. Their Panzerters replied with ball-mounted machine guns and Panzerter-sized rifles. The dropships dodged the rifle fire and ignored the machinegun fire.

Reiter swore softly as the Lowe swung its rotary cannons over each shoulder. *Well, at least I get to use the big guns.* The cannons roared, a sound not unlike a sheet of canvas being constantly torn. The dropships flew right into a curtain of metal. Shells the length of his hand and forearm punched right through their armor plating. Flaming wrecks crashed to the ground at the foot of the hill.

"Is everyone okay?" Reiter asked.

"Blue's good," Webb replied.

"Black's up," Wesser said.

"White took some damage," Major replied. "Nothing too serious, though."

"Gold's searching the wrecks," LT Rudman said. "You know, just in case."

Reiter sighed. "Good, so nobody died," he said. "All units, prepare for exfil, and stay on guard." He looked up as their own dropships approached from the West, *Lazy Sue* leading the way. When they lifted off, Reiter could see a few Union artillery pieces hanging off their undersides from cables. *And to the victor go the spoils.*

The moment the dropships had left his sight, Reiter began moving the rest of the company. Panzerters crashed through trees like creatures from fairy tales while infantry-fighting vehicles nipped at their heels. Reiter took up his own position in the center of the massive formation. They turned west, back towards the firebase their regiment operated out of.

As they crossed into Firebase Kozma, Reiter finally relaxed. *Good, we made it. Now, after the debriefs, I'll put up my hammock, receive the next mission. Wash my face, begin planning. Maybe tonight I'll get to read my book a little.* He smiled at the sight of soldiers running over and tossing camouflage nets onto their Panzerters, taking a knee inside the positions engineers had dug for them.

Shivering, he realized his air conditioning had made the once muggy cockpit much cooler than he needed it to be. He tried in vain to reduce the fan speed, realized the knob was broken, and sighed. As he turned the system off, he leaned back to stretch. The memorial journal hung over his head. *No more names for the book today. I wonder how much longer that lasts.*

———

THANK YOU FOR READING! IF YOU'VE ENJOYED THE STORY SO FAR, you can find Enemy Front available for Kindle here.

www.ingramcontent.com/pod-product-compliance
Lightning Source LLC
Chambersburg PA
CBHW072025020726
47501CB00006B/1967